The Secret Power

The Secret Power
Marie Corelli

MINT EDITIONS

The Secret Power was first published in 1921.

This edition published by Mint Editions 2021.

ISBN 9781513280110 | E-ISBN 9781513285139

Published by Mint Editions®

MINT
EDITIONS

minteditionsbooks.com

Publishing Director: Jennifer Newens
Design & Production: Rachel Lopez Metzger
Project Manager: Micaela Clark
Typesetting: Westchester Publishing Services

Contents

I

A cloud floated slowly above the mountain peak. Vast, fleecy and white as the crested foam of a sea-wave, it sailed through the sky with a divine air of majesty, seeming almost to express a consciousness of its own grandeur. Over a spacious tract of Southern California it extended its snowy canopy, moving from the distant Pacific Ocean across the heights of the Sierra Madre, now and then catching fire at its extreme edge from the sinking sun, which burned like a red brand flung on the roof of a roughly built hut situated on the side of a sloping hollow in one of the smaller hills. The door of the hut stood open; there were a couple of benches on the burnt grass outside, one serving as a table, the other as a chair. Papers and books were neatly piled on the table,—and on the chair, if chair it might be called, a man sat reading. His appearance was not prepossessing at a first glance, though his actual features could hardly be seen, so concealed were they by a heavy growth of beard. In the way of clothing he had little to trouble him. Loose woollen trousers, a white shirt, and a leathern belt to keep the two garments in place, formed his complete outfit, finished off by wide canvas shoes. A thatch of dark hair, thick and ill combed, apparently served all his need of head covering, and he seemed unconscious of, or else indifferent to, the hot glare of the summer sky which was hardly tempered by the long shadow of the floating cloud. At some moments he was absorbed in reading,—at others in writing. Close within his reach was a small note-book in which from time to time he jotted down certain numerals and made rapid calculations, frowning impatiently as though the very act of writing was too slow for the speed of his thought. There was a wonderful silence everywhere,—a silence such as can hardly be comprehended by anyone who has never visited wide-spreading country, over-canopied by large stretches of open sky, and barricaded from the further world by mountain ranges which are like huge walls built by a race of Titans. The dwellers in such regions are few—there is no traffic save the coming and going of occasional pack-mules across the hill tracks—no sign of modern civilisation. Among such deep and solemn solitudes the sight of a living human being is strange and incongruous, yet the man seated outside his hut had an air of ease and satisfied proprietorship not always found with wealthy owners of mansions and park-lands. He was so thoroughly engrossed in his books and papers that he hardly saw, and certainly did not hear, the approach of a woman who came climbing wearily up the edge of the sloping hill against which his cabin presented itself to the view as a sort of fitment, and advanced towards him carrying a tin pail full of milk. This she set down within a yard or so of him, and then, straightening her back, she rested her hands on her hips and drew a long breath. For a minute or two he took no notice of her. She waited. She was a big handsome creature, sun-browned and black-haired, with flashing dark eyes lit by a spark that was not originally caught from heaven. Presently, becoming conscious of her presence, he threw his book aside and looked up.

"Well! So you've come after all! Yesterday you said you wouldn't."

She shrugged her shoulders.

"I do not wish you to starve."

"Very kind of you! But nothing can starve me."

"If you had no food—"

"I should find some"—he said—"Yes!—I should find some,—somewhere! I want very little."

He rose, stretching his arms lazily above his head,—then, stooping, he lifted the pail of milk and carried it into his cabin. Disappearing for a moment, he returned, bringing back the pail empty.

"I have enough for two days now," he said—"and longer. What you brought me at the beginning of the week has turned beautifully sour,—a 'lovely curd' as our cook at home used to say—, and with that 'lovely curd' and plenty of fruit I'm living in luxury." Here he felt in his pockets and took out a handful of coins. "That's right, isn't it?"

She counted them over as he gave them to her—bit one with her strong white teeth and nodded.

"You don't pay ME"—she said, emphatically—"It's the Plaza you pay."

"How many times will you remind me of that!" he replied, with a laugh—"Of course I know I don't pay You! Of course I know I pay the Plaza!—that amazing hotel and 'sanatorium' with a tropical garden and no comfort—"

"It is more comfortable than this"—she said, with a disparaging glance at his log dwelling.

"How do You know?" and he laughed again—"What have You ever experienced in the line of hotels? You are employed at the Plaza to fetch and carry;—to wait on the wretched invalids who come to California for a 'cure' of diseases incurable—"

"You are not an invalid!" she said with a slight accent of contempt.

"No! I only pretend to be!"

"Why do you pretend?"

"Oh, Manella! What a question! Why do we all pretend?—all!—every human being from the child to the dotard! Simply because we dare not face the truth! For example, consider the sun! It is a furnace with flames five thousand miles high, but we 'pretend' it is our beautiful orb of day! We must pretend! If we didn't we should go mad!"

Manella knitted her black brows perplexedly.

"I do not understand you"—she said—"Why do you talk nonsense about the sun? I suppose you ARE ill after all,—you have an illness of the head."

He nodded with mock solemnity.

"That's it! You're a wise woman, Manella! That's why I'm here. Not tubercles on the lungs,—tubercles on the brain! Oh, those tubercles! They could never stand the Plaza!—the gaiety, the brilliancy—the—the all-too dazzling social round! . . ." he paused, and a gleam of even white teeth under his dark moustache gave the suggestion of a smile—"That's why I stay up here."

"You make fun of the Plaza"—said Manella, biting her lips vexedly—"And of me, too. I am nothing to you!"

"Absolutely nothing, dear! But why should you be any thing?"

A warm flush turned her sunburnt skin to a deeper tinge.

"Men are often fond of women"—she said.

"Often? Oh, more than often! Too often! But what does that matter?"

She twisted the ends of her rose-coloured neckerchief nervously with one hand.

"You are a man"—she replied, curtly—"You should have a woman."

He laughed—a deep, mellow, hearty laugh of pleasure.

"Should I? You really think so? Wonderful Manella? Come here!—come quite close to me!"

She obeyed, moving with the soft tread of a forest animal, and, face to face with him, looked up. He smiled kindly into her dark fierce eyes, and noted with artistic approval the unspoiled beauty of natural lines in her form, and the proud poise of her handsome head on her full throat and splendid shoulders.

"You are very good-looking, Manella"—he then remarked, lazily—"Quite the model for a Juno. Be satisfied with yourself. You should have scores of lovers!"

She stamped her foot suddenly and impatiently.

"I have none!" she said—"And you know it! But you do not care!"

He shook a reproachful forefinger at her.

"Manella, Manella, you are naughty! Temper, temper! Of course I do not care! Be reasonable! Why should I?"

She pressed both hands tightly against her bosom, seeking to control her quick, excited breathing.

"Why should you? I do not know! But *I* care! I would be your woman! I would be your slave! I would wait upon you and serve you faithfully! I would obey your every wish. I am a good servant,—I can cook and sew and wash and sweep—I can do everything in a house and you should have no trouble. You should write and read all day,—I would not speak a word to disturb you. I would guard you like a dog that loves his master!"

He listened, with a strange look in his eyes,—a look of wonder and something of compassion. There was a pause. The silence of the hills was, or seemed more intense and impressive—the great white cloud still spread itself in large leisure along the miles of slowly darkening sky. Presently he spoke. "And what wages, Manella? What wages should I have to pay for such a servant?—such a dog?"

Her head drooped, she avoided his steady, searching gaze.

"What wages, Manella? None, you would say, except—love! You tell me you would be my woman,—and I know you mean it. You would be my slave—you mean that, too. But you would want me to love you! Manella, there is no such thing as love!—not in this world! There is animal attraction,—the magnetism of the male for the female, the female for the male,—the magnetism that pulls the opposite sexes together in order to keep this planet supplied with an ever new crop of fools,—but love! No, Manella! There is no such thing!"

Here he gently took her two hands away from their tightly folded position on her bosom and held them in his own.

"No such thing, my dear!" he went on, speaking softly and soothingly, as though to a child—"Except in the dreams of poets, and you—fortunately!—know nothing about poetry! The wild animal in you is attracted to the tame, ruminating animal in me,—and you would be my woman, though I would not be your man. I quite believe that it is the natural instinct of the female to select her mate,—but, though the rule may hold good in the forest world, it doesn't always work among the human herd. Man considers that he has the right of selection—

quite a mistake of his I'm sure, for he has no real sense of beauty or fitness, and generally selects most vilely. All the same he is an obstinate brute, and sticks to his brutish ideas as a snail sticks to its shell. *I* am an obstinate brute!—I am absolutely convinced that I have the right to choose my own woman, if I want one—which I don't,—or if ever I do want one—which I never shall!"

She drew her hands quickly from his grasp. There were tears in her splendid dark eyes.

"You talk, you talk!" she said, with a kind of sob in her voice—"It is all talk with you—talk which I cannot understand! I don't WANT to understand!—I am only a poor, ignorant girl. I cannot talk—but I can love! Ah yes, I can love! You say there is no such thing as love! What is it then, when one prays every night and morning for a man?—when one would work one's fingers to the bone for him?—when one would die to keep him from sickness and harm? What do you call it?"

He smiled.

"Self-delusion, Manella! The beautiful self-delusion of every nature-bred woman when her fancy is attracted by a particular sort of man. She makes an ideal of him in her mind and imagines him to be a god, when he is nothing but a devil!"

Something sinister and cruel in his look startled her,—she made the sign of the cross on her bosom.

"A devil?" she murmured—"a devil—?"

"Ah, now you are frightened!" he said, with a flash of amusement in his eyes—"You are a good Catholic, and you believe in devils. So you make the sign of the cross as a protection. That's right! That's the way to defend yourself from my evil influence! Wise Manella!"

The light mockery of his tone roused her pride,—that pride which had been suppressed in her by the force of a passionate emotion she could not restrain. She lifted her head and regarded him with an air of sorrow and scorn.

"After all, I think you must be a wicked man!" she said—"You have no heart! You are not worthy to be loved!"

"Quite true, Manella! You've hit the bull's eye in the very middle three times! I am a wicked man,—I have no heart,—I'm not worthy to be loved. No I'm not. I should find it a bore!"

"Bore?" she echoed—"What is that?"

"What is that? It is itself, Manella! 'Bore' is just 'bore.' It means tiredness—worn-out-ness—a state in which you wish yourself in a hot bath or a cold one, so that nobody can come near you. To be 'loved' would finish me off in a month!"

Her big eyes opened more widely than their wont in piteous perplexity.

"But how?" she asked.

"How? Why, just as you have put it,—to be prayed for night and morning,—to be worked for and waited on till fingers turned to bones,—to be guarded from sickness and harm,—heavens!—think of it! No more adventures in life,—no more freedom!—just love, love, love, which would not be love at all but the chains of a miserable wretch in prison!"

She flushed an angry crimson.

"Who is it that would chain you?" she demanded, "Not I! You could do as you liked with me—you know it!—and when you go away from this place, you could leave me and forget me,—I should never trouble you or remind you that I lived!! I should have had my happiness,— enough for my day!"

The pathos in her voice moved him though he was not easily moved. On a sudden impulse he put an arm about her, drew her to him and kissed her. She trembled at his caress, while he smiled at her emotion.

"A kiss is nothing, Manella!" he said—"We kiss children as I kiss you! You are a child,—a child-woman. Physically you are a Juno,— mentally you are an infant! By and by you will grow up,—and you will be glad I did no more than kiss you! It's getting late,—you must go home."

He released her and put her gently away from him. Then, as he saw her eyes still uplifted questioningly to his face, he laughed.

"Upon my word!" he exclaimed—"I am making a nice fool of myself! Actually wasting time on a woman. Go home, Manella, go home! If you are wise you won't stop here another minute! See now! You are full of curiosity—all women are! You want to know why I stay up here in this hill cabin by myself instead of staying at the 'Plaza.' You think I'm a rich Englishman. I'm not. No Englishman is ever rich,—not up to his own desires. He wants the earth and all that therein is—does the Englishman, and of course he can't have it. He rather grudges America her large slice of rich plum-pudding territory, forgetting that he could have had it himself for the price of tea. But I don't grudge anybody anything—America is welcome to the whole bulk as far as

I'm concerned—Britain ditto,—let them both eat and be filled. All *I* want is to be left alone. Do you hear that, Manella? To be left alone! Particularly by women. That's one reason why I came here. This cabin is supposed to be a sort of tuberculosis 'shelter,' where a patient in hopeless condition comes with a special nurse to die. I don't want a nurse, and I'm not going to die. Tubercles don't touch me—they don't flourish on my soil. So this solitude just suits me. If I were at the 'Plaza' I should have to meet a lot of women—"

"No, you wouldn't," interrupted Manella, suddenly and sharply— "only one woman."

"Only one? You?"

She sighed, and moved impatiently.

"Oh, no! Not me. A stranger."

He looked at her with a touch of inquisitiveness.

"An invalid?"

"She may be. I don't know. She has golden hair."

He gave a gesture of dislike.

"Dreadful! That's enough! I can imagine her,—a die-away creature with a cough and a straw-coloured wig. Yes!—that will do, Manella! You'd better go and wait upon her. I've got all I want for a couple of days at least." He seated himself and took up his note-book. She turned away.

"Stop a minute, Manella!"

She obeyed.

"Golden hair, you said?"

She nodded.

"Old or young?"

"She might be either"—and Manella gazed dreamily at the darkening sky—"There is nobody old nowadays—or so it seems to me."

"An invalid?"

"I don't think so. She looks quite well. She arrived at the Plaza only yesterday."

"Ah! Well, good-night, Manella! And if you want to know anything more about me, I don't mind telling you this,—that there's nothing in the world I so utterly detest as a woman with golden hair! There!"

She looked at him, surprised at his harsh tone. He shook his forefinger at her.

"Fact!" he said—"Fact as hard as nails! A woman with golden hair is a demon—a witch—a mischief and a curse! See? Always has been and always will be! Good-night!"

But Manella paused, meditatively.

"She looks like a witch," she said slowly—"One of those creatures they put in pictures of fairy tales,—small and white. Very small,—I could carry her."

"I wouldn't try it if I were you"—he answered, with visible impatience—"Off you go! Good-night!"

She gave him one lingering glance; then, turning abruptly picked up her empty milk pail and started down the hill at a run.

The man she left gave a sigh, deep and long of intense relief. Evening had fallen rapidly, and the purple darkness enveloped him in its warm, dense gloom. He sat absorbed in thought, his eyes turned towards the east, where the last stretches of the afternoon's great cloud trailed filmy threads of woolly black through space. His figure seemed gradually drawn within the coming night so as almost to become part of it, and the stillness around him had a touch of awe in its impalpable heaviness. One would have thought that in a place of such utter loneliness, the natural human spirit of a man would instinctively desire movement,— action of some sort, to shake off the insidious depression which crept through the air like a creeping shadow, but the solitary being, seated somewhat like an Aryan idol, hands on knees and face bent forwards, had no inclination to stir. His brain was busy; and half unconsciously his thoughts spoke aloud in words—

"Have we come to the former old stopping place?" he said, as though questioning some invisible companion; "Must we cry 'halt!' for the thousand millionth time? Or can we go on? Dare we go on? If actually we discover the secret—wrapped up like the minutest speck of a kernel in the nut of an electron,—what then? Will it be well or ill? Shall we find it worth while to live on here with nothing to do?—nothing to trouble us or compel us to labour? Without pain shall we be conscious of health?—without sorrow shall we understand joy?"

A sudden whiteness flooded the dark landscape, and a full moon leaped to the edge of the receding cloud. Its rising had been veiled in the drift of black woolly vapour, and its silver glare, sweeping through the darkness flashed over the land with astonishing abruptness. The man lifted his eyes.

"One would think that done for effect!" he said, half aloud—"If the moon were the goddess Cynthia beloved of Endymion, as woman and goddess in an impulse of vanity she would certainly have done that for effect! As it is—"

Here he paused,—an instinctive feeling warned him that some one was looking at him, and he turned his head quickly. On the slope of the hill where Manella had lately stood, there was a figure, white as the white moonlight itself, outlined delicately against the dark background. It seemed to be poised on the earth like a bird just lightly descended; in the stirless air its garments appeared closed about it fold on fold like the petals of an unopened magnolia flower. As he looked, it came gliding towards him with the floating ease of an air bubble, and the strong radiance of the large moon showed its woman's face, pale with the moonbeam pallor, and set in a wave of hair that swept back from the brows and fell in a loosely twisted coil like a shining snake stealthily losing itself in folds of misty drapery. He rose to meet the advancing phantom.

"Entirely for effect!" he said, "Well planned and quite worthy of you! All for effect!"

II

A laugh, clear and cold as a sleigh-bell on a frosty night rang out on the silence.

"Why did you run away from me?"

He replied at once, and brusquely.

"Because I was tired of you!"

She laughed again. A strange white elf as she looked In the spreading moonbeams she was woman to the core, and the disdainful movement of her small uplifted head plainly expressed her utter indifference to his answer.

"I followed you"—she said—"I knew I should find you! What are you doing up here? Shamming to be ill?"

"Precisely! 'Sham' is as much in my line as yours. I have to 'pretend' in order to be real!"

"Paradoxical as usual!" and she shrugged her shoulders—"Anyway you've chosen a good place to do your shamming in. It's quite lovely up here,—much better than the Plaza. I am at the Plaza."

"Automobile and all I suppose!" he said, sarcastically—"How many servants?—how many boxes with how many dresses?"

She laughed again.

"That's no concern of yours!" she replied—"I am my own mistress."

"More's the pity!" he retorted.

They faced each other. The moon, now soaring high in clear space, shed a luminous rain of silver over all the visible breadth of wild country, and their two figures looked mere dark silhouettes half drowned in the pearly glamour.

"It's worth travelling all the long miles to see!" she declared, stretching her arms out with an enthusiastic gesture—"Oh, beautiful big moon of California! I'm glad I came!"

He was silent.

"You are not glad!" she continued—"You are a bear-man in hiding, and the moon says nothing to you!"

"It says nothing because it Is nothing"—he answered, impatiently—"It is a dead planet without heart,—a mere shell of extinct volcanoes where fire once burned, and its light is but the reflection of the sun on its barren surface. It is like all women,—but mostly like You!"

She made him a sweeping curtsy so exquisitely graceful that

the action resembled nothing so much as the sway of a lily in a light wind.

"Thanks, gentle Knight!—flower of chivalry!" she said—"I see you love me in spite of yourself!"

He made a quick stride towards her,—then stopped. "Love you!" he echoed,—then laughed loudly and derisively-"Great God! Love you? You? If I did I should be mad! When will you learn the truth of me?—that women are less in my estimation than the insects crawling on a blade of grass or spawning in a stagnant pond?—that they have no power to move me to the smallest pulse of passion or desire?—and that you, of all your sex, seem to my mind the most—"

"Hateful?" she suggested, smilingly.

"No—the most complete and unmitigated bore!"

"Dreadful!" and she made a face at him like that of a naughty child,—then she sank down on the sun-baked turf in an easy half-reclining attitude—"It's certainly much worse to be a bore than to be hated. Hate is quite a live sentiment,—besides it always means, or HAS meant—love! You can't hate anything that is quite indifferent to you, but of course you CAN be bored! You are bored by me and I am bored by You!—and we are absolutely indifferent to each other! What a comedy it is! Isn't it?"

He stood still and sombre, gazing down at the figure resting on the ground at his feet, its white garments gathering about it as though they were sentiently aware that they must keep the line of classic beauty in every fold.

"Boredom is the trouble"—she went on—"No one escapes it. The very babies of to-day are bored. We all know too much. People used to be happy because they were ignorant—they had no sort of idea why they were born, or what they came into the world for. Now they've learned the horrid truth that they are only here just as the trees and flowers are here—to breed other trees and flowers and then go out of it—for no purpose, apparently. They are 'disillusioned.' They say 'what's the use?' To put up with so much trouble and labour for the folks coming after us whom we shall never see,—it seems perfectly foolish and futile. They used to believe in another life after this—but that hope has been knocked out of them. Besides it's quite open to question whether any of us would care to live again. Probably it might mean more boredom. There's really nothing left. That's why so many of us go reckless—it's just to escape being bored."

He listened in cold silence. After a pause—

"Have you done?" he said.

She looked up at him. The moonbeams set tiny frosty sparkles in her eyes.

"Have I done?" she echoed—"No,—not quite! I love talking—and it's a new and amusing sensation for me to talk to a man in his shirt-sleeves on a hill in California by the light of the moon! So wild and picturesque you know! All the men I've ever met have been dressed to death! Have you had your dinner?"

"I never dine," he replied.

"Really! Don't you eat and drink at all?"

"I live simply,"—he said—"Bread and milk are enough for me, and I have these."

She laughed and clapped her hands.

"Like a baby!" she exclaimed—"A big bearded baby! It's too delicious! And you're doing all this just to get away from ME! What a compliment!"

With angry impetus he bent over her reclining figure and seized her two hands.

"Get up!" he said harshly—"Don't lie there like a fallen angel!"

She yielded to his powerful grasp as he pulled her to her feet—then looked at him still laughing.

"Plenty of muscle!" she said—"Well?"

He held her hands still and gripped them fiercely. She gave a little cry.

"Don't! You forget my rings,—they hurt!"

At once he loosened his hold, and gazed moodily at her small fingers on which two or three superb diamond circlets glittered like drops of dew.

"Your rings!" he said—"Yes—I forgot them! Wonderful rings!—emblems of your inordinate vanity and vulgar wealth—I forgot them! How they sparkle in this wide moonlight, don't they? Just a drifting of nature's refuse matter, turned into jewels for women! Strange ordinance of strange elements! There!" and he let her hands go free—"They are not injured, nor are you."

She was silent pouting her under-lip like a spoilt child, and rubbing one finger where a ring had dinted her flesh.

"So you actually think I have come here to get away from YOU?" he went on—"Well for once your ineffable conceit is mistaken. You think yourself a personage of importance—but you are nothing,—less than nothing to me, I never give you a thought—I have come here to study—

to escape from the crazy noise of modern life—the hurtling to and fro of the masses of modern humanity,—I want to work out certain problems which may revolutionise the world and its course of living—"

"Why revolutionise it?" she interrupted—"Who wants it to be revolutionised? We are all very well as we are—it's a breeding place and a dying place—voila tout!"

She gave a French shrug of her shoulder and waved her hands expressively. Then she pushed back her flowing hair,—the moonbeams trickled like water over it, making a network of silver on gold.

"What did you come here for?" he asked, abruptly.

"To see you!" she answered smilingly—"And to tell you that I'm 'on the war-path' as they say, taking scalps as I go. This means that I'm travelling about,—possibly I may go to Europe—"

"To pick up a bankrupt nobleman!" he suggested.

She laughed.

"Dear, no! Nothing quite so stupid! Neither noblemen nor bankrupts attract me. No! I'm doing a scientific 'prowl,' like you. I believe I've discovered something with which I could annihilate you—so!" and she made a round O of her curved fingers and blew through it—"One breath!—from a distance, too! and hey presto!—the bear-man on the hills of California eating bread and milk is gone!—a complete vanishing trick—no more of him anywhere!" The bear-man, as she called him, gloomed upon her with a scowl.

"You'd better leave such things alone!" he said, angrily—"Women have no business with science."

"No, of course not!" she agreed—"Not in men's opinion. That's why they never mention Madame Curie without the poor Monsieur! SHE found radium and he didn't,—but 'he' is always first mentioned."

He gave an impatient gesture.

"Enough of all this!" he said—"Do you know it's nearly ten o'clock at night?—I suppose you do know!—and the people at the Plaza—"

"THEY know!"—she interrupted, nodding sagaciously—"They know I am rich—rich—rich! It doesn't matter what I do, because I am rich! I might stay out all night with a bear-man, and nobody would say a word against me, because I am rich! I might sit on the roof of the Plaza and swing my legs over the visitors' windows and it would be called 'charming' because I am rich! I can appear at the table d'hote in a bath-wrap and eat peas with a hair-pin if I like—and my conduct will be admired, because I am rich! When I go to Europe my photo will be in all the London pictorials with the grinning chorus-girls, because I am rich! And I shall be called 'the beautiful,' 'the exquisite'—'the fascinating' by all the unwashed penny journalists because I am rich! O-ooh!" and she gave a comic little screw of her mouth and eyes—"It's great fun to be rich if you know what to do with your riches!"

"Do You?" he enquired, sarcastically.

"I think so!" here she put her head on one side like a meditative bird and her wonderful hair fell aslant like a golden wing—"I amuse myself—as much as I can. I learn all that can be done with greedy, stupid humanity for so much cash down! I would,"—here she paused, and with a sudden feline swiftness of movement came close up to him—"I would have married You!—if you would have had me! I would have given you all my money to play with,—you could have got everything you want for your inventions and experiments, and I would have helped you,—and then—then—you could have blown up the world and me with it, so long as you gave me time to look at the magnificent sight! And I wouldn't have married you for love, mind you!—only for curiosity!"

He withdrew from her a couple of paces,—a glimmer of white teeth between his dark moustache and beard gave his face the expression of a snarl more than a smile.

"For curiosity!" she repeated, stretching out a hand and touching his arm—"To see what the thing that calls itself a man is made of! I did my very best with you, didn't I?—uncouth as you always were and are!—but I did my best! And all Washington thought it was settled! Why wouldn't you do what Washington expected?"

The light of the moon fell full on her upturned face. It was a wonderful face,—not beautiful according to the monotonous press-camera type, but radiant with such a light of daring intelligence as to make beauty itself seem cheap and meretricious in comparison with its glowing animation. He moved away from her another step, and shook his arm free from her touch.

"Why wouldn't you?" she reiterated softly; then with a sudden ripple of laughter, she clasped her hands and uplifted them in an attitude of prayer—"Why wouldn't he? Oh, big moon of California, why? Oh, pagan gods and goddesses and fauns and fairies, tell me why? Why wouldn't he?"

He gave her a glance of cool contempt.

"You should have been on the stage!" he said.

"'All the world's a stage,'" she quoted, letting her upraised arms fall languidly at her sides—"And ours is a real comedy! Not 'As You Like It' but 'As You Don't Like It!' Poor Shakespeare!—he never imagined such characters as we are! Now, suppose you had satisfied the expectations of all Washington City and married me, of course we should have bored each other dreadfully—but with plenty of money we could have run away from each other whenever we liked—they all do it nowadays!"

"Yes—they all do it!" he repeated, mechanically.

"They don't 'love' you know!" she went on—"Love is too much of a bore. You would find it so!"

"I should, indeed!" he said, with sudden energy—"It would be worse than any imaginable torture!—to be 'loved' and looked after, and watched and coddled and kissed—"

"Oh, surely no woman would want to kiss you!" she exclaimed—"Never! THAT would be too much of a good thing!"

And she gave a little peal of laughter, merry as the lilt of a sky-lark in the dawn. He stared at her angrily, moved by an insensate desire to seize her and throw her down the hill like a bundle of rubbish.

"To kiss You," she said, "one would have to wear a lip-shield of leather! As well kiss a bunch of nettles! No, no! I have quite a nice little mouth—soft and rosy! I shouldn't like to spoil it by scratching it against yours! It's curious how all men imagine women LIKE to kiss them! They never grasp an idea of the frequent unpleasantness of the operation! Now I'm going!"

"Thank God!" he exclaimed fervently.

"And don't worry yourself"—she continued, airily—"I shall not stay long at the Plaza."

"Thank God again!" he interpolated.

"It would be too dull,—especially as I'm not shamming to be ill, like you. Besides, I have work to do!—wonderful work! and I don't believe in doing it shut up like a hermit. Humanity is my crucible! Good-night,—good-bye!"

He checked her movement by a quick, imperious gesture.

"Wait!" he said—"Before you go I want you to know a bit of my mind—"

"Is it necessary?" she queried.

"I think so," he answered—"It will save you the trouble of ever trying to see me again, which will be a relief to me, if not to you. Listen!—and look at yourself with MY eyes—"

"Too difficult!" she declared—"I can look at nothing with your eyes any more than you can with mine!"

"Madam—"

She uttered a little laughing "Oh!" and put her hand to her ears.

"Not 'Madam' for heaven's sake!" she exclaimed; "It sounds as if I were either a queen or a dressmaker!"

His sombre eyes had no smile in them.

"How should you be addressed?" he demanded, "A woman of such wealth and independence as you possess can hardly be called 'Miss' as if she were in parental leading-strings!"

She looked up at the clear dark sky where the moon hung like a huge silver air-ball.

"No, I suppose not!" she replied—"The old English word was 'Mistress.' So quaint and pretty, don't you think?"

> *'Oh mistress mine, where are you roaming?*
> *Oh stay and hear! your true love's coming!'*

She sang the two lines in a deliciously entrancing voice, full of youth and tenderness. With one quick stride he advanced upon her and caught her by the shoulders.

"My God, I could shake the life out of you!" he said, fiercely—"I wonder you are not afraid of me!"

She laughed, careless of his grasp.

"Why should I be? You couldn't kill me if you tried—and if you could—"

"If I could—ah, if I could!" he muttered, fiercely.

"Why then there would be another murderer added to the general world of murderers!" she said—"That's all! It's not worth it!"

Still he held her in his grip.

"See here!" he said—"Before you go I want you to know a thing or two,—you may as well learn once for all my views on women. They're brief, but they're fixed. And they're straight! Women are nothing—just necessary for the continuation of the race—no more. They may be beautiful or homely—it's all one—they serve the same purpose. I'm under no delusions about them. Without men they are utterly useless,—mere waste on the wind! To idealise them is a stupid mistake. To think that they can do anything original, intellectual or imaginative is to set one's self down an idiot. You,—you the spoilt only child of one of the biggest rascal financiers in New York,—You, left alone in the world with a fortune so vast as to be almost criminal—you think you are something superlative in the way of women,—you play the Cleopatra,—you are convinced you can draw men after you—but it's your money that draws them,—not You! Can't you see that?—or are you too vain to see it? And you've no mercy on them,—you make them believe you care for them and then you throw them over like empty nutshells! That's your way! But you never fooled Me,—and you never will!"

He released her as suddenly as he had grasped her,—she drew her white draperies round her shoulders with a statuesque grace, and lifted her head, smiling.

"Empty nutshells are a very good description of men who come after a woman for her money"—she observed, placidly—"and it's quite natural that the woman should throw them over her shoulder. There's nothing in them—not even a flavour! No—never fooled you,—you fooled yourself—you are fooling yourself now, only you don't know it. But there!—let's finish talking! I like the romance of the situation—you in your shirt-sleeves on a hill in California, and I in silken stuff and diamonds paying you a moonlight visit— it's really quite novel and charming!—but it can't go on for ever! Just now you said you wanted me to know a thing or two, and I presume you have explained yourself. What you think or what you don't think about women doesn't interest me. I'm one of the 'wastes on the wind!' I shall not aid in the continuation of the race,—heaven forbid! The race is too stupid and too miserable to merit continuance. Everything has been done for it that can be done, over and over again, from the beginning—till now,—and now—Now!" She paused, and despite himself the tone of her voice sent a thrill through his blood of something like fear.

"Now?—well! What Now?" he demanded.

She lifted one hand and pointed upwards. Her face in the moonbeams looked austere and almost spectral in outline.

"Now—the Change!" she answered—"The Change when all things shall be made new!"

A silence followed her words,—a strange and heavy silence.

It was broken by her voice hushed to an extreme softness, yet clearly audible.

"Good-night!—good-bye!"

He turned impatiently away to avoid further leave-taking—then, on a sudden impulse, his mood changed.

"Morgana!"

The call echoed through emptiness. She was gone. He called again,—the long vowel in the strange name sounding like "Mor-ga-ar-na" as a shivering note on the G string of a violin may sound at the conclusion of a musical phrase. There was no reply. He was—as he had desired to be,—alone.

III

"S he left New York several weeks ago,—didn't you know it? Dear me!—I thought everybody was convulsed at the news!"

The speaker, a young woman fashionably attired and seated in a rocking chair in the verandah of a favourite summer hotel on Long Island, raised her eyes and shrugged her shoulders expressively as she uttered these words to a man standing near her with a newspaper in his hand. He was a very stiff-jointed upright personage with iron grey hair and features hard enough to suggest their having been carved out of wood.

"No—I didn't know it"—he said, enunciating his words in the deliberate dictatorial manner common to a certain type of American— "If I had I should have taken steps to prevent it."

"You can't take steps to prevent anything Morgana Royal decides to do!" declared his companion. "She's a law to herself and to nobody else. I guess You couldn't stop her, Mr. Sam Gwent!"

Mr. Sam Gwent permitted himself to smile. It was a smile that merely stretched the corners of his mouth a little,—it had no geniality.

"Possibly not!" he answered—"But I should have had a try! I should certainly have pointed out to her the folly of her present adventure."

"Do you know what it is?"

He paused before replying.

"Well,—hardly! But I have a guess!"

"Is that so? Then I'll admit you're cleverer than I am!"

"Thats a great compliment! But even Miss Lydia Herbert, brilliant woman of the world as she is, doesn't know EVERYTHING!"

"Not quite!" she replied, stifling a tiny yawn—"Nor do you! But most things that are worth knowing I know. There's a lot one need never learn. The chief business of life nowadays is to have heaps of money and know how to spend it. That's Morgana's way."

Mr. Sam Gwent folded up his newspaper, flattened it into a neat parcel, and put it in his pocket.

"She has a great deal too much money"—he said, "and-to my thinking—she does NOT know how to spend it,—not in the right womanly way. She has gone off in the midst of many duties to society at a time when she should have stayed—"

Miss Herbert opened her brown, rather insolent eyes wide at this and laughed.

"Does it matter?" she asked. "The old man left his pile to her 'absolutely and unconditionally'—without any orders as to society duties. And I don't believe You'VE any authority over her, have you? Or are you suddenly turning up as a trustee?"

He surveyed her with a kind of admiring sarcasm.

"No. I'm only an uncle,"—he said—"Uncle of the boy that shot himself this morning for her sake!"

Miss Herbert uttered a sharp cry. She was startled and horrified.

"What! . . . Jack? . . . Shot himself? . . . Oh, how dreadful!—I'm— I'm sorry—!"

"You're not!"—retorted Gwent—"So don't pretend. No one is sorry for anybody else nowadays. There's no time. And no inclination. Jack was always a fool—perhaps he's best out of it. I've just seen him—dead. He's better-looking so than when alive."

She sprang up from her rocking chair in a blaze of indignation.

"You are brutal!" she exclaimed, with a half sob—"Positively brutal!"

"Not at all!" he answered, composedly—"Only commonplace. It is you advanced women that are brutal,—not we left-behind men. Jack was a fool, I say—he staked the whole of his game on Morgana Royal, and he lost. That was the last straw. If he could have married her he would have cleared all his debts over and over—and that's what he had hoped for. The disappointment was too much for him."

"But—didn't he LOVE her?" Lydia Herbert put the question almost imperatively.

Mr. Sam Gwent raised his eyebrows quizzically. "I guess you came out of the Middle Ages!" he observed—"What's 'love'? Did you ever know a woman with millions of money who got 'loved'? Not a bit of it! Her MONEY is loved—but not herself. She's the encumbrance to the cash."

"Then—then—you mean to tell me Jack was only after the money—?"

"What else should he be after? The woman? There are thousands of women,—all to be had for the asking—they pitch themselves at men headlong—no hesitation or modesty about them nowadays! Jack's asking would never have been refused by any one of them. But the millions of Morgana Royal are not to be got every day!"

Miss Herbert's rather thin lips tightened into a close line,—she flicked some light tear-drops away from her eyes with a handkerchief as fine as a cobweb delicately perfumed, and stood silently looking out on the view from the verandah.

　　　　　　　　　　　　　　MARIE CORELLI

"You see," pursued Gwent, in his cold, deliberate accents, "Jack was ruined financially. And he has all but ruined ME. Now he has taken himself out of the way with a pistol shot, and left me to face the music for him. Morgana Royal was his only chance. She led him on,—she certainly led him on. He thought he had her,—then—just as he was about to pin the butterfly to his specimen card, away it flew!"

"Cute butterfly!" interjected Miss Herbert.

"Maybe. Maybe not. We shall see. Anyway Jack's game is finished."

"And I suppose this is why, as you say, Morgana has gone off 'in the midst of many social duties'? Was Jack one of her social duties?"

Gwent gazed at her with an unrevealing placidity.

"No. Not exactly," he replied—"I give her credit for not knowing anything of his intention to clear out. Though I don't think she would have tried to alter his intention if she had."

Miss Herbert still surveyed the scenery.

"Well,—I don't feel so sorry for him now you tell me it was only the money he was after"—she said—"I thought he was a finer character—"

"You're talking 'Middle Ages' again,"—interrupted Gwent—"Who wants fine characters nowadays? The object of life is to LIVE, isn't it? And to 'live' means to get all you can for your own pleasure and profit,—take care of Number One!—and let the rest of the world do as it likes. It's quite YOUR method,—though you pretend it isn't!"

"You're not very polite!" she said.

"Now, why should I be?" he pursued, argumentatively—"What's politeness worth unless you want to flatter something for yourself out of somebody? I never flatter, and I'm never polite. I know just how you feel,—you haven't got as much money as you want and you're looking about for a fellow who HAS. Then you'll marry him—if you can. You, as a woman, are doing just what Jack did as a man. But,—if you miss your game, I don't think you'll commit suicide. You're too well-balanced for that. And I think you'll succeed in your aims—if you're careful!"

"If I'm careful?" she echoed, questioningly.

"Yes—if you want a millionaire. Especially the old rascal you're after. Don't dress too 'loud.' Don't show ALL your back—leave some for him to think about. Don't paint your face,—let it alone. And be, or pretend to be, very considerate of folks' feelings. That'll do!"

"Here endeth the first lesson!" she said. "Thanks, preacher Gwent! I guess I'll worry through!"

"I guess you will!"—he answered, slowly. "I wish I was as certain of anything in the world as I am of THAT!"

She was silent. The corners of her mouth twitched slightly as though she sought to conceal a smile. She watched her companion furtively as he took a cigar from a case in his pocket and lit it.

"I must go and fix up the funeral business"—he said, "Jack has gone, and his remains must be disposed of. That's my affair. Just now his mother's crying over him,—and I can't stand that sort of thing. It gets over me."

"Then you actually HAVE a heart?" she suggested.

"I suppose so. I used to have. But it isn't the heart,—that's only a pumping muscle. I conclude it's the head."

He puffed two or three rings of smoke into the clear air.

"You know where she's gone?" he asked, suddenly.

"Morgana?"

"Yes."

Lydia Herbert hesitated.

"I THINK I know," she replied at last—"But I'm not sure."

"Well, I'M sure"—said Gwent—"She's after the special quarry that has given her the slip,—Roger Seaton. He went to California a month ago."

"Then she's in California?"

"Certain!"

Mr. Gwent took another puff at his cigar.

"You must have been in Washington when every one thought that he and she were going to make a matrimonial tie of it"—he went on—"Why, nothing else was talked of!"

She nodded.

"I know! I was there. But a man who has set his soul on science doesn't want a wife."

"And what about a woman who has set her soul in the same direction?" he asked.

She shrugged her shoulders.

"Oh, that's all popcorn! Morgana is not a scientist,—she's hardly a student. She just 'imagines' she can do things. But she can't."

"Well! I'm not so sure!" and Gwent looked ruminative—"She's got a smart way of settling problems while the rest of us are talking about them."

"To her own satisfaction only"—said Miss Herbert, ironically,—"Certainly not to the satisfaction of anybody else! She talks the wildest nonsense about controlling the world! Imagine it! A world controlled by Morgana!" She gave an impatient little shake of her skirts. "I do hate these sorts of mysterious, philosophising women, don't you? The old days must have been ever so much better! When it was all poetry and romance and beautiful idealism! When Dante and Beatrice were possible!"

Gwent smiled sourly.

"They never WERE possible!" he retorted—"Dante was, like all poets, a regular humbug. Any peg served to hang his stuff on,—from a child of nine to a girl of eighteen. The stupidest thing ever written is what he called his 'New Life' or 'Vita Nuova.' I read it once, and it made me pretty nigh sick. Think of all that twaddle about Beatrice 'denying him her most gracious salutation'! That any creature claiming to be a man could drivel along in such a style beats me altogether!"

"It's perfectly lovely!" declared Miss Herbert—"You've no taste in literature, Mr. Gwent!"

"I've no taste for humbug"—he answered—"That's so! I guess I know the difference between tragedy and comedy, even when I see them side by side." He flicked a long burnt ash from his cigar. "I've had a bit of comedy with you this morning—now I'm going to take up tragedy! I tell you there's more written in Jack's dead face than in all Dante!"

"The tragedy of a lost gamble for money!" she said, with a scornful uplift of her eyebrows.

He nodded.

"That's so! It upsets the mental balance of a man more than a lost gamble for love!"

And he walked away.

Lydia Herbert, left to herself, played idly with the leaves of the vine that clambered about the high wooden columns of the verandah where she stood, admiring the sparkle of her diamond bangle which, like a thin circlet of dewdrops, glittered on her slim wrist. Now and then she looked far out to the sea gleaming in the burning sun, and allowed her thoughts to wander from herself and her elegant clothes to some of the social incidents in which she had taken part during the past couple of months. She recalled the magnificent ball given by Morgana Royal at her regal home, when all the fashion and frivolity of the noted "Four Hundred" were assembled, and when the one whispered topic of conversation among gossips was the possibility of the marriage of one of the richest women in the world to a shabbily clothed scientist without a penny, save what he earned with considerable difficulty. Morgana herself played the part of an enigma. She laughed, shook her head, and moved her daintily attired person through the crowd of her guests with all the gliding grace of a fairy vision in white draperies showered with diamonds, but gave no hint of special favour or attention to any man, not even to Roger Seaton, the scientist in question, who stood apart from the dancing throng, in a kind of frowning disdain, looking on, much as one might fancy a forest animal looking at the last gambols of prey It purposed to devour. He had taken the first convenient interval to disappear, and as he did not return, Miss Herbert had asked her hostess what had become of him? Morgana, her cheeks flushed prettily by a just-finished dance, smiled in surprise at the question.

"How should I know?" she replied—"I am not his keeper?"

"But—but—you are interested in him?" Lydia suggested.

"Interested? Oh, yes! Who would not be interested in a man who says he can destroy half the world if he wants to! He assumes to be a sort of deity, you know!—Jove and his thunderbolts in the shape of a man in a badly cut suit of modern clothes! Isn't it fun!" She gave a little peal of laughter. "And every one in the room to-night thinks I am going to marry him!"

"And are you not?"

"Can you imagine it! Me, married? Lydia, Lydia, do you take me for a fool!" She laughed again—then grew suddenly serious. "To think of such a thing! Fancy Me!—giving my life into the keeping of a scientific wizard who, if he chose, could reduce me to a little heap of dust in two minutes, and no one any the wiser! Thank you! The sensational press has been pretty full lately of men's brutalities to women,—and I've no intention of adding myself to the list of victims! Men Are brutes! They were born brutes, and brutes they will remain!"

"Then you don't like him?" persisted Lydia, moved, in spite of herself, by curiosity, and also by a vague wonder at the strange brilliancy of complexion and eyes which gave to Morgana a beauty quite unattainable by features only—"You're not set on him?"

Morgana held up a finger.

"Listen!" she said—"Isn't that a lovely valse? Doesn't the music seem to sweep round and tie us all up in a garland of melody! How far, far above all these twirling human microbes it is!—as far as heaven from earth! If we could really obey the call of that music we should rise on wings and fly to such wonderful worlds!—as it is, we can only hop round and round like motes in a sunbeam and imagine we are enjoying ourselves for an hour or two! But the music means so much more!" She paused, enrapt;—then in a lighter tone went on—"And you think I would marry? I would not marry an emperor if there were one worth having—which there isn't!—and as for Roger Seaton, I certainly am not 'set' on him as you so elegantly put it! And he's not 'set' on me. We're both 'set' on something else!"

She was standing near an open window as she spoke, and she looked up at the dark purple sky sprinkled with stars. She continued slowly, and with emphasis—

"I might—possibly I might—have helped him to that something else—if I had not discovered something more!"

She lifted her hand with a commanding gesture as though unconsciously,—then let it drop at her side. Lydia Herbert looked at her perplexedly.

"You talk so very strangely!" she said.

Morgana smiled.

"Yes, I know I do!" she admitted—"I am what old Scotswomen call 'fey'! You know I was born away in the Hebrides,—my father was a poor herder of sheep at one time before he came over to the States. I was only a baby when I was carried away from the islands of mist and rain—but I was 'fey' from my birth—"

"What is fey?" interrupted Miss Herbert.

"It's just everything that everybody else is Not"—Morgana replied—"'Fey' people are magic people; they see what no one else sees,—they hear voices that no one else hears—voices that whisper secrets and tell of wonders as yet undiscovered—" She broke off suddenly. "We must not stay talking here"—she resumed-"All the folks will say we are planning the bridesmaids' dresses and that the very day of the ceremony is fixed! But you can be sure that I am not going to marry anybody—least of all Roger Seaton!"

"You like him though! I can see you like him!"

"Of course I like him! He's a human magnet,—he 'draws'! You fly towards him as if he were a bit of rubbed sealing-wax and you a snippet of paper! But you soon drop off! Oh, that valse! Isn't it entrancing!"

And, swinging herself round lightly like a bell-flower in a breeze she danced off alone and vanished in the crowd of her guests.

Lydia Herbert recalled this conversation now, as she stood looking from the vine-clad verandah of her hotel towards the sea, and again saw, as in a vision, the face and eyes of her "fey" friend,—a face by no means beautiful in feature, but full of a sparkling attraction which was almost irresistible.

"Nothing in her!" had declared New York society generally—"Except her money! And her hair—but not even that unless she lets it down!"

Lydia had seen it so "let down," once, and only once, and the sight of such a glistening rope of gold had fairly startled her.

"All your own?" she had gasped.

And with a twinkling smile, and comic hesitation of manner Morgana had answered.

"I—I THINK it is! It seems so! I don't believe it will come off unless you pull VERY hard!"

Lydia had not pulled hard, but she had felt the soft rippling mass falling from head to far below the knee, and had silently envied the owner its possession.

"It's a great bother," Morgana declared—"I never know what to do with it. I can't dress it 'fashionably' one bit, and when I twist it up it's so fine it goes into nothing and never looks the quantity it is. However, we must all have our troubles!—with some it's teeth—with others it's ankles—we're never QUITE all right! The thing is to endure without complaining!"

"And this curious creature who talked "so very strangely," possessed millions of money! Her father, who had arrived in the States from the wildest north of Scotland with practically not a penny, had so gathered and garnered every opportunity that came in his way that every investment he touched seemed to turn to five times its first value under his fingers. When his wife died very soon after his wealth began to accumulate, he was beset by women of beauty and position eager to take her place, but he was adamant against all their blandishments and remained a widower, devoting his entire care to the one child he had brought with him as an infant from the Highland hills, and to whom he gave a brilliant but desultory and uncommon education. Life seemed to swirl round him in a glittering ring of gold of which he made himself the centre,—and when he died suddenly "from overstrain" as the doctors said, people were almost frightened to name the vast fortune his daughter inherited, accustomed as they were to the counting of many millions. And now—?"

"California!" mused Lydia—"Sam Gwent thinks she has gone there after Roger Seaton. But what can be her object if she doesn't care for him? It's far more likely she's started for Sicily—she's having a palace built there for her small self to live in 'all by her lonesome'! Well! She can afford it!"

And with a short sigh she let go her train of thought and left the verandah,—it was time to change her costume and prepare "effects" to dazzle and bewilder the uncertain mind of a crafty old Croesus who, having freely enjoyed himself as a bachelor up to his present age of seventy-four, was now looking about for a young strong woman to manage his house and be a nurse and attendant for him in his declining years, for which service, should she be suitable, he would concede to her the name of "wife" in order to give stability to her position. And Lydia Herbert herself was privately quite aware of his views. Moreover she was entirely willing to accommodate herself to them for the sake of riches and a luxurious life, and the "settlement" she meant to insist upon if her plans ripened to fulfilment. She had no great ambitions; few women of her social class have. To be well housed, well fed and well clothed, and enabled to do the fashionable round without hindrance—this was all she sought, and of romance, sentiment, emotion or idealism she had none. Now and again she caught the flash of a thought in her brain higher than the level of material needs, but dismissed it more quickly than it came as—"Ridiculous! Absolute nonsense! Like Morgana!"

And to be like Morgana, meant to be like what cynics designate "an impossible woman,"—independent of opinions and therefore "not understood of the people."

IV

W hy do you stare at me? You have such big eyes!"

Morgana, dotted only in a white silk nightgown, sitting on the edge of her bed with her small rosy toes peeping out beneath the tiny frill of her thin garment, looked at the broad-shouldered handsome girl Manella who had just brought in her breakfast tray and now stood regarding her with an odd expression of mingled admiration and shyness.

"Such big eyes!" she repeated—"Like great head-lamps flaring out of that motor-brain of yours! What do you see in me?"

Manella's brown skin flushed crimson.

"Something I have never seen before!" she answered—"You are so small and white! Not like a woman at all!"

Morgana laughed merrily.

"Not like a woman! Oh dear! What am I like then?"

Manella's eyes grew darker than ever in the effort to explain her thought.

"I do not know"—she said, hesitatingly—"But—once—here in this garden—we found a wonderful butterfly with white wings—all white,— and it was resting on a scarlet flower. We all went out to look at it, because it was unlike any other butterfly we had ever seen,—its wings were like velvet or swansdown. You remind me of that butterfly."

Morgana smiled.

"Did it fly away?"

"Oh, yes. Very soon! And an hour or so after it had flown, the scarlet flower where it had rested was dead."

"Most thrilling!" And Morgana gave a little yawn. "Is that breakfast? Yes? Stay with me while I have it! Are you the head chambermaid at the Plaza?"

Manella shrugged her shoulders.

"I do not know what I am! I do everything I am asked to do as well as I can."

"Obliging creature! And are you well paid?"

"As much as I want"—Manella answered, indifferently. "But there is no pleasure in the work."

"Is there pleasure in ANY work?"

"If one works for a person one loves,—surely yes!" the girl murmured as if she were speaking to herself, "The days would be too short for all the work to be done!"

Morgana glanced at her, and the flash of her eyes had the grey-blue of lightning. Then she poured out the coffee and tasted it.

"Not bad!" she commented—"Did you make it?"

Manella nodded, and went on talking at random.

"I daresay it's not as good as it ought to be"—she said—"If you had brought your own maid I should have asked HER to make it. Women of your class like their food served differently to us poor folk, and I don't know their ways."

Morgana laughed.

"You quaint, handsome thing! What do you know about it? What, in your opinion, Is my class?"

Manella pulled nervously at the ends of the bright coloured kerchief she wore knotted across her bosom, and hesitated a moment.

"Well, for one thing you are rich"—she said, at last—"There is no mistaking that. Your lovely clothes—you must spend a fortune on them! Then—all the people here wonder at your automobile—and your chauffeur says it is the most perfect one ever made! And all these riches make you think you ought to have everything just as you fancy it. I suppose you ought—I'm not sure! I don't believe you have much feeling,—you couldn't, you know! It is not as if you wanted something very badly and there was no chance of your getting it,— your money would buy all you could desire. It would even buy you a man!"

Morgana paused in the act of pouring out a second cup of coffee, and her face dimpled with amusement.

"Buy me a man!" she echoed—"You think it would?"

"Of course it would!" Manella averred—"If you wanted one, which I daresay you don't. For all I know, you may be like the man who is living in the consumption hut on the hill,—he ought to have a woman, but he doesn't want one."

Morgana buttered her little breakfast roll very delicately.

"The man who lives in the consumption hut on the hill!" she repeated, slowly, and with a smile—"What man is that?"

"I don't know—" and Manella's large dark eyes filled with a strangely wistful perplexity. "He is a stranger—and he's not ill at all. He is big and strong and healthy. But he has chosen to live in the 'house of the dying,' as it is sometimes called—where people from the Plaza go when there's no more hope for them. He likes to be quite alone—he thinks and writes all day. I take him milk and bread,—it is all he orders from the Plaza. I would be his woman. I would work for him from morning till night. But he will not have me."

Morgana raised her eyes, glittering with the "fey" light in them that often bewildered and rather scared her friends.

"You would be his woman? You are in love with him?" she said.

Something in her look checked Manella's natural impulse to confide in one of her own sex.

"No, I am not!"—she answered coldly—"I have said too much."

Morgana smiled, and stretching out her small white hand, adorned with its sparkling rings, laid it caressingly on the girl's brown wrist.

"You are a dear!"—she murmured, lazily—"Just a dear! A big, beautiful creature with a heart! That's the trouble—your heart! You've found a man living selfishly alone, scribbling what he perhaps thinks are the most wonderful things ever put on paper, when they are very likely nothing but rubbish, and it enters into your head that he wants mothering and loving! He doesn't want anything of the sort! And You want to love and mother him! Oh heavens!—have you ever thought what loving and mothering mean?"

Manella drew a quick soft breath.

"All the world, surely!" she answered, with emotion—"To love!—to possess the one we love, body and soul!—and to mother a life born of such love!—THAT must be heaven!"

The smile flitted away from Morgana's lips, and her expression became almost sorrowful.

"You are like a trusting animal!" she said—"An animal all innocent of guns and steel-traps! You poor girl! I should like you to come with me out of these mountain solitudes into the world! What is your name?"

"Manella."

"Manella—what?"

"Manella Soriso"—the girl answered—"I am Spanish by both parents,—they are dead now. I was born at Monterey."

Morgana began to hum softly—

> "Under the walls of Monterey
> At dawn the bugles began to play
> Come forth to thy death
> Victor Galbraith."

MARIE CORELLI

She broke off,—then said—

"You have not seen many men?"

"Oh, yes, I have!" and Manella tossed her head airily—"Men all more or less alike—greedy for dollars, fond of smoke and cinema women,—I do not care for them. Some have asked me to marry, but I would rather hang myself than be wife to one of them!"

Morgana slid off the edge of her bed and stood upright, her white silk nightgown falling symmetrically round her small figure. With a dexterous movement she loosened the knot into which she had twisted her hair for the night, and it fell in a sinuous coil like a golden snake from head to knee. Manella stepped back in amazement.

"Oh!" she cried—"How beautiful! I have quite as much in quantity, but it is black and heavy—ugly!—no good. And he,—that man who lives in the hut on the hill—says there is nothing he hates so much as a woman with golden hair! How can he hate such a lovely thing!"

Morgana shrugged her shoulders.

"Each one to his taste!" she said, airily—"Some like black hair—some red—some gold—some nut-brown. But does it matter at all what men think or care for? To me it is perfectly indifferent! And you are quite right to prefer hanging to marriage—I do, myself!"

Fascinated by her wonderful elfin look as she stood like a white iris in its silken sheath, her small body's outline showing dimly through the folds of her garment, Manella drew nearer, somewhat timidly.

"Ah, but I do not mean that I prefer hanging to real, true marriage!" she said—"When one loves, it is different! In love I would rather hang than not give myself to the man I love—give myself in all I am, and all I have! And You—you who look so pretty and wonderful—almost like a fairy!—do You not feel like that too?"

Morgana laughed—a little laugh sweet and cold as rain tinkling on glass.

"No, indeed!" she answered—"I have never felt like THAT! I hope I shall never feel like THAT! To feel like THAT is to feel like the female beasts of the field who only wait and live to be used by the males, giving 'all they are and all they have,' poor creatures! The bull does not 'love' the cow—he gives her a calf. When the calf is born and old enough to get along by itself, it forgets its mother just as its mother forgets IT, while the sire is blissfully indifferent to both! It's really the same thing with human animals,—especially nowadays—only we haven't the honesty to admit it! No, Manella Soriso!—with your good looks you ought to be far above 'feeling like THAT!'—you are a nobler creature than a cow! No wonder men despise women who are always on the cow level!"

She laughed again, and tripped lightly to the looking-glass.

"I must dress;"—she said—"And you can take a message to my chauffeur and tell him to get everything ready to start. I've had a lovely night's rest and am quite fit for a long run."

"Oh, are you going?" and Manella gave a little cry of pain—"I am sorry! I do want you to stay!"

Morgana's eyes flashed mingled humour and disdain. "You quaint creature! Why should I stay? There's nothing to stay for!"

"If there's nothing to stay for, why did you come?"

This was an unexpected question, the result of a subconscious suggestion in Manella's mind which she herself could not have explained.

Morgana seemed amused.

"What did I come for? Really, I hardly know! I am full of odd whims and fancies, and I like to humour myself in my various ways. I think I wanted to see a bit of California,—that's all!"

"Then why not see more of it?" persisted Manella.

"Enough is better than too much!" laughed Morgana—"I am easily bored! This Plaza hotel would bore me to death! What do you want me to stay for? To see your man on the mountain?"

"No!" Manella replied with sudden sharpness—"No! I would not like you to see him! He would either hate you or love you!"

The grey-blue lightning flash glittered in Morgana's eyes.

"You ARE a curious girl!" she said, slowly—"You might be a tragic actress and make your fortune on the stage, with that voice and that look! And yet you stay here as 'help' in a Sanatorium! Well! It's a dull, dreary way of living, but I suppose you like it!"

"I DON'T like it!" declared Manella, vehemently, "I hate it! But what am I to do? I have no home and no money. I must earn my living somehow."

"Will you come away with me?" said Morgana—"I'll take you at once if you like!"

Manella stared in a kind of child-like wonderment,—her big dusky eyes grew brilliant,—then clouded with a sombre sadness.

"Thank you, Senora!" she answered, pronouncing the Spanish form of address with a lingering sweetness, "It is very good of you! But I should not please you. I do not know the world, and I am not quick to learn. I am better where I am."

A little smile, dreamy and mysterious, crept round Morgana's lips.

"Yes!-perhaps you are!" she said—"I understand! You would not like to leave HIM! I am sure that is so! You want to feed your big bear regularly with bread and milk—yes, you poor deluded child! Courage! You may still have a chance to be, as you say, 'his woman!' And when you are I wonder how you will like it!"

She laughed, and began to brush her shining hair out in two silky lengths on either side. Manella gazed and gazed at the glittering splendour till she could gaze no more for sheer envy, and then she turned slowly and left the room.

Alone, Morgana continued brushing her hair meditatively,—then, twisting it up in a great coil out of her way, she proceeded with her toilette. Everything of the very finest and daintiest was hers to wear, from the silken hose to the delicate lace camisole, and when she reached the finishing point in her admirably cut summer serge gown and becoming close-fitting hat, she studied herself from head to foot in the mirror with fastidious care to be sure that every detail of her costume was perfect. She was fully aware that she was not a newspaper camera "beauty" and that she had subtle points of attraction which no camera could ever catch, and it was just these points which she knew how to emphasise.

"I hate untidy travellers!"—she would say—"Horrors of men and women in oil-skins, smelling of petrol! No goblin ever seen in a nightmare could be uglier than the ordinary motorist!"

She had no luggage with her, save an adaptable suitcase which, she declared "held everything." This she quickly packed and locked, ready for her journey. Then she stepped to the window and waved her hand towards the near hill and the "hut of the dying."

"Fool of a bear man!" she said, apostrophising the individual she chose to call by that name—"Here you come along to a wild place in California running away from ME,—and here you find a sort of untutored female savage eager and willing to be your 'woman!' Well, why not? She's just the kind of thing you want—to fetch wood, draw water, cook food, and—bear children! And when the children come they'll run about the hill like savages themselves, and yell and dance and be greedy and dirty—and you'll presently wonder whether you are a civilised man or a species of unthinking baboon! You will be living the baboon life,—and your brain will grow thicker and harder as you grow older,—and your great scientific discovery will be buried in the thickness and hardness and never see the light of day! All this, IF she is 'your woman!' It's a great 'if' of course!—but she's big and handsome, with a beautiful body and splendid strength, and I never heard of a man who could resist beauty and strength together. As for ME and my 'vulgar wealth' as you call it, I'm a little wisp of straw not worth your thought!—or so you assume—no, good Bear!—not till we come to a tussle—if we ever do!"

She took up her gloves and hand-bag and went downstairs, entering the broad, airy flower-bordered lounge of the Plaza with a friendly nod and smile to the book-keeper in the office where she paid her bill. Her chauffeur, a smart Frenchman in quiet livery, was awaiting her with an assistant groom or page beside him.

"We go on to-day, Madame?" he enquired.

"Yes,—we go on"—she replied—"as quickly and as far as possible. Just fetch my valise—it's ready packed in my room."

The groom hurried away to obey this order, and Morgana glancing around her saw that she was an object of intense curiosity to some of the hotel inmates who were in the lounge—men and women both. Her grey-blue eyes flashed over them all carelessly and lighted on Manella who stood shrinking aside in a corner. To her she beckoned smilingly.

"Come and see me off!" she said—"Take a look at my car and see how you'd like to travel in it!"

Manella pursed her lips and shook her head.

"I'd rather not!" she murmured—"It's no use looking at what one can never have!"

Morgana laughed.

"As you please!" she said—"You are an odd girl, but you are quite beautiful! Don't forget that! Tell the man on the mountain that I said so!—quite beautiful! Good-bye!"

She passed through the lounge with a swift grace of movement and entered her sumptuous limousine, lined richly in corded rose silk and fitted with every imaginable luxury like a queen's boudoir on wheels, while Manella craned her neck forward to see the last of her. Her valise was quickly strapped in place, and in another minute to the sound of a high silvery bugle note (which was the only sort of "hooter" she would tolerate) the car glided noiselessly away down the broad, dusty white road, its polished enamel and silver points glittering like streaks of light vanishing into deeper light as it disappeared.

"There goes the richest woman in America!" said the hotel clerk for the benefit of anyone who might care to listen to the announcement,— "Morgana Royal!"

"Is that so?" drawled a sallow-faced man, reclining in an invalid chair—"She's not much to look at!"

And he yawned expansively.

He was right. She was not much to look at. But she was more than looks ever made. So, with sorrow and with envy, thought Manella, who instinctively felt that though she herself might be something to look at and "quite beautiful," she was nothing else. She had never heard the word "fey." The mystic glamour of the Western Highlands was shut away from her by the wide barrier of many seas and curtains of cloud. And therefore she did not know that "fey" women are a race apart from all other women in the world.

V

That evening at sunset Manella made her way towards the hill and the "House of the Dying," moved by she knew not what strange impulse. She had no excuse whatever for going; she knew that the man living up there in whom she was so much interested had as much food for three days as he asked for or desired, and that he was likely to be vexed at the very sight of her. Yet she had an eager wish to tell him something about the wonderful little creature with lightning eyes who had left the Plaza that morning and had told her, Manella, that she was "quite beautiful." Pride, and an innocent feminine vanity thrilled her; "if another woman thinks so, it must be so,"—she argued, being aware that women seldom admire each other. She walked swiftly, with head bent,—and was brought to a startled halt by meeting and almost running against the very individual she sought, who in his noiseless canvas shoes and with his panther-like tread had come upon her unawares. Checked in her progress she stood still, her eyes quickly lifted, her lips apart. In her adoration of the strength and magnificent physique of the stranger whom she knew only as a stranger, she thought he looked splendid as a god descending from the hill. Far from feeling god-like, he frowned as he saw her.

"Where are you going?" he demanded, brusquely.

The rich colour warmed her cheeks to a rose-red that matched the sunset.

"I was going—to see if you—if you wanted anything"—she stammered, almost humbly.

"You know I do not"—he said—"You can spare yourself the trouble."

She drew herself up with a slight air of offence.

"If you want nothing why do you come down into the valley?" she asked. "You say you hate the Plaza!"

"I do!" and he spoke almost vindictively—"But, at the moment, there's some one there I want to see."

Her black eyes opened inquisitively.

"A man?"

"No. Strange to say, a woman."

A sudden light flashed on her mind.

"I know!" she exclaimed—"But you will not see her! She has gone!"

"What do you mean?" he asked, impatiently—"What do you know?"

"Oh, I know nothing!" and there was a sobbing note of pathos in her voice—"But I feel Here!"—and she pressed her hands against her bosom—"something tells me that you have seen Her—the little wonderful white woman, sweetly perfumed like a rose,—with her silks and jewels and her fairy car!—and her golden hair. . . ah!—you said you hated a woman with golden hair! Is that the woman you hate?"

He stood looking at her with an amused, half scornful expression.

"Hate is too strong a word"—he answered—"She isn't worth hating!"

Her brows contracted in a frown.

"I do not believe That!"—she said—"You are not speaking truly. More likely it is, I think, you love her!"

He caught her roughly by the arm.

"Stop that!" he exclaimed, angrily—"You are foolish and insolent! Whether I love or hate anybody or anything is no affair of yours! How dare you speak to me as if it were!"

She shrank away from him. Her lips quivered, and tears welled through her lashes.

"Forgive me! . . . oh, forgive!" she murmured, pleadingly—"I am sorry! . . ."

"So you ought to be!" he retorted—"You—Manella—imagine yourself in love with me. . . yes, you do!—and you cannot leave me alone! No amorous man ever cadged round for love as much or as shamelessly as an amorous woman! Then you see another woman on the scene, and though she's nothing but a stray visitor at the Plaza where you help wash up the plates and dishes, you suddenly conceive a lot of romantic foolery in your head and imagine me to be mysteriously connected with her! Oh, for God's sake don't cry! It's the most awful bore! There's nothing to cry for. You've set me up like a sort of doll in a shrine and you want to worship me—well!—I simply won't be worshipped. As for your 'little wonderful white woman sweetly perfumed like a rose,' I don't mind saying that I know her. And I don't mind also telling you that she came up the hill last night to ferret me out."

Step by step Manella drew nearer, her eyes blazing.

"She went to see you?—She did That!—In the darkness?—like a thief or a serpent!"

He laughed aloud.

"No thief and no serpent in it!" he said—"And no darkness, but in the full light of the moon! Such a moon it was, too! A regular stage moon! A perfect setting for such an actress, in her white gown and her rope of gold hair! Yes—it was very well planned!—effective in its way, though it left me cold!"

"Ah, but it did Not leave you cold!" cried Manella; "Else you would not have come down to see her to-day! You say she went 'to ferret you out'—"

"Of course she did"—he interrupted her—"She would ferret out any man she wanted for the moment. Forests could not hide him,—caves could not cover him if she made up her mind to find him. I had hoped she would not find Me—but she has—however,—you say she has gone—"

The colour had fled from Manella's face,—she was pale and rigid.

"She will come back," she said stiffly.

"I hope not!" And he threw himself carelessly down on the turf to rest—"Come and sit beside me here and tell me what she said to you!"

But Manella was silent. Her dark, passionate eyes rested upon him with a world of scorn and sorrow in their glowing depths.

"Come!" he repeated—"Don't stare at me as if I were some new sort of reptile!"

"I think you are!" she said, coldly—"You seem to be a man, but you have not the feelings of a man!"

"Oh, have I not!" and he gave a light gesture of indifference—"I have the feelings of a modern man,—the 'Kultur' of a perfect super-German! Yes, that is so! Sentiment is the mere fly-trap of sensuality—the feeler thrust out to scent the prey, but once the fly is caught, the trap closes. Do you understand? No, of course you don't! You are a dreadfully primitive woman!"

"I did not think you were German," she said.

"Nor did I!" and he laughed—"Nor am I. I said just now that I had the 'Kultur' of a super-German—and a super-German means something above every other male creature except himself. He cannot get away from himself—nor can I! That's the trouble! Come, obey me, Manella! Sit down here beside me!"

Very slowly and very reluctantly she did as he requested. She sat on the grass some three or four paces off. He stretched out a hand to touch her, but she pushed it back very decidedly. He smiled.

"I mustn't make love to you this morning, eh?" he queried. "All right! I don't want to make love—it doesn't interest me—I only want to put you in a good temper! You are like a rumpled pussy-cat—your fur must be stroked the right way."

"You will not stroke it so!" said Manella, disdainfully.

"No?"

"No. Never again!"

"Oh, dire tragedy!" And he stretched himself out on the turf with his arms above his head—"But what does it matter! Give me your news, silly child! What did the 'little wonderful white woman' say to you?"

"You want to know?"

"I think so! I am conscious of a certain barbaric spirit of curiosity, like that of a savage who sees a photograph of himself for the first time! Yes! I want to know what the modern feminine said to the primitive!"

Manella gave an impatient gesture.

"I do not understand all your fine words"—she said—"But I will answer you. I told her about you—how you had come to live in the hut for the dying on the hill rather than at the Plaza—and how I took to you all the food you asked for, and she seemed amused—"

"Amused?" he echoed.

"Yes—amused. She laughed,—she looks very pretty when she laughs. And—and she seemed to fancy—"

He lifted himself upright in a sitting posture.

"Seemed to fancy? . . . what?—"

"That I was not bad to look at—" and Manella, gathering sudden boldness, lifted her dark eyes to his face—"She said I could tell you that she thinks me quite beautiful! Yes!—quite beautiful!"

He smiled—a smile that was more like a sneer.

"So you are! I've told you so, often. 'There needs no ghost come from the grave' to emphasise the fact. But she—the purring cat!—she told you to repeat her opinion to me, because—can you guess why?"

"No!"

"Simpleton! Because she wishes you to convey to me the message that she considers me your lover and that she admires my taste! Now she'll go back to New York full of the story! Subtle little devil! But I am not your lover, and never shall be,—not even for half an hour!"

Manella sprang up from the turf where she had been sitting.

"I know that!" she said, and her splendid eyes flashed proud defiance—"I know I have been a fool to let myself care for you! I do not know why I did—it was an illness! But I am well now!"

"You are well now? Good! O let us be joyful! Keep well, Manella!—and be 'quite beautiful'—as you are! To be quite beautiful is a fine thing—not so fine as it used to be in the Greek period—still, it has its advantages! I wonder what you will do with your beauty?"

As he spoke, he rose, stretching and shaking him self like a forest animal.

"What will you do with it?" he repeated—"You must give it to somebody! You must transmit it to your offspring! That's the old law of nature—it's getting a bit monotonous, still it's the law! Now she—the wonderful white woman—she's all for upsetting the law! Fortunately she's not beautiful—"

"She Is!" exclaimed Manella—"I think her so!" He looked down upon her from his superior height with a tolerant amusement.

"Really! You think her so! And She thinks you so! Quite a mutual admiration society! And both of you obsessed by the same one man! I pity that man! The only thing for him to do is to keep out of it! No, Manella!—think as you like, she is not beautiful. You Are beautiful. But She is clever, You are Not clever. You may thank God for that! She is outrageously, unnaturally, cursedly clever! And her cleverness makes her see the sham of life all through; the absurdity of birth that ends in death—the freakishness of civilisation to no purpose—and she's out for something else. She wants some thing newer than sex-attraction and family life. A husband would bore her to extinction—the care of children would send her into a lunatic asylum!"

Manella looked bewildered.

"I cannot understand!" she said—"A woman lives for husband and children!"

"Some women do!" he answered—"Not all! There are a good few who don't want to stay on the animal level. Men try to keep them there—but it's a losing game nowadays. ('Foxes have holes and birds of the air have nests'—but we cannot fail to see that when Mother Fox has reared her puppies she sends them off about their own business and doesn't know them any more—likewise Mother Bird does the same. Nature has no sentiment.) We have, because we cultivate artificial feelings— we imagine we 'love,' when we only want something that pleases us for the moment. To live, as you say, for husband and children would make a woman a slave—a great many women are slaves—but they are beginning to get emancipated—the woman with the gold hair, whom you so much admire, is emancipated."

Manella gave a slight disdainful movement of her head.

"That only means she is free to do as she likes"—she said—"To marry or not to marry—to love or not to love. I think if she loved at all, she would love very greatly. Why did she go so secretly in the evening to see you? I suppose she loves you!"

A sudden red flush of anger coloured his brow.

"Yes"—he answered with a kind of vindictive slowness—"I suppose she does! You, Manella, are after me as a man merely—she is after me as a Brain! You would steal my physical liberty,—she would steal my innermost thought! And you will both be disappointed! Neither my body nor my brain shall ever be dominated by any woman!"

He turned from her abruptly and began the ascent that led to his solitary retreat. Once he looked back—

"Don't let me see you for two days at least!" he called—"I've more than enough food to keep me going."

He strode on, and Manella stood watching him, her tall handsome figure silhouetted against the burning sky. Her dark eyes were moist with suppressed tears of shame and suffering,—she felt herself to be wronged and slighted undeservedly. And beneath this personal emotion came now a smarting sense of jealousy, for in spite of all he had said, she felt that there was some secret between him and "the little wonderful white woman," which she could not guess and which was probably the reason of his self-sought exile and seclusion.

"I wish now I had gone with her!" she mused—"for if I am 'quite beautiful,' as she said, she might have helped me in the world,—I might have become a lady!"

She walked slowly and dejectedly back to the Plaza, knowing in her heart that lady or no lady, her rich beauty was useless to her, inasmuch as it made no effect on the one man she had elected to care for, unwanted and unasked. Certain physiologists teach that the law of natural selection is that the female should choose her mate, but the difficulty along this line of argument is that she may choose where her choice is unwelcome and irresponsive. Manella was a splendid type of primitive womanhood,—healthy, warm-blooded and full of hymeneal passion,—as a wife she would have been devoted,—as a mother superb in her tenderness; but, measured by modern standards of advanced and restless femininity she was a mere drudge, without the ability to think for herself or to analyse subtleties of emotion. Intellectuality had no part in her; most people's talk was for her meaningless, and she had not the patience to listen to any conversation that rose above the food and business of the day. She was confused and bewildered by everything the strange recluse on the hill said to her,—she could not follow him at all,—and yet, the purely physical attraction he exercised over her nature drew her to him like a magnet and kept her in a state of feverish craving for a love she knew she could never win. She would have gladly been his servant on the mere chance and hope that possibly in some moment of abandonment he might have yielded to the importunity of her tenderness; Adonis himself in all the freshness of his youth never exercised a more potent spell upon enamoured Venus than this plain, big bearded man over the lonely, untutored Californian girl with the large loveliness of a goddess and the soul of a little child. What was the singular fascination which like the "pull" of a magnetic storm on telegraph wires, forced a woman's tender heart under the careless foot of a rough creature as indifferent to it as to a flower he trampled in his path? Nature might explain it in some unguarded moment of self-betrayal,—but Nature is jealous of her secrets,—they have to be coaxed out of her in the slow course of centuries. And with all the coaxing, the subtle work of her woven threads between the Like and the Unlike remains an unsolved mystery.

VI

From California to Sicily is a long way. It used to be considered far longer than it is now but in these magical days of aerial and motor travelling, distance counts but little,—indeed as almost nothing to the mind of any man or woman brought up in America and therefore accustomed to "hustle." Morgana Royal had "hustled" the whole business, staying in Paris a few days only,—in Rome but two nights; and now here she was, as if she had been spirited over sea and land by supernatural power, seated in a perfect paradise-garden of flowers and looking out on the blue Mediterranean with dreamy eyes in which the lightning flash was nearly if not wholly subdued. About quarter of a mile distant, and seen through the waving tops of pines and branching oleander, stood the house to which the garden belonged,—a "restored" palace of ancient days, built of rose-marble on the classic lines of Greek architecture. Its "restoration" was not quite finished; numbers of busy workmen were employed on the facade and surrounded loggia; and now and again she turned to watch them with a touch of invisible impatience in her movement. A slight smile sweetened her mouth as she presently perceived one figure approaching her,—a lithe, dark, handsome man, who, when he drew near enough, lifted his hat with a profoundly marked reverence, and, as she extended her hand, raised it to his lips.

"A thousand welcomes, Madama!" he said, speaking in English with a scarcely noticeable foreign accent—"Last night I heard you had arrived, but could hardly believe the good fortune! You must have travelled quickly?"

"Never quickly enough for my mind!" she answered—"The whole world moves too slowly for me!"

"You must carry that complaint to the buon Dio!" he said, gaily—"Perhaps He will condescend to spin this rolling planet a little faster! But in my mind, time flies far too rapidly! I have worked—we all have worked—to get this place finished for you, yet much remains to be done—"

She interrupted him.

"The interior is quite perfect"—she said—"You have carried out my instructions more thoroughly than I imagined could be possible. It is now an abode for fairies to live in,—for poets to dream in—"

"For women to love in!" he said, with a sudden warmth in his dark eyes.

She looked at him, laughing.

"You poor Marchese!"—she said—"Still you think of love! I really believe Italians keep all the sentiment of le moyen age in their hearts,—other peoples are gradually letting it go. You are like a child believing in childish things! You imagine I could be happy with a lover—or several lovers! To moon all day and embrace all night! Oh fie! What a waste of time! And in the end nothing is so fatiguing!" She broke off a spray of flowering laurel and hit him with it playfully on the hand. "Don't moon or spoon, caro amico! What is it all about? Do I leave you nothing on which to write poetry? I find you out in Sicily—a delightful poor nobleman with a family history going back to the Caesars!—handsome, clever, with beautiful ideas—and I choose and commission you to restore and rebuild for me a fairy palace out of a half-ruined ancient one, because you have taste and skill, and I know you can do everything when money is no object—and you have done, and are doing it all perfectly. Why then spoil it by falling in love with me? Fie, fie!"

She laughed again and rising, gave him her hand.

"Hold that!" she said—"And while you hold it, tell me of my other palace—the one with wings!"

He clasped her small white fingers in his own sun-browned palm and walked beside her bare-headed.

"Ah!" And he drew a deep breath—"That is a miracle! What we called your 'impossible' plan has been made possible! But who would have thought that a woman—"

"Stop there!" she interrupted—"Do not repeat the old gander-cackle of barbaric man, who, while owing his every comfort as well as the continuance of his race, to woman, denied her every intellectual initiative! 'Who would have thought that a woman'—could do anything but bend low before a man with grovelling humility saying 'My lord, here am I, the waiting vessel of your lordship's pleasure!—possess me or I die!' We have changed that beggarly attitude!"

Her eyes flashed,—her voice rang out—the little fingers he held, stiffened resolutely in his clasp. He looked at her with a touch of anxiety.

"Pardon me!—I did not mean—" he stammered.

In a second her mood changed, and she laughed.

"No!—Of course you 'did not mean' anything, Marchese! You are naturally surprised that my 'idea' which was little more than an idea, has resolved itself into a scientific fact—but you would have been just as surprised if the conception had been that of a man instead of a woman. Only you would not have said so!"

She laughed again,—a laugh of real enjoyment,—then went on—

"Now tell me—what of my White Eagle?—what movement?—what speed?"

"Amazing!" and the Marchese lowered his voice to almost a whisper—"I hardly dare speak of it!—it is like something supernatural! We have carried out your instructions to the letter—the thing is LIVING, in all respects save life. I made the test with the fluid you gave me—I charged the cells secretly—none of the mechanics saw what I did—and when she rose in air they were terrified—"

"Brave souls!" said Morgana, and now she withdrew her hand from his grasp—"So you went up alone?"

"I did. The steering was easy—she obeyed the helm,—it was as though she were a light yacht in a sea,—wind and tide in her favour. But her speed outran every air-ship I have ever known—as also the height to which she ascends."

"We will take a trip in her tomorrow pour passer le temps"—said Morgana, "You shall choose a place for us to go. Nothing can stop us—nothing on earth or in the air!—and nothing can destroy us. I can guarantee that!"

Giulio Rivardi gazed at her wonderingly,—his dark deep Southern eyes expressed admiration with a questioning doubt commingled.

"You are very sure of yourself"—he said, gently. "Of course one cannot but marvel that your brain should have grasped in so short a time what men all over the world are still trying to discover—"

"Men are slow animals!" she said, lightly. "They spend years in talking instead of in doing. Then again, when one of them really does something, all the rest are up in arms against him, and more years are wasted in trying to prove him right or wrong. I, as a mere woman, ask nobody for an opinion—I risk my own existence—spend my own money—and have nothing to do with governments. If I succeed I shall be sought after fast enough!—but I do not propose to either give or sell my discovery."

"Surely you will not keep it to yourself?"

"Why not? The world is too full of inventions as it is—and it is not the least grateful to its inventors or explorers. It would make the fool of a film a three-fold millionaire—but it would leave a great scientist or a noble thinker to starve. No, no! Let It swing on its own round—I shall not enlighten it!"

She walked on, gathering a flower here and there, and he kept pace beside her.

"The men who are working here"—he at last ventured to say—"are deeply interested. You can hardly expect them not to talk among each other and in the outside clubs and meeting-places of the wonderful mechanism on which they have been engaged. They have been at it now steadily for fifteen months."

"Do I not know it?" And she turned her head to him, smiling, "Have I not paid their salaries regularly?—and yours? I do not care how they talk or where,—they have built the White Eagle, but they cannot make her fly!—not without Me! You were as brave as I thought you would be when you decided to fly alone, trusting to the means I gave you and which I alone can give!"

She broke off and was silent for a moment, then laying her hand lightly on his arm, she added—

"I thank you for your confidence in me! As I have said, you were brave!—you must have felt that you risked your life on a chance!—nevertheless, for once, you allowed yourself to believe in a woman!"

"Not only for once but for always would I so believe!—in Such a woman—if she would permit me!" he answered in a low tone of intense passion. She smiled.

"Ah! The old story! My dear Marchese, do not fret your intellectual perception uselessly! Think what we have in store for us!—such wonders as none have yet explored,—the mysteries of the high and the low—the light and the dark—and in those far-off spaces strewn with stars, we may even hear things that no mortal has yet heard—"

"And what is the use of it all?" he suddenly demanded.

She opened her deep blue eyes in amaze.

"The use of it? . . . You ask the use of it?—"

"Yes—the use of it—without love!" he answered, his voice shaken with a sudden emotion—"Madonna, forgive me!—Listen with patience for one moment!—and think of the whole world mastered and possessed—but without anyone to love in it—without anyone to love You! Suppose you could command the elements—suppose every force that science could bestow were yours, and yet!—no love for you—no love in yourself for anyone—what would be the use of it all? Think, Madonna!"

She raised her delicate eyebrows in a little surprise,—a faint smile was on her lips.

"Dear Marchese, I Do think! I Have thought!" she answered—"And I have observed! Love—such as I imagined it when I was quite a young girl—does not exist. The passion called by that name is too petty and personal for me. Men have made love to me often—not as prettily perhaps as you do!—but in America at least love means dollars! Yes, truly! Any man would love my dollars, and take me with them, just thrown in! You, perhaps—"

"I should love you if you were quite poor!" he interposed vehemently.

She laughed.

"Would you? Don't be angry if I doubt it! If I were 'quite poor' I could not have given you your big commission here—this house would not have been restored to its former beauty, and the White Eagle would be still a bird of the brain and not of the air! No, you very charming Marchese!—I should not have the same fascination for you without my dollars!—and I may tell you that the only man I ever felt disposed to like,—just a little,—is a kind of rude brute who despises my dollars and me!"

His brows knitted involuntarily.

"Then there Is some man you like?" he asked, stiffly.

"I'm not sure!" she answered, lightly—"I said I felt 'disposed' to like him! But that's only in the spirit of contradiction, because he detests Me! And it's a sort of duel between us of sheer intellectuality, because he is trying to discover—in the usual slow, laborious, calculating methods of man—the very thing I Have discovered! He's on the verge—But not across it!"

"And so—he may outstrip you?" And the Marchese's eyes glittered with sudden anger—"He may claim Your discovery as his own?"

Morgana smiled. She was ascending the steps of the loggia, and she paused a moment in the full glare of the Sicilian sunshine, her wonderful gold hair shining in it with the hue of a daffodil.

"I think not!" she said—"Though of course it depends on the use he makes of it. He—like all men—wishes to destroy; I, like all women, wish to create!"

One or two of the workmen who were busy polishing the rose-marble pilasters of the loggia, here saluted her—she returned their salutations with an enchanting smile.

"How delightful it all is!" she said—"I feel the real use of dollars at last! This beautiful 'palazzo,' in one of the loveliest places in the world—all the delicious flowers running down in garlands to the very shore of the sea-and liberty to enjoy life as one wishes to enjoy it, without hindrance or argument—without even the hindrance and argument of—love!" She laughed, and gave a mirthful upward glance at the Marchese's somewhat sullen countenance. "Come and have luncheon with me! You are the major-domo for the present—you have engaged the servants and you know the run of the house—you must show me everything and tell me everything! I have quite a nice chaperone—such a dear old English lady 'of title' as they say in the 'Morning Post'—so it's all quite right and proper—only she doesn't know a word of Italian and very little French. But that's quite British you know!"

She passed, smiling, into the house, and he followed.

.

VII

Perhaps there is no lovelier effect in all nature than a Sicilian sunset, when the sky is one rich blaze of colour and the sea below reflects every vivid hue as in a mirror,—when the very air breathes voluptuous indolence, and all the restless work of man seems an impertinence rather than a necessity. Morgana, for once in her quick restless life, felt the sudden charm of sweet peace and holy tranquility, as she sat, or rather reclined at ease in a long lounge chair after dinner in her rose-marble loggia facing the sea and watching the intense radiance of the heavens burning into the still waters beneath. She had passed the afternoon going over her whole house and gardens, and to the Marchese Giulio Rivardi had expressed herself completely satisfied,—while he, to whom unlimited means had been entrusted to carry out her wishes, wondered silently as to the real extent of her fortune, and why she should have spent so much in restoring a "palazzo" for herself alone. An occasional thought of "the only man" she had said she was "disposed" to like, teased his brain; but he was not petty-minded or jealous. He was keenly and sincerely interested in her intellectual capacity, and he knew, or thought he knew, the nature of woman. He watched her now as she reclined, a small slim figure in white, with the red glow of the sun playing on the gold uptwisted coil of her hair,—a few people of the neighbourhood had joined her at dinner, and these were seated about, sipping coffee and chatting in the usual frivolous way of after-dinner guests—one or two of them were English who had made their home in Sicily,—the others were travelling Americans.

"I guess you're pretty satisfied with your location, Miss Royal"—said one of these, a pleasant-faced grey-haired man, who for four or five years past had wintered in Sicily with his wife, a frail little creature always on the verge of the next world—"It would be difficult to match this place anywhere! You only want one thing to complete it!"

Morgana turned her lovely eyes indolently towards him over the top of the soft feather fan she was waving lightly to and fro.

"One thing? What is that?" she queried.

"A husband!"

She smiled.

"The usual appendage!" she said—"To my mind, quite unnecessary, and likely to spoil the most perfect environment! Though the Marchese

Rivardi DID ask me to-day what was the use of my pretty 'palazzo' and gardens without love! A sort of ethical conundrum!"

She glanced at Rivardi as she spoke—he was rolling a cigarette in his slim brown fingers and his face was impassively intent on his occupation.

"Well, that's so!"—and her American friend looked at her kindly—"Even a fairy palace and a fairy garden might prove lonesome for one!"

"And boresome for two!" laughed Morgana—"My dear Colonel Boyd! It is not every one who is fitted for matrimony—and there exist so many that ARE,—eminently fitted—we can surely allow a few exceptions! I am one of those exceptions. A husband would be excessively tiresome to me, and very much in my way!"

Colonel Boyd laughed heartily.

"You won't always think so!" he said—"Such a charming little woman must have a heart somewhere!"

"Oh, yes, dear!" chimed in his fragile invalid wife, "I am sure you have a heart!"

Morgana raised herself on her cushions to a sitting posture and looked round her with a curious little air or defiance.

"A heart I MUST have!" she said—"otherwise I could not live. It is a necessary muscle. But what YOU call 'heart'—and what the dear elusive poets write about, is simply brain,—that is to say, an impulsive movement of the brain, suggesting the desirability of a particular person's companionship—and we elect to call that 'love'! On that mere impulse people marry."

"It's a good impulse"—said Colonel Boyd, still smiling broadly—"It founds families and continues the race!"

"Ah, yes! But I often wonder why the race should be continued at all!" said Morgana—"The time is ripe for a new creation!"

A slow footfall sounded on the garden path, and the tall figure of a man clad in the everyday ecclesiastical garb of the Roman Church ascended the steps of the loggia.

"Don Aloysius!" quickly exclaimed the Marchese, and every one rose to greet the newcomer, Morgana receiving him with a profound reverence. He laid his hand on her head with a kindly touch of benediction.

"So the dreamer has come to her dream!" he said, in soft accents—"And it has not broken like an air-bubble!—it still floats and shines!" As he spoke he courteously saluted all present by a bend of his head,—

and stood for a moment gazing at the view of the sea and the dying sunset. He was a very striking figure of a man—tall, and commanding in air and attitude, with a fine face which might be called almost beautiful. The features were such as one sees in classic marbles—the full clear eyes were set somewhat widely apart under shelving brows that denoted a brain with intelligence to use it, and the smile that lightened his expression as he looked from, the sea to his fair hostess was of a benignant sweetness.

"Yes"—he continued—"you have realised your vision of loveliness, have you not? Our friend Giulio Rivardi has carried out all your plans?"

"Everything is perfect!" said Morgana—"Or will be when it is finished. The workmen still have things to do."

"All workmen always have things to do!" said Don Aloysius, tranquilly—"And nothing is ever finished! And you, dear child!—you are happy?"

She flushed and paled under his deep, steady gaze.

"I—I think so!" she murmured—"I ought to be!"

The priest smiled and after a pause took the chair which the Marchese Rivardi offered him. The other guests in the loggia looked at him with interest, fascinated by his grave charm of manner. Morgana resumed her seat.

"I ought to be happy"—she said—"And of course I am—or I shall be!"

"'Man never is but always to be blest'!" quoted Colonel Boyd—"And woman the same! I have been telling this lady, reverend father, that maybe she will find her 'palazzo' a bit lonesome without some one to share its pleasures."

Don Aloysius looked round with a questioning glance.

"What does she herself think about it?" he asked, mildly.

"I have not thought at all"—said Morgana, quickly, "I can always fill it with friends. No end of people are glad to winter in Sicily."

"But will such 'friends' care for You or Your happiness?" suggested the Marchese, pointedly.

Morgana laughed.

"Oh, no, I do not expect that! Nowadays no one really cares for anybody else's happiness but their own. Besides, I shall be much too busy to want company. I'm bent on all sorts of discoveries, you know!—I want to dive 'deeper than ever plummet sounded'!"

"You will only find deeper depths!" said Don Aloysius, slowly—"And in the very deepest depth of all is God!"

There was a sudden hush as he spoke. He went on in gentle accents.

"How wonderful it is that He should be THERE,—and yet HERE! No one need 'dive deep' to find Him. He is close to us as our very breathing! Ah!" and he sighed—"I am sorry for all the busy 'discoverers'—they will never arrive at the end,—and meanwhile they miss the clue—the little secret by the way!"

Another pause ensued. Then Morgana spoke, in a very quiet and submissive tone.

"Dear Don Aloysius, you are a 'religious' as they say—and naturally you mistrust all seekers of science—science which is upsetting to your doctrine."

Aloysius raised a deprecating hand.

"My child, there is no science that can upset the Source of all science! The greatest mathematician that lives did not institute mathematics—he only copies the existing Divine law."

"That is perfectly true"—said the Marchese Rivardi—"But la Signora Royal means that the dogma of the Church is in opposition to scientific discovery—"

"I have not found it so"—said Don Aloysius, tranquilly—"We have believed in what you call your 'wireless telephony'—for centuries;—when the Sanctus bell rings at Mass, we think and hope a message from Our Lord comes to every worshipper whose soul is 'in tune' with the heavenly current; that is one of your 'scientific discoveries'—and there are hundreds of others which the Church has incorporated through a mystic fore-knowledge and prophetic instinct. No—I find nothing upsetting in science,—the only students who are truly upset both physically and morally, are they who seek to discover God while denying His existence."

There followed a silence. The group in the loggia seemed for the moment mesmerised by the priest's suave calm voice, steady eyes and noble expression, A bell rang slowly and sweetly—a call to prayer in some not far distant monastery, and the first glimmer of the stars began to sparkle faintly in the darkening heavens. A little sigh from Morgana stirred the stillness.

"If one could always live in this sort of mood!" she suddenly exclaimed—"This lovely peace in the glow of the sunset and the perfume of the flowers!—and you, Don Aloysius, talking beautiful things!—why then, one would be perpetually happy and good! But such living would not be life!—one must go with the time—"

Don Aloysius smiled indulgently.

"Must one? Is it so vitally necessary? If I might take the liberty to go on speaking I would tell you a story—a mere tradition—but it might weary you—"

A general chorus of protest from all present assured him of their eagerness to hear.

"As if You could weary anybody!" Morgana said. "You never do— only you have an effect upon ME which is not very flattering to my self-love!—you make me feel so small!"

You ARE small, physically"—said Don Aloysius—Do you mind that? Small things are always sweetest!"

She flushed, and turned her head away as she caught the Marchese Rivardi's eyes fixed upon her.

"You should not make pretty compliments to a woman, reverend father!" she said, lightly—"It is not your vocation!"

His grave face brightened and he laughed with real heartiness.

"Dear lady, what do you know of my vocation?" he asked—"Will you teach it to me? No!—I am sure you will not try! Listen now!—as you all give me permission—let me tell you of certain people who once 'went with the time'—and decided to stop en route, and are still at the stopping-place. Perhaps some of you who travel far and often, have heard of the Brazen City?"

Each one looked at the other enquiringly, but with no responsive result.

"Those who visit the East know of it"—went on Aloysius—"And some say they have seen a glimpse of its shining towers and cupolas in the far distance. However this may be, tradition declares that it exists, and that it was founded by St. John, the 'beloved disciple.' You will recall that when Our Lord was asked when and how John should die He answered—'If I will that he tarry till I come, what is that to thee?' So—as we read—the rumour went forth that John was the one disciple for whom there should be no death. And now—to go on with the legend—it is believed by many, that deep in the as yet unexplored depths of the deserts of Egypt—miles and miles over rolling sand-waves which once formed the bed of a vast ocean, there stands a great city whose roofs and towers are seemingly of brass,—a city barricaded and built in by walls of brass and guarded by gates of brass. Here dwells a race apart—a race of beautiful human creatures who have discovered the secret of perpetual youth and immortality on this earth.

They have seen the centuries come and go,—the flight of time touches them not,—they only await the day when the whole world will be free to them—that 'world to come' which is not made for the 'many,' but the 'few.' All the discoveries of our modern science are known to them—our inventions are their common everyday appliances—and on the wings of air and rays of light they hear and know all that goes on in every country. Our wars and politics are no more to them than the wars and politics of ants in ant-hills,—they have passed beyond all trivialities such as these. They have discovered the secret of life's true enjoyment—and—they enjoy!"

"That's a fine story if true!" said Colonel Boyd—

"But all the same, it must be dull work living shut up in a city with nothing to do,—doomed to be young and to last for ever!"

Morgana had listened intently,—her eyes were brilliant.

"Yes—I think it would be dull after a couple of hundred years or so"— she said—"One would have tested all life's possibilities and pleasures by then."

"I am not so sure of that!" put in the Marchese Rivardi—"With youth nothing could become tiresome—youth knows no ennui."

Some of the other listeners to the conversation laughed.

"I cannot quite agree to that"—said a lady who had not yet spoken— "Nowadays the very children are 'bored' and ever looking for something new—it is just as if the world were 'played out'—and another form of planet expected."

"That is where we retain the vitality of our faith—" said Don Aloysius—"We expect—we hope! We believe in an immortal progress towards an ever Higher Good."

"But I think even a soul may grow tired!" said Morgana, suddenly— "so tired that even the Highest Good may seem hardly worth possessing!"

There was a moment's silence.

"Povera figlia!" murmured Aloysius, hardly above his breath,—but she caught the whisper, and smiled.

"I am too analytical and pessimistic," she said—"Let us all go for a ramble among the flowers and down to the sea! Nature is the best talker, for the very reason that she has no speech!"

The party broke up in twos and threes and left the loggia for the garden. Rivardi remained a moment behind, obeying a slight sign from Aloysius.

"She is not happy!" said the priest—"With all her wealth, and all her gifts of intelligence she is not happy, nor is she satisfied. Do you not find it so?"

"No woman is happy or satisfied till love has kissed her on the mouth and eyes!" answered Rivardi, with a touch of passion in his voice,— "But who will convince her of that? She is satisfied with her beautiful surroundings,—all the work I have designed for her has pleased her,— she has found no fault—"

"And she has paid you loyally!" interpolated Aloysius—"Do not forget that! She has made your fortune. And no doubt she expects you to stop at that and go no further in an attempt to possess herself as well as her millions!"

The Marchese flushed hotly under the quiet gaze of the priest's steady dark eyes.

"It is a great temptation," went on Aloysius, gently—"But you must resist it, my son! I know what it would mean to you—the restoration of your grand old home—that home which received a Roman Emperor in the long ago days of history and which presents now to your eyes so desolate a picture with its crumbling walls and decaying gardens beautiful in their wild desolation!—yes, I know all this!—I know how you would like to rehabilitate the ancient family and make the venerable genealogical tree sprout forth into fresh leaves and branches by marriage with this strange little creature whose vast wealth sets her apart in such loneliness,—but I doubt the wisdom or the honour of such a course—I also doubt whether she would make a fitting wife for you or for any man!"

The Marchese raised his eyebrows expressively with the slightest shrug of his shoulders.

"You may doubt that of every modern woman!" he said—"Few are really 'fitting' for marriage nowadays. They want something different— something new!—God alone knows what they want!"

Don Aloysius sighed.

"Aye! God alone knows! And God alone will decide what to give them!"

"It must be something more 'sensational' than husband and children!" said Rivardi a trifle bitterly—"Only a primitive woman will care for these!"

The priest laid a gentle hand on his shoulder.

"Come, come! Do not be cynical, my son! I think with you that if anything can find an entrance to a woman's soul it is love—but the woman must be capable of loving. That is the difficulty with the little millionairess Royal. She is not capable!"

He uttered the last words slowly and with emphasis.

Rivardi gave him a quick searching glance.

"You seem to know that as a certainty"—he said, "How and why do you know it?"

Aloysius raised his eyes and looked straight ahead of him with a curious, far-off, yet searching intensity.

"I cannot tell you how or why"—he answered—"You would not believe me if I told you that sometimes in this wonderful world of ours, beings are born who are neither man nor woman, and who partake of a nature that is not so much human as elemental and ethereal—or might one not almost say, atmospheric? That is, though generated of flesh and blood, they are not altogether flesh and blood, but possess other untested and unproved essences mingled in their composition, of which as yet we can form no idea. We grope in utter ignorance of the greatest of mysteries—Life!—and with all our modern advancement, we are utterly unable to measure or to account for life's many and various manifestations. In the very early days of imaginative prophecy, the 'elemental' nature of certain beings was accepted by men accounted wise in their own time,—in the long ago discredited assertions of the Count de Gabalis and others of his mystic cult,—and I am not entirely sure that there does not exist some ground for their beliefs. Life is many-sided;—humanity can only be one facet of the diamond."

Giulio Rivardi had listened with surprised attention.

"You seem to imply then"—he said—"that this rich woman, Morgana Royal, is hardly a woman at all?—a kind of sexless creature incapable of love?"

"Incapable of the usual kind of so-called 'love'—yes!" answered Aloysius—"But of love in other forms I can say nothing, for I know nothing!—she may be capable of a passion deep and mysterious as life itself. But come!—we might talk all night and arrive no closer to the solving of this little feminine problem! You are fortunate in your vocation of artist and designer, to have been chosen by her to carry out her conceptions of structural and picturesque beauty—let the romance stay there!—and do not try to become the husband of a Sphinx!"

He smiled, resting his hand on the Marchese's shoulder with easy familiarity.

"See where she stands!" he continued,—and they both looked towards the beautiful flower-bordered terrace at the verge of the gardens overhanging the sea where for the moment Morgana stood alone, a small white figure bathed in the deep rose afterglow of the sunken sun—"Like a pearl dropped in a cup of red wine!—ready to dissolve and disappear!"

His voice had a strange thrill in it, and Giulio looked at him curiously.

"You admire her very much, my father!" he said, with a touch of delicate irony in his tone.

"I do, my son!" responded Aloysius, composedly, "But only as a poor priest may—at a distance!"

The Marchese glanced at him again quickly,—almost suspiciously— and seemed about to say something further, but checked himself,—and the two walked on to join their hostess, side by side together.

VIII

Early dawn peered through the dark sky like the silvery light of a pale lamp carried by an advancing watchman,—and faintly illumined the outline of a long, high, vastly extending wooden building which, at about a mile distant from Morgana's "palazzo" ran parallel with the sea-shore. The star-sparkle of electric lamps within showed it to be occupied—and the murmur of men's voices and tinkle of working tools suggested that the occupants were busy. The scarcely visible sea made pleasant little kissing murmurs on the lip-edges of the sand, and Nature, drowsing in misty space, seemed no more than the formless void of the traditional beginning of things.

Outside the building which, by its shape, though but dimly defined among shadows, was easily recognisable as a huge aerodrome, the tall figure of Giulio Rivardi paced slowly up and down like a sentinel on guard. He, whose Marquisate was inherited from many noble Sicilian houses renowned in Caesar's day, apparently found as much satisfaction in this occupation as any warrior of a Roman Legion might have experienced in guarding the tent of his Emperor,—and every now and then he lifted his eyes to the sky with a sense of impatience at the slowness of the sun's rising. In his mind he reviewed the whole chapter of events which during the past three years had made him the paid vassal of a rich woman's fancy—his entire time taken up, and all the resources of his inventive and artistic nature (which were exceptionally great) drawn upon for the purpose of carrying out designs which at first seemed freakish and impossible, but which later astonished him by the extraordinary scientific acumen they displayed, as well as by their adaptability to the forces of nature. Then, the money!—the immense sums which this strange creature, Morgana Royal, had entrusted to him!—and with it all, the keen, business aptitude she had displayed, knowing to a centime how much she had spent, though there seemed no limit to how much she yet intended to spend! He looked back to the time he had first seen her, when on visiting Sicily apparently as an American tourist only, she had taken a fancy to a ruined "palazzo" once an emperor's delight, but crumbling slowly away among its glorious gardens, and had purchased the whole thing then and there. Her guide to the ruins at that period had been Don Aloysius, a learned priest, famous for his archaeological knowledge—and it was through Don

Aloysius that he, the Marchese Rivardi, had obtained the commission to restore to something of its pristine grace and beauty the palace of ancient days. And now everything was done, or nearly done; but much more than the "palazzo" had been undertaken and completed, for the lady of many millions had commanded an air-ship to be built for her own personal use and private pleasure with an aerodrome for its safe keeping and anchorage. This airship was the crux of the whole business, for the men employed to build it were confident that it would never fly, and laughed with one another as they worked to carry out a woman's idea and a woman's design. How could it fly without an engine?—they very sensibly demanded,—for engine there was none! However, they were paid punctually and most royally for their labours; and when, despite their ominous predictions, the ship was released on her trial trip, manipulated by Giulio Rivardi, who ascended in her alone, sailing the ship with an ease and celerity hitherto unprecedented, they were more scared than enthusiastic. Surely some devil was in it!—for how could the thing fly without any apparent force to propel it? How was it that its enormous wings spread out on either side as by self-volition and moved rhythmically like the wings of a bird in full flight? Every man who had worked at the design was more or less mystified. They had, according to plan and instructions received, "plumed" the airship for electricity in a new and curious manner, but there was no battery to generate a current. Two small boxes or chambers, made of some mysterious metal which would not "fuse" under the strongest heat, were fixed, one at either end of the ship;—these had been manufactured secretly in another country and sent to Sicily by Morgana herself,—but so far, they contained nothing. They seemed unimportant—they were hardly as large as an ordinary petrol-can holding a gallon. When Rivardi had made a trial ascent he had inserted in each of these boxes a cylindrical tube made to fit an interior socket as a candle fits into a candle-stick,—all the workmen watched him, waiting for a revelation, but he made none. He was only particular and precise as to the firm closing down of the boxes when the tubes were in. And then in a few minutes the whole machine began to palpitate noiselessly like a living thing with a beating heart,—and to the amazement and almost fear of all who witnessed what seemed to be a miracle, the ship sprang up like a bird springing from the ground, and soared free and away into space, its vast white wings cleaving the air with a steady rise and fall of rhythmic power. Once aloft she sailed in level flight, apparently at perfect ease—and after several rapid "runs," and circlings, descended slowly and gracefully, landing her pilot without shock or jar. He was at once surrounded and was asked a thousand questions which it was evident he could not answer.

"How can I tell!" he replied, to all interrogations. "The secret is the secret of a woman!"

A woman! Man's pretty toy!—man's patient slave! How should a woman master any secret! Engineers and mechanics laughed scornfully and shrugged their shoulders—yet—yet—the great airship stared them in the face as a thing created,—a thing of such power and possibility as seemed wholly incredible. And now the creator,—the woman—had arrived,—the woman whose rough designs on paper had been carefully followed and elaborated into actual shape;—and there was a tense state of expectation among all the workers awaiting her presence. Meanwhile the lantern-gleam in the sky broadened and the web of mist which veiled the sea began to lift and Giulio Rivardi, pacing to and fro, halted every now and then to look in the direction of a path winding downward from the mainland to the shore, in watchful expectation of seeing an elfin figure, more spiritlike than mortal, floating towards him through the dividing vapours of the morning. The words of Don Aloysius haunted him strangely, though his common sense sharply rejected the fantastic notions to which they had given rise. She,—Morgana Royal,—was "not capable" of love, the priest had implied,—and yet, at times—only at times,—she seemed eminently lovable. At times,—again, only at times—he was conscious of a sweeping passion of admiration for her that well-nigh robbed him of his self-control. But a strong sense of honour held him in check—he never forgot that he was her paid employe, and that her wealth was so enormous that any man presuming too personally upon her indulgence could hardly be exonerated from ulterior sordid aims. And while he mused, somewhat vexedly, on all the circumstances of his position, the light widened in the heavens, showing the very faintest flush of rose in the east as an indication of the coming sun. He lifted his eyes. . .

"At last!" he exclaimed, with relief, as he saw a small gliding shadow among shadows approaching him,—he figure of Morgana so wrapped in a grey cloak and hood as to almost seem part of the slowly dispersing mists of the morning. She pushed back the hood as she came near, showing a small eager white face in which the eyes glittered with an almost unearthly brightness.

"I have slept till now,"—she said—"Imagine!—all night through without waking! So lazy of me!—but the long rest has done me good and I'm ready for anything! Are you? You look very solemn and morose!—like a warrior in bronze! Anything gone wrong?"

"Not that I am aware of"—he replied—"The men are finishing some small detail of ornament. I have only looked in to tell them you are coming."

"And are they pleased?"

"Madama, they are not of a class to be either pleased or displeased"—he said—"They are instructed to perform certain work, and they perform it. In all that they have been doing for you, according to your orders, I truly think they are more curious than interested."

A streak of rose and silver flared through the sky flushing the pallor of Morgana's face as she lifted it towards him, smiling.

"Quite natural!" she said—"No man is ever 'interested' in woman's work, but he is always 'curious.' Woman is a many-cornered maze—and man is always peeping round one corner or another in the hope to discover her—but he never does!"

Rivardi gave an almost imperceptible shrug.

"Never?" he queried.

"Never!" she affirmed, emphatically—"Don't be sarcastic, amico!—even in this dim morning light I can see the scornful curve of your upper lip!—you are really very good-looking, you know!—and you imply the same old Garden of Eden story of man giving away woman as a wholly incomprehensible bad job! Adam flung her back as a reproach to her Creator—'the woman thou gavest me;'—oh, that woman and that apple! But he had to confess 'I did eat.' He always eats,—he eats everything woman can give him—he will even eat HER if he gets the chance!" She laughed and pointed to the brightening sky. "See? ''Tis almost morning!' as Shakespeare's Juliet remarked—but I would not 'have thee gone'—not unless I go also. Whither shall we fly?"

He looked at her, moved as he often was by a thrill of admiration and wonder.

"It is for you to decide"—he answered—"You know best the possibilities-and the risks—"

"I know the possibilities perfectly,"—she said—"But I know nothing of risks—there are none. This is our safety"—and she drew out from the folds of her cloak, two small packets of cylindrical form—"This emanation of Nature's greatest force will keep us going for a year if needful! Oh man!—I do not mean YOU particularly, but man generally!—

why could you not light on this little, little clue!—why was it left to a woman! Come!—let us see the White Eagle in its nest,—it shall spread its wings and soar to-day—we will give it full liberty!"

The dawn was spreading in threads of gold and silver and blue all over the heavens, and the sea flushed softly under the deepening light, as she went towards the aerodrome, he walking slowly by her side.

"Are you so sure?" he said—"Will you not risk your life in this attempt?"

She stopped abruptly.

"My life? What is it? The life of a midge in the sun! It is no good to me unless I do something with it! I would live for ever if I could!—here, on this dear little ball of Earth—I do not want a better heaven. The heaven which the clergy promise us is so remarkably unattractive! But I run no risk of losing my life or yours in our aerial adventures; we carry the very essence of vitality with us. Come!—I want to see my flying palace! When I was a small child I used to feed my fancy on the 'Arabian Nights,' and most dearly did I love the story of Aladdin and his palace that was transported through the air. I used to say 'I will have a flying palace myself!' And now I have realised my dream."

"That remains to be proved"—said Rivardi—"With all our work we may not have entirely carried out your plan."

"If not, it will HAVE to be carried out"—returned Morgana, tranquilly—"There is no reason, moral or scientific, why it should NOT be carried out—we have all the forces of Nature on our side."

He was silent, and accompanied her as she walked to the aerodrome and entered it. There were half a dozen or more men within, all working—but they ceased every movement as they saw her,—while she, on her part, scarcely seemed to note their presence. Her eyes were uplifted and fixed on a vast, smooth oblong object, like the body of a great bird with shut wings, which swung from the roof of the aerodrome and swayed lightly to and fro as though impelled by some mysterious breathing force. Morgana's swift glance travelled from its one end to the other with a flash of appreciation, while at the same time she received the salutations of all the men who advanced to greet her.

"You have done well, my friends!"—she said, speaking in fluent French—"This beautiful creature you have made seems a perfect thing,—from the OUTSIDE. What of the interior?"

A small, dark, intelligent looking man, in evident command of the rest, smiled and shrugged his shoulders.

"Ah, Signora! It is as you commanded!" he answered—"It is beautiful—like a chrysalis for a butterfly. But a butterfly has the advantage—it comes to LIFE, to use its wings!"

"Quite true, Monsieur Gaspard!" and Morgana gave him a smile as sunny as his own. "But what is life? Is it not a composition of many elements? And should we not learn to combine such elements to vitalise our 'White Eagle'? It is possible!"

"With God all things are possible!" quoted the Marchese Rivardi—"But with man—"

"We are taught that God made man 'in His image. In the image of God created He him.' If this is true, all things should be possible to man"—said Morgana, quietly—"To man,—and to that second thought of the Creator—Woman! And we mustn't forget that second thoughts are best!" She laughed, while the man called Gaspard stared at her and laughed also for company. "Now let me see how I shall be housed in air!" and with very little assistance she climbed into the great bird-shaped vessel through an entrance so deftly contrived that it was scarcely visible,—an entrance which closed almost hermetically when the ship was ready to start, air being obtained through other channels.

Once inside it was easy to believe in Fairyland. Not a scrap of any sort of mechanism could be seen. There were two exquisitely furnished saloons—one a kind of boudoir or drawing-room where everything that money could buy or luxury suggest as needful or ornamental was collected and arranged with thoughtful selection and perfect taste. A short passage from these apartments led at one end to some small, daintily fitted sleeping-rooms beyond,—at the other was the steering cabin and accommodation for the pilot and observer. The whole interior was lined with what seemed to be a thick rose-coloured silk of a singularly smooth and shining quality, but at a sign from Morgana, Rivardi and Gaspard touched some hidden spring which caused this interior covering to roll up completely, thus disclosing a strange and mysterious "installation" beneath. Every inch of wall-space was fitted with small circular plates of some thin, shining substance, set close together so that their edges touched, and in the center of each plate or disc was a tiny white knob resembling the button of an ordinary electric bell. There seemed to be at least two or three thousand of these discs— seen all together in a close mass they somewhat resembled the "suckers" on the tentacles of a giant octopus. Morgana, seating herself in an easy chair of the richly carpeted "drawing-room" of her "air palace," studied every line, turn and configuration of this extraordinary arrangement with a keenly observant and criticising eye. The Marchese Rivardi and Gaspard watched her expression anxiously.

"You are satisfied?" asked Rivardi, at last—"It is as you planned?"

She turned towards Gaspard with a smile.

"What do You think about it?" she queried—"You are an expert in modern scientific work—you understand many of the secrets of natural force—what do You think?"

"Madama, I think as I have always thought!—a body without soul!"

"What Is soul?" she said—"Is it not breath?—the breath of life? Is it not said that God 'made man of the dust of the ground and breathed into his nostrils the breath of life and man became a living soul!' And what is the breath of life? Is it not composed of such elements as are in the universe and which we may all discover if we will, and use to our advantage? You cannot deny this! Come, Marchese!—and you, Monsieur Gaspard! Call to them below to set this Eagle free; we will fly into the sunrise for an hour or two,—no farther, as we are not provisioned."

"Madama!" stammered Gaspard—"I am not prepared—"

"You are frightened, my friend!" and Morgana smiled, laying her little white hand soothingly on his arm—"But if I tell you there is no cause for fear, will you not believe me? Do you not think I love my own life? Oh yes, I love it so much that I seek to prolong it, not risk it by sudden loss. Nor would I risk Your life—or His!" and she looked towards Rivardi—"He is not frightened—he will come with me wherever I go! Now, Monsieur Gaspard, see! Here is our breath of life!" And she held up before his eyes the two cylindrically shaped packages she had previously shown to Rivardi—"The Marchese has already had some experience of it"—here she unfastened the wrappings of the packages, and took out two tubes made of some metallic substance which shone like purest polished gold—"I will fix these in myself—will you open the lower end chamber first, please?"

Silently the two men obeyed her gesture and opened the small compartment fixed at what might be called the hull end of the airship. The interior was seen to be lined with the same round discs which covered the walls of the vessel, every disc closely touching its neighbour. With extreme caution and delicacy Morgana set one of the tubes she held upright in the socket made to receive it, and as she did this, fine sharp, needle like flashes of light broke from it in a complete circle, filling the whole receptacle with vibrating rays which instantly ran round each disc, and glittered in and out among them like a stream of quicksilver. As soon as this manifestation occurred, Morgana beckoned to her two assistants to shut the compartment. They did so with scarcely an effort, yet it closed down with a silent force and tenacity that suggested some enormous outward pressure, yet pressure there seemed none. And now a sudden throbbing movement pulsated through the vessel—its huge folded wings stirred.

"Quick! Tell them below to lose no time! Open the shed and let her rise!—when the contact is once established there will not be half a second to spare!"

Hurriedly the man Gaspard, though obviously terrified, shouted the necessary orders, while Morgana went to the other end of the ship where Rivardi opened for her the second compartment into which she fixed the second tube. Once again the circular flashes broke out, but this time directly the compartment was closed down, the shining stream of light was seen to run rapidly and completely round the interior of the vessel, touching every disc that lined the walls as with the sparkling point of a jewel. The wings of the ship palpitated as with life and began to spread open. . .

"Let her go!" cried Morgana—"Away to your place, pilot!" and she waved a commanding hand as Rivardi sprang to the steering gear— "Hold her fast! . . . Keep her steady! Straight towards the sun-rise!"

As she spoke, a wonderful thing happened—every disc that lined the interior of the ship started throbbing like a pulse,—every little white knob in the centre of each disc vibrated with an extraordinary rapidity of motion which dazzled the eyes like the glittering of swiftly falling snow, and Gaspard, obeying Morgana's sign, drew down at once all the rose silk covering which completely hid the strange mechanism from view. There was absolutely no noise in this intense vibration,— and there was no start or jar, or any kind of difficulty, when the air-ship, released from bondage, suddenly rose, and like an actual living bird sprang through the vast opening gateway of the aerodrome and as it sprang, spread out its wings as though by its own volition. In one moment, it soared straight upright, far far into space, and the men who were left behind stood staring amazedly after it, themselves looking no more than tiny black pin-heads down below,—then, with a slow diving grace it righted itself as it were, and as if it had of its own will selected the particular current of air on which to sail. It travelled with a steady swiftness in absolute silence,—its great wings moved up and down with a noiseless power and rhythm for which there seemed no possible explanation,—and Morgana turned her face, now delicately flushed with triumph, on the pale and almost breathless Gaspard, smiling as she looked at him, her eyes questioning his. He seemed stricken dumb with astonishment,—his lips moved, but no word issued from them.

"You believe me now, do you not?" she said—"We have nothing further to do but to steer. The force we use re-creates itself as it works—it cannot become exhausted. To slow down and descend to earth one need only open the compartments at either end—then the vibration grows less and less, and like a living creature the 'White Eagle' sinks gently to rest. You see there is no cause for fear!"

While she yet spoke, the light of the newly risen sun bathed her in its golden glory, the long dazzling beams filtering through mysterious apertures inserted cunningly in the roof of the vessel and mingling with the roseate hues of the silken sheathing that covered its walls. So fired with light she looked ethereal—a very spirit of air or of flame; and Rivardi, just able to see her from his steering place, began to think there was some truth an the strange words of Don Aloysius—"Sometimes in this wonderful world of ours beings are born who are neither man nor woman and who partake of a nature that is not so much human as elemental—or, might not one almost say atmospheric?"

At the moment Morgana seemed truly "atmospheric"—a small creature so fine and fair as to almost suggest an evanescent form about to melt away in mist. Some sudden thrill of superstitious fear moved Gaspard to make the sign of the cross and mutter an "Ave,"—Morgana heard him and smiled kindly.

"I am not an evil spirit, my friend!" she said—"You need not exorcise me! I am nothing but a student with a little more imagination than is common, and in the moving force which carries our ship along I am only using a substance which, as our scientists explain, 'has an exceptional capacity for receiving the waves of energy emanating from the sun and giving them off.' On the 'giving off' of those waves we move—it is all natural and easy, and, like every power existent in the universe, is meant for our comprehension and use. You cannot say you feel any sense of danger?—we are sailing with greater steadiness than any ship at sea—there is scarcely any consciousness of movement—and without looking out and down, we should not realise we are so far from earth. Indeed we are going too far now—we do not realize our speed."

"Too far!" said Gaspard, nervously—"Madama, if we go too far we may also go too high—we may not be able to breathe! . . ."

She laughed.

"That is a very remote possibility!" she said—"The waves of energy which bear us along are concerned in our own life-supply,—they make our air to breathe—our heat to warm. All the same it is time we returned—we are not provisioned."

She called to Rivardi, and he, with the slightest turn of the wheel, altered the direction in which the air-ship moved, so that it travelled back again on the route by which it had commenced its flight. Soon, very soon, the dainty plot of earth, looking no more than a gay flower-bed, where Morgana's palazzo was situated, appeared below—and then, acting on instructions, Gaspard opened the compartments at either end of the vessel. The vibrating rays within dwindled by slow degrees—their light became less and less intense—their vibration less powerful,—till very gradually with a perfectly beautiful motion expressing absolute grace and lightness the vessel descended towards the aerodrome it had lately left, and all the men who were waiting for its return gave a simultaneous shout of astonishment and admiration, as it sank slowly towards them, folding its wings as it came with the quiet ease of a nesting-bird flying home. So admirably was the distance measured between itself and the great shed of its local habitation, that it glided into place as though it had eyes to see its exact whereabouts, and came to a standstill within a few seconds of its arrival. Morgana descended, and her two companions followed. The other men stood silent, visibly inquisitive yet afraid to express their curiosity. Morgana's eyes flashed over them all with a bright, half-laughing tolerance.

"I thank you, my friends!" she said—"You have done well the work I entrusted you to do under the guidance of the Marchese Rivardi, and you can now judge for yourselves the result It mystifies you I can see! You think it is a kind of 'black magic'? Not so!—unless all our modern science is 'black magic' as well, born of the influence of those evil spirits who, as we are told in tradition, descended in rebellion from heaven and lived with the daughters of men! From these strange lovers sprang a race of giants,—symbolical I think of the birth of the sciences, which mingle in their composition the active elements of good and evil. You have built this airship of mine on lines which have never before been attempted;—you have given it wings which are plumed like the wings of a bird, not with quills, but with channels many and minute, to carry the runlets of the 'emanation' from the substance held in the containers at either end of the vessel,—its easy flight therefore should not surprise you. Briefly—we have filled a piece of mechanism with the composition or essence of Life!—that is the only answer I can give to your enquiring looks!—let it be enough!"

"But, Madama"—ventured Gaspard—"that composition or essence of Life!—what is it?"

There was an instant's silence. Every man's head craned forward eagerly to hear the reply. Morgana smiled strangely.

"That," she said—"is My secret!"

IX

A nd now you have attained your object, what is the use of it?" said Don Aloysius.

The priest was pacing slowly up and down the old half-ruined cloister of an old half-ruined monastery, and beside his stately, black-robed figure moved the small aerial form of Morgana, clad in summer garments of pure white, her golden head uncovered to the strong Sicilian sunshine which came piercing in sword-like rays through the arches of the cloister, and filtered among the clustering leaves which hung in cool twining bunches from every crumbling grey pillar of stone.

"What is the use of it?" he repeated, his calm eyes resting gravely on the little creature gliding sylph-like beside him. "Suppose your invention out-reaped every limit of known possibility—suppose your air-ship to be invulnerable, and surpassing in speed and safety everything ever experienced,—suppose it could travel to heights unimaginable, what then? Suppose even that you could alight on another star—another world than this—what purpose is served?—what peace is gained?— what happens?"

Morgana stopped abruptly in her walk beside him.

"I have not worked for peace or happiness,"—she said and there was a thrill of sadness in her voice—"because to my mind neither peace nor happiness exist. From all we can see, and from the little we can learn, I think the Maker of the universe never meant us to be happy or peaceful. All Nature is at strife with itself, incessantly labouring for such attainment as can hardly be won,—all things seem to be haunted by fear and sorrow. And yet it seems to me that there are remedies for most of our evils in the very composition of the elements—if we were not ignorant and stupid enough to discourage our discoverers on the verge of discovery. My application of a certain substance, known to scientists, but scarcely understood, is an attempt to solve the problem of swift aerial motion by light and heat—light and heat being the chiefest supports of life. To use a force giving out light and heat continuously seemed to me the way to create and command equally continuous movement. I have—I think and hope—fairly succeeded, and in order to accomplish my design I have used wealth that would not have been at the service of most inventors,—wealth which my father left to me quite unconditionally,—but were I able to fly with my 'White Eagle' to the remotest parts of the Milky Way itself, I should not look to find peace or happiness!"

"Why?"

The priest's simple query had a note of tender pity in it. Morgana looked up at him with a little smile, but her eyes were tearful.

"Dear Don Aloysius, how can I tell 'why'? Nobody is really happy, and I cannot expect to have what is denied to the whole world!"

Aloysius resumed his slow walk to and fro, and she kept quiet pace with him.

"Have you ever thought what happiness is?" he asked, then—"Have you ever felt it for a passing moment?"

"Yes"—she answered quickly—"But only at rare intervals—oh so rare! . . ."

"Poor little rich child!" he said, kindly—"Tell me some of those 'intervals'! Cannot they be repeated? Let us sit here"—and he moved towards a stone bench which fronted an ancient disused well in the middle square of the cloistered court,—a well round which a crimson passion-flower twined in a perfect arch of blossom—"What was the first 'interval'?"

He sat down, and the sunshine sent a dazzling ray on the silver crucifix he wore, giving it the gleam of a great jewel. Morgana took her seat beside him.

"Interval one!" he said, playfully—"What was this little lady's first experience of happiness? When she played with her dolls?"

"No, oh no!" cried Morgana, with sudden energy—"That was anything but happiness! I hated dolls!—abominable little effigies!"

Don Aloysius raised his eyebrows in surprise and amusement.

"Horrid little stuffed things of wood and wax and saw-dust!" continued Morgana, emphatically—"With great beads for eyes—or eyes made to look like beads—and red cheeks,—and red lips with a silly smile on them! Of course they are given to girl-children to encourage the 'maternal instinct' as it is called—to make them think of babies,— but *I* never had any 'maternal instinct'!—and real babies have always seemed to me as uninteresting as sham ones!"

"Dear child, you were a baby yourself once!"—said Aloysius gently.

A shadow swept over her face.

"Do you think I was?" she queried meditatively—"I cannot imagine it! I suppose I must have been, but I never remember being a child at all.

I had no children to play with me—my father suspected all children of either disease or wickedness, and imagined I would catch infection of body or of soul by association with them. I was always alone—alone!—yet not lonely!" She broke off a moment, and her eyes grew dark with the intensity of her thought "No—never lonely! And the very earliest 'interval' of happiness I can recall was when I first saw the inside of a sun-ray!"

Don Aloysius turned to look at her, but said nothing. She laughed.

"Dear Father Aloysius, what a wise priest you are! Not a word falls from those beautifully set lips of yours! If you were a fool—(so many men are!) you would have repeated my phrase, 'the inside of a sun-ray,' with an accent of scornful incredulity, and you would have stared at me with all a fool's contempt! But you are not a fool,—you know or you perceive instinctively exactly what I mean. The inside of a sun-ray!—it was disclosed to me suddenly—a veritable miracle! I have seen it many times since, but not with all the wonder and ecstasy of the first revelation. I was so young, too! I told a renowned professor at one of the American colleges just what I saw, and he was so amazed and confounded at my description of rays that had taken the best scientists years to discover, that he begged to be allowed to examine my eyes! He thought there must be something unusual about them. In fact there Is!—and after his examination he seemed more puzzled than ever. He said something about 'an exceptionally strong power of vision,' but frankly admitted that power of vision alone would not account for it. Anyhow I plainly saw all the rays within one ray—there were seven. The ray itself was—or so I fancied—the octave of colour. I was little more than a child when this 'interval' of happiness—PERFECT happiness!—was granted to me—I felt as if a window had been opened for me to look through it into heaven!"

"Do you believe in heaven?" asked Aloysius, suddenly.

She hesitated.

"I used to,—in those days. As I have just said I was only a child, and heaven was a real place to me,—even the angels were real presences—"

"And you have lost them now?"

She gave a little gesture of resignation.

"They left me"—she answered—"I did not lose them. They simply went."

He was silent. His fine, calm features expressed a certain grave patience, but nothing more.

She resumed—

"That was my first experience of real 'happiness.' Till then I had lived the usual monotonous life of childhood, doing what I was told, and going whither I was taken, but the disclosure of the sun-ray was a key to individuality, and seemed to unlock my prison doors. I began to think for myself, and to find my own character as a creature apart from others. My second experience was years after,—just when I left school and when my father took me to see the place where I was born, in the north of Scotland. Oh, it is such a wild corner of the world! Beautiful craggy hills and dark, deep lakes—rough moorlands purple with heather and such wonderful skies at sunset! The cottage where my father had lived as a boy when he herded sheep is still there—I have bought it for myself now,—it is a little stone hut of three rooms,—and another one about a mile off where he took my mother to live, and where I came into the world!—I have bought that too. Yes—I felt a great thrill of happiness when I stood there knee-deep among the heather, my father clasping my hand, and looking, with me, on those early scenes of his boyhood when he had scarcely a penny to call his own! Yet HE was sad!—very sad! and told me then that he would give all his riches to feel as light of heart and free from care as he did in those old days! And then—then we went to see old Alison—" Here she broke off,—a strange light came into her eyes and she smiled a little. "I think I had better not tell you about old Alison!" she said.

"Why not?" and Don Aloysius returned her smile. "If old Alison has anything to do with your happiness I should like to hear."

"Well, you see, you are a priest," went on Morgana, slowly, "and she is a witch. Oh yes, truly!—a real witch! There is no one in all that part of the Highlands that does not know of her, and the power she has! She is very, very old—some folks say she is more than a hundred. She knew my father and grandfather—she came to my father's cottage the night I was born, and said strange things about a 'May child'—I was born in May. We went—as I tell you—to see her, and found her spinning. She looked up from her wheel as we entered—but she did not seem surprised at our coming. Her eyes were very bright—not like the eyes of an old person. She spoke to my father at once—her voice was very clear and musical. 'Is it you, John Royal?' she said—'and you have brought your fey lass along with you!' That was the first time I ever heard the word 'fey.' I did not understand it then."

"And do you understand it now?" asked Aloysius.

"Yes"—she replied,—"I understand it now! It is a wonderful thing to be born 'fey'! But it is a kind of witchcraft,—and you would be displeased—"

"At what should I be displeased?" and the priest bent his eyes very searchingly upon her—"At the fact,—which none can disprove,—that 'there are things in heaven and earth' which are beyond our immediate knowledge? That there are women strangely endowed with premonitory instincts land preternatural gifts? Dear child, there is nothing in all this that can or could displease me! My faith—the faith of my Church—is founded on the preternatural endowment of a woman!"

She lifted her eyes to his, and a little sigh came from her lips.

"Yes, I know what you mean!"—she said—"But I am sure you cannot possibly realise the weird nature of old Alison! She made me stand before her, just where the light of the sun streamed through the open doorway, and she looked at me for a long time with such a steady piercing glance that I felt as if her eyes were boring through my flesh. Then she got up from her spinning and pushed away the wheel, and stretched out both her hands towards me, crying out in quite a strange, wild voice—'Morgana! Morgana! Go your ways, child begotten of the sun and shower!—go your ways! Little had mortal father or mother to do with your making, for you are of the fey folk! Go your ways with your own people!—you shall hear them whispering in the night and singing in the morning,—and they shall command you and you shall obey!—they shall beckon and you shall follow! Nothing of mortal flesh and blood shall hold you—no love shall bind you,—no hate shall wound you!—the clue is given into your hand,—the secret is disclosed—and the spirits of air and fire and water have opened a door that you may enter in! Hark!—I can hear their voices calling "Morgana! Morgana!" Go your ways, child!—go hence and far!—the world is too small for your wings!' She looked so fierce and grand and terrible that I was frightened—I was only a girl of sixteen, and I ran to my father and caught his hand. He spoke quite gently to Alison, but she seemed quite beyond herself and unable to listen. 'Your way lies down a different road, John Royal'—she said—'You that herded sheep on these hills and that now hoard millions of money—of what use to you is your wealth? You are but the worker,—gathering gold for HER—the "fey" child born in an hour of May moonlight! You must go, but she must stay,—her own folk have work for her to do!' Then my father said, 'Dear Alison, don't frighten the child!' and she suddenly changed in her tone and manner.

'Frighten her?' she muttered. 'I would not frighten her for the world!' And my father pushed me towards her and whispered—'Ask her to bless you before you go.' So I just knelt before her, trembling very much, and said, 'Dear Alison, bless me!'—and she stared at me and lifted her old brown wrinkled hands and laid them on my head. Then she spoke some words in a strange language as to herself, and afterwards she said, 'Spirit of all that is and ever shall be, bless this child who belongs to thee, and not to man! Give her the power to do what is commanded, to the end.' And at this she stopped suddenly and bending down she lifted my head in her two hands and looked at me hard—'Poor child, poor child! Never a love for you—never a love! Alone you are, alone you must be! Never a love for a "fey" woman!' And she let me go, and sat down again to her spinning-wheel, nor would she say another word—neither to me nor to my father."

"And you call THIS your second experience of happiness?" said Don Aloysius, wonderingly—"What happiness did you gain by your interview with this old Alison?"

"Ah!" and Morgana smiled—"You would not understand me if I tried to explain! Everything came to me!—yes, everything! I began to live in a world of my own—" she paused, and her eyes grew dark and pensive, "and I have lived in it ever since. That is why I say my visit to old Alison was my second experience of happiness. I've seen her again many times since then, but not with quite the same impression."

"She is alive still?"

"Oh, yes! I often fancy she will never die!"

There was a silence of some minutes. Morgana rose, and crossing over to the old well, studied the crimson passion-flowers which twined about it, with almost loving scrutiny.

"How beautiful they are!" she said—"And they seem to serve no purpose save that of simple beauty!"

"That is enough for many of God's creatures"—said Aloysius—"To give joy and re-create joy is the mission of perfection."

She looked at him wistfully.

"Alas, poor me!" she sighed—"I can neither give joy nor create it!"

"Not even with all your wealth?"

"Not even with all my wealth!" she echoed. "Surely you—a priest—know what a delusion wealth really is so far as happiness goes?—mere happiness? course you can buy everything with it—and there's the trouble! When everything is bought there's nothing left! And if you try to help the poor they resent it—they think you are doing it because you are afraid of them! Perhaps the worst of all things to do is to help artists—artists of every kind!—for THEY say you want to advertise yourself as a 'generous patron'! Oh, I've tried it all and it's no use. I was just crazy to help all the scientists,—once!—but they argued and quarrelled so much as to which 'society' deserved most money that I dropped the whole offer, and started 'scientising' myself. There is one man I tried to lift out of his brain-bog,—but he would have none of me, and he is still in his bog!"

"Oh! There is one man!" said Aloysius, with a smile.

"Yes, good father!" And Morgana left the passion-flowers and moved slowly back to her seat on the stone-bench—"There is one man! He was my third and last experience of happiness. When I first met him, my whole heart gave itself in one big pulsation—but like a wave of the sea, the pulsation recoiled, and never again beat on the grim rock of human egoism!" She laughed gaily, and a delicate colour flushed her face. "But I was happy while the 'wave' lasted,—and when it broke, I still played on the shore with its pretty foam-bells."

"You loved this man?" and the priest's grave eyes dwelt on her searchingly.

"I suppose so—for the moment! Yet no,—it was not love—it was just an 'attraction'—he was—he Is—clever, and thinks he can change the face of the world. But he is fooling with fire! I tell you I tried to help him—for he is deadly poor. But he would have none of me nor of what he calls my 'vulgar wealth.' This is a case in point where wealth is useless! You see?"

Don Aloysius was silent.

"Then"—Morgana went on—"Alison is right. The witchery of the Northern Highlands is in my blood,—never a love for me—alone I am—alone I must be!—never a love for a 'fey' woman!"

Over the priest's face there passed a quiver as of sudden pain.

"You wrong yourself, my child"—he said, slowly—"You wrong yourself very greatly! You have a power of which you appear to be unconscious—a great, a terrible power!—you compel interest—you attract the love of others even if you yourself love no one—you draw the very soul out of a man—"

He paused, abruptly.

Morgana raised her eyes,—the blue lightning gleam flashed in their depths.

"Ah, yes!" she half whispered—"I know I have THAT power!"

Don Aloysius rose to his feet.

"Then,—if you know it,—in God's name do not exercise it!" he said.

His voice shook—and with his right hand he gripped the crucifix he wore as though it were a weapon of self-defence. Morgana looked at him wonderingly for a moment,—then drooped her head with a strange little air of sudden penitence. Aloysius drew a quick sharp breath as of one in effort,—then he spoke again, unsteadily—

"I mean"—he said, smiling forcedly—"I mean that you should not—you should not break the heart of—of—the poor Giulio for instance! . . . it would not be kind."

She lifted her eyes again and fixed them on him.

"No, it would not be kind!" she said, softly—"Dear Don Aloysius, I understand! And I will remember!" She glanced at a tiny diamond-set watch-bracelet on her wrist—"How late it is!—nearly all the morning gone! I have kept you so long listening to my talk—forgive me! I will run away now and leave you to think about my 'intervals' of happiness,—will you?—they are so few compared to yours!"

"Mine?" he echoed amazedly.

"Yes, indeed!—yours! Your whole life is an interval of happiness between this world and the next, because you are satisfied in the service of God!"

"A poor service!" he said, turning his gaze away from her elfin figure and shining hair—"Unworthy,—shameful!—marred by sin at every moment! A priest of the Church must learn to do without happiness such as ordinary life can give—and without love,—such as woman may give—but—after all—the sacrifice is little."

She smiled at him, sweetly—tenderly,

"Very little!" she said—"So little that it is not worth a regret! Good-bye! But not for long! Come and see me soon!"

Moving across the cloister with her light step she seemed to float through the sunshine like a part of it, and as she disappeared a kind of shadow fell, though no cloud obscured the sun. Don Aloysius watched her till she had vanished,—then turned aside into a small chapel opening out on the cloistered square—a chapel which formed part of the monastic house to which he belonged as Superior,—and there, within that still, incense-sweetened sanctuary, he knelt before the noble, pictured Head of the Man of Sorrows in silent confession and prayer.

X

Roger Seaton was a man of many philosophies. He had one for every day in the week, yet none wherewith to thoroughly satisfy himself. While still a mere lad he had taken to the study of science as a duck takes to water,—no new discovery or even suggestion of a new discovery missed his instant and close attention. His avidity for learning was insatiable,—his intense and insistent curiosity on all matters of chemistry gave a knife-like edge to the quality of his brain, making it sharp, brilliant and incisive. To him the ordinary social and political interests of the world were simply absurd. The idea that the greater majority of men should be created for no higher purpose than those of an insect, just to live, eat, breed, and die, was to him preposterous.

"Think of it!" he would exclaim—"All this wondrous organisation of our planet for THAT! For a biped so stupid as to see nothing in his surroundings but conveniences for satisfying his stomach and his passions! We men are educated chiefly in order to learn how to make money, and all we can do with the money WHEN made, is to build houses to live in, eat as much as we want and more, and breed children to whom we leave all the stuff we have earned, and who either waste it or add to it, whichever suits their selfishness best. Such lives are absolutely useless,—they repeat the same old round, leading nowhere. Occasionally, in the course of centuries a real Brain is born—and at once, all who are merely Bodies leap up against it, like famished wolves, striving to tear it to pieces and devour it—if it survives the attack its worth is only recognised long after its owner has perished. The whole scheme is manifestly unintelligent and ludicrous, but it is not intended to be so—of that I am sure. THERE MUST BE SOMETHING ELSE!"

When urged to explain what he conceived as this "something else," he would answer—

"There has always been 'something else' in our environment,—something that stupid humanity has taken centuries to discover. Sound-waves for example—light-rays,—electricity—these have been freely at our service from the beginning. Electricity might have been used ages ago, had not dull-witted man refused to find anything better for lighting purposes than an oil-lamp or a tallow candle! If, in past periods, he had been told 'there is something else'—he would have laughed his informant to scorn. So with our blundering methods of living—'there is something else'—not after death, but Now and HERE. We are going about in the darkness with a candle when a great force of wider light is all round us, only awaiting connection and application to our uses."

Those who heard him speak in this way—(and they were few, for Seaton seldom discussed his theories with others)—convinced themselves that he was either a fool or a madman,—the usual verdict given for any human being who dares break away from convention and adopt an original line of thought and action. But they came to the conclusion that as he was direfully poor, and nevertheless refused various opportunities of making money, his folly or his madness would be brought home to him sooner or later by strong necessity, and that he would then either arrive at a sane every-day realisation of "things as they are"—or else be put away in an asylum and quietly forgotten. This being the sagacious opinion of those who knew him best, there was a considerable flutter in such limited American circles as call themselves "upper" when the wealthiest young woman in the States, Morgana Royal, suddenly elected to know him and to bring him into prominent notice at her parties as "the most wonderful genius of the time"—"a man whose scientific discoveries might change the very face of the globe"—and other fantastically exaggerated descriptions of her own which he himself strongly repudiated and resented. Gossip ran amok concerning the two, and it was generally agreed that if the "madman" of science were to become the husband of a woman multi-millionaire, he would not have to be considered so mad after all! But the expected romance did not materialise,—there came apparently a gradual "cooling off" in the sentiments of both parties concerned,—and though Roger Seaton was still occasionally seen with Morgana in her automobile, in her opera-box, or at her receptions, his appearances were fewer, and other men, in fact many other men, were more openly encouraged and flattered,—Morgana herself showing as much indifference towards him as she had at first shown interest. When, therefore, he suddenly left the social scene of action, his acquaintances surmised that he had got an abrupt dismissal, or as they more brusquely expressed it—"the game's up"!

"He's lost his chance!" they said, shaking their heads forlornly— "And he's poorer than Job! He'll be selling newspapers in the cars for a living by and by!"

However, he was never met engaged in this lucrative way of business,—he simply turned his back on everybody, Morgana Royal included, and so far as "society" was concerned, just disappeared. In the "hut of the dying" on that lonely hill-slope in California he was happy, feeling a relief from infinite boredom, and thankful to be alone. He had much to think about and much to do—inhabited places and the movement of people were to him tedious and fatiguing, and he decided that nature,—wild nature in a solitary and savage aspect,—would suit his speculative and creative tendencies best. Yet, like all human beings, he had his odd, almost child-like moods, inexplicable even to himself—moods illogical, almost pettish, and wholly incongruous with his own accepted principles of reasoning. For instance, he maintained that women had neither attraction nor interest for him—yet he found himself singularly displeased when after two or three days of utter solitude, and when he was rather eagerly expecting Manella to arrive with the new milk which was his staple food, a lanky, red-haired ugly boy appeared instead of her—a boy who slouched along, swinging the milk pail in one hand and clutching a half-munched slice of pine-apple in the other.

"Hello—o!" called this individual. "Not dead yet?"

For answer Seaton strode forward and taking the milk-pail from him gripped him by the dirty cotton shirt and gave him a brief but severe shaking.

"No,—not dead yet!" he said—"You insolent young monkey! Who are you?"

The boy wriggled in his captor's clutch, and tried to squirm himself out of it.

"I'm—I'm Jake—they calls me Irish Jake"—he gasped—"O Blessed Mary!—my breath! I clean the knives at the Plaza—"

"I'll clean knives for you presently!" remarked Seaton, with a threatening gesture—"Yes, Irish Jake, I will! Who sent you here?"

"SHE did—oh, Mary mother!" and the youth gave a further wriggle—"Miss Soriso—the girl they call Manella. She told me to say she's too busy to come herself."

Seaton let go the handful of shirt he had held.

"Too busy to come herself!" he repeated, slowly—then smiled—"Well! That's all right!" Here he lifted the pail of milk, took it into his hut and brought it back empty, while "Irish Jake," as the boy had called himself, stood staring—"Tell Miss Soriso that I quite understand! And that I'm delighted to hear she is so busy! Now, let us see!" Here he pulled some money out of his pocket, and fingered a few dirty paper notes—"There, Irish Jake! You'll find that's correct. And when you come here again don't forget your manners! See? Then you may be able to keep that disgraceful shirt of yours on! Otherwise it's likely to be torn off! If you are Irish you should remember that in very ancient days there used to be manners in the Emerald Isle. Yes, positively! Fine, gracious, lovely manners! It doesn't look as if that will be ever any more—but we live in hope. Anyway, You—you young offspring of an Irish hybrid gorilla—you'd best remember what *I* say, or there'll be trouble! And"— here he made a mock solemn bow—"My compliments to Miss Soriso!"

The red-haired youth remained for a moment stock-still with mouth and eyes open,—then, snatching up the empty milk-pail he scampered down the hill-slope at a lightning quick run.

Seaton looked after him with an air of contemptuous amusement.

"Ugly little devil!" he soliloquised—"And yet Nature made him,—as she makes many hideous things—in a hurry, I presume, without any time for details or artistic finish. Well!"—here he stretched his arms out with a long sigh—"And the silly girl is 'too busy' to come! As if I could not see through THAT little game! She'd give her eyes to come!—fine eyes they are, too! She just thinks she'll pay me out for being rough with her the other day—she's got an idea that she'll vex me, and make me want to see her. She's right,—I AM vexed!—and I Do want to see her!"

It was mid-morning, and the sun blazed down upon the hill-side with the scorching breath of a volcano. He turned into his hut,—it was a dark, cool little dwelling, comfortable enough for a single inhabitant. There was a camp-bed in one corner—and there were a couple of wicker chairs made for easy transposition into full-length couches if so required, A good sized deal table occupied the centre of the living-room,—and on the table was a clear crystal bowl full of what appeared at a first glance to be plain water, but which on closer observation showed a totally different quality. Unlike water it was never still,—some interior bubbling perpetually moved it to sway and sparkle, throwing out tiny flashes as though the smallest diamond cuttings were striving to escape from it—while it exhaled around itself an atmosphere of extreme coldness and freshness like that of ice. Seaton threw himself indolently into one of wicker chairs by the window—a window which was broad and wide, commanding a full view of distant mountains, and far away to the left a glimpse of sea.

"I am vexed, and I want to see her"—he repeated, speaking aloud to himself—"Now—WHY? Why am I vexed?—and why do I want to see her? Reason gives no answer! If she were here she would bore me to death. I could do nothing. She would ask me questions—and if I answered them she would not understand,—she is too stupid. She has no comprehension of any thing beyond simple primitive animalism. Now if it were Morgana—"

He stopped in his talk, and started as if he had been stung. Some subtle influence stole over him like the perfumed mist of incense—he leaned back in his chair and half closed his eyes. What was the stealthy, creeping magnetic power that like an invisible hand touched his brain and pulled at his memory, and forced him to see before him a small elf-like figure clad in white, with a rope of gold hair twisting, snake-like, down over its shoulders and glistening in the light of the moon? For the moment he lost his usual iron mastery of will and let himself go on the white flood of a dream. He recalled his first meeting with Morgana,—one of accident, not design—in the great laboratory of a distinguished scientist,—he had taken her for a little girl student trying to master a few principles of chemistry, and was astonished and incredulous when the distinguished scientist himself had introduced her as "one of our most brilliant theorists on the future development of radio activity." Such a description seemed altogether absurd, applied to a little fair creature with beseeching blue eyes and gold hair! They had left the laboratory together, walking some way in company and charmed with each other's conversation, then, when closer acquaintance followed, and he had learned her true position in social circles and the power she wielded owing to her vast wealth, he at once withdrew from her as much as was civilly possible, disliking the suggestion of any sordid motive for his friendship. But she had so sweetly reproached him for this, and had enticed him on—yes!—he swore it within himself,—she had enticed him on in a thousand ways,—most especially by the amazing "grip" she had of scientific problems in which he was interested and which puzzled him, but which she seemed to unravel as easily as she might unravel a skein of wool. Her clear brightness of brain and logical precision of argument first surprised him into unqualified admiration, calling to his mind the assertion of a renowned physiologist that "From the beginning woman had lived in another world than man. Formed of finer vibrations and consequently finer chemical atoms she is in touch with more subtle planes of existence and of sensation and ideation. She holds unchallenged the code of Life." Then admiration yielded to the usual under-sense of masculine resentment against feminine intellectuality, and a kind of smouldering wrath and opposition took the place of his former chivalry and the almost tender pleasure he had previously felt in her exceptional genius and ability. And there came an evening—why did he think of it now, he wondered?—when, after a brilliant summer ball given at the beautiful residence of a noted society woman on Long Island, he had taken Morgana out into their hostess's garden which sloped to the sea, and they had strolled together almost unknowingly down to the shore where, under the light of the moon, the Atlantic waves, sunken to little dainty frills of lace-like foam, broke murmuringly at their feet,—and he, turning suddenly to his companion, was all at once smitten by a sense of witchery in her looks as she stood garmented in her white, vaporous ball-gown, with diamonds in her hair and on her bosom—smitten with an overpowering lightning-stroke of passion which burnt his soul as a desert is burnt by the hot breath of the simoon, and, yielding to its force, he had caught the small, fine, fairy creature in his arms and kissed her wildly on lips and eyes and hair. And she,—she had not resisted. Then—as swiftly as he had clasped her he let her go—and stood before her in a strange spirit of defiance.

"Forgive me!" he said, in low uneven tones—"I—I did not mean it!"

She lifted her eyes to his, half proudly half appealingly.

"You did not mean it?" she asked, quietly.

An amazed scorn flashed into her face, clouding its former sweetness— then she smiled coldly, turned away and left him. In a kind of stupor he watched her go, her light figure disappearing by degrees, as she went up the ascending path from the sea to the house where gay music was still sounding for dancers not yet grown weary. And from that evening a kind of silence fell between them,—they were separated as by an ice-floe. They met often in the social round, but scarcely spoke more than the ordinary words of conventional civility, and Morgana apparently gave herself up to frivolity, coquetting with her numerous admirers and would-be husbands in a casual, not to say heartless, manner which provoked Seaton past endurance,—so much so that he worked himself up to a kind of cynical detestation and contempt for her, both as a student of science and a woman of wealth. And yet—and yet—he had almost loved her! And a thing that goaded him to the quick was that so far as scientific knowledge and attainment were concerned she was more than his equal. Irritated by his own quarrelsome set of sentiments which pulled him first this way and then that, he decided that the only thing possible for him was to put a "great divide" of distance between himself

MARIE CORELLI

and her. This he had done—and to what purpose? Apparently merely to excite her ridicule!—and to prick her humor up to the mischievous prank of finding out where he had fled and following him! And she—even she—who had kept him aloof ever since that fatal moment on the seashore,—had discovered him on this lonely hill-side, and had taunted him with her light mockery—and actually said that "to kiss him would be like kissing a bunch of nettles!"—She said that!—she who for one wild moment he had held in his arms—bah!—he sprang up from his chair in a kind of rage with himself, as his thoughts crowded thick and fast one on the other—why did he think of her at all! It was as if some external commanding force compelled him to do so. Then—she had seen Manella, and had naturally drawn her own conclusions, based on the girl's rich beauty which was so temptingly set within his reach. He began to talk to himself aloud once more, picking up the thread of his broken converse where he had left it—

"If it were Morgana it would be far worse than if it were Manella!" he said—"The one is too stupid—the other too clever. But the stupid woman would make the best wife—if I wanted one—which I do not; and the best mother, if I desired children,—which I do not. The question is,—what Do I want? I think I know—but supposing I get it, shall I be satisfied? Will it fulfil my life's desire? What Is my life's desire?"

He stood inert—his tall figure erect—his eyes full of strange and meditative earnestness, and for a moment he seemed to gather his mental forces together with an effort. Turning towards the table where the bowl of constantly sparkling fluid danced in tiny flashing eddies within its crystal prison, he watched its movement.

"There's the clue!" he said—"so little—yet so much! Life that cannot cease—force that cannot die! For me—for me alone this secret!—to do with it what I will—to destroy or to re-create! How shall I use it? If I could sweep the planet clean of its greedy, contentious human microbes, and found a new race I might be a power for good,—but should I care to do this? If God does not care, why should I?"

He lost himself anew in musing—then, rousing his mind to work, he put paper, pens and ink on the table, and started writing busily—only interrupting himself once for a light meal of dry bread and milk during a stretch of six or seven hours. At the end of his self-appointed time, he went out of the hut to see, as he often expressed it, "what the sky was doing." It was not doing much, being a mere hot glare in which the sun was beginning to roll westwards slowly like a sinking fire-ball.

He brought out one of the wicker chairs from the hut and set it in the only patch of shade by the door, stretching himself full length upon it, and closing his eyes, composed himself to sleep. His face in repose was a remarkably handsome one,—a little hard in outline, but strong, nobly featured and expressive of power,—an ambitious sculptor would have rejoiced in him as a model for Achilles. He was as unlike the modern hideous type of man as he could well be,—and most particularly unlike any specimen of American that could be found on the whole huge continent. In truth he was purely and essentially English of England,— one of the fine old breed of men nurtured among the winds and waves of the north, for whom no labour was too hard, no service too exacting, no death too difficult, provided "the word was the bond." His natural gifts of intellect were very great, and profound study had ripened and rounded them to fruition,—certain discoveries in chemistry which he had tested were brought to the attention of his own country's scientists, who in their usual way of accepting new light on old subjects smiled placidly, shook their heads, pooh-poohed, and finally set aside the matter "for future discussion." But Roger Seaton was not of a nature to sink under a rebuff. If the Wise Men of Gotham in England refused to take first advantage of the knowledge he had to offer them, then the Wise Men of Gotham in Germany or the United States should have their chance. He tried the United States and was received with open arms and open minds. So he resolved to stay there, for a few years at any rate, and managed to secure a position with the tireless magician Edison, in whose workshops he toiled patiently as an underling, obtaining deeper grasp of his own instinctive knowledge, and further insight into an immense nature secret which he had determined to master alone. He had not mastered it yet—but felt fairly confident that he was near the goal. As he slept peacefully, with the still shade of a heavily foliaged vine which ramped over the roof of the hut, sheltering his face from the sun, his whole form in its relaxed, easy attitude expressed force in repose,—physical energy held in leash.

The sun sank lower, its hue changing from poppy red to burning orange—and presently a woman's figure appeared on the hill slope, and cautiously approached the sleeper—a beautiful figure of classic mould and line, clothed in a simple white linen garb, with a red rose at its breast. It was Manella. She had taken extraordinary pains with her attire, plain though it was—something dainty and artistic in the manner of its wearing made its simplicity picturesque,—and the red rose at her bosom was effectively supplemented by another in her hair, showing brilliantly against its rich blackness. She stopped when about three paces away from the sleeping man and watched him with a wonderful tenderness. Her lips quivered sweetly—her lovely eyes shone with a soft wistfulness,—she looked indeed, as Morgana had said of her, "quite beautiful." Instinctively aware in slumber that he was not alone, Seaton stirred—opened his eyes, and sprang up.

"What! Manella!" he exclaimed—"I thought you were too busy to come!"

She hung her head a little shamefacedly.

"I HAD to come"—she answered—"There was no one else ready to bring this—for you."

She held out a telegram. He opened and read it. It was very brief— "Shall be with you tomorrow. Gwent."

He folded it and put it in his pocket. Then he turned to Manella, smiling.

"Very good of you to bring this!" he said—"Why didn't you send Irish Jake?"

"He is taking luggage down from the rooms," she answered—"Many people are going away to-day."

"Is that why you are 'so busy'"? he asked, the smile still dancing in his eyes.

She gave a little toss of her head but said nothing.

"And how fine we are to-day!" he said, glancing over her with an air of undisguised admiration—"White suits you, Manella! You should always wear it! For what fortunate man have you dressed yourself so prettily?"

She shrugged her shoulders expressively—

"For you!"

"For me? Oh, Manella! What a frank confession! And what a contradiction you are to yourself! For did you not send word by that Irish monkey that you were 'too busy to come'? And yet you dress yourself in white, with red roses, for ME! And you come after all! Capricious child! Oh Senora Soriso, how greatly honoured I am!"

She looked straight at him.

"You laugh, you laugh!" she said—"But I do not care! You can laugh at me all the time if you like. But—you cannot help looking at me! Ah yes!—you cannot help THAT!"

A triumphant glory flashed in her eyes—her red lips parted in a ravishing smile.

"You cannot help it!" she repeated—"That little white lady—that friend of yours whom you hate and love at the same time!—she told me I was 'quite beautiful!' I know I am!—and you know it too!"

He bent his eyes upon her gravely.

"I have always known it—yes!"—he said, then paused—"Dear child, beauty is nothing—"

She made a swift step towards him and laid a hand on his arm. Her ardent, glowing face was next to his.

"You speak not truly!" and her voice was tremulous—"To a man it is everything!"

Her physical fascination was magnetic, and for a moment he had some trouble to resist its spell. Very gently he put an arm round her,—and with a tender delicacy of touch unfastened the rose she wore at her bosom.

"There, dear!" he said—"I will keep this with me for company! It is like you—except that it doesn't talk and doesn't ask for love—"

"It has it without asking!" she murmured.

He smiled.

"Has it? Well,—perhaps it has!" He paused—then stooping his tall head kissed her once on the lips as a brother might have kissed her. "And perhaps—one day—when the right man comes along, you will have it too!"

XI

M r. Sam Gwent stood in what was known as the "floral hall" of the Plaza Hotel, so called because it was built in colonnades which opened into various vistas of flowers and clambering vines growing with all the luxuriance common to California. He had just arrived, and while divesting himself of a light dust overcoat interrogated the official at the enquiry office.

"So he doesn't live here after all,"—he said—"Then where's he to be found?"

"Mr. Seaton has taken the hill hut"—replied the book-keeper—"'The hut of the dying' it is sometimes called. He prefers it to the hotel. The air is better for his lungs."

"Air? Lungs?"—Gwent sniffed contemptuously. "There's very little the matter with his lungs if he's the man *I* know! Where's this hut of the dying? Can I get there straight?"

The bookkeeper touched a bell, and Manella appeared. Gwent stared openly. Here—if "prize beauties" were anything—was a real winner!

"This gentleman wants Mr. Seaton"—said the bookkeeper—"Just show him the way up the hill."

"Sorry to trouble you!" said Gwent, raising his hat with a courtesy not common to his manner.

"Oh, it is no trouble!" and Manella smiled at him in the most ravishing way—"The path is quite easy to follow."

She preceded him out of the "floral hall," and across the great gardens, now in their most brilliant bloom to a gate which she opened, pointing with one hand towards the hill where the flat outline of the "hut of the dying" could be seen clear against the sky.

"There it is"—she explained—"It's nothing of a climb, even on the warmest day. And the air is quite different up there to what it is down here."

"Better, I suppose?"

"Oh, yes! Much better!"

"And is that why Mr. Seaton lives in the hut? On account of the air?"

Manella waved her hands expressively with a charming Spanish gesture of indifference.

"I suppose so! How should I know? He is here for his health."

Sam Gwent uttered a curious inward sound, something between a grunt and a cough.

"Ah! I should like to know how long he's been ill!"

Manella again gave her graceful gesture.

"Surely you Do know if you are a friend of his?" she said.

He looked keenly at her.

"Are You a friend of his?"

She smiled—almost laughed.

"I? I am only a help in the Plaza—I take him his food—"

"Take him his food!" Sam Gwent growled out something like an oath—"What! Can't he come and get it for himself? Is he treated like a bear in a cage or a baby in a cradle?"

Manella gazed at him with reproachful soft eyes.

"Oh, you are rough!" she said—"He pays for whatever little trouble he gives. Indeed it is no trouble! He lives very simply—only on new milk and bread. I expect his health will not stand anything else—though truly he does not look ill—"

Gwent cut her description short.

"Well, thank you for showing me the way, Senora or Senorita, whichever you are—I think you must be Spanish—"

"Senorita"—she said, with gentle emphasis—"I am not married. You are right that I am Spanish."

"Such eyes as yours were never born of any blood but Spanish!" said Gwent—"I knew that at once! That you are not married is a bit of luck for some man—the man you WILL marry! For the moment adios! I shall dine at the Plaza this evening, and shall very likely bring my friend with me."

She shook her head smiling.

"You will not!"

"How so?"

"Because he will not come!"

She turned away, back towards the Hotel, and Gwent started to ascend the hill alone.

"Here's a new sort of game!"—he thought—"A game I should never have imagined possible to a man like Roger Seaton! Hiding himself up here in a consumption hut, and getting a beautiful woman to wait on him and 'take him his food'! It beats most things I've heard of! Dollar sensation books aren't in it! I wonder what Morgana Royal would say to it, if she knew! He's given her the slip this time!"

Half-way up the hill he paused to rest, and saw Seaton striding down at a rapid pace to meet him.

"Hullo, Gwent!"

"Hullo!"

The two men shook hands.

"I got your wire at the beginning of the week"—said Gwent—"and came as soon as I could get away. It's been a stiff journey too—but I wouldn't keep you waiting."

"Thanks,—it's as much your affair as mine"—said Seaton—"The thing is ripe for action if you care to act. It's quite in your hands, I hardly thought you'd come—"

"But I sent you a reply wire?"

"Oh, yes—that's all right! But reply wires don't always clinch business. Yours arrived last night."

"I wonder if it was ever delivered!" grumbled Gwent—"It was addressed to the Plaza Hotel—not to a hut on a hill!"

Seaton laughed.

"You've heard all about it I see! But the hut on the hill is a 'dependence' of the Plaza—a sort of annex where dying men are put away to die peaceably—"

"You are not a dying man!" said Gwent, very meaningly—"And I can't make out why you pretend to be one!"

Again Seaton laughed.

"I'm not pretending!—my dear Gwent, we're all dying men! One may die a little faster than another, but it's all the same sort of 'rot, and rot, and thereby hangs a tale!' What's the news in Washington?"

They walked up the hill slowly, side by side.

"Not startling"—answered Gwent—then paused—and repeated—"Not startling—there's nothing startling nowadays—though some folks made a very good show of being startled when my nephew Jack shot himself."

Seaton stopped in his walk.

"Shot himself? That lad? Was he insane?"

"Of course!—according to the coroner. Everybody is called 'insane' who gets out of the world when it's too difficult to live in. Some people would call it sane. I call it just—cowardice! Jack had lost his last chance, you see. Morgana Royal threw him over."

Seaton paced along with a velvet-footed stride like a tiger on a trail.

"Had she led him on?"

"Rather! She leads all men 'on'—or they think she does. She led You on at one time!"

Seaton turned upon him with a quick, savage movement.

"Never! I saw through her from the first! She could never make a fool of Me!"

Sam Gwent gave a short cough, expressing incredulity.

"Well! Washington thought you were the favoured 'catch' and envied your luck! Certainly she showed a great preference for you—"

"Can't you talk of something else?" interposed Seaton, impatiently.

Gwent gave him an amused side-glance.

"Why, of course I can!" he responded—"But I thought I'd tell you about Jack—"

"I'm sorry!" said Seaton, hastily, conscious that he had been lacking in sympathy—"He was your heir, I believe?"

"Yes,—he might have been, had he kept a bit straighter"—said Gwent—"But heirs are no good anywhere or anyhow. They only spend what they inherit and waste the honest work of a life-time. Is that your prize palace?"

He pointed to the hut which they had almost reached.

"That's it!" answered Seaton—"And I prefer it to any palace ever built. No servants, no furniture, no useless lumber—just a place to live in—enough for any man."

"A tub was enough for Diogenes"—commented Gwent—"If we all lived in his way or your way it would be a poor look-out for trade! However, I presume you'll escape taxation here!"

Seaton made no reply, but led the way into his dwelling, offering his visitor a chair.

"I hope you've had breakfast"—he said—"For I haven't any to give you. You can have a glass of milk if you like?"

Gwent made a wry face.

"I'm not a good subject for primitive nourishment"—he said—"I've been weaned too long for it to agree with me!"

He sat down. His eyes were at once attracted by the bowl of restless fluid on the table.

"What's that?" he asked.

Roger Seaton smiled enigmatically.

"Only a trifle"—he answered—"Just health! It's a sort of talisman;—germ-proof, dust-proof, disease-proof! No microbe of mischief, however infinitesimal, can exist near it, and a few drops, taken into the system, revivify the whole."

"If that's so, your fortune's made"—said Gwent, "Give your discovery, or recipe, or whatever it is, to the world—"

"To keep the world alive? No, thank you!" And the look of dark scorn on Seaton's face was astonishing in its almost satanic expression—"That is precisely what I wish to avoid! The world is over-ripe and over-rotten,—and it is over-crowded with a festering humanity that is Inhuman, and worse than bestial in its furious grappling for self and greed. One remedy for the evil would be that no children should be born in it for the next thirty or forty years—the relief would be incalculable,—a monstrous burden would be lifted, and there would be some chance of betterment,—but as this can never be, other remedies must be sought and found. It's pure hypocrisy to talk of love for children, when every day we read of mothers selling their offspring for so much cash down,—lately in China during a spell of famine parents killed their daughters like young calves, for food. Ugly facts like these have to be looked in the face—it's no use putting them behind one's back, and murmuring beautiful lies about 'mother-love' and such nonsense. As for the old Mosaic commandment 'Honour thy father and mother'—it's ordinary newspaper reading to hear of boys and girls attacking and murdering their parents for the sake of a few dollars."

"You've got the ugly facts by heart"—said Gwent slowly—"But there's another and more cheerful outlook—if you choose to consider it. Newspaper reading always gives the worst and dirtiest side of everything—it wouldn't be newspaper stuff if it was clean. Newspapers remind me of the rotting heaps in gardens—all the rubbish piled together till the smell becomes a nuisance—then a good burning takes place of the whole collection and it makes a sort of fourth-rate manure." He paused a moment—then went on—

"I'm not given to sentiment, but I dare say there are still a few folks who love each other in this world,—and it's good to know of when they do. My sister"—he paused again, as if something stuck in his throat; "My sister loved her boy,—Jack. His death has driven her silly for the time—doctors say she will recover—that it's only 'shock.' 'Shock' is answerable for a good many tragedies since the European war."

Seaton moved impatiently, but said nothing,

"You're a bit on the fidgets"—resumed Gwent, placidly—"You want me to come to business—and I will. May I smoke?"

His companion nodded, and he drew out his cigar-case, selecting from it a particularly fragrant Havana.

"You don't do this sort of thing, or I'd offer you one,"—he said,—"Pity you don't, it soothes the nerves. But I know your 'fads'; you are too closely acquainted with the human organism to either smoke or drink. Well—every man to his own method! Now what you want me to do is this—to represent the force and meaning of a certain substance which you have discovered, to the government of the United States and induce them to purchase it. Is that so?"

"That is so!" and Roger Seaton fixed his eyes on Gwent's hard, lantern-jawed face with a fiery intensity—"Remember, it's not child's play! Whoever takes what I can give, holds the mastery of the world! I offer it to the United States—but I would have preferred to offer it to Great Britain, being as I am, an Englishman. But the dilatory British men of science have snubbed me once—and I do not intend them to have the chance of doing it again. Briefly—I offer the United States the power to end wars, and all thought or possibility of war for ever. No Treaty of Versailles or any other treaty will ever be necessary. The only thing I ask in reward for my discovery is the government pledge to use it. That is, of course, should occasion arise. For my material needs, which are small, an allowance of a sum per annum as long as I live, will satisfy my ambition. The allowance may be as much or as little as is found convenient. The pledge to Use my discovery is the one all-important point—it must be a solemn, binding pledge—never to be broken."

Gwent puffed slowly at his cigar.

"It's a bit puzzling!"—he said—"When and where should it be used?"

Seaton stretched out a hand argumentatively.

"Now listen!" he said—"Suppose two nations quarrel—or rather, their governments and their press force them to quarrel—the United States (possessing my discovery) steps between and says—'Very well! The first move towards war—the first gun fired—means annihilation for one of you or both! We hold the power to do this!'"

Gwent drew his cigar from his lips.

"Annihilation!" he murmured—"Annihilation? For one or both!"

"Just so—absolute annihilation!" and Seaton smiled with a pleasant air of triumph—"A holocaust of microbes! The United States must let the whole world know of their ability to do this (without giving away my discovery). They must say to the nations 'We will have no more wars.

If innocent people are to be killed, they can be killed quite as easily in one way as another, and our way will cost nothing—neither ships nor ammunition nor guns.' And, of course, the disputants will be given time to decide their own fate for themselves."

Sam Gwent, holding his cigar between his fingers and looking meditatively at its glowing end, smiled shrewdly.

"All very well!"—he said—"But you forget money interests. Money interests always start a war—it isn't nations that do it, it's 'companies.' Your stuff won't annihilate companies all over the globe. Governments are not likely to damage their own financial moves. Suppose the United States government agreed to your proposition and took the sole possession and proprietorship of your discovery, and gave you their written, signed and sealed pledge to use it, it doesn't at all follow that they would not break that pledge at the first opportunity. In these days governments break promises as easily as eggshells. And there would be ample excuse for breaking the pledge to you—simply on the ground of inhumanity."

"War is inhumanity"—said Seaton—"The use of my discovery would be no worse than war."

"Granted!—but war makes money for certain sections of the community,—you must think of that!" and Gwent's little shrewd eyes gleamed like bits of steel.—"Money!—money! Stores—food, clothing—transport—all these things in war mean fortunes to the contractors—while the wiping out of a nation in YOUR way would mean loss of money. Loss of life wouldn't matter,—it never does really matter—not to governments!—but loss of money—ah, well!—that's a very different and much more serious affair!"

A cynical smile twisted his features as he spoke, and Roger Seaton, standing opposite to him with his fine head well thrown back on his shoulders and his whole face alive with the power of thought, looked rather like a Viking expostulating with some refractory vassal.

"So you think the United States wouldn't take my 'discovery?'" he said—"Or—if they took it—couldn't be trusted to keep a pledged word?"

Gwent shrugged his shoulders.

"Of course our government could be trusted as much as any other government in the world,"—he said—"Perhaps more. But it would exonerate itself for breaking even a pledged word which necessitated an inhuman act involving loss of money! See? War is an inhuman act, but it brings considerable gain to those who engineer it,—this makes all the difference between humanity and Inhumanity!"

"Well!—you are a senator, and you ought to know!" replied Seaton— "And if your opinion is against my offer, I will not urge you to make it. But—as I live and stand here talking to you, you may bet every dollar you possess that if neither the United States nor any other government will accept the chance I give it of holding the nations like dogs in leash, I'll hold them myself! I! One single unit of the overteeming millions! Yes, Mr. Senator Gwent, I swear it! I'll be master of the world!"

XII

G went was silent. With methodical care he flicked off the burnt end of his cigar and watched it where it fell, as though it were something rare and curious. He wanted a few minutes to think. He gave a quick upward glance at the tall athletic figure above him, with its magnificent head and flashing eyes,—and the words "I'll be master of the world" gave him an unpleasant thrill. One man on the planet with power to destroy nations seemed quite a fantastic idea—yet science made it actually possible! He bethought himself of a book he had lately read concerning radio-activity, in which he had been struck by the following passage—"Radio-activity is an explosion of great violence; the energy exerted is millions of times more powerful than the highest explosive substance yet made in our laboratories; one bomb loaded with such energy would be equal to millions of bombs of the same size and energy as used in the trenches. One's mind stands aghast at the thought of what could be possible if such power were used for destructive purposes; a single aeroplane could carry sufficient to annihilate a whole army, or lay the biggest city in ruins with the death of all its inhabitants." The writer of the book in question had stated that, so far, no means had been found of conserving and concentrating this tremendous force for such uses,—but Gwent, looking at Roger Seaton, said within himself— "He's got it!" And this impression, urging itself strongly in on his brain, was sufficiently startling to give him a touch of what is called "nerves."

After a considerably long pause he said, slowly—"Well, 'master of the world' is a pretty tall order! Now, look here, Seaton—you're a plain, straight man, and so am I, as much as my business will let me. What are you after, anyway? What is your aim and end? You say you don't want money—yet money is the chief goal of all men's ambition. You don't care for fame, though you could have it for the lifting of a finger, and I suppose you don't want love—"

Seaton laughed heartily, pushing back with a ruffling hand the thick hair from his broad open brow.

"All three propositions are nil to me"—he said—"I suppose it is because I can have them for the asking! And what satisfaction is there in any one of them? A man only needs one dinner a day, a place to sleep in and ordinary clothes to wear—very little money is required for the actual necessaries of life—enough can be earned by any day-labourer.

As for fame—whosoever reads the life of even one 'famous' man will never be such a fool as to wish for the capricious plaudits of a fool-public. And love!—love does not exist—not what *I* call love!"

"Oh! May I have your definition?"

"Why yes!—of course you may! Love, to my thinking, means complete harmony between two souls—like two notes that make a perfect chord. The man must feel that he can thoroughly trust and reverence the woman,—the woman must feel the same towards the man. And the sense of 'reverence' is perhaps the best and most binding quality. But nowadays what woman will you find worth reverence?—what man so free from drink and debauchery as to command it? The human beings of our day are often less respectable than the beasts! I can imagine love,—what it might be—what it should be—but till we have a very different and more spiritualised world, the thing is impossible."

Again, Gwent was silent for some minutes. Then he said—

"Apparently the spirit of destructiveness is strong in you. As 'master of the world'—to quote your own words, I presume that in the event of a nation or nations deciding on war, you would give them a time-limit to consider and hold conference, with their allies—and then—if they were resolved to begin hostilities—"

"Then I could—and WOULD—wipe them off the face of the earth in twenty-four hours!" said Seaton, calmly—"From nations they should become mere dust-heaps! War makes its own dust-heaps, but with infinitely more cost and trouble—the way of exit I offer would be cheap in comparison!"

Gwent smiled a grim smile.

"Well, I come back to my former question"—he said—"Suppose the occasion arose, and you did all this, what pleasure to yourself do you foresee?"

"The pleasure of clearing the poor old earth of some of its pestilential microbes!"—answered Seaton, "Something of the same thankful satisfaction Sir Ronald Ross must have experienced when he discovered the mosquito-breeders of yellow fever and malaria, and caused them to be stamped out. The men who organise national disputes are a sort of mosquito, infecting their fellow-creatures with perverted mentality and disease,—they should be exterminated."

"Why not begin with the newspaper offices?" suggested Gwent—"The purlieus of cheap journalism are the breeding-places of the human malaria-mosquito."

"True! And it wouldn't be a bad idea to stamp them out," here Seaton threw back his head with the challenging gesture which was characteristic of his temperament—"But what is called 'the liberty of the press'(it should be called 'the license of the press') is more of an octopus than a mosquito. Cut off one tentacle, it grows another. It's entirely octopus in character, too,—it only lives to fill its stomach."

"Oh, come, come!" and Gwent's little steely eyes sparkled—"It's the 'safe-guard of nations' don't you know?—it stands for honest free speech, truth, patriotism, justice—"

"Good God!" burst out Seaton, impatiently—"When it does, then the 'new world' about which men talk so much may get a beginning! 'Honest free speech—truth!' Why, modern journalism is one GREAT LIE advertised on hoardings from one end of the world to the other!"

"I agree!" said Gwent—"And there you have the root and cause of war! No need to exterminate nations with your destructive stuff,—you should get at the microbes who undermine the nations first. When you can do THAT, you will destroy the guilty and spare the innocent,— whereas your plan of withering a nation into a dust-heap involves the innocent along with the guilty."

"War does that,"—said Seaton, curtly.

"It does. And your aim is to do away with all chance or possibility of war for ever. Good! But you need to attack the actual root of the evil."

Seaton's brow clouded into a frown.

"You're a careful man, Gwent,"—he said—"And, in the main, you are right. I know as well as you do that the license of the press is the devil's finger in the caldron of affairs, stirring up strife between nations that would probably be excellent friends and allies, if it were not for this 'licensed' mischief. But so long as the mob read the lies, so long will the liars flourish. And my argument is that if any two peoples are so brainless as to be led into war by their press, they are not fit to live—no more fit than the mosquitoes that once made Panama a graveyard."

Gwent smoked leisurely, regarding his companion with unfeigned interest.

"Apparently you haven't much respect for life?" he said.

"Not when it is diseased life—not when it is perverted life;"— returned Seaton—"Then it is mere deformity and encumbrance. For life itself in all its plenitude, health and beauty I have the deepest, most passionate respect. It is the outward ray or reflex of the image of God—"

"Stop there!" interrupted Gwent—"You believe in God?"

"I do,—most utterly! That is to say I believe in an all-pervading Mind originating and commanding the plan of the Universe. We talk of 'ions' and 'electrons'—but we are driven to confess that a Supreme Intelligence has the creation of electrons, and directs them as to the formation of all existing things. To that Mind—to that Intelligence—I submit my soul! And I do NOT believe that this Supreme Mind desires evil or sorrow,—we create disaster ourselves, and it is ourselves that must destroy it, We are given free-will—if we 'will' to create disease, we must equally 'will' to exterminate it by every means in our power."

"I think I follow you"—said Gwent, slowly—"But now, as regards this Supreme Intelligence, I suppose you will admit that the plan of creation is a dual sort of scheme—that is to say 'male and female created He them'?"

"Why, of course!" and Seaton smiled—"The question is superfluous!"

"I asked it," went on Gwent—"because you seem to eliminate the female element from your life altogether. Therefore, so I take it, you are not at your full strength, either as a scientist or philosopher. You are a kind of eagle, trying to fly high on one wing. You'll need the other! There, don't look at me in that savage way! I'm merely making my own comments on your position,—you needn't mind them. I want to get out of the tangle-up of things you have suggested. You fancy it would be easy to get the United States Government to purchase your discovery and pledge themselves to use it on occasion for the complete wiping out of a nation,—any nation—that decided to go to war,—and, failing their acceptance, or the acceptance of any government on these lines, you purpose doing the deed yourself. Well!—I can tell you straight away it's no use my trying to negotiate such a business, The inhumanity of it is to palpable."

"What of the inhumanity of war?" asked Seaton.

"That PAYS!" replied Gwent, with emphasis—"You don't, or won't, seem to recognise that blistering fact! The inhumanity of war pays everybody concerned in it except the fellows who fight to order. They are the 'raw material.' They get used up. YOUR business WOULDN'T 'pay.' And what won't 'pay' is no good to anybody in this present sort of world."

Seaton, still standing erect, bent his eyes on the lean hard features of his companion with eloquent scorn.

"So! Everything must be measured and tested by money!" he said—"And yet you senators talk of reform!—of a 'new' world!—of a higher code of conduct between man and man—"

"Yes, we talk"—interrupted Gwent—"But we don't mean what we say!—we should never think of meaning it!"

"'Scribes and Pharisees, hypocrites!'" quoted Seaton with passionate emphasis.

"Just so! The Lord Christ said it two thousand years ago, and it's true to-day! We haven't improved!"

With an impatient movement, Seaton strode to the door of his hut and looked out at the wide sky,—then turned back again. Gwent watched him critically.

"After all," he said, "It isn't as if you wanted anything of anybody. Money is no object of yours. If it were I should advise your selling your discovery to Morgana Royal,—she'd buy it—and, I tell you what!— She'd Use It!"

"Thanks!" and Seaton nodded curtly—"I can use it myself!"

"True!" And Gwent looked interestedly at his dwindling Havana— "You can!" There followed a pause during which Gwent thought of the strange predicament in which the world might find itself, under the scientific rule of one man who had it in his power to create a terrific catastrophe without even "showing his hand." "Anyway, Seaton, you surely want to make something out of life for yourself, don't you?"

"What Is there to be made out of it?" he asked.

"Well!-happiness—the physical pleasure of living—"

"I Am happy"—declared Seaton—"and I entirely appreciate the physical pleasure of living. But I should be happier and better pleased with life if I could rid the earth of some of its mischief, disease and sorrow—"

"How about leaving that to the Supreme Intelligence?" interposed Gwent.

"That's just it! The Supreme Intelligence led me to the discovery I have made—and I feel that it has been given into my hands for a purpose. Gwent, I am positive that this same Supreme Intelligence expects his creature, Man, to help Him in the evolvement and work of the Universe! It is the only reasonable cause for Man's existence. We must help, not hinder, the scheme of which we are a part. And wherever hindrance comes in we are bound to remove and destroy it!"

The last ash of Gwent's cigar fell to the floor, and Gwent himself rose from his chair.

"Well, I suppose we've had our talk out"—he said; "I came here prepared to offer you a considerable sum for your discovery—but I can't go so far as a Government pledge. So I must leave you to it. You know"—here he hesitated—"you know a good many people would consider you mad—"

Seaton laughed.

"Oh, that goes without saying! Did you ever hear of any scientist possessing a secret drawn from the soul of nature that was not called 'mad' at once by his compeers and the public? I can stand THAT accusation! Pray Heaven I never get as mad as a Wall Street gambler!"

"You will, if you gamble with the lives of nations!" said Gwent.

"Let the nations beware how they gamble with their own lives!" retorted Seaton—"You say war is a method of money-making—let them take heed how they touch money coined in human blood! I—one man only,—but an instrument of the Supreme Intelligence,—I say and swear there shall be no more wars!"

As he uttered these words there was something almost supernatural in the expression of his face—his attitude, proudly erect, offered a kind of defiance to the world,—and involuntarily Gwent, looking at him, thought of the verse in the Third Psalm—

"I laid me down and slept; I awaked for the Lord sustained me. I will not be afraid of ten thousands of the people that have set themselves against me round about."

"No—he would not be afraid!" Gwent mused—"He is a man for whom there is no such thing as fear! But—if it knew—the world might be afraid of HIM!"

Aloud he said—"Well, you may put an end to war, but you will never put an end to men's hatred and envy of one another, and if they can't 'let the steam off' in fighting, they'll find some other way which may be worse. If you come to consider it, all nature is at war with itself,—it's a perpetual struggle to live, and it's evident that the struggle was intended and ordained as universal law. Life would be pretty dull without effort— and effort means war."

"War against what?—against whom?" asked Seaton.

"Against whatever or whoever opposes the effort," replied Gwent, promptly—"There must be opposition, otherwise effort would be unnecessary. My good fellow, you've got an idea that you can alter the fixed plan of things, but you can't. The cleverest of us are only like goldfish in a glass bowl—they see the light through, but they cannot get to it. The old ship of the world will sail on its appointed way to its destined port,—and the happiest creatures are those who are content to sail with it in the faith that God is at the helm!" He broke off, smiling at his own sudden eloquence, then added—"By-the-by, where is your laboratory?"

"Haven't got one!" replied Seaton, briefly.

"What! Haven't got one! Why, how do you make your stuff?"

Seaton laughed.

"You think I'm going to tell you? Mr. Senator Gwent, you take me for a greater fool than I am! My 'stuff' needs neither fire nor crucible,— the formula was fairly complete before I left Washington, but I wanted quiet and solitude to finish what I had begun. It is finished now. That's why I sent for you to make the proposition which you say you cannot carry through."

"Finished, is it?" queried Gwent, abstractedly—"And you have it here?—in a finished state?"

Seaton nodded affirmatively.

"Then I suppose"—said Gwent with a nervous laugh—"you could 'finish' ME, if it suited your humour?"

"I could, certainly!" and Seaton gave him quite an encouraging smile—"I could reduce Mr. Senator Gwent into a small pinch of grey dust in about forty seconds, without pain! You wouldn't feel it I assure you! It would be too swift for feeling."

"Thanks! Much obliged!" said Gwent—"I won't trouble you this morning! I rather enjoy being alive."

"So do I!" declared Seaton, still smiling—"I only state what I Could do."

Gwent stood at the door of the hut and surveyed the scenery.

"You've a fine, wild view here"—he said—"I think I shall stay at the Plaza a day or two before returning to Washington. There's a very attractive girl there."

"Oh, you mean Manella"—said Seaton, carelessly; "Yes, she's quite a beauty. She's the maid, waitress or 'help' of some sort at the hotel."

"She's a good 'draw' for male visitors"—said Gwent—"Many a man I know would pay a hundred dollars a day to have her wait upon him!"

"Would You?" asked Seaton, amused.

"Well!—perhaps not a hundred dollars a day, but pretty near it! Her eyes are the finest I've ever seen."

Seaton made no comment.

"You'll come and dine with me to-night, won't you?" went on Gwent—"You can spare me an hour or two of your company?"

"No, thanks"—Seaton replied—"Don't think me a churlish brute—but I don't like hotels or the people who frequent them. Besides—we've done our business."

"Unfortunately there was no business doing!" said Gwent—"Sorry I couldn't take it on."

"Don't be sorry! I'll take it on myself when the moment comes. I would have preferred the fiat of a great government to that of one unauthorised man—but if there's no help for it then the one man must act."

Gwent looked at him with a grave intentness which he meant to be impressive.

"Seaton, these new scientific discoveries are dangerous tools!" he said—"If they are not handled carefully they may work more mischief than we dream of. Be on your guard! Why, we might break up the very planet we live on, some day!"

"Very possible!" answered Seaton, lightly—"But it wouldn't be missed! Come,—I'll walk with you half way down the hill."

He threw on a broad palmetto hat as a shield against the blazing sun, for it was now the full heat of the afternoon, while Gwent solemnly unfurled a white canvas umbrella which, folded, served him on occasion as a walking-stick. A greater contrast could hardly be imagined than that afforded by the two men,—the conventionally clothed, stiff-jointed Washington senator, and the fine, easy supple figure of his roughly garbed companion; and Manella, watching them descend the hill from a coign of vantage in the Plaza gardens, criticised their appearance in her own special way.

"Poof!" she said to herself, snapping her fingers in air—"He is so ugly!—that one man—so dry and yellow and old! But the other—he is a god!"

And she snapped her fingers again,—then kissed them towards the object of her adoration,—an object as unconscious and indifferent as any senseless idol ever worshipped by blind devotees.

XIII

On his return to the Plaza Mr. Sam Gwent tried to get some conversation with Manella, but found it difficult. She did not wait on the visitors in the dining-room, and Gwent imagined he knew the reason why. Her beauty was of too brilliant and riante a type to escape the notice and admiration of men, whose open attentions were likely to be embarrassing to her, and annoying to her employers. She was therefore kept very much out of the way, serving on the upper floors, and was only seen flitting up and down the staircase or passing through the various corridors and balconies. However, when evening fell and its dark, still heat made even the hotel lounge, cooled as it was by a fountain in full play, almost unbearable, Gwent, strolling forth into the garden, found her there standing near a thick hedge of myrtle which exhaled a heavy scent as if every leaf were being crushed between invisible fingers. She looked up as she saw him approaching and smiled.

"You found your friend well?" she said.

"Very well, indeed!" replied Gwent, promptly—"In fact, I never knew he was ill!"

Manella gave her peculiar little uplift of the head which was one of her many fascinating gestures.

"He is not ill"—she said—"He only pretends! That is all! He has some reason for pretending. I think it is love!"

Gwent laughed.

"Not a bit of it! He's the last man in the world to worry himself about love!"

Manella glanced him over with quite a superior air.

"Ah, perhaps you do not know!" And she waved her hands expressively. "There was a wonderful lady came here to see him some weeks ago—she stole up the hill at night, like a spirit—a little, little fairy woman with golden hair—"

Gwent pricked up his ears and stood at attention.

"Yes? Really? You don't say so! 'A little fairy woman'? Sounds like a story!"

"She wore the most lovely clothes"—went on Manella, clasping her hands in ecstasy—"She stayed at the Plaza one night—I waited upon her. I saw her in her bed—she had skin like satin, and eyes like blue stars—her hair fell nearly to her ankles—she was like a dream! And she went up the hill by moonlight all by herself, to find HIM!"

Gwent listened with close interest.

"And I presume she found him?"

Manella nodded, and a sigh escaped her.

"Oh, yes, she found him! He told me that. And I am sure—something tells me HERE" and she pressed one hand against her heart—"by the way he spoke—that he loves her!"

"You seem to be a very observant young woman," said Gwent, smiling—"One would think you were in love with him yourself!"

She raised her large dark eyes to his with perfect frankness.

"I am!" she said—"I see no shame in that! He is a fine man—it is good to love him!"

Gwent was completely taken aback. Here was primitive passion with a vengeance!—passion which admitted its own craving without subterfuge. Manella's eyes were still uplifted in a kind of childlike confidence.

"I am happy to love him!" she went on—"I wish only to serve him. He does not love ME—oh, no!—he loves HER! But he hates her too—ah!" and she gave a little shivering movement of her shoulders—"There is no love without hate!—and when one loves and hates with the same heartbeat, THAT is a love for life and death!" She checked herself abruptly— then with a simplicity which was not without dignity added—"I am saying too much, perhaps? But you are his friend—and I think he must be very lonely up there!"

Mr. Senator Gwent was perplexed. He had not looked to stumble on a romantic episode, yet here was one ready made to his hand. His nature was ill attuned to romance of any kind, but he felt a certain compassion for this girl, so richly dowered with physical beauty, and smitten with love for a man like Roger Seaton who, according to his own account, had no belief in love's existence. And the "fairy woman" she spoke of— who could that be but Morgana Royal? After his recent interview with Seaton his thoughts were rather in a whirl, and he sought for a bit of commonplace to which he could fasten them without the risk of their drifting into greater confusion. Yet that bit of commonplace was hard to find with a woman's lovely passionate eyes looking straight into his, and the woman herself, a warm-blooded embodiment of exquisite physical beauty, framed like a picture among the scented myrtle boughs under the dusky violet sky, where glittered a few stars with that large fiery brilliance so often seen in California. He coughed—it was a convenient thing to cough—it cleared the throat and helped utterance.

"I—I—well!—I hardly think he is lonely"—he said at last, hesitatingly—"Perhaps you don't know it—but he's a very clever man— an inventor—a great thinker with new ideas—"

He stopped. How could this girl understand him? What would she know of "inventors"—and "thinkers with new ideas"? A trifle embarrassed, he looked at her. She nodded her dark head and smiled.

"I know!" she said—"He is a god!"

Sam Gwent almost jumped. A god! Oh, these women! Of what fantastic exaggerations they are capable!

"A god!" she repeated, nodding again, complacently; "He can do anything! I feel that all the time. He could rule the whole world!"

Gwent's nerves "jumped" for the second time. Roger Seaton's own words—"I'll be master of the world" knocked repeatingly on his brain with an uncomfortable thrill. He gathered up the straying threads of his common sense and twisted them into a tough string.

"That's all nonsense!" he said, as gruffly as he could—"He's not a god by any means! I'm afraid you think too much of him, Miss—Miss—er—"

"Soriso," finished Manella, gently—"Manella Soriso."

"Thank you!" and Gwent sought for a helpful cigar which he lit— "You have a very charming name! Yes—believe me, you think too much of him!"

"You say that? But—are you not his friend?"

Her tone was reproachful.

But Gwent was now nearly his normal business self again.

"No,—I am scarcely his friend"—he replied—"'Friend' is a big word,—it implies more than most men ever mean. I just know him— I've met him several times, and I know he worked for a while under Edison—and—and that's about all. Then I THINK"—he was cautious here—"I THINK I've seen him at the house of a very wealthy lady in New York—a Miss Royal—"

"Ah!" exclaimed Manella—"That is the name of the fairy woman who came here!"

Gwent went on without heeding her.

"She, too, is very clever,—she is also an inventor and a scientist—and if it was she who came here—(I daresay it was!) it was probably because she wished to ask his advice and opinion on some of the difficult things she studies—"

Manella snapped her fingers as though they were castanets.

"Ah—bah!" she exclaimed—"Not at all! No difficult thing takes a woman out by moonlight, all in soft white and diamonds to see a man!—no difficult thing at all, except to tempt him to love! Yes! That is the way it is done! I begin to learn! And you, if you are not his friend, what are you here for?"

Gwent began to feel impatient with this irrepressible "prize" beauty.

"I came to see him at his own request on business;" he answered curtly—"The business is concluded and I go away tomorrow."

Manella was silent. The low chirping of a cicada hidden in the myrtle thicket made monotonous sweetness on the stillness.

Moved by some sudden instinct which he did not attempt to explain to himself, Gwent decided to venture on a little paternal advice.

"Now don't you fly off in a rage at what I'm going to say,"—he began, slowly—"You're only a child to me—so I'm just taking the liberty of talking to you as a child. Don't give too much of your time or your thought to the man you call a 'god.' He's no more a god than I am. But I tell you one thing—he's a dangerous customer!"

Manella's great bright eyes opened wide like stars in the darkness.

"Dangerous?—How?—I do not understand—!"

"Dangerous!"—repeated Gwent, shaking his head at her—"Not to you, perhaps,—for you probably wouldn't mind if he killed you, so long as he kissed you first! Oh, yes, I know the ways of women! God made them trusting animals, ready to slave all their lives for the sake of a caress. You are one of that kind—you'd willingly make a door-mat of yourself for Seaton to wipe his boots on. I don't mean that he's dangerous in that way, because though *I* might think him so, You wouldn't. No,—what I mean is that he's dangerous to himself—likely to run risks of his life—"

Here he paused, checked by the sudden terror in the beautiful eyes that stared at him.

"His life!" and Manella's voice trembled—"You think he is here to kill himself—"

"No, no—bless my soul, he doesn't INTEND to kill himself"—said Gwent, testily—"He's not such a fool as all that! Now look here!—try and be a sensible girl! The man is busy with an invention—a discovery—which might do him harm—I don't say it WILL—but it MIGHT. You've heard of bombs, haven't you?—timed to explode at a given moment?"

Manella nodded—her lips trembled, and she clasped her hands nervously across her bosom.

"Well!—I believe—I won't say it for certain,—that he's got something worse than that!" said Gwent, impressively—"And that's why he was chosen to live up on that hill in the 'hut of the dying' away from everybody. See? And—of course—anything may happen at any moment. He's plucky enough, and is not the sort of man to involve any other man in trouble—and that's why he stays alone. Now you know! So you can put away your romantic notions of his being 'in love'! A very good thing for him if he were! It might draw him away from his present occupation. In fact, the best that could happen to him would be that you should make him fall in love with You!"

She gave a little cry.

"With Me?"

"Yes, with you! Why not? Why don't you manage it? A beautiful woman like you could win the game in less than a week?"

She shook her head sorrowfully.

"You do not know him!" she said—"But—He knows!"

"Knows what?"

She gave a despairing little gesture.

"That I love him!"

"Ah! That's a pity!" said Gwent—"Men are curious monsters in their love-appetites; they always refuse the offered dish and ask for something that isn't in the bill of fare. You should have pretended to hate him!"

"I could not pretend That!" said Manella, sadly—"But if I could, it would not matter. He does not want a woman."

"Oh, doesn't he?" Gwent was amused at her quaint way of putting it. "Well, he's the first man I ever heard of, that didn't! That's all bunkum, my good girl! Probably he's crying for the moon!"

"What is that?" she asked, wistfully.

"Crying for the moon? Just hankering after what can't be got. Lots of men are afflicted that way. But they've been known to give up crying and content themselves with something else."

"He would never content himself!" she said—"If she—the woman that came here, is the moon, he will always want her. Even I want her!"

"You?" exclaimed Gwent, amazed.

"Yes! I want to see her again!" A puzzled look contracted her brows. "Since she spoke to me I have always thought of her,—I cannot get her out of my mind! She just Holds me—yes!—in one of her little white hands! There are few women like that I think!—women who hold the souls of others as prisoners till they choose to let them go!"

Mr. Senator Gwent was fairly nonplussed. This dark-eyed Spanish beauty with her romantic notions was almost too much for him. Had he met her in a novel he would have derided the author of the book for delineating such an impossible character,—but coming in contact with her in real life, he was at a loss what to say. Especially as he himself was quite aware of the mysterious "hold" exercised by Morgana Royal on those whom she chose to influence either near or at a distance. After a few seconds of deliberation he answered—

"Yes—I should say there are very few women of that rather uncomfortable sort of habit,—the fewer the better, in my opinion. Now Miss Manella Soriso, remember what I say to you! Don't think about being 'held' by anybody except by a lover and husband! See? Play the game! With such looks as God has given you, it should be easy! Win your 'god' away from his thunderbolts before he begins havoc with them from his miniature Olympus. If he wants the 'moon' (and possibly he doesn't!) he won't say no to a star,—it's the next best thing. Seriously now,"—and Gwent threw away the end of his cigar and laid a hand gently on her arm—"be a good girl and think over what I've said to you. Marry him if you can!—it will be the making of him!"

Manella gazed about her in the darkness, bewildered. A glittering little mob of fire-flies danced above her head like a net of jewels.

"Oh, you talk so strangely!" she said—"You forget!—I am a poor girl—I have no money—"

"Neither has he,"—and Gwent gave a short laugh. "But he could make a million dollars tomorrow—if he chose. Having only himself to consider, he DOESN'T choose! If he had YOU, he'd change his opinion. Seaton's not the man to have a wife without keeping her in comfort. I tell you again, you can be the making of him. You can save his life!"

She clasped her hands nervously. A little gasping sigh came from her lips.

"Oh!—Santa Madonna!—to save his life!"

"Ah, just that!" said Gwent impressively—"Think of it! I'm not speaking lies—that's not my way. The man is making for himself what we in the European war called a 'danger zone,' where everybody not 'in the know' was warned off hidden mines. Hidden mines! He's got them! That's so! You can take my word! It's no good looking for them, no one will ever find them but himself, and he thinks of nothing else. But if he fell in love with YOU—"

She gave a hopeless gesture.

"He will not—he thinks nothing of me—nothing!—no!—though he says I am beautiful!"

"Oh, he says that, does he?" and Gwent smiled—"Well, he'd be a fool if he didn't!"

"Ah, but he does not care for beauty!" Manella went on. "He sees it and he smiles at it, but it does not move him!"

Gwent looked at her in perplexity, not knowing quite how to deal with the subject he himself had started. Truth to tell his nerves had been put distinctly "on edge" by Seaton's cool, calculating and seemingly callous assertion as to the powers he possessed to destroy, if he chose, a nation,—and all sorts of uncomfortable scraps of scientific information gleaned from books and treatises suggested themselves vividly to his mind at this particular moment when he would rather have forgotten them. As, for example—"A pound weight of radio-active energy, if it could be extracted in as short a time as we pleased, instead of in so many million years, could do the work of a hundred and fifty tons of dynamite." This agreeable fact stuck in his brain as a bone may stick in a throat, causing a sense of congestion. Then the words of one of the "pulpit thunderers" of New York rolled back on his ears—"This world will be destroyed, not by the hand of God, but by the wilful and devilish malingering of Man!" Another pleasant thought! And he felt himself to be a poor weak fool to even try to put up a girl's beauty, a girl's love as a barrier to the output of a destroying force engineered by a terrific human intention,—it was like the old story of the Scottish heroine who thrust a slender arm through the great staple of a door to hold back the would-be murderers of a King.

"Beauty does not move him!" she said.

She was right. Nothing was likely to move Roger Seaton from any purpose he had once resolved upon. What to him was beauty? Merely a "fortuitous concourse of atoms" moving for a time in one personality. What was a girl? Just the young "female of the species"—no more. And love? Sexual attraction, of which there was enough and too much in Seaton's opinion. And the puzzled Gwent wondered whether after all he would not have acted more wisely—or diplomatically—in accepting Seaton's proposal to part with his secret to the United States Government, even with the proviso and State pledge that it was to be "used" should occasion arise, rather than leave him to his own devices to do as he pleased with the apparently terrific potentiality of which he alone had the knowledge and the mastery. And while his thoughts thus buzzed in his head like swarming bees, Manella stood regarding him in a kind of pitiful questioning like a child with a broken toy who can not understand "why" it is broken. As he did not speak at once she took up the thread of conversation.

"You see how it is no use," she said. "No use to think of his ever loving ME! But love for HIM—ah!—that I have, and that I will ever keep in my heart!—and to save his life I would myself gladly die!"

Gwent uttered a sound between a grunt and a sigh.

"There it is! You women always run to extremes! 'Gladly die' indeed! Poor girl, why should you 'die' for him or for any man! That's sheer sentimental nonsense! There's not a man that ever lived, or that ever will live, that's worth the death of a woman! That's so! Men think too much of themselves—they've been killing women ever since they were born—it's time they stopped a bit."

Manella's beautiful eyes expressed bewilderment.

"Killing women? Is that what they do?"

"Yes, my good girl!—that is what they do! The silly trusting creatures go to them like lambs, and get their throats cut! In marriage or out of it—the throat-cutting goes on, for men are made of destructive stuff and love the sport of killing. They are never satisfied unless they can kill something—a bird, a fox or a woman. I'm a man myself and I know!"

"YOU would kill a woman?" Manella's voice was a horrified whisper.

Gwent laughed.

"No,—not I, my child! I'm too old. I've done with love-making and 'sport' of all kinds. I don't even drive a golf-ball, in make-believe that it's a woman I'm hitting as fast and far as I can. Oh, yes!—you stare!—you are wondering why, if I have such ideas, I should suggest love-making and marriage to YOU,—well, I don't actually recommend it!—but I'm rather thinking more of your 'god' than of you. You might possibly help him a bit—"

"Ah, I am not clever!" sighed Manella.

"No—you're not clever—thank God for it! But you're devoted—and devotion is sometimes more than cleverness." He paused, reflectively. "Well, I'll have to go away tomorrow—it wouldn't be any use my staying on here. In fact, I'd rather be out of the way. But I've a notion I may be able to do something for Seaton in Washington when I get back—in the meantime I'll leave a letter for you to give him—"

"You will not write of me in that letter!" interrupted the girl, hastily. "No—you must not—you could not!—"

Gwent raised a deprecating hand.

"Don't be afraid, my girl! I'm not a cad. I wouldn't give you away for the world! I've no right to say a word about you, and I shall not. My letter will be a merely business one—you shall read it if you like—"

"Oh no!"—she said at once, with proud frankness; "I would not doubt your word!"

Gwent gave her a comprehensively admiring glance. Even in the dusk of evening her beauty shone with the brilliance of a white flower among the dark foliage. "What a sensation she would make in New York!" he thought—"With those glorious eyes and that hair!"

And a vague regret for his lost youth moved him; he was a very wealthy man, and had he been in his prime he would have tried a matrimonial chance with this unspoilt beautiful creature,—it would have pleased him to robe her in queenly garments and to set the finest diamonds in her dark tresses, so that she should be the wonder and envy of all beholders. He answered her last remark with a kindly little nod and smile.

"Good! You needn't doubt it ever!"—he said—"If at any time you want a friend you can bet on Sam Gwent. I'm a member of Congress and you can always find me easily. But remember my advice—don't make a 'god' of any man;—he can't live up to it—"

As he spoke a sudden jagged flash of lightning tore the sky, followed almost instantaneously by a long, low snarl of thunder rolling through the valley. Great drops of rain began to fall.

"Come along! Let us get in!" and Gwent caught Manella's hand— "Run!"

And like children they ran together through the garden into the Plaza lounge, reaching it just before a second lightning flash and peal of thunder renewed double emphasis.

"Storm!" observed a long-faced invalid man in a rocking-chair, looking at them as they hurried in.

"Yes! Storm it is!" responded Gwent, releasing the hand of his companion—"Good-night, Miss Soriso!"

She inclined her head graceful, smiling.

"Good-night, Senor!"

XIV

Convention is still occasionally studied even in these unconventional days, and Morgana Royal, independent and wealthy young woman as she was, had subscribed to its rule and ordinance by engaging a chaperone,—a "dear old English lady of title," as she had described her to the Marchese Rivardi. Lady Kingswood merited the description thus given of her, for she was distinctly a dear old English lady, and her title was the least thing about her, especially in her own opinion. There was no taint of snobbery in her simple, kindly disposition, and when her late husband, a distinguished military officer, had been knighted for special and splendid service in the war, she had only deplored that the ruin of his health and disablement by wounds, prevented him from taking any personal pleasure in the "honour." His death followed soon after the King's recognition of his merit, and she was left with his pension to live upon, and a daughter who having married in haste repented at leisure, being deserted by a drunken husband and left with two small children to nourish and educate. Naturally, Lady Kingswood took much of their care upon herself—but the pension of a war widow will not stretch further than a given point, and she found it both necessary and urgent to think of some means by which she could augment her slender income. She was not a clever woman,—she had no special talents,—her eyes would not stand her in good stead for plain sewing, and she could not even manage a typing machine. But she had exquisitely gentle manners,—she was well-bred and tactful, and, rightly judging that good-breeding and tact are valuable assets in some quarters of the "new" society, she sought, through various private channels, for a post as companion or "chaperone" to "one lady." Just when she was rather losing hope as to the success of her effort, the "one lady" came along in the elfin personality of Morgana Royal, who, after a brief interview in London, selected her with a decision as rapid as it was inexplicable, offering her a salary of five hundred a year, which to Lady Kingswood was a small fortune.

"You will have nothing to do but just be pleasant!" Morgana had told her, smilingly, "And enjoy your self as you like. Of course I do not expect to be controlled or questioned,—I am an independent woman, and go my own way, but I'm not at all 'modern.' I don't drink or smoke or 'dope,' or crave for male society. I think you'll find yourself all right!"

And Lady Kingswood had indeed "found herself all right." Her own daughter had never been so thoughtful for her comfort as Morgana was, and she became day by day more interested and fascinated by the original turn of mind and the bewitching personality of the strange little creature for whom the ordinary amusements of society seemed to have no attraction. And now, installed in her own sumptuously fitted rooms in the Palazzo d'Oro, Morgana's Sicilian paradise, she almost forgot there was such a thing as poverty, or the sordid business of "making both ends meet." Walking up and down the rose-marble loggia and looking out to the exquisite blue of the sea, she inwardly thanked God for all His mercies, and wondered at the exceptional good luck that had brought her so much peace, combined with comfort and luxury in the evening of her days. She was a handsome old lady; her refined features, soft blue eyes and white hair were a "composition" for an eighteenth-century French miniature, and her dress combined quiet elegance with careful taste. She was inflexibly loyal to her stated position; she neither "questioned" nor "controlled" Morgana, or attempted to intrude an opinion as to her actions or movements,—and if, as was only natural, she felt a certain curiosity concerning the aims and doings of so brilliant and witch-like a personality she showed no sign of it. She was interested in the Marchese Rivardi, but still more so in the priest, Don Aloysius, to whom she felt singularly attracted, partly by his own dignified appearance and manner, and partly by the leaning she herself had towards the Catholic Faith where "Woman" is made sacred in the person of the Holy Virgin, and deemed worthy of making intercession with the Divine. She knew, as we all in our innermost souls know, that it is a symbol of the greatest truth that can ever be taught to humanity.

The special morning on which she walked, leaning slightly on a silver-knobbed stick, up and down the loggia and looked at the sea, was one of rare beauty even in Sicily, the sky being of that pure ethereal blue for which one can hardly find a comparison in colour, and the ocean below reflecting it, tone for tone, as in a mirror. In the terraced garden, half lost among the intertwining blossoms, Morgana moved to and fro, gathering roses,—her little figure like a white rose itself set in among the green leaves. Lady Kingswood watched her, with kindly, half compassionate eyes.

"It must be a terrible responsibility for her to have so much money!" she thought. "She can hardly know what to do with it! And somehow—I do not think she will marry."

At that moment Morgana came slowly up the steps cut in the grass bordered on either side by flowers, and approached her.

"Here are some roses for you, dear 'Duchess!'" she said, "Duchess" being the familiar or "pet" name she elected to call her by. "Specially selected, I assure you! Are you tired?—or may I have a talk?"

Lady Kingswood took the roses with a smile, touching Morgana's cheek playfully with one of the paler pink buds.

"A talk by all means!" she replied—"How can I be tired, dear child? I'm a lazy old woman, doing nothing all day but enjoy myself!"

Morgana nodded her golden head approvingly.

"That's right!—I'm glad!" she said. "That's what I want you to do! It's a pretty place, this Palazzo d'Oro, don't you think?"

"More than pretty—it's a perfect paradise!" declared Lady Kingswood, emphatically.

"Well, I'm glad you like it"—went on Morgana—"Because then you won't mind staying here and looking after it when I'm away. I'll have to go away quite soon."

Lady Kingswood controlled her first instinctive movement of surprise.

"Really?" she said—"That seems a pity as you only arrived so recently—"

Morgana gave a wistful glance round her at the beautiful gardens and blue sea beyond.

"Yes—perhaps it is a pity!" she said, with a light shrug of her shoulders—"But I have a great deal to do, and ever so much to learn. I told you, didn't I?—that I have had an air-ship built for me quite on my own lines?—an air-ship that moves like a bird and is quite different from any other air-ship ever made or known?"

"Yes, you told me something about it"—answered Lady Kingswood—"But you know, my dear, I am very stupid about all these wonderful new inventions. 'Progress of science' they call it. Well, I'm rather afraid of the 'progress of science.' I'm an old-fashioned woman and I cannot bear to hear of aeroplanes and air-ships and poor wretched people falling from the sky and being dashed to pieces. The solid earth is quite good enough for my old feet as long as they will support me!"

Morgana laughed.

"You dear Duchess!" she said, affectionately—"Don't worry! I'm not going to ask you to travel in my air-ship—I wouldn't so try your nerves for the world! Though it is an absolutely safe ship,—nothing"—and she emphasised the word—"NOTHING can upset it or drive it out of its course unless natural law is itself upset! Now let us sit here"—and she drew two wicker chairs into the cool shadow of the loggia and set them facing the sea—"and have our talk! I've begun it—I'll go on! Tell me"—and she nestled down among the cushions, watching Lady Kingswood seat herself in slower, less supple fashion—"tell me—what does it feel like to be married?"

Lady Kingswood opened her eyes, surprised and amused.

"What does it feel like? My dear—?"

"Oh, surely you know what I mean!" pursued Morgana—"You have been married. Well, when you were first married were you very, very happy? Did your husband love you entirely without a thought for anybody or anything else?—and were you all in all to each other?"

Lady Kingswood was quite taken aback by the personal directness of these questions, but deciding within herself that Morgana must be contemplating marriage on her own behalf, answered simply and truthfully—

"My husband and I were very fond of each other. We were the best of friends and good companions. Of course he had his military duties to attend to and was often absent—"

"And you stayed at home and kept house,"—interpolated Morgana, musingly—"I see! That is what all wives have to do! But I suppose he just adored you?"

Lady Kingswood smiled.

"'Adore' is a very strong word to use, my dear!" she said—"I doubt if any married people 'adore' each other! If they can be good friends and rub along pleasantly through all the sorrows and joys of life together, they should be satisfied."

"And you call that LOVE!" said Morgana, with a passionate thrill in her voice—"Love! 'Love that is blood within the veins of time!' Just 'rubbing along pleasantly together!' Dear 'Duchess,' that wouldn't suit ME!"

Lady Kingswood looked at her with interested, kind eyes.

"But then, what WOULD suit you?" she queried—"You know you mustn't expect the impossible!"

"What the world calls the impossible is always the possible"—said Morgana—"And only the impossible appeals to me!"

This was going beyond the boundary-line of Lady Kingswood's brain capacity, so she merely remained agreeably quiescent.

"And when your child was born"—pursued Morgana—"did you feel a wonderful ecstasy?—a beautiful peace and joy?—a love so great that it was as if God had given you something of His Own to hold and keep?"

Lady Kingswood laughed outright.

"My dear girl, you are too idealistic! Having a baby is not at all a romantic business!—quite the reverse! And babies are not interesting till they 'begin to take notice' as the nurses say. Then when they get older and have to go to school you soon find out that you have loved THEM far more than they have loved or ever WILL love YOU!"

As she said this her voice trembled a little and she sighed.

"I see! I think I quite understand!" said Morgana—"And it is just what I have always imagined—there is no great happiness in marriage. If it is only a matter of 'rubbing along pleasantly together' two friends can always do that without any 'sex' attraction, or tying themselves up together for life. And it's not much joy to bring children into the world and waste treasures of love on them, if after you have done all you can, they leave you without a regret,—like the birds that fly from a nest when once they know how to use their wings."

Lady Kingswood's eyes were sorrowful.

"My daughter was a very pretty girl,"—she said—"Her father and I were proud of her looks and her charm of manner. We spared every shilling we could to give her the best and most careful education—and we surrounded her with as much pleasure and comfort at home as possible,—but at the first experience of 'society,' and the flattery of strangers, she left us. Her choice of a husband was most unfortunate—but she would not listen to our advice, though we had loved her so much—she thought 'he' loved her more."

Morgana lifted her eyes. The "fey" light was glittering in them.

"Yes! She thought he loved her! That's what many a woman thinks—that 'he'—the particular 'he' loves her! But how seldom he does! How much more often he loves himself!"

"You must not be cynical, my dear!" said Lady Kingswood, gently—"Life is certainly full of disappointments, especially in love and marriage—but we must endure our sorrows patiently and believe that God does everything for the best."

This was the usual panacea which the excellent lady offered for all troubles, and Morgana smiled.

"Yes!—it must be hard work for God!" she said—"Cruel work! To do everything for the best and to find it being turned into the worst by the very creatures one seeks to benefit, must be positive torture! Well, dear 'Duchess,' I asked you all these questions about love and marriage just to know if you could say anything that might alter my views—but you have confirmed them. I feel that there is no such thing in the world as the love *I* want—and marriage without it would be worse than any imagined hell. So I shall not marry."

Lady Kingswood's face expressed a mild tolerance.

"You say that just now"—she said—"But I think you will alter your mind some day! You would not like to be quite alone always—not even in the Palazzo d'Oro."

"You are quite alone?"

"Ah, but I am an old woman, my dear! I have lived my day!"

"That's not true," said Morgana, decisively—"You have not 'lived your day' since you are living Now! And if you are old, that is just a reason why you should Not be alone. But you Are. Your husband is dead, and your daughter has other ties. So even marriage left you high and dry on the rocks as it were till my little boat came along and took you off them!"

"A very welcome little boat!" said Lady Kingswood, with feeling—"A rescue in the nick of time!"

"Never mind that!" and Morgan waved her pretty hand expressively— "My point is that marriage—just marriage—has not done much for you. It is what women clamour for, and scheme for,—and nine out of ten regret the whole business when they have had their way. There are so many more things in life worth winning!"

Lady Kingswood looked at her interestedly. She made a pretty picture just then in her white morning gown, seated in a low basket chair with pale blue silk cushions behind her on which her golden head rested with the brightness of a daffodil.

"So many more things!" she repeated—"My air-ship for instance!— it's worth all the men and all the marriages I've ever heard of! My beloved 'White Eagle!'—my own creation—my baby—Such a baby!" She laughed. "But I must learn to fly with it alone!"

"I hope you will do nothing rash!"—said Lady Kingswood, mildly; she was very ignorant of modern discovery and invention, and all attempt to explain anything of the kind to her would have been a hope less business—"I understand that it is always necessary to take a pilot and an observer in these terrible sky-machines—"

She was interrupted by a gay little peal of laughter from Morgana.

"Terrible?—Oh, dear 'Duchess,' you are too funny! There's nothing 'terrible' about My 'sky-machine!' Do you ever read poetry? No?—Well then you don't know that lovely and prophetic line of Keats—"

'Beautiful things made new
For the surprise of the sky-children.'

"Poets are always prophetic,—that is, REAL poets, not modern verse mongers; and I fancy Keats must have imagined something in the far distant future like my 'White Eagle!' For it really Is 'a beautiful thing made new'—a beautiful natural force put to new uses—and who knows?—I may yet surprise those 'sky-children!'"

Lady Kingswood's mind floundered helplessly in this flood of what, to her, was incomprehensibility. Morgana went on in the sweet fluting voice which was one of her special charms.

"If you haven't read Keats, you must have read at some time or other the 'Arabian Nights' and the story of 'Sindbad the Sailor'? Yes? You think you have? Well, you know how poor Sindbad got into the Valley of Diamonds and waited for an eagle to fly down and carry him off! That's just like me! I've been dropped into a Valley of Diamonds and often wondered how I should escape—but the Eagle has arrived!"

"I'm afraid I don't quite follow you"—said Lady Kingswood—"I'm rather dense, you know! Surely your Valley of Diamonds—if you mean wealth—has made your 'Eagle' possible?"

Morgana nodded.

"Exactly! If there had been no Valley of Diamonds there would have been no Eagle! But, all the same, this little female Sindbad is glad to get out of the valley!"

Lady Kingswood laughed.

"My dear child, if you are making a sort of allegory on your wealth, you are not 'out of the valley' nor are you likely to be!"

Morgana sighed.

"My vulgar wealth!" she murmured.

"What? Vulgar?"

"Yes. A man told me it was."

"A vulgar man himself, I should imagine!" said Lady Kingswood, warmly.

Morgana shrugged her shoulders carelessly.

"Oh, no, he isn't. He's eccentric, but not vulgar. He's aristocratic to the tips of his toes—and English. That accounts for his rudeness. Sometimes, you know—only sometimes—Englishmen can be VERY rude! But I'd rather have them so—it's a sort of well-bred clumsiness, like the manners of a Newfoundland dog. It's not the 'make-a-dollar' air of American men."

"You are quite English yourself, aren't you?" queried her companion.

"No—not English in any sense. I'm pure Celtic of Celt, from the farthest Highlands of Scotland. But I hate to say I'm 'Scotch,' as slangy people use that word for whisky! I'm just Highland-born. My father and mother were the same, and I came to life a wild moor, among mists and mountains and stormy seas—I'm always glad of that! I'm glad my eyes did not look their first on a city! There's a tradition in the part of Scotland where I was born which tells of a history far far back in time when sailors from Phoenicia came to our shores,—men greatly civilised when we all were but savages, and they made love to the Highland women and had children by them,—then when they went away back to Egypt they left many traces of Eastern customs and habits which remain to this day. My father used always to say that he could count his ancestry back to Egypt!—it pleased him to think so and it did nobody any harm!"

"Have you ever been to the East?" asked Lady Kingswood.

"No—but I'm going! My 'White Eagle' will take me there in a very short time! But, as I've already told you, I must learn to fly alone."

"What does the Marchese Rivardi say to that?"

"I don't ask him!" replied Morgana, indifferently—"What I may decide to do is not his business." She broke off abruptly—then continued—"He is coming to luncheon,—and afterwards you shall see my air-ship. I won't persuade you to go up in it!"

"I COULDN'T!" said Lady Kingswood, emphatically—"I've no nerve for such an adventure."

Morgana rose from her chair, smiling kindly.

"Dear 'Duchess' be quite easy in your mind!" she said—"I want you very much on land, but I shall not want you in the air! You will be quite safe and happy here in the Palazzo d'Oro"—she turned as she saw the shadow of a man's tall figure fall on the smooth marble pavement of the loggia—"Ah! Here is the Marchese! We were just speaking of you!"

"Tropp' onore!" he murmured, as he kissed the little hand she held out to him in the Sicilian fashion of gallantry—"I fear I am perhaps too early?"

"Oh no! We were about to go in to luncheon—I know the hour by the bell of the monastery down there—you hear it?"

A soft "ting-ting tong"—rang from the olive and ilex woods below the Palazzo,—and Morgana, listening, smiled.

"Poor Don Aloysius!" she said—"He will now go to his soup maigre—and we to our poulet, sauce bechamel,—and he will be quite as contented as we are!"

"More so, probably!" said Rivardi, as he courteously assisted Lady Kingswood, who was slightly lame, to rise from her chair—"He is one of the few men who in life have found peace."

Morgana gave him a keen glance.

"You think he has really found it?"

"I think so,—yes! He has faith in God—a great support that has given way for most of the peoples of this world."

Lady Kingswood looked pained.

"I am sorry to hear you say that!"

"I am sorry myself to say it, miladi, but I fear it is true!" he rejoined—"It is one sign of a general break-up."

"Oh, you are right! You are very right!" exclaimed Morgana suddenly, and with emphasis—"We know that when even one human being is unable to recognise his best friend we say—'Poor man! His brain is gone!' It's the same thing with a nation. Or a world! When it is so ailing that it cannot recognise the Friend who brought it into being, who feeds it, keeps it, and gives it all it has, we must say the same thing—'Its brain is gone!'"

Rivardi was surprised at the passionate energy she threw into these words.

"You feel that deeply?" he said—"And yet—pardon me!—you do not assume to be religious?"

"Marchese, I 'assume' nothing!" she answered—"I cannot 'pretend'! To 'assume' or to 'pretend' would hardly serve the Creator adequately. Creative or Natural Force is so far away from sham that one must do more than 'assume'—one must BE!"

Her voice thrilled on the air, and Lady Kingswood, who was crossing the loggia, leaning on her stick, paused to look at the eloquent speaker. She was worth looking at just then, for she seemed inspired. Her eyes were extraordinarily brilliant, and her whole personality expressed a singular vitality coupled with an ethereal grace that suggested some thing almost superhuman.

"Yes—one must be!" she repeated—"I have not BEEN A STUDENT OF SCIENCE SO LONG WITHOUT LEARNING that there is no 'assuming' anything in the universe. One must SEE straight, and THINK straight too! I could not 'assume' religion, because I FEEL it—in the very depths of my soul! As Don Aloysius said the other day, it is marvellous how close we are to the Source of all life, and yet we imagine we are far away! If we could only realise the truth of the Divine Nearness, and work WITH it and IN it, we should make discoveries worth knowing! We work too much WITH ourselves and OF ourselves." She paused,—then added slowly and seriously—"I have never done any work that way. I have always considered myself Nothing,—the Force I have obeyed was and is Everything."

"And so—being Nothing—you still made your air-ship possible!" said Rivardi, smiling indulgently at her fantastic speech.

She answered him with unmoved and patient gravity.

"It is as you say,—being Nothing myself, and owning myself to be Nothing; the Force that is Everything made my air-ship possible!"

XV

Two or three hours later the "White Eagle" was high in air above the Palazzo d'Oro. Down below Lady Kingswood stood on the seashore by the aerodrome, watching the wonderful ship of the sky with dazzled, scared eyes—amazed at the lightning speed of its ascent and the steadiness of its level flight. She had seen it spread its great wings as by self-volition and soar out of the aerodrome with Morgana seated inside like an elfin queen in a fairy car—she had seen the Marchese Giulio Rivardi "take the helm" with the assistant Gaspard, now no longer a prey to fear, beside him. Up, up and away they had flown, waving to her till she could see their forms no longer—till the "White Eagle" itself looked no bigger than a dove soaring in the blue. And while she waited, even this faint dove-image vanished! She looked in every direction, but the skies were empty. To her there was something very terrifying in this complete disappearance of human beings in the vast stretches of the air—they had gone so silently, too, for the "White Eagle's" flight made no sound, and though the afternoon was warm and balmy she felt chilled with the cold of nervous apprehension. Yet they had all assured her there was no cause for alarm,—they were only going on a short trial trip and would be back to dinner.

"Nothing more than a run in a motor-car!" Morgana said, gaily.

Nothing more,—but to Lady Kingswood it seemed much more. She belonged to simple Victorian days—days of quiet home-life and home affections, now voted "deadly dull!" and all the rushing to and fro and gadding about of modern men and women worried and distressed her, for she had the plain common sense to perceive that it did no good either to health or morals, and led nowhere. She looked wistfully out to sea,—the blue Sicilian sea so exquisite in tone and play of pure reflections,—and thought how happy a life lived after the old sweet ways might be for a brilliant little creature like Morgana, if she could win "a good man's love" as Shakespeare puts it. And yet—was not this rather harking back to mere sentiment, often proved delusive? Her own "good man's love" had been very precious to her,—but it had not fulfilled all her heart's longing, though she considered herself an entirely commonplace woman. And what sort of a man would it be that could hold Morgana? As well try to control a sunbeam or a lightning flash as the restless vital and intellectual spirit that had, for the time being, entered into feminine form, showing itself nevertheless as something utterly different and superior to women as they are generally known. Some thoughts such as these, though vague and disconnected, passed through Lady Kingswood's mind as she turned away from the sea-shore to re-ascend the flower-bordered terraces of the Palazzo d'Oro,—and it was with real pleasure that she perceived on the summit of the last flight of grassy steps, the figure of Don Aloysius. He was awaiting her approach, and came down a little way to meet her.

"I saw the air-ship flying over the monastery,"—he explained, greeting her—"And I was anxious to know whether la Signora had gone away into the skies or was still on earth! She has gone, I suppose?"

"Yes, she has gone!" sighed Lady Kingswood—"and the Marchese with her, and one assistant. Her 'nerve' is simply astonishing!"

"You did not think of venturing on a trip with her yourself?"—and the priest smiled kindly, as he assisted her to ascend the last flight of steps to the loggia.

"No indeed! I really could not! I feel I ought to be braver—but I cannot summon up sufficient courage to leave terra firma. It seems altogether unnatural."

"Then what will you do when you are an angel, dear lady?" queried Aloysius, playfully—"You will have to leave terra firma then! Have you ever thought of that?"

She smiled.

"I'm afraid I don't think!" she said—"I take my life on trust. I always believe that God who brought me HERE will take care of me THERE!— wherever 'there' is. You understand me, don't you? You speak English so well that I'm sure you do."

"Yes—I understand you perfectly"—he replied—"That I speak English is quite natural, for I was educated at Stonyhurst, in England. I was then for a time at Fort Augustus in Scotland, and studied a great many of the strange traditions of the Highland Celts, to which mystic people Miss Royal by birth belongs. Her ancestry has a good deal to do with her courage and character."

While he spoke Lady Kingswood gazed anxiously into the sky, searching it north, south, east, west, for the first glimpse of the returning "White Eagle," but there was no sign of it.

"You must not worry yourself,"—went on the priest, putting a chair for her in the loggia, and taking one himself—"If we sit here we shall see the air-ship returning, I fancy, by the western line,—certainly near the sunset. In any case let me assure you there is no danger!" "No danger?"

"Absolutely none!"

Lady Kingswood looked at him in bewildered amazement.

"Surely there MUST be danger?" she said—"The terrible accidents that happen every day to these flying machines—"

"Yes—but you speak of ordinary flying machines," said Aloysius,— "This 'White Eagle' is not an ordinary thing. It is the only one of its kind in the world—the only one scientifically devised to work with the laws of Nature. You saw it ascend?"

"I did."

"It made no sound?"

"None."

"Then how did its engines move, if it HAD engines?" pursued Aloysius—"Had you no curiosity about it?"

"I'm afraid I hadn't—I was really too nervous! Morgana begged me to go inside, but I could not!"

Don Aloysius was silent for a minute or two, out of gentle tolerance. He recognised that Lady Kingswood belonged to the ordinary class of good, kindly women not overburdened with brains, to whom thought, particularly of a scientific or reflective nature, would be a kind of physical suffering. And how fortunate it is that there are, and always will be such women! Many of them are gifted with the supreme talent of making happiness around themselves,—and in this way they benefit humanity more than the often too self-absorbed student of things which are frequently "past finding out."

"I understand your feeling";—he said, at last—"And I hardly wonder at your very natural fears. I must admit that I think human daring is going too fast and too far—the science of to-day is not tending to make men and women happier—and after all, happiness is the great goal."

A slight sigh escaped him, and Lady Kingswood looked at his fine, composed features with deep interest.

"Do you think God meant us to be happy?" she asked, gently.

"It is a dubious question!" he answered—"When we view the majesty and loveliness of nature—we cannot but believe we were intended to enjoy the splendid treasures of beauty freely spread out before us,— then again, if we look back thousands of years and consider the great civilisations of the past that have withered into dust and are now forgotten, we cannot help wondering why there should be such a waste of life for apparently no purpose. I speak in a secular sense,—of course my Church has but one reply to doubt, or what we call 'despair of God's mercy'—that it is sin. We are not permitted to criticise or to question the Divine."

"And surely that is best!" said Lady Kingswood, "and surely you have found happiness, or what is nearest to happiness, in your beautiful Faith?"

His eyes were shadowed by deep gravity.

"Miladi, I have never sought happiness," he replied; "From my earliest boyhood I felt it was not for me. Among the comrades of my youth many started the race of life with me—happiness was the winning post they had in view—and they tried many ways to reach it—some through ambition, some through wealth, some through love—but I have never chanced to meet one of them who was either happy or satisfied. My mind was set on nothing for myself—except this—to grope through the darkness for the Great Mind behind the Universe—to drop my own 'ego' into it, as a drop of rain into the sea—and so—to be content! And in this way I have learned much,—more than I consider myself worthy to know. Modern science of the surface kind—(not the true deep discoveries)—has done its best to detach the rain-drop from the sea!—but it has failed. I stay where I have plunged my soul!"

He spoke as it were to himself with the air of one inspired; he had almost forgotten the presence of Lady Kingswood, who was gazing at him in a rapture of attention.

"Oh, if I could only think as you do!" she said, in a low tone—"Is it truly the Catholic Church that teaches these things?"

"The Catholic Church is the sign and watchword of all these things!" he answered—"Not only that, but its sacred symbols, though ancient enough to have been adopted from Babylonia and Chaldea, are actually the symbols of our most modern science. Catholicism itself does not as yet recognise this. Like a blind child stumbling towards the light it has FELT the discoveries of science long before discovery. In our sacraments there are the hints of the transmutation of elements,—the 'Sanctus' bell suggests wireless telegraphy or telepathy, that is to say, communication between ourselves and the divine Unseen,—and if we are permitted to go deeper, we shall unravel the mystery of that 'rising from the dead' which means renewed life. I am a 'prejudiced' priest, of course,"—and he smiled, gravely—"but with all its mistakes, errors, crimes (if you will) that it is answerable for since its institution, through the sins of unworthy servants, Catholicism is the only creed with the true seed of spiritual life within it—the only creed left standing on a firm foundation in this shaking world!"

He uttered these words with passionate eloquence and added—

"There are only three things that can make a nation great,—the love of God, the truth of man, the purity of woman. Without these three the greatest civilisation existing must perish,—no matter how wide its power or how vast its wealth. Ignorant or vulgar persons may sneer at this as 'the obvious'—but it is the 'obvious' sun alone that rules the day."

Lady Kingswood's lips trembled; there were tears in her eyes.

"How truly you speak!" she murmured—"And yet we live in a time when such truths appear to have no influence with people at all. Every one is bent on pleasure—on self—"

"As every one was in the 'Cities of the Plain,'"—he said, "and we may well expect another rain of fire!"

Here, lifting his eyes, he saw in the soft blush rose of the approaching sunset a small object like a white bird flying homeward across the sea.

"Here it comes!" he exclaimed—"Not the rain of fire, but something more agreeable! I told you, did I not, miladi, that there was no danger? See!"

Lady Kingswood looked where he pointed.

"Surely that is not the air-ship?" she said—"It is too small!"

"At this distance it is small"—answered Aloysius—"But wait! Watch,—and you will soon perceive Its great wings! What a marvellous thing it is! Marvellous!—and a woman's work!"

They stood together, gazing into the reddening west, thrilled with expectancy,—while with a steady swiftness and accuracy of movement the bird-like object which at the first glimpse had seemed so small gradually loomed larger with nearer vision, its enormous wings spreading wide and beating the air rhythmically as though the true pulsation of life impelled their action. Neither Lady Kingswood nor Don Aloysius exchanged a word, so absorbed were they in watching the "White Eagle" arrive, and not till it began to descend towards the shore did they relax their attention and turn to each other with looks of admiration and amazement.

"How long have they been gone?" asked Aloysius then.

Lady Kingswood glanced at her watch.

"Barely two hours."

At that moment the "White Eagle" swooped suddenly over the gardens, noiselessly and with an enormous spread of wing that was like a white cloud in the sky—then gracefully swerved aside towards its "shed" or aerodrome, folding its huge pinions as of its own will and sliding into its quarters as easily as a hand may slide into a loose-fitting glove. The two interested watchers of its descent and swift "run home" had no time to exchange more than a few words of comment before Morgana ran lightly up the terrace, calling to them with all the gaiety of a child returning on a holiday.

"It was glorious!" she exclaimed—"Just glorious! We've been to Naples,—crowds gathered in the street to stare at us,—we were ever so high above them and they couldn't make us out, as we moved so silently! Then we hovered for a bit over Capri,—the island looked like a lovely jewel shining with sun and sea,—and now here we are!—home in plenty of time to dress for dinner! You see, dear 'Duchess'—you need not have been nervous,—the 'White Eagle' is safer than any railway train, and ever so much pleasanter!"

"Well, I'm glad you've come back all right"—said Lady Kingswood—"It's a great relief! I certainly was afraid—"

"Oh, you must never be afraid of anything!" laughed Morgana—"It does no good. We are all too much afraid of everything and everybody,—and often when there's nothing to be afraid of! Am I not right, most reverend Father Aloysius?" and she turned with a radiant smile to the priest whose serious dark eyes rested upon her with an expression of mingled admiration and wonder—"I'm so glad to find you here with Lady Kingswood—I'm sure you told her there was no danger for me, didn't you? Yes? I thought so! Now do stay and dine with us, please!—I want you to talk to the Marchese Rivardi—he's rather cross! He cannot bear me to have my own way!—I suppose all men are like that!—they want women to submit, not to command!" She laughed again. "See!—here he comes,—with the sulky air of a naughty boy!" this, as Rivardi slowly mounted the terrace steps and approached—"I'm off to dress for dinner—come, 'Duchess!' We'll leave the men to themselves!"

She slipped her arm through Lady Kingswood's and hurried her away. Don Aloysius was puzzled by her words,—and, as Rivardi came up to him raised his eyebrows interrogatively. The Marchese answered the unspoken query by an impatient shrug.

"Altro! She is impossible!" he said irritably—"Wild as the wind!—uncontrollable! She will kill herself!—but she does not care!"

"What has she done?" asked Aloysius, smiling a little—"Has she invented something new?—a parachute in which to fall gracefully like a falling star?"

"Nothing of the kind"—retorted Rivardi; vexed beyond all reason at the priest's tranquil air of good-humored tolerance—"But she insists on steering the air-ship herself! She took my place to-day."

"Well?"

"Well! You think that nothing? I tell you it is very serious—very foolhardy. She knows nothing of aerial navigation—"

"Was her steering faulty?"

Rivardi hesitated.

"No,—it was wonderful"—he admitted, reluctantly; "Especially for a first attempt. And now she declares she will travel with the 'White Eagle' alone! Alone! Think of it! That little creature alone in the air with a huge air-ship under her sole control! The very idea is madness!"

"Have patience, Giulio!" said Don Aloysius, gently—"I think she cannot mean what she says in this particular instance. She is naturally full of triumph at the success of her invention,—an amazing invention you must own!—and her triumph makes her bold. But be quite easy in your mind!—she will not travel alone!"

"She will—she will!" declared Rivardi, passionately—"She will do anything she has a mind to do! As well try to stop the wind as stop her! She has some scheme in her brain,—so fantastic vision of that Brazen City you spoke of the other day—"

Don Aloysius gave a sudden start.

"No!—not possible!" he said—"She will not pursue a phantasm,—a dream!"

He spoke nervously, and his face paled. Rivardi looked at him curiously.

"There is no such place then?" he asked—"It is only a legend?"

"Only a legend!" replied Aloysius, slowly—"Some travellers say it is a mirage of the desert,—others tell stories of having heard the bells in the brazen towers ring,—but no one—No One," and he repeated the words with emphasis—"has ever been able to reach even the traditional environs of the place. Our hostess," and he smiled—"is a very wonderful little person, but even she will hardly be able to discover the undiscoverable!"

"Can we say that anything is undiscoverable?" suggested Rivardi.

Don Aloysius thought a moment before replying.

"Perhaps not!"—he said, at last—"Our life all through is a voyage of discovery wherein we have no certainty of the port of arrival. The puzzling part of it is that we often 'discover' what has been discovered before in past ages where the discoverers seemed to make no use of their discoveries!—and so we lose ourselves in wonder—and often in weariness!" He sighed,—then added—"Had we not better go in and prepare to meet our hostess at dinner? And Giulio!—unbend your brows!—you must not get angry with your charming benefactress! If you do not let her have HER way, she will never let you have YOURS!"

Rivardi gave a resigned gesture.

"Oh, MINE! I must give up all hope—she will never think of me more than as a workman who has carried out her design. There is something very strange about her—she seems, at certain moments, to withdraw herself from all the interests of mere humanity. To-day, for instance, she looked down from the air-ship on the swarming crowds in the streets of Naples and said 'Poor little microbes! How sad it is to see them crawling about and festering down there! What Is the use of them! I wish I knew!' Then, when I ventured to suggest that possibly they were more than 'microbes,'—they were human beings that loved and worked and thought and created, she looked at me with those wonderful eyes of hers and answered—'Microbes do the same—only we don't take the trouble to think about them! But if we knew their lives and intentions, I dare say we should find they are quite as clever in their own line as we are in ours!' What is one to say to a woman who argues in this way?"

Don Aloysius laughed gently.

"But she argues quite correctly after all! My son, you are like the majority of men—they grow impatient with clever women,—they prefer stupid ones. In fact they deliberately choose stupid ones to be the mothers of their children—hence the ever increasing multitude of fools!" He moved towards the open doors of the beautiful lounge-hall of the Palazzo, Rivardi walking at his side. "But you will grant me a measure of wisdom in the advice I gave you the other day-the little millionairess is unlike other women—she is not capable of loving,—not in the way loving is understood in this world,—therefore do not seek from her what she cannot give!—As for her 'flying alone'—leave that to the fates!—I do not think she will attempt it."

They entered the Palazzo just as a servant was about to announce to them that dinner would be served in a quarter of an hour, and their talk, for the time being, ended. But the thoughts of both men were busy; and unknown to each other, centered round the enigmatical personality of one woman who had become more interesting to them than anything else in the world,—so much so indeed that each in his own private mind wondered what life would be worth without her!

XVI

That evening Morgana was in one of her most bewitching moods—even the old Highland word "fey" scarcely described her many brilliant variations from grave to gay, from gay to romantic, and from romantic to a kind of humorous-satiric vein which moved her to utter quick little witticisms which might have seemed barbed with too sharp a point were they not so quickly covered with a sweetness of manner which deprived them of all malice. She looked her best, too,—she had robed herself in a garment of pale shimmering blue which shone softly like the gleam of moonbeams through crystal—her wonderful hair was twisted up in a coronal held in place by a band of diamonds,—tiny diamonds twinkled in her ears, and a star of diamonds glittered on her breast. Her elfin beauty, totally unlike the beauty of accepted standards, exhaled a subtle influence as a lily exhales fragrance—and the knowledge she had of her own charm combined with her indifference as to its effect upon others gave her a dangerous attractiveness. As she sat at the head of her daintily adorned dinner-table she might have posed for a fairy queen in days when fairies were still believed in and queens were envied,—and Giulio Rivardi's thoughts were swept to and fro in his brain by cross-currents of emotion which were not altogether disinterested or virtuous. For years his spirit had been fretted and galled by poverty,—he, the descendant of a long line of proud Sicilian nobles, had been forced to earn a precarious livelihood as an art decorator and adviser to "newly rich" people who had neither taste nor judgment, teaching them how to build, restore or furnish their houses according to the pure canons of art, in the knowledge of which he excelled,—and now, when chance or providence had thrown Morgana in his way,—Morgana with her millions, and an enchanting personality,—he inwardly demanded why he should not win her to have and to hold for his own? He was a personable man, nobly born, finely educated,—was it possible that he had not sufficient resolution and force of character to take the precious citadel by storm? These ideas flitted vaguely across his mind as he watched his fair hostess talking, now to Don Aloysius, now to Lady Kingswood, and sometimes flinging him a light word of badinage to rally him on what she chose to call his "sulks."

"He can't get over it!" she declared, smiling—"Poor Marchese Giulio! That I should have dared to steer my own air-ship was too much for him, and he can't forgive me!"

"I cannot forgive your putting yourself into danger," said Rivardi—"You ran a great risk—you must pardon me if I hold your life too valuable to be lightly lost."

"It is good of you to think it valuable,"—and her wonderful blue eyes were suddenly shadowed with sadness—"To me it is valueless."

"My dear!" exclaimed Lady Kingswood—"How can you say such a thing!"

"Only because I feel it"—replied Morgana—"I dare say my life is not more valueless than other lives—they are all without ultimate meaning. If I knew, quite positively, that I was all in all to some ONE being who would be unhappy without me,—to whom I could be helper and inspirer, I dare say I should value my life more,—but unfortunately I have seen too much of the modern world to believe in the sincerity of even that 'one' being, could I find him—or her. I am very positively alone in life,—no woman was ever more alone than I!"

"But—is not that your own fault?" suggested Don Aloysius, gently.

"Quite!" she answered, smiling—"I fully admit it. I am what they call 'difficult' I know,—I do not like 'society' or its amusements, which to me seem very vulgar and senseless,—I do not like its conversation, which I find excessively banal and often coarse—I cannot set my soul on tennis or golf or bridge—so I'm quite an 'outsider.' But I'm not sorry!—I should not care to be INside the human menagerie. Too much barking, biting, scratching, and general howling among the animals!—it wouldn't suit me!"

She laughed lightly, and continued,—

"That's why I say my life is valueless to anyone but myself. And that's why I'm not afraid to risk it in flying the 'White Eagle' alone."

Her hearers were silent. Indeed there was nothing to be said. Whatever her will or caprice there was no one with any right to gainsay it. Rivardi was inwardly seething with suppressed irritation—but his handsome face showed no sign of annoyance save in an extreme pallor and gravity of expression.

"I think,"—said Don Aloysius, after a pause—"I think our hostess will do us the grace of believing that whatever she has experienced of the world in general, she has certainly won the regard and interest of those whom she honours with her company at the present moment!"—

and his voice had a thrill of irresistible kindness—"And whatever she chooses to do, and however she chooses to do it, she cannot avoid involving such affection and interest as those friends represent—"

"Dear Father Aloysius!" interrupted Morgana, quickly and impulsively—"Forgive me!—I did not think!—I am sure you and the Marchese and Lady Kingswood have the kindest feeling for me!—but—"

"But!"—and Aloysius smiled—"But—it is a little lady that will not be commanded or controlled! Yes—that is so! However this may be, let us not imagine that in the rush of commerce and the marvels of science the world is left empty of love! Love is still the strongest force in nature!"

Morgana's eyes flashed up, then drooped under their white lids fringed with gold.

"You think so?" she murmured—"To me, love leads nowhere!"

"Except to Heaven!" said Aloysius.

There followed a silence.

It was broken by the entrance of a servant announcing that coffee was served in the loggia. They left the dinner-table and went out into the wonder of a perfect Sicilian moonlight. All the gardens were illumined and the sea beyond, with wide strands of silver spreading on all sides, falling over the marble pavements and steps of the loggia and glistening on certain white flowering shrubs with the smooth sheen of polished pearl. The magical loveliness of the scene, made lovelier by the intense silence of the hour, held them as with a binding spell, and Morgana, standing by one of the slender columns which not only supported the loggia but the whole Palazzo d'Oro as with the petrified stems of trees, made a figure completely in harmony with her surroundings.

"Could anything be more enchantingly beautiful!" sighed Lady Kingswood—"One ought to thank God for eyes to see it!"

"And many people with eyes would not see it at all,"—said Don Aloysius—"They would go indoors, shut the shutters and play Bridge! But those who can see it are the happiest!"

And he quoted—

> "*On such a night as this,*
> *When the sweet wind did gently kiss the trees*
> *And they did make no noise,—on such a night*
> *Troilus, methinks, mounted the Trojan walls*

> *And sighed his soul towards the Grecian tents*
> *Where Cressid lay!'"*

"You know your Shakespeare!" said Rivardi.

"Who would not know him!" replied Aloysius—"One is not blind to the sun!"

"Ah, poor Shakespeare!" said Morgana—"What a lesson he gives us miserable little moderns in the worth of fame! So great, so unapproachable,—and yet!—doubted and slandered and reviled three hundred years after his death by envious detractors who cannot write a line!"

"But what does that matter?" returned Aloysius. "Envy and detraction in their blackness only emphasise his brightness, just as a star shines more brilliantly in a dark sky. One always recognises a great spirit by the littleness of those who strive to wound it,—if it were not great it would not be worth wounding!"

"Shakespeare might have imagined my air-ship!" said Morgana, suddenly—"He was perhaps dreaming vaguely of something like it when he wrote about—"

> *'A winged messenger of heaven*
> *When he bestrides the lazy-pacing clouds*
> *And sails upon the bosom of the air!'*

"The 'White Eagle' sails upon the bosom of the air!"

"Quite true"—said the Marchese Rivardi, looking at her as she stood, bathed in the moonlight, a nymph-like figure of purely feminine charm, as unlike the accepted idea of a "science" scholar as could well be imagined—"And the manner of its sailing is a mystery which you only can explain! Surely you will reveal this secret?—especially when so many rush into the air-craft business without any idea of the scientific laws by which you uphold your great design? Much has been said and written concerning new schemes for air-vessels moved by steam—"

"That is so like men!" interrupted Morgana, with a laugh—"They will think of steam power when they are actually in possession of electricity!—and they will stick to electricity without moving the one step further which would give them the full use of radio-activity! They will 'bungle' to the end!—and their bungling is always brought about by an ineffable conceit of their own so-called 'logical' conclusions! Poor dears!—they 'get there' at last—and in the course of centuries find out what they could have discovered in a month if they had opened their minds as well as their eyes!"

"Well, then,—help them now," said Rivardi—"Give them the chance to learn your secret!"

Morgana moved away from the column where she had leaned, and came more fully into the broad moonlight.

"My dear Marchese Giulio!" she said, indulgently, "You really are a positive child in your very optimistic look-out on the world of to-day! Suppose I were to 'give them the chance,' as you suggest, to learn my secret, how do you think I should be received? I might go to the great scientific institutions of London and Paris and I might ask to be heard—I might offer to give a 'demonstration,'" here she began to laugh; "Oh dear!—it would never do for a woman to 'demonstrate' and terrify all the male professors, would it! No!—well, I should probably have to wait months before being 'heard,'—then I should probably meet with the chill repudiation dealt out to that wonderful Hindu scientist, Jagadis Bose, by Burdon Sanderson when the brilliant Indian savant tried to teach men what they never knew before about the life of plants. Not only that, I should be met with incredulity and ridicule—'a woman! a WOMAN dares to assume knowledge superior to ours!' and so forth. No, no! Let the wise men try their steam air-ships and spoil the skies by smoke and vapour, so that agriculture becomes more and more difficult, and sunshine an almost forgotten benediction!—let them go their own foolish way till they learn wisdom of themselves—no one could ever teach them what they refuse to learn, till they tumble into a bog or quicksand of dilemma and have to be forcibly dragged out."

"By a woman?" hinted Don Aloysius, with a smile.

She shrugged her shoulders carelessly.

"Very often! Marja Sklodowska Curie, for example, has pulled many scientists out of the mud, but they are not grateful enough to acknowledge it. One of the greatest women of the age, she is allowed to remain in comparative obscurity,—even Anatole France, though he called her a 'genius,' had not the generosity or largeness of mind to praise her as she deserves. Though, of course, like all really great souls she is indifferent to praise or blame—the notice of the decadent press, noisy and vulgar like the beating of the cheap-jack's drum at a country fair, has no attraction for her. Nothing is known of her private life,—not a photograph of her is obtainable—she has the lovely dignity of complete reserve. She is one of my heroines in this life—she does not offer herself to the cheap journalist like a milliner's mannequin or a film face. She will not give herself away—neither will I!"

"But you might benefit the human race"—said Rivardi—"Would not that thought weigh with you?"

"Not in the least!"—and she smiled—"The human race in its present condition is 'an unweeded garden, things rank and gross in nature possess it merely,' and it wants clearing. I have no wish to benefit it. It has always murdered its benefactors. It deludes itself with the idea that the universe is for IT alone,—it ignores the fact that there are many other sharers in its privileges and surroundings—presences and personalities as real as itself. I am almost a believer in what the old-time magicians called 'elementals'—especially now."

Don Aloysius rose from his chair and put aside his emptied coffee-cup. His tall fine figure silhouetted more densely black by the whiteness of the moon-rays had a singularly imposing effect.

"Why especially now?" he asked, almost imperatively—"What has chanced to make you accept the idea—an old idea, older than the lost continent of Atlantis!—of creatures built up of finer life-cells than ours?"

Morgana looked at him, vaguely surprised by his tone and manner.

"Nothing has chanced that causes me any wonder," she said—"or that would 'make' me accept any theory which I could not put to the test for myself. But, out in New York while I have been away, a fellow-student of mine—just a boy,—has found out the means of 'creating energy from some unknown source'—that is, unknown to the scientists of rule-and-line. They call his electric apparatus 'an atmospheric generator.' Naturally this implies that the atmosphere has something to 'generate' which has till now remained hidden and undeveloped. I knew this long ago. Had I NOT known it I could not have thought out the secret of the 'White Eagle'!"

She paused to allow the murmured exclamations of her hearers to subside,—then she went on—"You can easily understand that if atmosphere generates ONE form of energy it is capable of many other forms,—and on these lines there is nothing to be said, against the possibility of 'elementals.' I feel quite 'elemental' myself in this glorious moonlight!—just as if I could slip out of my body like a butterfly out of a chrysalis and spread my wings!"

She lifted her fair arms upward with a kind of expansive rapture,— the moonbeams seemed to filter through the delicate tissue of her garments adding brightness to their folds and sparkling frostily on the diamonds in her hair,—and even Lady Kingswood's very placid nature was conscious of an unusual thrill, half of surprise and half of fear, at the quite "other world" appearance she thus presented.

"You have rather the look of a butterfly!" she said, kindly—"One of those beautiful tropical things—or a fairy!—only we don't know what fairies are like as we have never seen any!"

Morgana laughed, and let her arms drop at her sides. She felt rather than saw the admiring eyes of the two men upon her and her mood changed.

"Yes—it is a lovely night,—for Sicily,"—she said. "But it would be lovelier in California!"

"In California!" echoed Rivardi—"Why California?"

"Why? Oh, I don't know why! I often think of California—it is so vast! Sicily is a speck of garden-land compared with it—and when the moon rises full over the great hills and spreads a wide sheet of silver over the Pacific Ocean you begin to realise a something beyond ordinary nature—it helps you to get to the 'beyond' yourself if you have the will to try!"

Just then the soft slow tolling of a bell struck through the air and Don Aloysius prepared to take his leave.

"The 'beyond' calls to me from the monastery," he said, smiling—"I have been too long absent. Will you walk with me, Giulio?"

"Willingly!" and the Marchese bowed over Lady Kingswood's hand as he bade her "Good night."

"I will accompany you both to the gate,"—said Morgana, suddenly—"and then—when you are both gone I shall wander a little by myself in the light of the moon!"

Lady Kingswood looked dubiously at her, but was too tactful to offer any objection such as the "danger of catching cold" which the ordinary duenna would have suggested, and which would have seemed absurd in the warmth and softness of such a summer night. Besides, if Morgana chose to "wander by the light of the moon" who could prevent her? No one! She stepped off the loggia on to the velvety turf below with an aerial grace more characteristic of flying than walking, and glided along between the tall figures of the Marchese and Don Aloysius like a dream-spirit of the air, and Lady Kingswood, watching her as she descended the garden terraces and gradually disappeared among the trees, was impressed, as she had often been before, by a strange sense of the supernatural,—as if some being wholly unconnected with ordinary mortal happenings were visiting the world by a mere chance. She was a little ashamed of this "uncanny" feeling,—and after a few minutes' hesitation she decided to retire within the house and to her own apartments, rightly judging that Morgana would be better pleased to find her so gone than waiting for her return like a sentinel on guard. She gave a lingering look at the exquisite beauty of the moonlit scene, and thought with a sigh—

"What it would be if one were young once more!"

And then she turned, slowly pacing across the loggia and entering the Palazzo, where the gleam of electric lamps within rivalled the moonbeams and drew her out of sight.

Meanwhile, Morgana, between her two escorts stepped lightly along, playfully arguing with them both on their silence.

"You are so very serious, you good Padre Aloysius!" she said—"And you, Marchese—you who are generally so charming!—to-night you are a very morose companion! You are still in the dumps about my steering the 'White Eagle!'—how cross of you!"

"Madama, I think of your safety,"—he said, curtly.

"It is kind of you! But if I do not care for my safety?"

"I do!" he said, decisively.

"And I also!"—said Aloysius, earnestly—"Dear lady, be advised! Think no more of flying in the vast spaces of air alone—alone with an enormous piece of mechanism which might fail at any moment—"

"It cannot fail unless the laws of nature fail!"—said Morgana, emphatically—"How strange it is that neither of you seems to realise that the force which moves the 'White Eagle' is natural force alone! However—you are but men!" Here she stopped in her walk, and her brilliant eyes flashed from one to the other—"Men!—with pre-conceived ideas wedged in obstinacy!—yes!—you cannot help yourselves! Even Father Aloysius—" she paused, as she met his grave eyes fixed full upon her.

"Well!" he said gently—"What of Father Aloysius? He is 'but man' as you say!—a poor priest having nothing in common with your wealth or your self-will, my child!—one whose soul admits no other instruction than that of the Great Intelligence ruling the universe, and from whose ordinance comes forth joy or sorrow, wisdom or ignorance. We are but dust on the wind before this mighty power!—even you, with all your study and attainment are but a little phantom on the air!"

She smiled as he spoke.

"True!" she said—"And you would save this phantom from vanishing into air utterly?"

"I would!" he answered—"I would fain place you in God's keeping,"— and with a gesture infinitely tender and solemn, he made the sign of the cross above her head—"with a prayer that you may be guided out of the tangled ways of life as lived in these days, to the true realisation of happiness!"

She caught his hand and impulsively kissed it.

"You are good!—far too good!" she said—"And I am wild and wilful—forgive me! I will say good night here—we are just at the gate. Good night, Marchese! I promise you shall fly with me to the East—I will not go alone. There!—be satisfied!" And she gave him a bewitching smile—then with another markedly gentle "Good night" to Aloysius, she turned away and left them, choosing a path back to the house which was thickly overgrown with trees, so that her figure was almost immediately lost to view.

The two men looked at each other in silence.

"You will not succeed by thwarting her!"—said Aloysius, warningly.

Rivardi gave an impatient gesture.

"And you?"

"I? My son, I have no aim in view with regard to her! I should like to see her happy—she has great wealth, and great gifts of intellect and ability—but these do not make real happiness for a woman. And yet—I doubt whether she could ever be happy in the ordinary woman's way."

"No, because she is not an 'ordinary' woman," said Rivardi, quickly— "More's the pity I think—for HER!"

"And for you!" added Aloysius, meaningly.

Rivardi made no answer, and they walked on in silence, the priest parting with his companion at the gate of the monastery, and the Marchese going on to his own half-ruined villa lifting its crumbling walls out of wild verdure and suggesting the historic past, when a Caesar spent festal hours in its great gardens which were now a wilderness.

Meanwhile, Morgana, the subject of their mutual thoughts, followed the path she had taken down to the seashore. Alone there, she stood absorbed,—a fairylike figure in her shimmering soft robe and the diamonds flashing in her hair—now looking at the moonlit water,— now back to the beautiful outline of the Palazzo d'Oro, lifted on its rocky height and surrounded by a paradise of flowers and foliage—

then to the long wide structure of the huge shed where her wonderful air-ship lay, as it were, in harbour. She stretched out her arms with a fatigued, appealing gesture.

"I have all I want!"—she said softly aloud,—"All!—all that money can buy—more than money has ever bought!—and yet—the unknown quantity called happiness is not in the bargain. What is it? Why is it? I am like the princess in the 'Arabian Nights' who was quite satisfied with her beautiful palace till an old woman came along and told her that it wanted a roc's egg to make it perfect. And she became at once miserable and discontented because she had not the roc's egg! I thought her a fool when I read that story in my childhood—but I am as great a fool as she to-day. I want that roc's egg!"

She laughed to herself and looked up at the splendid moon, round as a golden shield in heaven.

"How the moon shone that night in California!" she murmured— "And Roger Seaton—bear-man as he is—would have given worlds to hold me in his arms and kiss me as he did once when he 'didn't mean it!' Ah! I wonder if he ever WILL mean it! Perhaps—when it is too late!"

And there swept over her mind the memory of Manella—her rich, warm, dark beauty—her frank abandonment to passions purely primitive,—and she smiled, a cold little weird smile.

"He may marry her,"—she said—"And yet—I think not! But—if he does marry her he will never love her—as he loves ME! How we play at cross-purposes in our lives!—he is not a marrying man—I am not a marrying woman—we are both out for conquest on other lines,—and if either of us wins our way, what then? Shall we be content to live on a triumph of power,—without love?"

XVII

S o the man from Washington told you to bring this to me?"

Roger Seaton asked the question of Manella, twirling in his hand an unopened letter she had just given him. She nodded in the affirmative. He looked at her critically, amused at the evident pains she had taken with her dress and general appearance. He twirled the letter again like a toy in his fingers.

"I wonder what it's all about? Do you know?"

Manella shrugged her shoulders with a charming air of indifference.

"I? How should I know? He is your friend I suppose?"

"Not a bit of it!" and Roger stretched himself lazily and yawned—"He's the friend of nobody who is poor. But he's the comrade of everybody with plenty of cash. He's as hard as a dried old walnut, without the shred of a heart—"

"You are wrong!" said Manella, flushing up suddenly—"You are wrong and unjust! He is an ugly old man, but he is very kind."

Seaton threw back his head and laughed heartily with real enjoyment.

"Manella, oh, Manella!" he exclaimed—"What has he said or done to you to win your good opinion? Has he made you some pretty compliments, and told you that you are beautiful? Every one can tell you that, my dear! It does not need Mr. Senator Gwent's assurance to emphasise the fact! That you find him an ugly old man is natural—but that you should also think him 'very kind' Does surprise me!"

Manella gazed at him seriously—her lovely eyes gleaming like jewels under her long black lashes.

"You mock at everything,"—she said—"It is a pity!"

Her tone was faintly reproachful. He smiled.

"My dear girl, I really cannot regard Mr. Senator Gwent as a figure to be reverenced!"—he said—"He's one of the dustiest, driest old dollar-grabbers in the States. I gave him the chance of fresh grab—but he was too much afraid to take it—"

"Afraid of what?" asked Manella, quickly.

"Of shadows!—shadows of coming events!—yes, they scared him! Now if you are a good girl, and will sit very quiet, you can come into my hut out of this scorching sun, and sit down while I read the letter—I may have to write an answer—and if so you can post it at the Plaza."

He went before her into the hut, and she followed. He bade her sit down in the chair by the window,—she obeyed, and glanced about her shyly, yet curiously. The room was not untidy, as she expected it would be without a woman's hand to set it in order,—on the contrary it was the perfection of neatness and cleanliness. Her gaze was quickly attracted by the bowl of perpetually moving fluid in the center of the table.

"What is that?" she asked.

"That? Oh, nothing! An invention of mine—just to look pretty and cool in warm weather! It reminds me of women's caprices and fancies— always on the jump! Yes!—don't frown, Manella!—that is so! Now—let me see what Mr. Sam Gwent has to say that he didn't say before—" and seating himself, he opened the letter and began to read.

Manella watched him from under the shadow of her long-fringed eyelids—her heart beat quickly and uncomfortably. She was fearful lest Gwent should have broken faith with her after all, and have written of her and her vain passion, to the man who already knew of it only too well. She waited patiently for the "god of her idolatry" to look up. At last he did so. But he seemed to have forgotten her presence. His brows were knitted in a frown, and he spoke aloud, as to himself—

"A syndicate! Old humbug! He knows perfectly well that the thing could not be run by a syndicate! It must be a State's own single possession—a State's special secret. If I were as bent on sheer destructiveness as he imagines me to be, I should waste no more time, but offer it to Germany. Germany would take it at once—Germany would require no persuasion to use it!—Germany would make me a millionaire twice over for the monopoly of such a force!—that is, if I wanted to be a millionaire, which I don't. But Gwent's a fool—I must have scared him out of his wits, or he wouldn't write all this stuff about risks to my life, advising me to marry quickly and settle down! Good God! I?—Marry and settle down? What a tame ending to a life's adventure! Hello, Manella!"

His eyes lighted upon her as if he had only just seen her. He rose from his chair and went over to where she sat by the window.

"Patient girl!" he said, patting her dark head with his big sun-browned hand—"As good as gold and quieter than a mouse! Well! You may go now. I've read the letter and there's no answer. Nothing for me to write, or for you to post!" She lifted her brilliant eyes to his—what glorious eyes they were! He would not have been man had he not been conscious of their amorous fire. He patted her head again in quite a paternal way.

"Nothing for me to write or for you to post"—he repeated, abstractedly—"and how satisfactory that is!"

"Then you are pleased?" she said.

"Pleased? My dear, there is nothing to be pleased or displeased about! The ugly old man whom you found so 'very kind' tells me to take care of myself—which I always do. Also—to marry and settle down—which I always don't!"

She stood upright, turning her head away from the touch of his hand. She had never looked more attractive than at that moment,—she wore the white gown in which he had before admired her, and a cluster of roses which were pinned to her bodice gave rich contrast to the soft tone of her smooth, suntanned skin, and swayed lightly with the unquiet heaving of the beautiful bosom which might have served a sculptor as a perfect model. A faint, quivering smile was on her lips.

"You always don't? That sounds very droll! You will be unlike every man in the world, then,—they all marry!"

"Oh, do they? You know all about it? Wise Manella!"

And he looked at her, smiling. Her passionate eyes, full of glowing ardour, met his,—a flashing fire seemed to leap from them into his own soul, and for the moment he almost lost his self-possession.

"Wise Manella!" he repeated, his voice shaking a little, while he fought with the insidious temptation which beset him,—the temptation to draw her into his arms and take his fill of the love she was so ready to give—"They always marry? No dear, they do NOT! Many of them avoid marriage—" he paused, then continued—"and do you know why?"

She shook her head.

"Because it is the end of romance! Because it rings down the curtain on a beautiful Play! The music ceases—the lights are put out—the audience goes home,—and the actors take off their fascinating costumes, wash away their paint and powder and sit down to supper—possibly fried steak and onions and a pot of beer. The fried steak and onions—also the beer—make a very good ordinary 'marriage.'"

In this flippant talk he gained the mastery over himself he had feared to lose—and laughed heartily as he saw Manella's expression of utter bewilderment.

"I do not understand!" she said, plaintively—"What is steak and onions?—how do they make a marriage? You say such strange things!"

He laughed again, thoroughly amused.

"Yes, don't I!" he rejoined—"But not half such strange things as I could say if I were so inclined! I'm a queer fellow!"

He touched her hair gently, putting back a stray curl that had fallen across her forehead.

"Now, dear," he continued, "It's time you went. You'll be wanted at the Plaza—and they mustn't think I'm keeping you up here, making love to you!"

She tossed her head back, and her eyes flashed almost angrily.

"There's no danger of that!" she said, with a little suppressed tremor in her throat like the sob of a nightingale at the close of its song.

"Isn't there?" and putting his arm round her, he drew her close to himself and looked full in her eyes—"Manella—there Was!—a moment ago!"

She remained still and passive in his arms—hardly daring to breathe, so rapt was she in a sudden ecstasy, but he could feel the wild beating of her heart against his own.

"A moment ago!" he repeated, in a half whisper. "A moment ago I could have made such desperate love to you as would have astonished myself!—and You! And I should have regretted it ever afterwards—and so would you!"

The struggling emotion in her found utterance.

"No, no—not I!" she said, in quick little passionate murmurs—"I could not regret it!—If you loved me for an hour it would be the joy of my life-time!—You might leave me,—you might forget!—but that would not take away my pride and gladness! You might kill me—I would die gladly if it saved Your life!—ah, you do not understand love—not the love of Manella!"

And she lifted her face to his—a face so lovely, so young, so warm with her soul's inward rapture that its glowing beauty might have made a lover of an anchorite. But with Roger Seaton the impulses of passion were brief—the momentary flame had gone out in vapour, and the spirit of the anchorite prevailed. He looked at the dewy red lips, delicately parted like rose petals—but he did not kiss them, and the clasp of his arms round her gradually relaxed.

"Hush, hush Manella!" he said, with a mild kindness, which in her overwrought state was more distracting than angry words would have been—"Hush! You talk foolishness—beautiful foolishness—all women do when they set their fancies on men. It is nature, of course,—You think it is love, but, my dear girl, there is no such thing as love! There!—now you are cross!" for she drew herself quickly away from his hold and stood apart, her eyes sparkling, her breast heaving, with the air of a goddess enraged,—"You are cross because I tell you the truth—"

"It is not the truth," she said, in a low voice quivering with intense feeling—"you tell me lies to disguise yourself. But I can see! You yourself love a woman—but you have not my courage!—you are afraid to own it! You would give the world to hold her in your arms as you just now held ME—but you will not admit it—not even to yourself—and you pretend to hate when you are mad for love!—just as you pretend to be ill when you are well! You should be ashamed to say there is no such thing as love! What mean you then by playing so false with yourself?—with me?—and with HER?"

She looked lovelier than ever in her anger, and he was taken by surprise at the impetuous and instinctive guess she had made at the complexity of his moods, which he himself scarcely understood. For a moment he stood inert, embarrassed by her straight, half-scornful glance—then he regained his usual mental poise and smiled with provoking good humour and tolerance.

"Temper, Manella!—temper again! A pity, a pity! Your Spanish blood is too fiery, Manella!—it is indeed! You have been very rude—do you know how rude you have been? But there! I forgive you! You are only a naughty child! As for love—"

He paused, and going to the door of the hut looked out.

"Manella, there is a big cloud in the west just over the ocean. It is shaped like a great white eagle and its wings are edged with gold,—it is the beginning of a fine sunset. Come and look at it,—and while we watch it floating along I will talk to you about love!"

She hesitated,—her whole spirit was up in arms against this man whom she loved, and who, so she argued with herself, had allowed her to love HIM, while having no love for HER; and yet,—since Gwent had told her that his mysterious occupation might result in disaster and danger to his life, her devotion had received a new impetus which was wholly unselfish,—that of watchful guardianship such as inspires a faithful dog to defend its master. And, moved by this thought, she obeyed his beckoning hand, and stood with him on the sward outside the hut, looking at the cloud he described. It was singularly white,—new-fallen snow could be no whiter,—and, shaped like a huge bird, its great wings spread out to north and south were edged with a red-gold fire.

Seaton pushed an old tree stump into position and sat down upon it, making Manella sit beside him.

"Now for this talk!" he said—"Love is the subject,—Love the theme! We are taught that we must love God and love our neighbor—but we don't, because we can't! In the case of God we cannot love what we don't know and don't see,—and we cannot love our neighbor because he is often a person whom we Do know and Can see, and who is extremely offensive. Now let us consider what Is love? You, Manella, are angry because I say there is no such thing—and you accuse me of indulging in love for a woman myself. Yet—I still declare, in spite of you, there is no such thing as love! I ought to be ashamed of myself for saying this—so You think!—but I'm not ashamed. I know I'm right! Love is a divine idea, never realised. It is like a ninth new note in the musical scale—not to be attained. It is suggested in the highest forms of poetry and art, but the suggestion can never be carried out. What men and women call 'love' is the ordinary attraction of sex,—the same attraction that pulls all male and female living things together and makes them mate. It is very unromantic! And to a man of my mind, very useless."

She looked at him in a kind of sorrowful perplexity.

"You have much talk"—she said—"and no doubt you are clever. But I think you are all wrong!"

"You do? Wise child! Now listen to my much talk a little longer! Have you ever watched silkworms? No? They are typical examples of humanity. A silkworm, while it is a worm, feeds to repletion,—you can never get it as many mulberry leaves as it would like to eat—then when it is gorged, it builds itself a beautiful house of silk (which is taken away from it in due course) and comes out at the door in wings!—wings it hardly uses and seems not to understand—then, if it is a female moth, it looks about for 'love' from the male. If the male 'loves' it, the female produces a considerable number of eggs like pin-heads—and then?— what then? Why she promptly dies, and there's an end of her! Her sole aim and end of being was to produce eggs, which in their turn become worms and repeat the same dull routine of business. Now—think me as brutal as you like—I say a woman is very like a female silkworm,—she comes out of her beautiful silken cocoon of maidenhood with wings which she doesn't know how to use—she merely flutters about waiting to be 'loved'—and when this dream she calls 'love' comes to her, she doesn't dream any longer—she wakes—to find her life finished!— finished, Manella!—dry as a gourd with all the juice run out!"

Manella rose from her seat beside him. The warm light in her eyes had gone—her face was pale, and as she drew herself up to her stately height she made a picture of noble scorn.

"I am sorry for you!" she said. "If you think these things your thoughts are quite dreadful! You are a cruel man after all! I am sorry I spoke of the beautiful little lady who came here to see you—you do not love her—you cannot!—I felt sure you did—but I am wrong!—there is no love in you except for yourself and your own will!"

She spoke, breathing quickly, and trembling with suppressed emotion. He smiled,—and, rising, saluted her with a profound bow.

"Thank you, Manella! You give me a true character!—Myself and my own will are certainly the chief factors in my life—and they may work wonders yet!—who knows! And there is no love in me—no!—not what You call love!—but—as concerns the 'beautiful little lady,' you may know this much of me—That I Want Her!"

He threw out his hands with a gesture that was almost tragic, and such an expression came into his face of savagery and tenderness commingled that Manella retreated from him in vague terror.

"I want her!" he repeated—"And why? Not to 'love' her,—but to break her wings,—for she, unlike a silkworm moth, knows how to use them! I want her, to make her proud mind bend to My will and way!—I want her to show her how a man can, shall, and Must be master of a woman's brain and soul!"

A sudden heat of pent-up feeling broke out in this impulsive rush of words;—he checked himself,—and seeing Manella's pale, scared face he went up to her and took her hand.

"You see, Manella?" he said, in quiet tones—"There is no such thing as 'love,' but there is such a thing as 'wanting.' And—for the most selfish reasons man ever had—I want Her—not you!"

The colour rushed back to her cheeks in a warm glow—her great dark eyes were ablaze with indignation. She drew her hand quickly from his hold.

"And I hope you will never get her!" she said, passionately—"I will pray the Holy Virgin to save her from you! For you are wicked! She is like an angel—and you are a devil!—yes, surely you must be, or you could not say such horrible things! You do not want me, you say? I know that! I am a fool to have shown you my heart—you have broken it, but you do not care—you could have been master of my brain and soul whenever you pleased—"

"Ah yes, dear!" he interrupted, with a smile—"That would be so easy!"

The touch of satire in these words was lost on her,—she took them quite literally, and a sudden softness sweetened her anger.

"Yes!—quite easy!" she said—"And you would be pleased! You would do as you wished with me—men like to rule women!"

"When it is worth while!" he thought, looking at her with a curious pitifulness as one might look at a struggling animal caught in a net. Aloud he said—

"Yes, Manella!—men like to rule women. It is their special privilege—they have enjoyed it always, even in the days when the Indian 'braves' beat their squaws out here in California, and killed them outright if they dared to complain of the beating! Women are busy just now trying to rule men—it's an experiment, but it won't do! Men are the masters of life! They expect to be obeyed by all the rest of creation. *I* expect to be obeyed!—and so, Manella, when I tell you to go home, you must go! Yes!—love, tempers and all!—you must go!"

She met his eyes with a resolved look in her own.

"I am going!" she answered—"But I shall come again. Oh, yes! And yet again! and very often! I shall come even if it is only to find you dead on this hill—killed by your own secret! Yes—I shall come!"

He gave an involuntary movement of surprise and annoyance. Had Mr. Senator Gwent discussed his affairs with this beautiful foolish girl who, like some forest animal, cared for nothing but the satisfaction of mating where her wishes inclined.

"What do you mean, Manella?" he demanded, imperatively—"Do you expect to find me dead?"

She nodded vehemently. Tears were in her eyes and she turned her head away that he might not see them.

"What a cheerful prospect!" he exclaimed, gaily—"And I'm to be killed by my own secret, am I? I wonder what it is! Ah, Manella, Manella! That stupid old Gwent has been at you, stuffing your mind with a lot of nonsense—don't you believe him! I've no 'secret' that will kill me—I don't want to be killed; No, Manella! Though you come 'again and yet again and ever so often' as you say, you will not find me dead! I'm too strong!"

But Manella, yielding to her inward excitement, pointed a hand at him with a warning air of a tragedy queen.

"Do not boast!" she said—"God is always listening! No man is too strong for God! I am not clever—I have no knowledge of what you do—

but this I will tell you surely! You may have a secret,—or you may not have it,—but if you play with the powers of God you will be punished! Yes!—of that I am quite certain! And this I will also say—if you were to pull all the clouds down upon you and the thunders and the lightnings and all the terrible things of destruction in the world, I would be there! And you would know what love is!—Yes!"—her voice choked, and then pealed out like that of a Sybilline prophetess, "If God struck you down to hell, I would be there!"

And with a wild, sobbing cry she rushed away from him down the hill before he could move or utter a word.

XVIII

A red sky burned over Egypt,—red with deep intensity of spreading fire. The slow-creeping waters of the Nile washed patches of dull crimson against the oozy mud-banks, tipping palms and swaying reeds with colour as though touched with vermilion, and here and there long stretches of wet sand gleamed with a tawny gold. All Cairo was out, inhabitants and strangers alike, strangers especially, conceiving it part of their "money's worth" never to miss a sunset,—and beyond Cairo, where the Pyramids lifted their summits aloft,—stern points of warning or menace from the past to the present and the future,—a crowd of tourists with their Arab guides were assembled, staring upward in, amazement at a white wonder in the red sky, a great air-ship, which, unlike other air-ships, was noiseless, and that moved vast wings up and down with the steady, swift rhythm of a bird's flight, as though of its own volition. It soared at an immense height so that it was quite impossible to see any pilot or passenger. It hung over the Pyramids almost motionless for three or four minutes as if about to descend, and the watching groups below made the usual alarmist prognostications of evil, taking care to look about for the safest place of shelter for themselves should the huge piece of mechanism above them suddenly escape control and take a downward dive. But apparently nothing was further from the intention of its invisible guides. Its pause above the Pyramids was brief—and almost before any of the observers had time to realise its departure it had floated away with an easy grace, silence and swiftness, miraculous to all who saw it vanish into space towards the Libyan desert and beyond. The Pyramids, even the Sphinx—lost interest for the time being, every eye being strained to watch the strange aerial visitant till it disappeared. Then a babble of question and comment began in all languages among the travellers from many lands, who, though most of them were fairly well accustomed to aeroplanes, air-ships and aerial navigation as having become part of modern civilisation, found themselves nonplussed by the absolute silence and lightning swiftness of this huge bird-shaped thing that had appeared with extraordinary suddenness in the deep rose glow of the Egyptian sunset sky. Meanwhile the object of their wonder and admiration had sped many miles away, and was sailing above a desert which, from the height it had attained, looked little more than a small stretch of sand such as children play upon by the sea. Its speed gradually slackened—and its occupants, Morgana, the Marchese Rivardi and their expert mechanic, Gaspard, gazed down on the unfolding panorama below them with close and eager interest. There was nothing much to see. Every sign of humanity seemed blotted out. The red sky burning on the little stretch of sand was all.

"How small the world looks from the air!" said Morgana—"It's not worth half the fuss made about it! And yet—it's such a pretty little God's toy!"

She smiled,—and in her smiling expressed a lovely sweetness. Rivardi raised his eyes from his steering gear.

"You are not tired, Madama?" he asked.

"Tired? No, indeed! How can I be tired with so short a journey!"

"Yet we have travelled a thousand miles since we left Sicily this morning"—said Rivardi—"We have kept up the pace, have we not, Gaspard?—or rather, the 'White Eagle' has proved its speed?"

Gaspard looked up from his place at the end of the ship.

"About two hundred and fifty to three hundred miles an hour,"—he said—"One does not realise it in the movement."

"But you realise that the flight is as safe as it is quick?" said Morgana—"Do you not?"

"Madama, I confess my knowledge is outdistanced by yours,"—replied Gaspard—"I am baffled by your secret—but I freely admit its power and success."

"Good! Now let us dine!" said Morgana, opening a leather case such as is used for provisions in motoring, set plates, glasses, wine and food on the table—"A cold collation—but we'll have hot coffee to finish. We could have dined in Cairo, but it would have been a bore! Marchese, we'll stop here, suspended in mid-air, and the stars shall be our festal lamps, vying with our own!" and she turned on a switch which illumined the whole interior of the air-ship with a soft bright radiance—"Whereabouts are we? Still over the Libyan desert?"

Rivardi consulted the chart which was spread open in his steering-cabin.

"No—I think not. We have passed beyond it. We are over the Sahara. Just now we can take no observations—the sunset is dying rapidly and in a few minutes it will be quite dark."

As he spoke he brought the ship to a standstill—it remained absolutely motionless except for the slight swaying as though touched by wave-like ripples of air. Morgana went to the window aperture of her silken-lined "drawing-room" and looked out. All round the great air-ship were the illimitable spaces of the sky, now of a dense dark violet hue with here and there a streak of dull red remaining of the glow of the vanished sun,—below there was only blackness. For the first time a nervous thrill ran through her frame at the look of this dark chaos—and she turned quickly back to the table where Rivardi and Gaspard awaited her before sitting down to their meal. Something quite foreign to her courageous spirit chilled her blood, but she fought against it, and seating herself became the charming hostess to her two companions as they ate and drank, though she took scarcely anything herself. For most unquestionably there was something uncanny in a meal served under such strange circumstances, and so far as the two men were concerned it was only eaten to sustain strength.

"Well, now, have I not been very good?" she asked suddenly of Rivardi—"Did I not say you should fly with me to the East, and are you not here? I have not come alone—though that was my wish,—I have even brought Gaspard who had no great taste for the trip!"

Gaspard moved uneasily.

"That is true, Madama,"—he said—"The art of flying is still in its infancy, and though in my profession as an engineer I have studied and worked out many problems, I dare not say I have fathomed all the mysteries of the air or the influences of atmosphere. I am glad that we have made this voyage safely so far—but I shall be still more glad when we return to Sicily!"

Morgana laughed.

"We can do that tomorrow, I dare say!" she said; "If there is nothing to see in the whole expanse of the desert but dark emptiness"—

"But—what do you expect to see, Madama?" enquired Gaspard, with lively curiosity.

She laughed again as she met Rivardi's keen glance.

"Why, ruins of temples—columns—colossi—a new Sphinx-all sorts of things!" she replied—"But at night, of course, we can see nothing—and we must move onward slowly—I cannot rest swaying like this in mid-air." She put aside the dinner things, and served them with hot coffee from one of the convenient flasks that hold fluids hot or cold for an interminable time, and when they had finished this, they went back to their separate posts. The great ship began to move—and she was relieved to feel it sailing steadily, though at almost a snail's pace "on the bosom of the air." The oppressive nervousness which affected her had not diminished; she could not account for it to herself,—and to rally her forces she went to the window, so-called, of her luxurious cabin. This was a wide aperture filled in with a transparent, crystal-clear material, which looked like glass, but which was wholly unbreakable, and through this she gazed, awe-smitten, at the magnificence of the starry sky. The millions upon millions of worlds which keep the mystery of their being veiled from humanity flashed upon her eyes and moved her mind to a profound sadness.

"What is the use of it all!" she thought—"If one could only find the purpose of this amazing creation! We learn a very little, only to see how much more there is to know! We live our lives, all hoping, searching, praying—and never an answer comes for all our prayers! From the very beginning—not a word from the mysterious Poet who has written the Poem! We are to breed and die—and there an end!—it seems strange and cruel, because so purposeless! Or is it our fault? Do we fail to discover the things we ought to know?"

So she mused, while her "White Eagle" ship sailed serenely on with a leisurely, majestic motion through a seeming wilderness of stars. Courageous as she was, with a veritable lion-heart beating in her delicate little body, and firm as was her resolve to discover what no woman had ever discovered before, to-night she was conscious of actual fear. Something—she knew not what—crept with a compelling influence through her blood,—she felt that some mysterious force she had never reckoned with was insidiously surrounding her with an invisible ring. She called to Rivardi—

"Are we not flying too high? Have you altered the course?"

"No, Madama," he replied at once—"We are on the same level."

She turned towards him. Her face was very pale.

"Well—be careful! To my mind we seem to be in a new atmosphere—there is a sensation of greater tension in the air—or—it is my fancy. We must not be too adventurous,—we must avoid the Great Nebula in Orion for example!"

"Madama, you jest! We are trillions upon trillions of miles distant from any great constellation—"

"Do I not know it? You are too literal, Marchese! Of course I jest—you could not suppose me to be in earnest! But I am sure we are passing through the waves of a new ether—not altogether suited to the average human being. The average human being is not made to inhabit the higher spaces of the upper air—hark!—What was that?"

She held up a warning hand, and listened. There was a distinct and persistent chiming of bells. Bells loud and soft,—bells mellow and deep, clear and silvery—clanging in bass and treble shocks of rising and falling rhythm and tune! "Do you hear?"

Rivardi and Gaspard simultaneously rose to their feet, amazed. Undoubtedly they heard! It was impossible NOT to hear such a clamour of concordant sound! Startled beyond all expression, Morgana sprang to the window of her cabin, and looking out uttered a cry of mingled terror and rapture. . . for there below her, in the previously inky blackness of the Great Desert, lay a great City, stretching out for miles, and glittering from end to end with a peculiarly deep golden light which seemed to bathe it in the lustre of a setting sun. Towers, cupolas, bridges, streets, squares, parks and gardens could be plainly seen from the air-ship, which had suddenly stopped, and now hung immovably in mid-air; though for some moments Morgana was too excited to notice this. Again she called to her companions—

"Look! Look!" she exclaimed—"We have found it! The Brazen City!"

But she called in vain. Turning for response, she saw, to her amazement and alarm, both men stretched on the floor, senseless! She ran to them and made every effort to rouse them,—they were breathing evenly and quietly as in profound and comfortable sleep—but it was beyond her skill to renew their consciousness. Then it flashed upon her that the "White Eagle" was no longer moving,—that it was, in fact, quite stationary,—and a quick rush of energy filled her as she realised that now she was as she had wished to be, alone with her air-ship to do with it as she would. All fear had left her,—her nerves were steady, and her daring spirit was fired with resolution. Whatever the mischance which had so swiftly overwhelmed Rivardi and Gaspard, she could not stop now to question, or determine it,—she was satisfied that they were not dead, or dying. She went to the steering-gear to take it in hand— but though the mysterious mechanism of the air-ship was silently and rapidly throbbing, the ship did not move. She grasped the propeller—it resisted her touch with hard and absolute inflexibility. All at once a low deep voice spoke close to her ear—

"Do not try to steer. You cannot proceed."

Her heart gave one wild bound,—then almost stood still from sheer terror. She felt herself swaying into unconsciousness, and made a violent effort to master the physical weakness that threatened her. That voice—what voice? Surely one evoked from her own imagination! It spoke again—this time with an intonation that was exquisitely soothing and tender.

"Why are you afraid? For you there is nothing to fear!"

She raised her eyes and looked about nervously. The soft luminance which lit the "White Eagle's" interior from end to end showed nothing new or alarming,—her dainty, rose-lined cabin held no strange or supernatural visitant,—all was as usual. After a pause she rallied strength enough to question the audible but invisible intruder.

"Who is it that speaks to me?" she asked, faintly.

"One from the city below,"—was the instant reply given in full clear accents—"I am speaking on the Sound Ray."

She held her breath in mute wonder, listening. The voice went on, equably—

"You know the use of wireless telephony—we have it as you have it, only your methods are imperfect. We speak on Sound Rays which are not yet discovered in your country. We need neither transmitter nor receiver. Wherever we send our messages, no matter how great the distance, they are always heard."

Slowly Morgana began to regain courage. By degrees she realised that she was attaining the wish of her heart—namely, to know what no woman had ever known before. Again she questioned the voice—

"You tell me I cannot proceed,"—she said—"Why?"

"Because our city is guarded and fortified by the air,"—was the answer—"We are surrounded by a belt of etheric force through which nothing can pass. A million bombs could not break it,—everything driven against it would be dashed to pieces. We saw you coming—we were surprised, for no air-ship has ever ventured so far—we rang the bells of the city to warn you, and stopped your flight."

The warm gentleness of the voice thrilled her with a sudden sympathy.

"That was kind!" she said, and smiled. Some one smiled in response—or she thought so. Presently she spoke again—

"Then you hold me here a prisoner?"

"No. You can return the way you came, quite freely."

"May I not come down and see your city?" "No."

"Why?"

"Because you are not one of us." The Voice hesitated. "And because you are not alone."

Morgana glanced at the prostrate and unconscious forms of Rivardi and Gaspard with a touch of pity.

"My companions are half dead!" she said.

"But not wholly!" was the prompt reply.

"Is it that force you speak of—the force which guards your city—that has struck them down?" she asked.

"Yes."

"Then why was I not also struck down?"

"Because you are what you are!" Then—after a silence—"You are Morgana!"

At this every nerve in her body started quivering like harp strings pulled by testing fingers. The unseen speaker knew her name!—and uttered it with a soft delicacy that made it sound more than musical. She leaned forward, extending a hand as though to touch the invisible.

"How do you know me?" she asked.

"As we all know you,"—came the answer—"Even as You have known the inside of a sun-ray!"

She listened, amazed—utterly mystified. Whoever or whatever it was that spoke knew not only her name, but the trend of her earliest studies and theories. The "inside of a sun-ray"! This was what she had only the other day explained to Father Aloysius as being her first experience of real happiness! She tried to set her thoughts in order—to realise her position. Here she was, a fragile human thing, in a flying ship of her own design, held fast by atmospheric force above an unknown city situate somewhere in the Great Desert,—and some one in that city was conversing with her by a method of "wireless" as yet undiscovered by admitted science,—yet communication was perfect and words distinct. Following up the suggestion presented to her she said—

"You are speaking to me in English. Are you all English folk in your city?"

A faint quiver as of laughter vibrated through the "Sound Ray."

"No, indeed! We have no nationality."

"No nationality?"

"None. We are one people. But we speak every language that ever has been spoken in the past, or is spoken in the present. I speak English to you because it is your manner of talk, though not your manner of life."

"How do you know it is not my manner of life?"

"Because you are not happy in it. Your manner of life is ours. It has nothing to do with nations or peoples. You are Morgana."

"And you?" she cried with sudden eagerness—"Oh, who are you that speak to me?—man, woman, or angel? What are the dwellers in your city, if it is in truth a city, and not a dream!"

"Look again and see!" answered the Voice—"Convince yourself!—do not be deceived! You are not dreaming—Look and make yourself sure!"

Impelled to movement, she went to the window which she had left to take up the steering-gear,—and from there saw again the wonderful scene spread out below, the towers, spires, cupolas and bridges, all lit with that mysterious golden luminance like smouldering sunset fire.

"It is beautiful!" she said—"It seems true—it seems real—"

"It Is true-it Is real!"—the Voice replied—"It has been seen by many travellers,—but because they can never approach it they call it a desert 'mirage.' It is more real and more lasting than any other city in the world."

"Can I never enter it?" she asked, appealingly—"Will you never let me in?"

There was a silence, which seemed to her very long. Still standing at the window of her cabin she looked down on the shining city, a broad stretch of splendid gold luminance under the canopy of the dark sky with its millions of stars. Then the Voice answered her—

"Yes—if you come alone!"

These words sounded so close to her ear that she felt sure the speaker must be standing beside her.

"I will come!" she said, impulsively—"Somehow—some way!—no matter how difficult or dangerous! I will come!"

As she spoke she was conscious of a curious vibration round her, as though some other thing than the ceaseless, silent throbbing of the air-ship's mechanism had disturbed the atmosphere.

"Wait!" said the Voice—"You say this without thought. You do not realise the meaning of your words. For—if you come, you must stay!"

A thrill ran through her blood.

"I must stay!" she echoed—"Why?"

"Because you have learned the Life-Secret,"—answered the Voice—"And, as you have learned it, so must you live. I will tell you more if you care to hear—"

An inrush of energy came to her as she listened—she felt that the unseen speaker acknowledged the power which she herself knew she possessed.

"With all my soul I care to hear!" she said—"But where do you speak from? And who are you that speak?"

"I speak from the central Watch-Tower,"—the Voice replied—"The City is guarded from that point—and from there we can send messages all over the world in every known language. Sometimes they are understood—more often they are ignored,—but we, who have lived since before the coming of Christ, have no concern with such as do not or will not hear. Our business is to wait and watch while the ages go by,— wait and watch till we are called forth to the new world. Sometimes our messages cross the 'wireless' Marconi system—and some confusion happens—but generally the 'Sound Ray' carries straight to its mark. You must well understand all that is implied when you say you will come to us,—it means that you leave the human race as you have known it and unite yourself with another human race as yet unknown to the world!"

Here was an overwhelming mystery—but, nothing daunted, Morgana pursued her enquiry.

"You can talk to me on the Sound Ray"—she said—"And I understand its possibility. You should equally be able to project your own portrait—a true similitude of yourself—on a Light Ray. Let me see you!"

"You are something of a wilful spirit!" answered the Voice—"But you know many secrets of our science and their results. So—as you wish it—"

Another second, and the cabin was filled with a pearly lustre like the vapour which sweeps across the hills in an early summer dawn—and in the center of this as in an aureole stood a nobly proportioned figure, clad in gold-coloured garments fashioned after the early Greek models. Presumably this personage was human,—but never was a semblance of humanity so transfigured. The face and form were those of a beautiful youth,—the eyes were deep and brilliant,—and the expression of the features was one of fine serenity and kindliness. Morgana gazed and gazed, bending herself towards her wonderful visitor with all her soul in her eyes,—when suddenly the vision, if so it might be called, paled and vanished. She uttered a little cry.

"Oh, why have you gone so soon?" she exclaimed.

"It is not I who have gone,"—replied the Voice—"It is only the reflection of me. We cannot project a light picture too far or too long. And even now—when you come to us—if you ever do come!—do you think you will remember me?"

"How could I forget anyone so beautiful!" she said, with passionate enthusiasm.

This time the Sound Ray conveyed a vibration of musical laughter.

"Where every being has beauty for a birthright, how should you know me more than another!" said the Voice—"Beauty is common to all in our city—as common as health, because we obey the Divine laws of both."

She stretched out her hands appealingly.

"Oh, if I could only come to you now!" she murmured.

"Patience!" and the Voice grew softer—"There is something for you to do in the world. You must lose a love before you find it!"

She drew a quick breath. What could these words mean?

"It is time for you now to turn homeward,"—went on the Voice—"You must not be seen above this City at dawn. You would be attacked and instantly destroyed, as having received a warning which you refused to heed."

"Do you attack and destroy all strangers so?" she asked—"Is that your rule?"

"It is our rule to keep away the mischief of the modern world"—replied the Voice—"As well admit a pestilence as the men and women of to-day!"

"I am a woman of to-day,"—said Morgana.

"No, you are not,—you are a woman of the future!" and the Voice was grave and insistent—"You are one of the new race. At the appointed hour you will take your part with us in the new world?"

"When will be that hour?"

There was a pause. Then, with an exceeding sweetness and solemnity the Voice replied—

"If He will that we tarry till He come, what is that to thee?"

A sense of great awe swept over her, oppressive and humiliating. She looked once more through her cabin window at the city spread out below, and saw that some of the lights were being extinguished in the taller buildings and on the bridges which connected streets and avenues in a network of architectural beauty.

The Voice spoke again—

"We are releasing you from the barrier. You are free to depart."

She sighed.

"I have no wish to go!" she said.

"You must!" The Voice became commanding. "If you stay now, you and your companions are doomed to perish. There is no alternative. Be satisfied that we know you—we watch you—we shall expect you sooner or later. Meanwhile—guide your ship!—the way is open."

Quickly she sprang to the steering-gear—she felt the "White Eagle" moving, and lifting its vast wings for flight.

"Farewell!" she cried, with a sense of tears in her throat—"Farewell!"

"Not farewell!" came the reply, spoken softly and with tenderness— "We shall meet again soon! I will speak to you in Sicily!"

"In Sicily!" she exclaimed, joyfully—"You will speak to me there?"

"There and everywhere!" answered the Voice—"The Sound Ray knows no distance. I shall speak—and you shall hear—whenever you will!"

The last syllables died away like faintly sung music—and in a few more seconds the great air-ship was sailing steadily in a level line and at a swift pace onward,—the last shining glimpse of the mysterious City vanished, and the "White Eagle" soared over a sable blackness of empty desert, through a dark space besprinkled with stars. Filled with a new sense of power and gladness, Morgana held the vessel in the guidance of her slight but strong hands, and it had flown many miles before the Marchese Rivardi sprang up suddenly from where he had lain lost in unconsciousness and stared around him amazed and confused.

"A thousand pardons, Madama!" he stammered—"I shall never forgive myself! I have been asleep!"

XIX

A t almost the same moment Gaspard stumbled to his feet.

"Asleep—asleep!" he exclaimed—"*Mon Dieu!*—the shame of it!—the shame! What pigs are men! To sleep after food and wine, and to leave a woman alone like this! . . . the shame!"

Morgana, quietly steering the "White Eagle," smiled.

"Poor Gaspard!" she said—"You could not help it! You were so tired! And you, Marchese! You were both quite worn out! I was glad to see you sleeping—there is no shame in it! As I have often told you, I can manage the ship alone."

But Rivardi was white with anger and self-reproach.

"Gross pigs we are!" he said, hotly—"Gaspard is right! And yet—" here he passed a hand across his brow and tried to collect his thoughts—"yes!—surely something unusual must have happened! We heard bells ringing—"

Morgana watched him closely, her hand on her air-vessel's helm.

"Yes—we all thought we heard bells"—she said—"But that was a noise in our own brains—the clamour of our own blood brought on by pressure—we were flying at too great a height and the tension was too strong—"

Gaspard threw out his hands with a half defiant gesture.

"No, Madama! It could not be so! I swear we never left our own level! What happened I cannot tell—but I felt that I was struck by a sudden blow—and I fell without force to recover—"

"Sleep struck you that sudden blow, you poor Gaspard!" said Morgana, "And you have not slept so long—barely an hour—just long enough for me to hover a while above this black desert and then turn homeward,—I want no more of the Sahara!"

Rivardi, smarting under a sense of loss and incompetency, went up to her.

"Give me the helm!" he said, almost sharply—"You have done enough!"

She resigned her place to him, smiling at his irritation.

"You are sure you are quite rested?" she asked.

"Rested!" he echoed the word disdainfully—"I should never have rested at all had I been half the man I profess to be! Why do you turn back? I thought you were bent on exploring the Great Desert!—that you meant to try and find the traditional Brazen City?"

She shrugged her shoulders.

"I do not like the prospect"—she said—"There is nothing but sand—interminable billows of sand! I can well believe it was all ocean once,—when the earth gave a sudden tilt, and all the water was thrown off from one surface to another. If we could dig deep enough below the sand I think we should find remains of wrecked ships, with the skeletons of antediluvian men and animals, remains of one of the many wasted civilisations—"

"You do not answer me—" interrupted Rivardi with impatience—"What of your search for the Brazen City?"

She raised her lovely, mysterious eyes and looked full at him.

"Do you believe it exists?" she asked.

He gave a gesture of annoyance.

"Whether I believe or not is of no importance,"—he answered—"You have some idea about it, and you have every means of proving the truth of your idea—yet, after making the journey from Sicily for the purpose, you suddenly turn back!"

Still she kept her eyes upon him.

"You must not mind the caprices of a woman!" she said, with a smile—"And do please remember the 'Brazen City' is not MY idea! The legend of this undiscovered place in the desert was related by your friend Don Aloysius—and he was careful to say it was 'only' a legend. Why should you think I accept it as a truth?"

"Surely it was the motive of your flight here?" he demanded, imperatively.

Her brows drew together in a slight frown.

"My dear Marchese, I allow no one to question my motives"—she said with sudden coldness—"That I have decided to go no farther in search of the Brazen City is my own affair."

"But—not even to wait for the full daylight!" he expostulated—"You could not see it by night even if it existed!"

"Not unless it was lit like other cities!" she said, smiling—"I suppose if such a city existed, its inhabitants would need some sort of illuminant—they would not grope about in the dark. In that case it would be seen from our ship as well by night as by day."

Gaspard, busy with some mechanical detail, looked up.

"Then why not make a search for it while we are here?" he said—"You evidently believe in it!"

"I have turned the 'White Eagle' homeward, and shall not turn again"—she said—"But I do not see any reason why such a city should not exist and be discovered some day. Explorers in tropical forests find the remains or beginnings of a different race of men from our own—pygmies, and such like beings—there is nothing really against the possibility of an undiscovered City in the Great Desert. We modern folk think we know a great deal—but our wisdom is very superficial and our knowledge limited. We have not mastered EVERYTHING under the sun!"

The Marchese Rivardi looked at her with something of defiance in his glance.

"I will adventure in search of the legendary city myself, alone!" he said.

Morgana laughed, her clear little cold laugh of disdain.

"Do so, my friend! Why not?" she said—"You are a daring airman on many forms of airships—I knew that,—before I entrusted you with the scheme of mine. Discover the legendary 'Brazen City' if you can!—I promise not to be jealous!—and return to the world of curiosity mongers—(also, if you CAN!) with a full report of its inhabitants and their manners and customs. And so—you will become famous! But you must not fall asleep on the way!"

He paled with anger and annoyance,—she still smiled.

"Do not be cross, AMICO!" she said, sweetly. "Think where we are!—in the wide spaces of heaven, pilgrims with the stars! This is no place for personal feeling of either disappointment or irritation. You asked me a while ago if I was tired—I thought I was Hot, but I am—very tired!—I am going to rest. And I trust you both to take care of me and the 'White Eagle'!"

"We are to make straight for Sicily?" he asked.

"Yes—straight for Sicily."

She retired into her sleeping-cabin and disappeared. The Marchese Rivardi looked at Gaspard questioningly.

"We must obey her, I suppose?"

"We could not think of disobeying!" returned Gaspard.

"She is a strange woman!" and as he spoke Rivardi gripped his steering-gear with a kind of vindictive force—"It seems absurd that we,—two men of fair intelligence and scientific attainment,—should be ruled by her whim,—her fancies—for after all she is made up of fancies—"

Gaspard shook his finger warningly.

"This air-ship is not a 'whim' or a 'fancy'"—he said, impressively—"It is the most wonderful thing of its kind ever invented! If it is given to the world it will revolutionise the whole system of aerial navigation. Here we are, flying at top speed in perfect ease and safety with no engine—nothing to catch fire—nothing to break or bust—and the whole mechanism mysteriously makes its own motive power as it goes. Radio-activity it may be—but its condensation and use for such a purpose is the secret invention of a woman—and surely we must admit her genius! As for our obedience—ECCELLENZA, we are both royally paid to obey!"

Rivardi flushed red.

"I know!" he said, curtly—"I never forget it. But money is not everything."

Gaspard's mobile French face lit up with a mirthful smile.

"It is most things!" he replied—"Without it even science is crippled. And this lady has so much of it!—it seems without end! Again,—it is seldom one meets with money and brains and beauty—all together!"

"Beauty?" Rivardi queried.

"Why, yes!—beauty that only flashes out at moments—of all beauty the most fascinating! A face that is always beautiful is fatiguing,—it is the changeful face with endless play of expression that enthralls,—or so it is to me!" And Gaspard gave an eloquent gesture—"This lady we both work for seems to have no lovers—but if she had, not one of them could ever forget her!"

Rivardi was silent.

"I should not wonder," ventured Gaspard, presently—"if—while we slept—she had seen her 'Brazen City'!"

Rivardi uttered something like an oath.

"Impossible!" he exclaimed—"She would have awakened us!"

"If she could, no doubt!" agreed Gaspard—"But if she could not, how then?"

For a moment Rivardi looked puzzled,—then he dismissed his companion's suggestion with a contemptuous shrug.

"Basta! There is no 'Brazen City'! When she heard the old tradition she was like a child with a fairy tale—a child who, reading of strawberries growing in the winter snow, goes out forthwith to find them—she did not really believe in it—but it pleased her to imagine she did. The mere sight of the arid empty desert has been enough for her."

"We certainly heard bells"—said Gaspard.

"In our brains! Such sounds often affect the nerves when flying for a long while at high speed. For all our cleverness we are only human. I have heard on the 'wireless,' sounds that do not seem of this world at all."

"So have I"—said Gaspard—"And though it may be my own brain talking, I'm not so obstinate in my own knowledge as to doubt a possible existing means of communication between one continent and another apart from OUR special 'wireless.' In fact I'm sure there is something of the kind,—though where it comes from and how it travels I cannot say. But certain people get news of occurring events somehow, from somewhere, long before it reaches Paris or London. I dare say the lady we are with could tell us something about it."

"Her powers are not limitless!" said Rivardi—"She is only a woman after all!"

Gaspard said no more, and there followed a silence,—a silence all the more tense and deep because of the amazing swiftness with which the "White Eagle" kept its steady level flight, making no sound despite the rapidity of its movement. Very gradually the darkness of night lifted, as it were, one corner of its sable curtain to show a grey peep-hole of dawn, and soon it became apparent that the ship was already far away from the mysterious land of Egypt—"The land shadowing with wings"—and was flying over the sea. There was something terrific in the complete noiselessness with which it sped through the air, and Rivardi, though now he had a good grip on his nerves, hardly dared allow himself to think of the adventurous business on which he was engaged. A certain sense of pride and triumph filled him, to realise that he had been selected from many applicants for the post he occupied—and yet with all his satisfaction there went a lurking spirit of envy and disappointed ambition. If he could win Morgana's love—if he could make the strange elfin creature with all her genius and inventive ability his own,—why then!—what then? He would share in her fame,—aye, more than share it, since it is the way of the world to give its honour to no woman whose life is connected with that of a man. The man receives the acknowledgment invariably, even if he has done nothing to deserve it, and herein is the reason why many gifted women do not marry, and prefer to stand alone in effort and achievement rather than have their hardly won renown filched from them by unjust hands. When Roger Seaton confessed to the girl Manella that his real desire was to bend and subdue Morgana's intellectuality to his own, he spoke the truth, not only for himself but for all men. Absolutely disinterested love for a brilliantly endowed woman would be difficult to find in any male nature,—men love what is inferior to themselves, not superior. Thus women who are endowed with more than common intellectual ability have to choose one of two alternatives—love, or what is called love, and child-bearing,—or fame, and lifelong loneliness.

The Marchese Rivardi, thinking along the usual line of masculine logic, had frequently turned over the problem of Morgana's complex character such as it appeared to him,—and had almost come to the conclusion that if he only had patience he would succeed in persuading her that wifehood and motherhood were more conducive to a woman's happiness than all the most amazing triumphs of scientific discovery and attainment. He was perfectly right according to simple natural law,—but he chose to forget that women's mental outlook has, in these modern days, been greatly widened,—whether for their gain or loss it is not yet easy to say. Even for men "much knowledge increaseth sorrow,"—and it may be hinted that women, with their often overstrung emotions and exaggerated sentiments, are not fit to plunge deeply into studies which tax the brain to its utmost capacity and try the nerves beyond the level of the calm which is essential to health. Though it has to be admitted that married life is less peaceful than hard study— and the bright woman who recently said, "A husband is more trying than any problem in Euclid," no doubt had good cause for the remark. Married or single, woman both physically and mentally is the greatest sufferer in the world—her time of youth and unthinking joy is brief, her martyrdom long—and it is hardly wonderful that she goes so often "to the bad" when there is so little offered to attract her towards the good.

Rivardi, letting himself go on the flood-tide of hope and ambition, pleased his mind with imaginary pictures of Morgana as his wife and as mother of his children, rehabilitating his fallen fortunes, restoring his once great house and building a fresh inheritance for its former renown. He saw no reason why this should not be,—yet—even while he indulged in his thoughts of her, he knew well enough that behind her small delicate personality there was a powerful intellectual "lens," so to speak, through which she examined the ins and outs of character in man or woman; and he felt that he was always more or less under this "lens," looked at as carefully as a scientist might study bacteria, and that as a matter of fact it was as unlikely as the descent of the moon-goddess to Endymion that she would ever submit herself to his possession. Nevertheless, he argued, stranger things had happened!

The grey peep of dawn widened into a silver rift, and the silver rift streamed into a bar of gold, and the gold broke up into long strands of blush pink and pale blue like festal banners hanging in heaven's bright pavilion, and the "White Eagle" flew on swiftly, steadily, securely, among all the glories of the dawn like a winged car for the conveyance of angels. And both Rivardi and Gaspard thought they were not far from the realisation of an angel when Morgana suddenly appeared at the door of her sleeping-cabin, attired in a fleecy-wool gown of purest white, her wonderful gold hair unbound and falling nearly to her feet.

"What a perfect morning!" she exclaimed—"All things seem new! And I have had such a good rest! The air is so pure and clean—surely we are over the sea?"

"We are some fifteen thousand feet above the Mediterranean"— answered Rivardi, looking at her as he spoke with unconcealed admiration;—never, he thought, had she seemed so charming, youthful and entirely lovable—"I am glad you have rested—you look quite refreshed and radiant. After all, it is a test of endurance—this journey to Egypt and back."

"Do you think so?" and Morgana smiled—"It should be nothing—it really is nothing! We ought to be quite ready and willing to travel like this for a week on end! But you and Gaspard are not yet absolutely sure of our motive power!—you cannot realise that as long as we keep going so long will our 'going' force be generated without effort—yet surely it is proved!"

Gaspard lifted his eyes towards her where she stood like a little white Madonna in a shrine.

"Yes, Madama, it is proved!" he said—"But the secret of its proving?—"

"Ah! That, for the present, remains locked up in the mystery box— here!" and she tapped her forehead with her finger—"The world is not ready for it. The world is a destructive savage, loving evil rather than good, and it would work mischief more than usefulness with such a force—if it knew! Now I will dress, and give you breakfast in ten minutes."

She waved a hand to them and disappeared, returning after a brief interval attired in her "aviation" costume and cap. Soon she had prepared quite a tempting breakfast on the table.

"Thermos coffee!" she said, gaily—"All hot and hot! We could have had Thermos tea, but I think coffee more inspiriting. Tea always reminds me of an afternoon at a country vicarage where good ladies sit round a table and talk of babies and rheumatism. Kind,—but so dull! Come—you must take it in turns—you, Marchese, first, while Gaspard steers—and Gaspard next—just as you did last night at what we called dinner, before you fell asleep! Men Do fall asleep after dinner you know!—it's quite ordinary. Married men especially!—I think they do it to avoid conversation with their wives!"

She laughed, and her eyes flashed mirthfully as Rivardi seated himself opposite to her at table.

"Well, *I* am not married"—he said, rather petulantly—"Nor is Gaspard. But some day we may fall into temptation and NOT be delivered from evil."

"Ah yes!" and Morgana shook her fair head at him with mock dolefulness—"And that will be very sad! Though nowadays it will not bind you to a fettered existence. Marriage has ceased to be a sacrament,—you can leave your wives as soon as you get tired of them,—or—they can leave YOU!"

Rivardi looked at her with reproach in his handsome face and dark eyes.

"You read the modern Press"—he said—"A pity you do!"

"Yes—it's a pity anyone reads it!"—she answered—"But what are we to read? If low-minded and illiterate scavengers are employed to write for the newspapers instead of well-educated men, we must put up with the mud the scavengers collect. We know well enough that every journal is more or less a calendar of lies,—all the same we cannot blind ourselves to the great change that has come over manners and morals—particularly in relation to marriage. Of course the Press always chronicles the worst items bearing on the subject—"

"The Press is chiefly to blame for it"—declared Rivardi.

"Oh, I think not!" and Morgana smiled as she poured out a second cup of coffee—"The Press cannot create a new universe. No—I think human nature alone is to blame—if blame there be. Human nature is tired."

"Tired?" echoed Rivardi—"In what way?"

"In every way!"—and a lovely light of tenderest pity filled her eyes as she spoke—"Tired of the same old round of working, mating, breeding and dying—for no results really worth having! Civilisation after civilisation has arisen—always with strife and difficulty, only to pass away, leaving, in many cases, scarce a memory. Human nature begins to weary of the continuous 'grind'—it demands the 'why' of its ceaseless labour. Latterly, poor striving men and women have been deprived of faith—they used to believe they had a loving Father in Heaven who cared for them,—but the monkeys of the race, the atheists, swinging from point to point of argument and chattering all the time, have persuaded them that they are as Tennyson once mournfully wrote—"

"Poor orphans of nothing—alone on that lonely shore,
Born of the brainless Nature who knew not that which she bore!"

"Can we wonder then that they are tired?—tired of pursuing a useless quest? Human nature is craving for a change—for a newer world—a newer race,—and those who see that Nature is Not 'brainless' but full of intelligent conception, are sure that the change will come!"

"And you are one of 'those who see'?—" said Rivardi, incredulously.

"I do not say I am,—that would be too much self-assertion"—she answered—"But I hope I am! I long to see the world endowed more richly with health and happiness. See how gloriously the sun has risen! In what splendour of light and air we are sailing! If we can do as much as this we ought to be able to do more!"

"We shall do more in time"—he said—"The advance of one step leads to another."

"In time!" echoed Morgana—"What time the human race has already taken to find out the simplest forces of nature! It is the horrible bulk of blank stupidity that hinders knowledge—the heavy obstinate bulk that declines to budge an inch out of its own fixity. Nowadays we triumph in our so-called 'discoveries' of wireless telegraphy and telephony, light-rays and other marvels—but these powers have always been with us from the beginning of things,—it is we, we only, who have refused to accept them as facts of the universe. Let us talk no more about it!—Stupidity is the only thing that moves me to despair!"

She rose from the little table, and called Gaspard to breakfast, while Rivardi went back to the business of steering. The day was now fully declared, and the great air-ship soared easily in a realm of ethereal blue—blue above, blue below—its vast wings moving up and down with perfect rhythm as if it were a living, sentient creature, revelling in the joys of flight. For the rest of the day Morgana was very silent, contenting herself to sit in her charming little rose-lined nest of a room, and read,—now and then looking out on the radiating space around her, and watching for the first slight downward movement of the "White Eagle" towards land. She had plenty to occupy her thoughts—and strange to say she did not consider as anything unexpected or remarkable, her brief communication with the "Brazen City." On the contrary it seemed quite a natural happening. Of course it had always been there, she said to herself,—only people were too dull and unenterprising to discover it,—besides, if they had ever found it (certain travellers having declared they had seen it in the distance) they would not have been allowed to approach it. This fact was the one point that chiefly dwelt in her mind—a secret of science which she puzzled her brain to fathom. What could be the unseen force that guarded the city?—girding it round with an unbreakable band from all exterior attack? A million bombs could not penetrate it,—so had said the Voice travelling to her ears on the mysterious Sound Ray. She thought of Shakespeare's lines on England—

> *"This precious stone set in the silver sea*
> *Which serves it in the office of a wall,*
> *Or as a moat defensive to a house*
> *Against the envy of less happy lands."*

Modern science had made the sea useless as a "wall" or "moat defensive" against attacks from the air,—but if there existed an atmospheric or "etheric" force which could be utilised and brought to such pressure as to encircle a city or a country with a protective ring that should resist all effort to break it, how great a security would be assured "against the envy of less happy lands"! Here was a problem for study,—study of the intricate character which she loved—and she became absorbed in what she called "thinking for results," a form of introspection which she knew, from experience, sometimes let in unexpected light on the creative cells of the brain and impelled them to the evolving of hitherto untried suggestions. She sat quietly with a book before her, not reading, but bent on seeking ways and means for the safety and protection of nations,—as bent as Roger Seaton was on a force for their destruction. So the hours passed swiftly, and no interruption or untoward obstacle hindered the progress of the "White Eagle" as it careered through the halcyon blue of the calmest, loveliest sky that ever made perfect weather, till late afternoon when it began to glide almost insensibly downward towards earth. Then she roused herself from her long abstraction and looked through the window of her cabin, watching what seemed to be the gradual rising of the land towards the air-ship, showing in little green and brown patches like the squares of a chess-board,—then the houses and towns, tiny as children's

MARIE CORELLI

toys—then the azure gleam of the sea and the boats dancing like bits of cork upon it,—then finally the plainer, broader view, wherein the earth with its woods and hills and rocky promontories appeared to heave up like a billow crowned with varying colours,—and so steadily, easily down to the pattern of grass and flowers from the centre of which the Palazzo d'Oro rose like a little white house for the abode of fairies.

"Well steered!" said Morgana, as the ship ran into its shed with the accuracy of a sword slipping into its sheath, and the soundless vibration of its mysterious motive-power ceased—"Home again safely!—and only away forty-eight hours! To the Sahara and back!—how far we have been, and what we have seen!"

"WE have seen nothing"—said Rivardi meaningly, as he assisted her to alight—"The seeing is all with You!"

"And the believing!" she answered, smiling—"All my thanks to you both for your skilful pilotage. You must be very tired—" here she gave her hand to them each in turn—"Again a thousand thanks! No air-ship could be better manned!"

"Or woman'd?" suggested Rivardi.

She laughed.

"IF you like! But I only steered while you slept. That is nothing! Good night!"

She left them, running up the garden path lightly like a child returning from a holiday, and disappeared.

"But that which she calls nothing"—said Gaspard as he watched her go—"is everything!"

XX

For some days after her adventurous voyage to the Great Desert and back Morgana chose to remain in absolute seclusion. Save for Lady Kingswood and her own household staff, she saw no one, and was not accessible even to Don Aloysius, who called several times, moved not only by interest, but genuine curiosity, to enquire how she fared. Many of the residents in the vicinity of the Palazzo d'Oro had gleaned scraps of information here and there concerning the wonderful airship which they had seen careering over their heads during its testing trials, and as a matter of course they had heard more than scraps in regard to its wealthy owner. But nowadays keen desire to know and to investigate has given place to a sort of civil apathy which passes for good form—that absolute indifferentism which is too much bored to care about other people's affairs, and which would not disturb itself if it heard of a neighbour deciding to cross the Atlantic in a washtub. "Nothing matters," is the general verdict on all events and circumstances. Nevertheless, the size, the swiftness and soundlessness of the "White Eagle" and the secrecy observed in its making, had somewhat moved the heavy lump of human dough called "society," and the whispered novelty of Morgana's invention had reached Rome and Paris, nay, almost London, without her consent or knowledge. So that she was more or less deluged with letters; and noted scientists, both in France and Italy, though all incredulous as to her attainment, made it a point of "business" to learn all they could about her, which was not much more than can be usually learned about any wealthy woman or man with a few whims to gratify. A murderer gains access to the whole press,—his look, his manner, his remarks, are all carefully noted and commented upon,—but a scientist, an explorer, a man or woman whose work is that of beneficence and use to humanity, is barely mentioned except in the way of a sneer. So it often chances that the public know nothing of its greatest till they have passed beyond the reach of worldly honour.

Morgana, however, had no desire that her knowledge or attainment should be admitted or praised. She was entirely destitute of ambition. She had read too much and studied too deeply to care for so-called "fame," which, as she knew, is the mere noise of one moment, to be lost in silence the next. She was self-centered and yet not selfish. She felt that to understand her own entity, its mental and physical composition, and the possibilities of its future development, was sufficient to fill her life—that life which she quite instinctively recognised as bearing within itself the seed of immortality. Her strange interview with the "Voice" from the City in the Desert, and the glimpse she had been permitted to see of the owner of that voice, had not so much surprised her as convinced her of a theory she had long held,—namely that there were other types of the human race existing, unknown to the generality of ordinary men and women—types that were higher in their organisation and mental capacity,—types which by reason of their very advancement kept themselves hidden and aloof from modern civilisation. And she forthwith plunged anew into the ocean of scientific problems, where she floated like a strong swimmer at ease with her mind upturned to the stars.

Yet she did not neglect the graceful comforts and elegancies of the Palazzo d'Oro, and life went on in that charming abode peacefully. Morgana always being the kindest of patrons to Lady Kingswood, and discoursing feminine commonplaces with her as though there were no other subjects of conversation in the world than embroidery and specific cures for rheumatism. She said little—indeed almost nothing,—of her aerial voyage to the East, except that she had enjoyed it, and that the Pyramids and the Sphinx were dwarfed into mere insignificant dots on the land as seen from the air,—she had apparently nothing more to describe, and Lady Kingswood was not sufficiently interested in air-travel to press enquiry. One bright sunny morning, after a week of her self-imposed seclusion, she announced her intention of calling at the monastery to see Don Aloysius.

"I have been rather rude"—she said—"Of course he has wanted to know how my flight to the East went off!—and I have given no sign and sent no message."

"He has called several times"—replied Lady Kingswood—"and I think he has been very much disappointed not to be received."

"Poor reverend Father!" and Morgana smiled—"He should not bother his mind about a woman! Well! I'm going to see him now."

Lady Kingswood looked at her critically. She was gowned in a simple white morning frock with touches of blue,—and she wore a broad-brimmed Tuscan straw hat with a fold of blue carelessly twined about it. She made a pretty picture—one of extraordinary youthfulness for any woman out of her 'teens—so much so that Lady Kingswood wondered if voyages in the air would be found to have a rejuvenating effect.

"They do not admit women into the actual monastery"—she went on—"Feminine frivolities are forbidden! But the ruined cloister is open to visitors and I shall ask to see Don Aloysius there."

She lightly waved adieu and went, leaving her amiable and contented chaperone to the soothing companionship of a strip of embroidery at which she worked with the leisurely tranquillity which such an occupation engenders.

The ruined cloister looked very beautiful that morning, with its crumbling arches crowned and festooned with roses climbing every way at their own sweet will, and Morgana's light figure gave just the touch of human interest to the solemn peacefulness of the scene. She waited but two or three minutes before Don Aloysius appeared—he had seen her arrive from the window of his own private library. He approached her slowly—there was a gravity in the expression of his face that almost amounted to coldness, and no smile lightened it as she met his keen, fixed glance.

"So you have come to me at last!" he said—"I have not merited your confidence till now! Why?"

His rich voice had a ring of deep reproach in its tone—and she was for a moment taken aback. Then her native self-possession and perfect assurance returned.

"Dear Father Aloysius, you do not want my confidence! You know all I can tell you!" she said—and drawing close to him she laid her hand on his arm—"Am I not right?"

A tremor shook him—gently he put her hand aside.

"You think I know!" he replied—"You imagine—"

"Oh, no, I imagine nothing!" and she smiled—"I am sure—yes, Sure!—that you have the secret of things that seem fabulous and yet are true! It was you who first told me of the Brazen City in the Great Desert,—you said it was a mere tradition—but you filled my mind with a desire to find it—"

"And you found it?" he interrupted, quickly—"You found it?"

"You know I did!" she replied—"Why ask the question? Messages on a Sound-Ray can reach You, as well as me!"

He moved to the stone bench which occupied a corner of the cloister and sat down. He was very pale and his eyes were feverishly bright. Presently he seemed to recover himself, and spoke more in his usual manner.

"Rivardi has been here every day"—he said—"He has talked of

nothing but you. He told me that he and Gaspard fell suddenly asleep—for which they were grievously ashamed of themselves—and that you took control of the air-ship and turned it homeward before you had given them any chance to explore the desert—"

"Quite true!" she answered, tranquilly—"And—You knew all that before he told you! You knew that I was compelled to turn the ship homeward because it was not allowed to proceed! Dear Father Aloysius, you cannot hide yourself from me! You are one of the few who have studied the secrets of the approaching future,—the 'change' which is imminent—the 'world to come' which is coming! Yes!—and you are brave to live as you do in the fetters of a conventional faith when you have such a far wider outlook—"

He stopped her by a gesture, rising from where he sat and extending a hand of warning and authority.

"Child, beware what you say!" and his voice had a ring of sternness in its mellow tone—"If I know what you think I know, on what ground do you suppose I have built my knowledge? Only on that faith which you call 'conventional'—that faith which has never been understood by the world's majority! That faith which teaches of the God-in-Man, done to death by the Man WITHOUT God in him!—and who, nevertheless, by the spiritual strength of a resurrection from the grave, proves that there is no death but only continuous renewal of life! This is no mere 'convention' of faith,—no imaginary or traditional tale—it is pure scientific fact. The virginal conception of divinity in woman, and the transfiguration of manhood, these things are true—and the advance of scientific discovery will prove them so beyond all denial. We have held the faith, As It Should Be Held, for centuries,—and it has led us, and continues to lead us, to all we know."

"We?" queried Morgana, softly—"We—of the Church?—or of the Brazen City?"

He looked at her for some moments without speaking. His tall fine figure seemed more than ever stately and imposing—and his features expressed a calm assurance and dignity of thought which gave them additional charm.

"Your question is bold!" he said—"Your enterprising spirit stops at nothing! You have learned much—you are resolved to learn more! Well,—I cannot prevent you,—nor do I see any reason why I should try! You are a resolved student,—you are also a woman:—a woman different to ordinary women and set apart from ordinary womanhood. So I say to you 'We of the Brazen City'—if you will! For more than three thousand years 'we' have existed—'we' have studied, 'we' have discovered—'we' have known. 'We,' the selected offspring of all the race that ever were born,—'we,' the pure blood of the earth,—'we,' the progenitors of the world To Be,—'we' have lived, watching temporary civilisations rise and fall,—seeing generations born and die, because, like weeds, they have grown without any root of purpose save to smother their neighbours and destroy. 'We' remain as commanded, waiting for the full declaration and culmination of those forces which are already advancing to the end,—when the 'Kingdom' comes!"

Morgana moved close to him, and looked up at his grave, dark face beseechingly.

"Then why are you here?" she asked—"If you know,—if you were ever in the 'Brazen City' how did it happen that you left it? How could it happen?"

He smiled down into the jewel-blue of her clear eyes.

"Little child!" he said—"Brilliant soul, that rejoiced in the perception that gave you what you called 'the inside of a sun-ray,'—you, for whom the things which interest men and women of the moment are mere toys of poor invention—you, of all others, ought to know that when the laws of the universe are understood and followed, there can be no fetters on the true liberty of the subject? If I were ever in the 'Brazen City'—mind! I say 'if'—there could be nothing to prevent my leaving it if I chose—"

She interrupted him by the uplifting of a hand.

"I was told"—she said slowly—"by a Voice that spoke to me—that if I went there I should have to stay there!"

"No doubt!" he answered—"For love would keep you!"

"Love!" she echoed.

"Even so! Such love as you have never dreamed of, dear soul weighted with millions of gold! Love!—the only force that pulls heaven to earth and binds them together!"

"But You—you—if you were in the Brazen City—"

"If!" he repeated, emphatically.

"If—yes! if"—she said—"If you were there, love did not hold You?"

"No!"

There was a silence. The sunshine burned down on the ancient grey flagstones of the cloister, and two gorgeous butterflies danced over the climbing roses that hung from the arches in festal wreaths of pink and white. A luminance deeper than that of the sun seemed to encircle the figures standing together—the one so elfin, light and delicate,—the other invested with a kind of inward royalty expressing itself outwardly in stateliness of look and bearing. Something mysteriously suggestive of super-humanity environed them; a spirit and personality higher than mortal. After some minutes Aloysius spoke again—

"The city is not a 'Brazen' City"—he said—"It has been called so by travellers who have seen its golden towers glistening afar off in a sudden refraction of light lasting but a few seconds. Gold often looks like brass and brass like gold, in human entities as in architectural results." He paused—then went on slowly and impressively—"Surely you remember,-you MUST remember, that it is written 'The city lieth four-square, and the length is as large as the breadth. The wall thereof is according to the measure of a man—that is, of the Angel. And the city is of pure gold.' Does that give you no hint of the measure of a man, that is, of the Angel?—of the 'new heavens and the new earth,' the old things being passed away? Dear child, you have studied deeply—you have adventured far and greatly!—continue your quest, but do not forget to take your guiding Light, the Faith which half the world and more ignores!"

She sprang to him impulsively and caught his hands.

"Oh, you must help me!" she cried—"You must teach me—I want to know what YOU know!—"

He held her gently and with reverent tenderness.

"I know no more than you,"—he answered—"you work by Science—I, by Faith, the bed-rock from Which all science proceeds—and we arrive at the same discoveries by different methods. I am a poor priest in the temple of the Divine, serving my turn—but I am not alone in service, for in every corner of the habitable globe there is one member of our 'City' who communicates with the rest. One!—but enough! To-day's commercial world uses old systems of wireless telegraphy and telephony which were known and done with thousands of years ago—but 'we' have the sound-ray—the light which carries music on its wings and creates form as it goes."

Here he released her hands.

"Knowing what you do know you have no need of my help"—he continued—"You have not found happiness yet, because that only comes through one source—Love. But I doubt not that God will give you that in His own good time." He paused—then went on—"As you go out, enter the chapel for a moment and send a prayer on the Sound-Ray to the Centre of all Knowledge,—the source of all discovery—have no fear but that it will arrive! The rest is for you to decide."

She hesitated.

"And—the Brazen City?" she queried.

"The Golden City!" he answered—"Well, you have had your experience! Your name is known there—and no doubt you can hear from it when you will."

"Do You hear from it?" she asked, pointedly.

He smiled gravely.

"I may not speak of what I hear"—he answered. "Nor may you!"

She was silent for a space—then looked up at him appealingly.

"The world is changed for me"—she said—"It will never be the same again! I do not seem to belong to it—other influences surround me,—how I live in it?—how shall I work—what shall I do?"

"You will do as you have always done—go your own way"—he replied—"The way which has led you to so much discovery and attainment. You must surely know in your own soul that you have been guided in that way—and your success is the result of allowing yourself to Be guided. In all things you will be guided now—have no fear for yourself! All will be well for you!"

"And for you?" she asked impulsively.

He smiled.

"Why think of me?" he said, gently—"I am nothing in your life—"

"You are!" she replied—"You are more than you imagine. I begin to realise—"

He held up his hand with a warning gesture.

"Hush!" he said—"There are things of which we must not speak!"

At that moment the monastery bell tolled the midday "Angelus." Don Aloysius bent his head—Morgana instinctively did the same. Within the building the deep voices of the brethren sounded, chanting,—

"Angelus Domini nuntiavit Maria Et concepit de Spiritu sancto."

As the salutation to heaven finished, the mellow music of the organ in the chapel sent a wave of solemn and prayerful tenderness on the air, and, moved by the emotion of the hour, Morgana's heart beat more quickly and tears filled her eyes.

"There must be beautiful music in the Golden City!" she said.

Don Aloysius smiled.

"There is! And when the other things of life give you pause to listen, you will often hear it!"

She smiled happily in response, and then, with a silent gesture of farewell, left the cloister and made her way to the chapel, part of which was kept open for public worship. It was empty, but the hidden organist was still playing. She went towards the High Altar and knelt in front of it. She was not of the Catholic faith,—she was truly of no faith at all save that which is taught by Science, which like a door opened in heaven shows all the wonders within,—but her keen sense of the beautiful was stirred by the solemn peace of the shut Tabernacle with the Cross above it, and the great lilies bending under their own weight of loveliness and fragrance on either side.

"It is the Symbol of a great Truth which is true for all time"—she thought, as she clasped her hands in an attitude of prayer—"And how sad and strange it is to feel that there are thousands among its best-intentioned worshippers and priests who have not discovered its mystic meaning. The God in Man, born of purity in woman! Is it only in the Golden City that they know?"

She raised her eyes in half unconscious appeal—and, as she did so, a brilliant Ray of light flashed downward from the summit of the Cross which surmounted the Altar, and remained extended slantwise towards her. She saw it,—and waited expectantly. Close to her ears a Voice spoke with extreme softness, yet very distinctly.

"Can you hear me?"

"Yes," she replied at once, with equal softness.

"Then, listen! I have a message for you!"

And Morgana listened,—listened intently,—the sapphire hue of the Ray lighting her gold hair, as she knelt, absorbed. What she heard filled her with a certain dread; and a tremor of premonition, like the darkness preceding storm, shook her nerves. But the inward spirit of her was as a warrior clothed in steel,—she was afraid of nothing—least of all of any event or incident passing for "supernatural," knowing beyond all doubt that the most seeming miraculous circumstances are all the result of natural movement and transmutation. There never had been anything surprising to her in the fact that light is a conveyor of sound; and that she was receiving a message by such means seemed no more extraordinary to her mind than receiving it by the accepted telephonic service. Every word spoken she heard with the closest attention—

until—as though a cloud had suddenly covered it,—the "Sound-Ray" vanished, and the Voice ceased.

She rose at once from her knees, alert and ready for action—her face was pale, her lips set, her eyes luminous.

"I must not hesitate"—she said—"If I can save him I will!"

She left the chapel and hurried home, where as soon as she reached her own private room she wrote to the Marchese Rivardi the following note, which was more than unpleasantly startling to him when he received it.

"I shall need you and Gaspard for a long journey in the 'White Eagle.' Prepare everything in the way of provisioning and other necessary details. No time must be lost, and no expense need be spared. We must start as quickly as possible."

This message written, sealed and dispatched by one of her servants to the Marchese's villa, she sat for some moments lost in thought, wistfully looking out on her flower-filled gardens and the shimmering blue of the Mediterranean beyond.

"I may be too late!" she said, speaking aloud to herself—"But I will take the risk! He will not care—no!—a man like that cares for nothing but himself. He would have broken my life—(had I given him the chance!)—for the sake of an experiment. Now—if I can—I will rescue his for the sake of an ideal!"

XXI

There shall be no more wars!—there CAN be none!"

Roger Seaton said these words aloud with defiant emphasis, addressing the dumb sky. It was early morning, but an intense heat had so scorched the earth that not the smallest drop of dew glittered on any leaf or blade of grass; it was all arid, brown and burned into a dryness as of fever. But Seaton was far too much engrossed with himself and his own business to note the landscape, or to be troubled by the suffocating closeness of the atmosphere,—he stood gazing with the idolatry of a passionate lover at a small, plain metal case, containing a dozen or more small plain metal cylinders, as small as women's thimbles, all neatly ranged side by side, divided from contact with one another by folded strips of cotton.

"There it is!" he went on, apostrophising the still air—"Complete,—perfected! If I sold that to any nation under the sun, that nation could rule the world!—could wipe out everything save itself and its own people! I have wrested the secret from the very womb of Nature!—it is mine—all mine! I would have given it to Britain—or to the United States—but neither will accept my terms—so therefore I hold it—I, only!—which is just as well! I—just I—am master of destiny!—the Power we call God, has put this tiling into my hands! What a marvel and shall I not use it? I will! Let Germany but stir an inch towards aggression, and Germany shall exist no longer!—The same with any other nation that starts a quarrel—I—I alone will settle it!"

His eyes blazed with the light of fanaticism—he was obsessed by the force of his own ideas and schemes, and the metal case on the table before him was, to his mind, time, life, present and future. He had arrived at that questionable point of intellectual attainment when man forgets that there is any existing force capable of opposing him, and imagines that he has but to go on in his own way to grasp all worlds and the secrets of their being. At this juncture, so often arrived at by many, a kind of super-sureness sets in, persuading the finite nature that it has reached the infinite. The whole mental organisation of the man thrilled with an awful consciousness of power. He said within himself "I hold the lives of millions at my mercy!"

Other thoughts—other dreams had passed away for the moment—he had forgotten life as it presents itself to the ordinary human being.

Now and again a flitting vision of Morgana vaguely troubled him,—her intellectual capacity annoyed him, and yet he would have been glad to discuss with her the scientific unfolding of his great secret—she would understand it in all its bearings,—she might advise—Advice!—no!—he did not need the advice of a woman! As for Manella, he had not seen her since her last violent outburst of what he called "temper"—and he had no wish for her presence. For now he had a thing to do which was of paramount importance,—and this was, to deposit the treasured discovery of his life in a secret hiding-place he had found for it, till he should be ready to remove it to safer quarters—or—TILL HE RESOLVED TO USE IT. Had he been a religious man, of such humility as should accompany true religion, he would have prayed that its use should never be called upon,—but he had trained himself into an attitude of such complete indifferentism towards life and the things of life, that to him it seemed useless to pray for what did not matter. Sometimes the thought, appalling in its truth, flashed across his brain that the force he had discovered and condensed within small compass might as easily destroy half the world as a nation! The fabled thunderbolts of Jove were child's play compared with those plain-looking, thimble-like cylinders which contained such terrific power! A touch of hesitation—of pure human dread affected his nerves for the moment,—he shivered in the sultry air as with cold, and looked about him right and left as though suspecting some hidden witness of his actions. There was not so much as a bird or a butterfly in sight, and he drew a long deep breath of relief. The day was treading in the steps of dawn with the full blazonry of burning Californian sunlight, and away in the distance the ridges and peaks of distant mountains stood out sharply clear against the intense blue of the sky. There was great stillness everywhere,—a pause, as it seemed, in the mechanism of the universe. The twitter of a bird or the cry of some wild animal would have been a relief,—so Seaton felt, though accustomed to deep silence.

"Better get through with this at once"—he said, aloud—"Now that a safe place is prepared." Here he looked at his watch. "In a couple of hours they will be sending up from the Plaza to know if I want anything—Irish Jake or Manilla will be coming on some trivial matter—I'd better take the opportunity of complete secrecy while I can."

For the next few minutes or so he hesitated. With the sudden fancy that he had forgotten something, he turned out his pockets, looking for he scarcely knew what. The contents were mixed and various, and among them was a crumpled letter which he had received some days since from Sam Gwent. He smoothed it out carefully and re-read it, especially one passage—

"I think the States will never get involved in another war, but I am fairly sure Germany will. If she joins up with Russia look out for squalls. In your old country, which appears to be peopled by madmen, there's a writing chap who spent a fortnight in Russia, not long enough to know the ins and outs of a village, yet assuming to know everything about the biggest territory in Europe, and the press is puffing up his ignorance as if it were wisdom. Germany has her finger on the spot—so perhaps your stuff will come in useful. But don't forget that if you make up your mind to use it you will ruin America, commercially speaking. And many other countries besides. So think it well over,—more than a hundred times! Lydia Herbert, whom perhaps you remember, and perhaps you don't, has caught her 'ancient mariner'—that is to say, her millionaire,—and all fashionable New York is going to the wedding, including yours truly. I had expected Morgana Royal to grace the function, but I hear she is quite engrossed with the decoration and furnishing of her Sicilian palace, as well as with her advising artist, a very good-looking Marquis or Marchese as he is called. It is also whispered that she has invented a wonderful air-ship which has no engines, and creates its own motive power as it goes! Sounds rather tall talk!—but this is an age of wonders and we never know what next. There is a new Light Ray just out which prospects for gold, oil and all ores and minerals, and finds them in a fifty-mile circuit—so probably nobody need be poor for the future. When we've all got most things we want, and there's nothing left to work for, I wonder what the world will be worth!"

Seaton left off reading and thrust the letter again in his pocket.

"What will the world be worth?" he soliloquised—"Why, nothing!"

Suddenly struck by this thought, which had not always presented itself with such sharp and clear precision as now, he took time to consider it. Capital and Labour, the two forces which are much more prone to rend each other than to co-operate—these would both possibly be non-existent if Science had its full way. If gold, silver and other precious minerals could be "picked up" as on the fabled Tom Tiddler's ground, by a ray of light, then the striving for wealth would cease and work would be reduced to a minimum. The prospect was stupendous, but hardly entirely pleasing. If there were no need for effort, then the powers of mind and body would sink into inertia.

"What object should we live for?" he mused—"Merely to propagate our own kind and bring more effortless beings into the world to cumber it? The very idea is horrible! Work is the very blood and bone of existence—without it we should rot! But one must work for something or some one—wife?—children?—Useless labour!—for in nine cases out often the wife becomes a bore,—and the children grow up ungrateful. Why waste strength and feeling on either?"

Thus mentally arguing, the exquisite lines of Tennyson's "Lotus Eaters" suddenly rang in his memory like a chime of bells from the old English village where he had lived as a boy, when his mother, one of the past sweet "old-fashioned" women, used to read to him and teach him much of the best in literature,—

> *"Death is the end of life; ah, why*
> *Should life all labour be?*
> *Let us alone. Time driveth onward fast*
> *And in a little while our lips are dumb,*
> *Let us alone. What is it that will last?*
> *All things are taken from us and become*
> *Portions and parcels of the dreadful Past,*
> *Let us alone. What pleasure can we have*
> *To war with evil? Is there any peace*
> *In ever climbing up the climbing wave?"*

An effortless existence would be the existence of such as these fabled Lotus Eaters—moreover, it was not possible it could go on, since all Nature shows effort without cessation. Roger Seaton knew this as all know it—but his soul's demand remained unsatisfied, for he sought to know the Cause of all the toil and trouble,—the "why" it should be. And at the back of his mind there was ever a teasing reminder of Morgana and her strange theories, some of which she had half imparted to him when their friendship had first begun. For her Tennyson's line— "Death is the end of life"—would be the statement of a foolish fallacy, as she held that there is no such thing as death, only failure to adapt the spirit to advancing and higher change in its physical organisation. To-day he remembered with curious clearness what she had said on this subject—

"Radio-activity is the chief secret of life. It is for us to learn how to absorb it into our systems as we grow,—to add by its means to our supplies of vitality and energy. It never gives out,—nor should we. The Nature-intention is that we should become better, stronger, more beautiful, more mentally and spiritually perfect—and that we do not fulfil this intention is our own fault. The decimation of the human race by wars and plagues and famines has always been traceable to human error. All accidents happen through those who make accidents possible,—diseases are bred through human dirt, greed, ignorance, and neglect. They are no part of the divine scheme of things. The plan is to advance and make progress from one point of excellence to another,— not to stop half way and turn back on the road. Humanity dies, because it will not learn how to live."

She had spoken these words with a quiet simplicity and earnestness that impressed him at the time as being almost child-like, considering the depth of thought into which she must have plunged, notwithstanding her youth and her sex—and on this morning of all others, this morning on which he had set himself a task for which he had made long and considerable preparation, he found himself half mechanically repeating her phrase—"Humanity dies because it will not learn how to live."

There was no fatalism,—no fixed destiny in this; only the force of Will was implied—the Will to learn,—the Will to know.

"And why should not humanity die?" he argued within himself— "If, in the long course of ages, it is proved that it will neither learn nor know,—why should it remain? Room should be made for a new race! A clever gardener can produce a perfectly beautiful flower from an insignificant and common weed,—surely this is a lesson to us that it may be possible to produce a god from a man!"

He bent his eyes lovingly on the case of small cylinders lying open before him;—the just risen sun brightened them to a glitter as of cold steel,—and for a moment he fancied they flashed upon him with an almost sinister gleam.

"Power of good or power of evil?" he questioned his inward spirit— "Who can decide? If it is good to destroy evil then the force is a good force—if it is evil to destroy good WITH evil, then it is an evil thing. But Nature makes no such particular discriminations—she destroys evil and good together at one blow. Why therefore should I—or anyone—offer to discriminate?—since evil is always the preponderating factor. When the 'Lusitania' was torpedoed neither God nor Nature interfered to save the innocent from the guilty—men, women and children were all plunged into the pitiless sea. I—as a part of Nature—if I destroy, I only follow her example. War is an evil,—an abominable crime—and those that attempt to make it should be swept from the face of the earth even if good and peace-loving units are swept along with them. This cannot be helped."

He went into his hut, and in a few minutes came out again clothed in thick garments of a dark, earth colour, and carrying a stout staff, steel-pointed at its end something after the fashion of a Swiss alpenstock. He brought with him a small metal box into which he placed the case of cylinders, covering it with a closely fitting lid. Then he put the package into a basket made of rough twigs and strips of bark, having a strong handle, to which he fastened a leather strap, and slung the whole thing over his shoulders like a knapsack. Then, casting another look round to make sure that there was no one about, he started to walk towards a steeper descent of the hill in a totally different direction from that which led to the "Plaza" hotel. He went swiftly, at a steady swinging pace,—and though his way took him among confused masses of rock, and fallen boulders, he thought nothing of these obstacles, vaulting lightly across them with the ease of a chamois, till he came to a point where there was a declivity running sheer down to invisible depths, from whence came the rumbling echo of falling water. In this almost perpendicular wall of rock were a few ledges, like the precarious rungs of a broken ladder, and down these he prepared to go. Clinging at first to the topmost edge of the precipice, he let himself down warily inch by inch till his figure entirely disappeared, sunken, as it were in darkness. As he vanished there was a sudden cry—a rush as of wings—and a woman sprang up from amid bushes where she had lain hidden,—it was Manella. For days and nights she had stolen away in the intervals of her work, to watch him—and nothing had chanced to excite her alarm till now—till now, when she had seen him emerge from his hut and pack up the mysterious box he carried,—and when she had heard him talking strangely to himself in a way she could not understand.

As soon as he started to walk she followed him, pushing through heavy brushwood and crawling along the ground where she could not be seen;—and now,—with dishevelled hair, and staring, terrified eyes she leaned over the edge of the precipice, baffled and desperate. Tearless sobs convulsed her throat,—

"Oh, God of mercy!" she moaned in suffocated accents—"How can I follow him down there! Oh, help me, Mary mother! Help me! I must—I must be with him!"

She gathered up her hair in a close coil and wound her skirts tightly about her, looking everywhere for a footing. She saw a deep cranny which had been hollowed out by some torrent of water—it cut sharply through the rock like a path,—she could risk that perhaps, she thought,—and yet her brain reeled—she felt sick and giddy—would it not be wiser to stay where she was and wait for the return of the reckless creature who had ventured all alone into one of the deepest canons of the whole country? While she hesitated she caught a sudden glimpse of him, stepping with apparent ease over huge heaps of stones and fallen pieces of rock at the bottom of the declivity,—she watched his movements in breathless suspense. On he went towards a vast aperture, shaped arch-wise like the entrance to a cavern—he paused a moment—then entered it. This was enough for Manella—her wild love and wilder terror gave her an almost supernatural strength and daring,—and all heedless now of results she sprang boldly towards the deep cutting in the rock, swinging herself from jagged point to point till—reaching the bottom of the declivity at last, bruised and bleeding, but undaunted,—she stopped, checked by a rushing stream which tumbled over great boulders and dashed its cold spray in her face. Looking about her she saw to her dismay that the vaulted cavern wherein Seaton had disappeared was on the other side of this stream—she stood almost opposite to it—but how to get across? Gazing despairingly in every direction she suddenly perceived the fallen trunk of a tree lying half in and half out of the brawling torrent—it was green with slippery moss and offered but a dangerous foothold,—nevertheless she resolved to attempt it.

"I said I would die for him!" she thought—"and I will!"

Getting astride the tree, it swayed under her,—but she found she could push one of the larger boughs forward to lengthen the extemporary bridge,—and so, as it were, riding the waters, which surged noisily around her, she managed by dint of super-human effort to reach the projection of pebbly shore where the entrance to the cavern yawned open before her, black and desolate. The sun in its full morning glory blazed slanting down upon the darkness of the canon, and as she stood shivering, wet through and utterly exhausted, wondering what next she should do, she caught sight of a form moving within the cave like a moving shadow, and ascending a steep natural stairway of columnar rocks piled one on top of the other. Affrighted as she was by the tomb-like aspect of the deep vault, she had not ventured so far that she should now shrink from further dangers or fail in her quest;—the cherished object of her constant watchful care was within that subterranean blackness,—for what purpose?—she did not dare to think! But there was an instinctive sense of dread foreknowledge upon her,—a warning of impending evil,—and had she not sworn to him— "If God struck you down to hell I would be there!" The entrance to the cavern looked like the mouth of hell itself, as she had seen it depicted in one of her Catholic early lesson books. There were serpents and dragons in the picture ready to devour the impenitent sinner,—there might be serpents and dragons in this cave, for all she knew! But what matter? If the man she loved were actually in hell she "would be there"—as she had said!—and would surely find it Heaven! And so,—seeing the mere outline of his form moving ghost-like in the gloom, it was to her a guiding presence,—a light amid darkness,—and when,—after a minute or two—her straining eyes perceived him climbing steadily up the steep and perilous rocks, seeming about to disappear altogether,— she mastered the tremor of her nerves and crept cautiously step by step into the sombre vault, blindly feeling her way through the damp, thick murkiness, reckless of all danger, and only bent on following him.

XXII

Of all the vagaries and humours of humanity when considered in crowds, there is nothing which appears more senseless and objectless than the way in which it congregates outside the door of a church at a fashionable or "society" wedding. The massed people pushing and shoving each other about have nothing whatever to do with either bride or bridegroom, the ceremony inside the sacred edifice has in most cases ceased to be a "sacrament"—and has become a mere show of dressed-up manikins and womenkins, many of the latter being mere OBJECT D'ART,—stands for the display of millinery. And yet—the crowds fight and jostle,—women scramble and scream,—all to catch a glimpse of the woman who is to be given to the man, and the man who has agreed to accept the woman. The wealthier the pair the wilder the frenzy to gaze upon them. Savages performing a crazy war-dance are decorous of behaviour in contrast with these "civilised" folk who tramp on each other's feet and are ready to squeeze each other into pulp for the chance of staring at two persons whom the majority of them have never seen before and are not likely to see again. The wedding of Miss Lydia Herbert with her "ancient mariner," a seventy-year-old millionaire reputed to be as wealthy as Rockefeller,—was one of these "sensations"—chiefly on account of the fact that every unmarried woman young and old, and every widow, had been hunting him in vain for fully five years. Miss Herbert had been voted "no chance," because she made no secret of her extravagant tastes in dress and jewels,—yet despite society croakers she had won the game. This in itself was interesting,—as the millionaire she had secured was known to be particularly close-fisted and parsimonious. Nevertheless he had shown remarkable signs of relaxing these tendencies; for he had literally showered jewels on his chosen bride, leaving no door open for any complaint in that quarter. Her diamonds were the talk of New York, and on the day of her wedding her gowns literally flashed like a firework with numerous dazzling points of light. "The Voice that breathed o'er Eden" had little to do with the magnificence of her attire, or with the brilliancy of the rose-wreathed bridesmaids, young girls of specially selected beauty and elegance who were all more or less disappointed in failing to win the millionaire themselves. For these youthful persons in their 'teens had social ambitions hidden in hearts harder than steel—"a good time" of self-indulgence and luxury was all they sought for in life—in fact, they had no conception of any higher ideal. The millionaire himself, though old, maintained a fairly middle-aged appearance—he was a thin, wiry, well-preserved man, his wizened and furrowed countenance chiefly showing the marks of Time's ploughshare. It would have been difficult to say why, out of all the feminine butterflies hovering around him, he had chosen Lydia Herbert,—but he was a shrewd judge of character in his way, and he had decided that as she was not in her first youth it would be more worth her while to conduct herself decorously as wife and housekeeper, and generally look after his health and comfort, than it would be for a less responsible woman. Then, she had "manner,"—her appearance was attractive and she wore her clothes well and stylishly. All this was enough for a man who wanted some one to attend to his house and entertain his friends, and he was perfectly satisfied with himself as he repeated after the clergyman the words, "With my body I thee worship, and with all my worldly goods I thee endow," knowing that "with his body" he had never worshipped anything, and that the "endowment" of his worldly goods was strictly limited to certain settlements. He felt himself to be superior to his old bachelor friend Sam Gwent, who supported him as "best man" at the ceremony, and who, as he stood, stiffly upright in immaculate "afternoon visiting attire" among the restlessly swaying, semi-whispering throng, was all the time thinking of the dusky night-gloom in the garden of the "Plaza" far away in California and a beautiful face set against the dark background of myrtle bushes exhaling rich perfume.

"What a startling contrast she would be to these dolls of fashion!" he thought—"What a sensation she would make! There's not a woman here who can compare with her! If I were only a bit younger I'd try my luck!—anyway I'm younger than to-day's bridegroom!—but she— Manella—would never look at any other man than Seaton, who doesn't care a rap for her or any other woman!" Here his thoughts took another turn.

"No," he repeated inwardly—"He doesn't care a rap for her or any other woman—except—perhaps—Morgana! And even if it were Morgana, it would be for himself and himself alone! While she—ah!— it would be a clever brain indeed that could worry out what SHE cares for! Nothing in this world, so far as I can see!"

Here the organ poured the rich strains of a soft and solemn prelude through the crowded church—the "sacred" part of the ceremony was over, and bride and bridegroom made their way to the vestry, there to sign the register in the presence of a selected group of friends. Sam Gwent was one of these,—and though he had attended many such functions before, he was more curiously impressed than usual by the unctuous and barefaced hypocrisy of the whole thing—the smiling humbug of the officiating clergy,—the affected delight of the "society" toadies fluttering like wasps round bride and bride-groom as though they were sweet dishes specially for stinging insects to feed upon, and in his mind he seemed to hear the warm, passionate voice of Manella in frank admission of her love for Seaton.

"It is good to love him!" she had said—"I am happy to love him. I wish only to serve him!"

This was primitive passion,—the passion of primitive woman for her mate whom she admitted to be stronger than herself, to whom she instinctively looked for shelter and protection, and round whose commanding force she sought to rear the lovely fabric of "Home,"—a state of feeling as far removed from the sentiments of modern women as the constellation of Orion is removed from earth. And Sam Gwent's fragmentary reflections flitting through his brain were more serious— one might say more romantic, than the consideration of dollars, which usually occupied all his faculties. He had always thought that there was a good deal in life which he had missed somehow, and which dollars could not purchase; and a certain irate contempt filled him for the man who, unlike himself, was in the prime of strength, and who, with all the glories of Nature about him and the love and beauty of an exquisite womanhood at his hand for possession, could nevertheless devote his energies to the science of destruction and the compassing of death without compunction, on the lines Roger Seaton had laid down as the remedy against all war.

"The kindest thing to think of him is that he's not quite sane,"— Gwent mused—"He has been obsessed by the horrible carnage of the Great War, and disgusted by the utter inefficiency of Governments since the armistice, and this appalling invention of his is the result."

The crashing chords of the Bridal March from "Lohengrin" put an end to his thoughts for the moment,—people began to crush and push out of church, or stand back on each other's toes to stare at the bride's diamonds as she moved very slowly and gracefully down the aisle on the arm of her elderly husband. She certainly looked very well,—and her smile suggested entire satisfaction with herself and the world. Press-camera men clambered about wherever they could find a footing, to catch and perpetuate that smile, which when enlarged and reproduced in newspapers would depict the grinning dental display so much associated with Woodrow Wilson and the Prince of Wales,— though more suggestive of a skull than anything else. Skulls invariably show their teeth, we know—but it has been left to the modern press-camera man to insist on the death-grin in faces that yet live. The crowd outside the church was far denser than the crowd within, and the fighting and scrambling for points of view became terrific, especially when the wedding guests' motor-cars began to make their way, with sundry hoots and snorts, through the densely packed mob. Women screamed,—some fainted—but none thought of giving way to others, or retiring from the wild scene of contest. Gwent judged it wisest to remain within the church portal till the crowd should clear, and there, safely ensconced, he watched the maddened mass of foolish sight-seers, all of whom had plainly left their daily avocations merely to stare at a man and woman wedded, with whom, personally, they had nothing whatever to do.

"People talk about unemployment!" he mused—"There's enough human material in this one street to make wealth for themselves and the whole community, yet they are idle by their own choice. If they had anything to do they wouldn't be here!"

He laughed grimly,—the utter stodginess and stupidity of humanity EN MASSE had of late struck him very forcibly, and he found every excuse for the so-called incapacity of Governments, seeing the kind of folk they are called upon to govern. He realised, as we all who read history, must do, that we are no worse and no better than the peoples of the past,—we are just as hypocritical, fraudulent, deceptive and cruel as ever they were in legalised torture-times, and just as ineradicably selfish. The pagans practised a religion which they did not truly believe in, and so do we. All through the ages God has been mocked;—all through the ages Divine vengeance has fallen on the mockers and the mockery.

"And after all," thought Gwent—"wars are as necessary as plagues to clear out a superabundant population, only most unfortunately Nature adopts such recklessness in her methods that it most often happens the best among us are taken, and the worst left. I tried to impress this on Seaton, whose system of destruction would involve the good as well as the bad—but these intellectual monsters of scientific appetite have no conscience and no sentiment. To prove their theories they would annihilate a continent."

MARIE CORELLI

Here a sudden ugly rush of the crowd, dangerous to both life and limb, pushed him back against the church portal with the force of a tidal wave,—it was not concerned with the bridal pair who had already driven away in their automobile, nor with the wedding guests who were following them to the great hotel where the bride's reception was held—it was caused by the wild dash of half a dozen or so of unkempt men and boys who tore a passage for themselves through the swaying mob of sightseers, waving newspapers aloft and shouting loudly with voices deep and shrill, clear and hoarse—

"Earthquake in California! Terrible loss of life! Thousands dead! Awful scenes! Earthquake in California!"

The people swayed again—then stopped in massed groups,—some clutching at the newsboys as they ran and buying the papers as fast as they could be sold, while all the time above the muffled roar of the city they sent their cries aloft, echoing near and far—

"Thousands dead! Awful scenes! Towns destroyed! Terrible Earthquake in California!"

Sam Gwent stepped out from the church portal, elbowing his way through the confusion,—the yells of the news vendors rang sharply in his ears and yet for the moment he scarcely grasped their meaning; "California" was the one word that caught him, as it were, with a hammer stroke,—then "Thousands dead!" Finding at last an open passage through the dispersing crowd, he went at something of a run after one of the newsboys, and snatched the last paper he had to sell out of his hand.

"What is it?" he demanded as he paid his money.

"Dunno!" the boy replied, breathlessly—"'Xpect everybody's dead down California way!"

Gwent unfolded the journal and stared at the great headlines, printed in fat black letters, still smelling strongly of printer's ink.

Appalling Earthquake In California!—Mountain Upheaval!—Towns Wiped Out!—Plaza Hotel Engulfed!—Frightful Loss of Life!

His eyes grew dim and dazzled—his brain swam,—he gazed up unseeingly at the blue sky, the tall "sky-scraper" houses, the sweep of human and vehicular traffic around him; and to his excited fancy the beautiful face of Manella came, like a phantom, between him and all else that was presented to his vision—that face warm and glowing with woman's tenderness—the splendid dark eyes aflame with love for a man whose indifference to her only strengthened her adoration and he seemed to hear the deep defiant voice of Roger Seaton ringing in his ears—

"Annihilation! A holocaust of microbes! I would—and could—wipe them off the face of the earth in twenty-four hours!" He could—and would!

"And by Heaven," said Gwent, within himself—"He's done it!"

XXIII

S truck by the hand of God! So men say when, after denying God's existence ail their lives, the seeming solid earth heaves up like a ship on a storm-billow, dragging down in its deep recoil their lives and habitations. An earthquake! Its irresistible rise and fall makes human beings more powerless than insects,—their houses and possessions have less stability than the spider's web which swings its frail threads across broken columns in greater safety than any man-made bridge of stone,—and terror, mad, hopeless, helpless terror, possesses every creature brought face to face with the dire cruelty of natural forces, which from the very beginning have played havoc with struggling mankind. Struck by the hand of God!—and with a merciless blow! All the sunny plains and undulating hills of the beautiful stretch of land in Southern California, in the centre of which the "Plaza" hotel and sanatorium had stood, were now unrecognisable,—the earth was torn asunder and thrown into vast heaps—great rocks and boulders were tumbled over each other pell-mell in appalling heights of confusion, and, for miles around, towns, camps and houses were laid in ruins. The scene was one of absolute horror,—there was no language to express or describe it—no word of hope or comfort that could be fitly used to lighten the blackness of despair and loss. Gangs of men were at relief work as soon as they could be summoned, and these busied themselves in extricating the dead, and rescuing the dying whose agonised cries and moans reproached the Power that made them for such an end,— and perhaps as terrible as any other sound was the savage roar and rush of a loosened torrent which came tearing furiously down from the cleft hills to the lower land, through the great canon beyond the site where the Plaza had stood,—a canon which had become enormously widened by the riving and the rending of the rocks, thus giving free passage to wild waters that had before been imprisoned in a narrow gorge. The persistent rush of the flood filled every inch of space with sound of an awful, even threatening character, suggesting further devastation and death. The men engaged in their dreadful task of lifting crushed corpses from under the stones that had fallen upon them, were almost overcome and rendered incapable of work by the appalling clamour, which was sufficient to torture the nerves of the strongest; and some of them, sickened at the frightful mutilation of the bodies they found gave up altogether and dropped from sheer fatigue and exhaustion into unconsciousness, despite the heroic encouragement of their director, a man well used to great emergencies. Late afternoon found him still organising and administering aid, with the assistance of two or three Catholic priests who went about seeking to comfort and sustain those who were passing "the line between." All the energetic helpers were prepared to work all night, delving into the vast suddenly made grave wherein were tumbled the living with the dead,—and it was verging towards sunset when one of the priests, chancing to raise his eyes from the chaos of earth around him to the clear and quiet sky, saw what at first he took to be a great eagle with outspread wings soaring slowly above the scene of devastation. It moved with singular lightness and ease,—now and then appearing to pause as though seeking some spot whereon to descend,—and after watching it for a minute or two he called the attention of some of the men around him to its appearance. They looked up wearily from their gruesome task of excavating the dead.

"That's an air-ship"—said one—"and a big thing, too!"

"An air-ship!" echoed the priest amazedly,—and then was silent, gazing at the shining expanse of sky through which the bird-shaped vessel made its leisurely way like the vision of a fairy tale more than any reality. There was something weirdly terrible in the contrast it made, moving so tranquilly through clear space in apparent safety, while down below on the so-called "solid" earth, all nature had been convulsed and overthrown. The wonderful result of human ingenuity as measured with the remorseless action of natural forces seemed too startling to be real to the mind of a Spanish priest who, despite all the evidences of triumphant materialism, still clung to the Cross and kept his simple, faithful soul high above the waves that threatened to engulf it. Turning anew to his melancholy duties, he bent over a dying youth just lifted from beneath a weight of stones that had crushed him. The boy's fast glazing eyes were upturned to the sky.

"See the angel coming?" he whispered, thickly—"Never used to believe in them!—but there's one sure enough! Glory—!" and his utterance ceased for ever.

The priest crossed his hands upon his breast and said a prayer—then again looked up to where the air-ship floated in the darkening blue. It was now directly over the canon,—immediately above the huge rift made by the earthquake, through which the clamorous rush of water poured. While he watched it, it suddenly stood still, then dived slowly

MARIE CORELLI

as though bent on descending into the very depths of the gully. He could not forbear uttering an exclamation, which made all the men about him look in the direction where his own gaze was fixed.

"That air-ship's going to kingdom-come!" said one—"Nothing can save it if it takes to nose-diving down there!"

They all stared amazed—but the dreadful work on which they were engaged left them no time for consideration of any other matter. The priest watched a few minutes longer, more or less held spell-bound with a kind of terror, for he saw that without doubt the great vessel was either purposely descending or being drawn into the vast abyss yawning black beneath it, and that falling thus it must be inevitably doomed to destruction. Whoever piloted it must surely be determined to invite this frightful end to its voyage, for nothing was ever steadier or more resolute than its downward movement towards the whirling waters that rushed through the canon. All suddenly it disappeared, whelmed as it seemed in darkness and the roaring flood, and the watching priest made the sign of the cross in air murmuring—

"God have mercy on their souls!"

Had he been able to see what happened he might have thought that the confused brain of the dying boy who had imagined the air-ship to be an angel, was not so far wrong, for no romancer or teller of wild tales could have pictured a stranger or more unearthly sight than the wonderful "White Eagle" poised at ease amid the tossed-up clouds of spray flung from the seething mass of waters, while at her prow stood a woman fair as any fabled goddess—a woman reckless of all danger, and keenly on the alert, with bright eyes searching every nook and cranny that could be discerned through the mist. Clear above the roaring torrent her voice rang like a silver trumpet as she called her instructions to the two men who, equally defying every peril, had ventured on this journey at her command,—Rivardi and Gaspard.

"Let her down very gently inch by inch!" she cried; "It must be here that we should seek!"

In absolute silence they obeyed. Both had given themselves up for lost and were resigned and ready to meet death at any moment. From the first they had made no effort to resist Morgana's orders—she and they had left Sicily at a couple of hours' notice—and their three days' journey across the ocean had been accomplished without adventure or accident, at such a speed that it was hardly to be thought of without a thrill of horror. No information had been given them as to the object of their long and rapid aerial voyage,—and only now when the "White Eagle," swooping over California, reached the scene of the terrific devastation wrought by the earthquake did they begin to think they had submitted their wills and lives to the caprice of a madwoman. However, there was no drawing back,—nothing for it but still to obey,—for even in the stress and terror naturally excited by their amazing position, they did not fail to see that the great air-ship was steadily controlled, and that whatever was the force controlling it, it maintained its level, its mysterious vibrating discs still throbbing with vital and incessant regularity. Apparently nothing could disturb its equilibrium or shatter its mechanism. And, according to its woman-designer's command, they lowered it gently till it was, so to say, almost immersed in the torrent and covered with spray—indeed Morgana's light figure itself at the prow looked like a fair spirit risen from the waters rather than any form of flesh and blood, so wreathed and transfigured it was by the dust of the ceaseless foam. She stood erect, bent on a quest that seemed hopeless, watching every eddying curve of water,—every flickering ripple,—her eyes, luminous as stars, searched the black and riven rocks with an eager passion of discovery,—when all suddenly as she gazed, a thin ray of light,—pure gold in colour,—struck sharply like a finger-point on a shallow pool immediately below her. She looked and uttered a cry, beckoning to Rivardi.

"Come! Come!"

He hurried to her side, Gaspard following. The pool on which her eyes were fixed was shallow enough to show the pebbly bed beneath the water—and there lay apparently two corpses—one of a man, the other of a woman whose body was half flung across that of the man.

Morgana pointed to them.

"They must be brought up here!" she said, insistently—"You must lift them! We have emergency ropes and pulleys—it is easily done! Why do you hesitate?"

"Because you demand the impossible!" said Rivardi—"You send us to death to rescue the already dead!"

She turned upon him with wrath in her eyes.

"You refuse to obey me?"

What a face confronted him! White as marble, and as terrible in expression as that of a Medusa, it had a paralysing effect on his nerves, and he shrank and trembled at her glance.

"You refuse to obey me?" she repeated—"Then—if you do—I destroy this air-ship and ourselves in less than two minutes! Choose! Obey, and live!—disobey and die!"

He staggered back from her in terror at her looks, which gave her a supernatural beauty and authority. The "fey" woman was "fey" indeed!—and the powers with which superstition endows the fairy folk seemed now to invest her with irresistible influence.

"Choose!" she reiterated.

Without another word he turned to Gaspard, who in equal silence got out the ropes and pulleys of which she had spoken. The air-ship stopped dead—suspended immovably over the wild waters and almost hidden in spray; and though the strange vibration of its multitudinous discs continued in itself it was fixed as a rock. A smile sweet as sunshine after storm changed and softened Morgana's features as she saw Rivardi swing over the vessel's side to the pool below, while Gaspard unwound the gear by which he would be able to lift and support the drowned creatures he was bidden to bring.

"That's a true noble!" she exclaimed—"I knew your courage would not fail! Believe me, no harm shall come to you!"

Inspirited by her words, he flung himself down—and raising the body of the woman first, was entangled by the wet thick strands of her long dark hair which, like sea-weed, caught about his feet and hands and impeded his movements. He had time just to see a face white as marble under the hair,—then he had enough to do to fasten ropes round the body and push it upward while Gaspard pulled—both men doubting whether the weight of it would not alter the balance of the air-ship despite its extraordinary fixity of position. Morgana, bending over from the vessel, watched every action,—she showed neither alarm nor impatience nor anxiety—and when Gaspard said suddenly—

"It is easier than I thought it would be!" she merely smiled as if she knew. Another few moments and the drowned woman's body was hauled into the cabin of the ship, where Morgana knelt down beside it. Parting the heavy masses of dark hair that enshrouded it she looked—and saw what she had expected to see—the face of Manella Soriso. But it was the death-mask of a face—strangely beautiful—but awful in its white rigidity. Morgana bent over it anxiously, but only for a moment, drawing a small phial from her bosom she forced a few drops of the liquid it contained between the set lips, and with a tiny syringe injected the same at the pulseless wrist and throat. While she busied herself with these restorative measures, the second body,—that of the man,—

was landed almost at her feet—and she found herself gazing in a sort of blank stupefaction at what seemed to be the graven image of Roger Seaton. No effigy of stone ever looked colder, harder, greyer than this inert figure of man,—uninjured apparently, for there were no visible marks of wounds or bruises upon his features, which appeared frozen into stiff rigidity, but a man as surely dead as death could make him! Morgana heard, as in a far-off dream, the Marchese Rivardi speaking—

"I have done your bidding because it was you who bade,"—he said, his voice shaking with the tremor and excitement of his daring effort—"And it was not so very difficult. But it is a vain rescue! They are past recall."

Morgana looked up from her awed contemplation of Seaton's rigid form. Her eyes were heavy with unshed tears.

"I think not,"—she said—"There is life in them—yes, there is life, though for the time it is paralysed. But"—here she gave him the loveliest smile of tenderness—"You brave Giulio!—you are exhausted and wet through—attend to yourself first—then you can help me with these unhappy ones—and you Gaspard,—Gaspard!"

"Here, Madama!"

"You have done so well!" she said—"Without fear or failure!"

"Only by God's mercy!" answered Gaspard—"If the rope had broken; if the ship had lost balance—"

She smiled.

"So many 'ifs' Gaspard? Have I not told you it CANNOT lose balance? And are not my words proved true? Now we have finished our rescue work we may go—we can start at once—"

He looked at her.

"There is more weight on board!" he said meaningly, "If we are to carry two dead bodies through the air, it may mean a heavenly funeral for all of us! The 'White Eagle' has not been tested for heavy transport."

She heard him patiently,—then turned to Rivardi and repeated her words—

"We can start at once. Steer upwards and onwards."

Like a man hypnotised he obeyed,—and in a few moments the air-ship, answering easily to the helm, rose lightly as a bubble from the depths of the canon, through the fiercely dashing showers of spray tossed by the foaming torrent, and soared aloft, high and ever higher, as swiftly as any living bird born for long and powerful flight. Night was falling; and through the dense purple shadows of the Californian sky a big white moon rose, bending ghost-like over the scene of destruction and chaos, lighting with a pale glare the tired and haggard faces of the relief men at their terrible work of digging out the living and the dead from the vast pits of earth into which they had been suddenly engulfed,—while far, far above them flew the "White Eagle," gradually lessening in size through distance till it looked no bigger than a dove on its homeward way. Some priests watching by a row of lifeless men, women and children killed in the earthquake, chanted the "Nunc Dimittis" as the evening grew darker,—and the only one among them who had first seen the air-ship over the canon, where it fell, as it were in the deep gulf surrounded by flood and foam, now raised his eyes in wonderment as he perceived it once more soaring at liberty towards the moon.

"Surely a miracle!" he exclaimed, under his breath—"An escape from destruction through God's mercy! God be praised!"

And he crossed himself devoutly, joining in the solemn chanting of his brethren, kneeling in the moonlight, which threw a ghastly lustre on the dead faces of the victims of the earthquake,—victims not "struck by the hand of God" but by the hand of man! And he who was responsible for the blow lay unconscious of having dealt it, and was borne through the air swiftly and safely away for ever from the tragic scene of the ruin and desolation he had himself wrought.

XXIV

A great silence pervaded the Palazzo d'Oro,—the strained silence of an intense activity weighted with suspense. Servants moved about here and there with noiseless rapidity,—Don Aloysius was seen constantly pacing up and down the loggia absorbed in anxious thought and prayer, and the Marchese Rivardi came and went on errands of which he alone knew the import. Overhead the sky was brilliantly blue and cloudless,—the sun flashed a round shield of dazzling gold all day long on the breast of the placid sea,—but within the house, blinds were drawn to shade and temper the light for eyes that perhaps might never again open to the blessing and glory of the day. A full week had passed since the "White Eagle" had returned from its long and adventurous flight over the vast stretches of ocean, bearing with it the two human creatures cast down to death in the deep Californian canon,—and only one of them had returned to the consciousness of life,—the other still stayed on the verge of the "Great Divide." Morgana had safely landed the heavy burden of seeming death her ship had carried,—and simply stating to Lady Kingswood and her household staff that it was a case of rescue from drowning, had caused the two corpses—(such as they truly appeared)—to be laid, each in a separate chamber, surrounded with every means that could be devised or thought of for their resuscitation. In an atmosphere glowing with mild warmth, on soft beds they were placed, inert and white as frozen clay, their condition being apparently so hopeless that it seemed mere imaginative folly to think that the least breath could ever again part their set lips or the smallest pulsation of blood stir colour through their veins. But Morgana never wavered in her belief that they lived, and hour after hour, day after day she watched with untiring patience, administering the mysterious balm or portion which she kept preciously in her own possession,—and not till the fifth day of her vigil, when Manella showed faint signs of returning consciousness, did she send to Rome for a famous scientist and physician with whom she had frequently corresponded. She entrusted the dispatch of this message to Rivardi, saying—

"It is now time for further aid than mine. The girl will recover—but the man—the man is still in the darkness!"

And her eyes grew heavy with a cloud of sorrow and regret which softened her delicate beauty and made it more than ever unearthly.

"What are they—what is HE—to you?" demanded Rivardi jealously.

"My friend, there was a time when I should have considered that question an impertinence from you!" she said, tranquilly—"But yours is the great share of the rescue—and your magnificent bravery wins you my pardon,—for many things!" And she smiled as she saw him flush under her quiet gaze—"What is this man to me, you ask? Why nothing!—not now! Once he was everything,—though he never knew it. Some quality in him struck the keynote of the scale of life for me,— he was the great delusion of a dream! The delusion is ended—the dream is over! But for that he WAS to me, though only in my own thoughts, I have tried to save his life—not for myself, but for the woman who loves him."

"The woman we rescued with him?—the woman who is here?"

She bent her head in assent. Rivardi's eyes dwelt on her with greater tenderness than he had ever felt before,—she looked so frail and fairy-like, and withal so solitary. He took her little hand and gently kissed it with courteous reverence.

"Then—after all—you have known love!" he said in a low voice— "You have felt what it is,—though you have assumed to despise it?"

"My good Giulio, I DO despise most heartily what the world generally understands as love"—she replied; "There is no baser or more selfish sentiment!—a sentiment made up half of animal desire and half of a personal seeking for admiration, appreciation and self-gratification! Yes, Giulio!—it is so, and I despise it for all these attributes—in truth it is not what I understand or accept as love at all—"

"What DO you understand and accept?" he asked, softly.

Her eyes shone kindly as she raised them to his face.

"Not what you can ever give, Giulio!" she said—"Love—to my mind—is the spiritual part of our being—it should be the complete union of two souls that move as one,—like the two wings of a bird making the body subservient to the highest flights, even as far as heaven! The physical mating of man and woman is seldom higher than the physical mating of any other animals under the sun,—the animals know nothing beyond—but we—we ought to know something!" She paused, then went on—"There is sometimes a great loftiness even in the physical way of so-called 'love'—such passion as the woman we have rescued has for the man she was ready to die with,—a primitive passion of primitive woman at her best. Such feeling is out of date in these days—we have passed that boundary line—and a great unexplored world lies open before us—who can say what we may find there! Perhaps we shall discover what all women have sought for from the beginning of things—"

"And that is?" he asked.

"Happiness!" she replied—"The perfect happiness of life in love!"

He had held her hand till now, when he released it.

"I wish I could give it to you!" he said.

"You cannot, Giulio! I am not made for any man—as men go!"

"It is a pity you think so"—he said—"For—after all—you are just—a woman!"

"Am I?" she murmured,—and a strange flitting smile brightened her features—"Perhaps!—and yet—perhaps not! Who knows!"

She left him puzzled and uneasy. Somehow she always managed to evade his efforts to become more intimate in his relations with her. Generous and kind-hearted as she was, she held him at a distance, and maintained her own aloof position inexorably. A less intelligent man than Rivardi would have adopted the cynic's attitude and averred that her rejection of love and marriage arose from her own unlovableness and unmarriageableness, but he knew better than that. He was wise enough to perceive the rareness and delicacy of her physical and mental organisation and temperament,—a temperament so finely strung as to make all other women seem gross and material beside her. He felt and knew her to be both his moral and intellectual superior,—and this very fact rendered it impossible that he could ever master her mind and tame it down to the subservience of married life. That dauntless spirit of hers would never bend to an inferior,—not even love (if she could feel it) would move her thus far. And the man she had adventured across ocean to rescue—what was he? She confessed that she had loved him, though that love was past. And now she had set herself to watch night and day by his dead body (for dead he surely was in Rivardi's opinion) sparing no pains to recover what seemed beyond recovery; while one of the greatest mysteries of the whole mysterious affair was just this—How had she known the man's life was in danger?

All these questions Rivardi discussed with Don Aloysius, who listened to him patiently without committing himself to any reply. Whatever Morgana had confided to him—(and she had confided much)—he kept his own counsel.

Within forty-eight hours of Morgana's summons the famous specialist from Rome, Professor Marco Ardini, noted all over the world for his miraculous cures of those whom other physicians had given up as past curing, arrived. He heard the story of the rescue of a man and woman from drowning with emotionless gravity, more taken for the moment by Morgana herself, whom he had never seen before, but with whom he had corresponded on current questions of scientific importance. From the extremely learned and incisive tone of her letters he had judged her to be an elderly woman of profound scholarship who had spent the greater part of her life in study, and his astonishment at the sight of the small, dainty creature who received him in the library of the Palazzo d'Oro was beyond all verbal expression,—in fact, he took some minutes to recover from the magnetic "shock" of her blue eyes and wistful smile.

"I must be quite frank with you,"—she said, after a preliminary conversation with the great man in his own Italian tongue—"These two people have suffered their injuries by drowning—but not altogether. They are the victims of an earthquake,—and were thrown by the earth's upheaval into a deep chasm flooded by water—"

The Professor interrupted her.

"Pardon, Signora! There has been no recent earthquake in Europe."

She gave a little gesture of assent.

"Not in Europe—no! But in America—in California there has been a terrible one!"

"In California!" he echoed amazedly-"Gran' Dio! You do not mean to say that you brought these people from California, across that vast extent of ocean?"

She smiled.

"By air-ship—yes! Really nothing so very remarkable! You will not ask for further details just now, Professor!" and she laid her pretty hand coaxingly on his arm—"You and I both know how advisable it is to say as little as possible of our own work or adventures, while any subject is awaiting treatment and every moment counts! I will answer any question you may ask when you have seen my patients. The girl is a beautiful creature—she is beginning to regain consciousness—but the man I fear is past even Your skill. Come!"

She led the way and Professor Ardini followed, marvelling at her ethereal grace and beauty, and more than interested in the "case" on which his opinion was sought. Entering a beautiful room glowing with light and warmth and colour, he saw, lying on a bed and slightly propped up by pillows, a lovely girl, pale as ivory, with dark hair loosely braided on either side of her head. Her eyes were closed, and the long black lashes swept the cheeks in a curved fringe,—the lips were faintly red, and the breath parted them slowly and reluctantly. The Professor bent over her and listened,—her heart beat slowly but regularly,—he felt her pulse.

"She will live!"—he said—"There are no injuries?"

"None"—Morgana replied, as he put his questions—"Some few bruises—but no bones broken—nothing serious."

"You have examined her?"

"Yes."

"You have no nurses?"

"No. I and my house people are sufficient." Her tone became slightly peremptory. "There is no need for outside interference. Whatever your orders are, they shall be carried out."

He looked at her. His face was a somewhat severe one, furrowed with thought and care,—but when he smiled, a wonderful benevolence gave it an almost handsome effect. And he smiled now.

"You shall not be interfered with,"—he said—"You have done very well! Complete rest, nourishment and your care are all that this patient needs. She will be quite herself in a very short time. She is extraordinarily beautiful!"

"I wish you could see her eyes!" said Morgana.

Almost as if the uttered wish had touched some recess of her stunned brain, Manella's eyelids quivered and lifted,—the great dark glory of the stars of her soul shone forth for an instant, giving sudden radiance to the pallor of her features—then they closed again as in utter weariness.

"Magnificent!" said Ardini, under his breath—"And full of the vital light,—she will live!"

"And she will love!" added Morgana, softly.

The Professor looked at her enquiringly.

"The man she loves is in the next room"—she continued—"We rescued him with her—if it can be called a rescue. He is the worst case. Only you may be able to bring him back to consciousness,—I have done my best in vain. If You fail then we must give up hope."

She preceded him into the adjoining chamber; as he entered it after her he paused—almost intimidated, despite his long medical and surgical experience, by the stone-like figure of man that lay before him. It was as if one should have unearthed a statue, grey with time—a statue nobly formed, with a powerful head and severe features sternly set,—

　　　　　　　　　　　　　　　MARIE CORELLI

the growth of beard revealing, rather than concealing, the somewhat cruel contour of mouth and chin. The Professor walked slowly up to the bed and looked at this strange effigy of a human being for many minutes in silence,—Morgana watching him with strained but quiet suspense. Presently he touched the forehead—it was stone-cold—then the throat, stone-cold and rigid—he bent down and listened for the heart's pulsations,—not a flutter—not a beat! Drawing back from this examination he looked at Morgana,—she met his eyes with the query in her own which she emphasised by the spoken word—

"Dead?"

"No!"—he answered—"I think not. It is very difficult for a man of this type to die at all. Granted favourable conditions—and barring accidents caused by the carelessness of others—he ought to be one of those destined to live for ever. But"—here he hesitated—"if I am right in my surmise,—of course it is only a first opinion—death would be the very best thing for him."

"Oh, why do you say that?" she asked, pitifully.

"Because the brain is damaged—hopelessly! This man—whoever he is—has been tampering with some chemical force he does not entirely understand,—his whole body is charged with its influence, and this it is that gives his form its unnatural appearance which, though death-like, is not death. If I leave him alone and untouched he will probably expire unconsciously in a few days,—but if—after what I have just told you—you wish me to set the life atoms going again,—even as a clock is wound up,—I can relax the tension which now paralyses the cells, muscles and nerves, and he will live—yes!—like most people without brains he will live a long time—probably too long!"

Morgana moved to the bedside and gazed with a solemn earnestness at the immobile, helpless form stretched out before her as though ready for burial. Her heart swelled with suppressed emotion,—she thought with anguish of the brilliant brain, the strong, self-sufficient nature brought to such ruin through too great an estimate of human capability. Tears rushed to her eyes—

"Oh, give him life!" she whispered—"Give him life for the sake of the woman who loves him more than life!"

The Professor gave her a quick, keen glance.

"You?"

She shivered at the question as though struck by a cold wind,—then conquering the momentary weakness, answered—

"No. The girl you have just seen. He is her world!"

Ardini's brows met in a saturnine frown.

"Her world will be an empty one!" he said, with an expressive gesture—"A world without fruit or flower,—without light or song! A dreary world! But such as it is,—such as it is bound to be,—it can live on,—a life-in-death."

"Are you quite sure of this?" Morgana asked—"Can any of us, however wise, be quite sure of anything?"

His frown relaxed and his whole features softened. He took her hand and patted it kindly.

"Signora, you know as well as I do, that the universe and all within it represents law and order. A man is a little universe in himself—and if the guiding law of his system is destroyed, there is chaos and darkness. We scientists can say 'Let there be light,' but the fulfilled result 'and there was light' comes from God alone!"

"Why should not God help in this case?" she suggested.

"Ah, why!" and Ardini shrugged his shoulders—"How can I tell? My long experience has taught me that wherever the law has been broken God does Not help! Who knows whether this frozen wreck of man has obeyed or disobeyed the law? I can do all that science allows—"

"And you will do it!" interrupted Morgana eagerly, "You will use your best skill and knowledge—everything you wish shall be at your service—name whatever fee your merit claims—"

He raised his hand with a deprecatory gesture.

"Money does not count with me, Signora!" he said—"Nor with you. The point with both of us in all our work is—success! Is it not so? Yes! And it is because I do not see a true success in this case that I hesitate; true success would mean the complete restoration of this man to life and intelligence,—but life without intelligence is no triumph for science. I can do all that science will allow—"

"And you Will do this 'all'"—said Morgana, eagerly—"You will forego triumph for simple pity!—pity for the girl who would surely die if he were dead!—and perhaps after all, God may help the recovery!"

"It shall be as you wish, Signora! I must stay here two or three days—"

"As long as you find it necessary"—said Morgana—"All your orders shall be obeyed."

"Good! Send me a trustworthy man-servant who can help to move and support the patient, and we can get to work. I left a few necessary appliances in your hall—I should like them brought into this room—

and then—" here he took her hand and pressed it kindly—"you can leave us to our task, and take some rest. You must be very tired."

"I am never tired"—she answered, gently—"I thank you in advance for all you are going to do!"

She left the room then, with one backward glance at the inert stiff figure on the bed,—and went to arrange matters with her household that the Professor's instructions should be strictly carried out. Lady Kingswood, deeply interested, heard her giving certain orders and asked—

"There is hope then? These two poor creatures will live?"

"I think so"—answered Morgana, with a thrill of sadness in her sweet voice—"They will live—pray God their lives may be worth living!"

She watched the man-servant whom she had chosen to wait on Ardini depart on his errand—she saw him open the door of the room where Seaton lay, and shut it—then there was a silence. Oppressed by a sudden heaviness of heart she thought of Manella, and entered her apartment softly to see how she fared. The girl's beautiful dark eyes were wide open and full of the light of life and consciousness. She smiled and stretched out her arms.

"It is my angel!" she murmured faintly—"My little white angel who came to me in the darkness! And this is Heaven!"

Swiftly and silently Morgana went to her side, and taking her outstretched arms put them round her own neck.

"Manella!" she said, tenderly—"Dear, beautiful Manella! Do you know me?"

The great loving eyes rested on her with glowing warmth and pleasure.

"Indeed I know you!" and Manella's voice, weak as that of a sick child, sounded ever so far away—"The little white lady of my dreams! Oh, I have wanted you!—wanted you so much! Why did you not come back sooner?"

Afraid to trouble her brain by the sudden shock of too rapidly recurring memories, Morgana made no reply, but merely soothed her with tender caresses, when all at once she made a violent struggle to rise from the bed.

"I must go!" she cried—"He is calling me! I must follow him—yes, even if he kills me for it—he is in danger!"

Morgana held her close and firmly.

"Hush, hush, dear!" she murmured—"Be quite still! He is safe—believe me! He is near you—in the next room!—out of all danger."

"Oh, no, it is not possible!" and the girl's eyes grew wild with terror—"He cannot be safe!—he is destroying himself! I have followed him every step of the way—I have watched him,—oh!—so long!—and he came out of the hut this morning—I was hidden among the trees—he could not see me—" she broke off, and a violent trembling shook her whole body. Morgana tried to calm her into silence, but she went on rambling incoherently. "There was something he carried as though it was precious to him—something that glittered like gold,—and he went away quickly—quickly to the canyon,—I followed him like a dog, crawling through the brushwood—I followed him across the deep water—to the cave where it was all dark—black as midnight!" She paused—then suddenly flung her arms round Morgana crying—"Oh, hold me!—hold me!—I am in this darkness trying to find him!—there!—there!—he turns and sees me by the light of a lamp he carries; he knows I have followed him, and he is angry! Oh, dear God, he is angry—he raises his arm to strike me!" She uttered a smothered shriek, and clung to Morgana in a kind of frenzy. "No mercy, no pity! That thing that glitters in his hand—it frightens me—what is it? I kneel to him on the cold stones—I pray him to forgive me—to come with me—but his arm is still raised to strike—he does not care—!"

Here a pale horror blanched her features—she drew herself away from Morgana's hold and put out her hands with the instinctive gesture of one who tries to escape falling from some great height. Morgana, alarmed at her looks, caught her again in her arms and held her tenderly, whereat a faint smile hovered on her lips and her distraught movements ceased.

"What is this?"—she asked—then murmured—"My little white lady, how did you come here? How could you cross the flood?—unless on wings? Ah!—you are a fairy and you can do all you wish to do—but you cannot save Him!—it is too late! He will not save himself—and he does not care,—he does not care—neither for me nor you!"

She drooped her head against Morgana's shoulder and her eyes closed in utter exhaustion. Morgana laid her back gently on her pillows, and pouring a few drops of the cordial she had used before, and of which she had the sole secret, into a wineglassful of water, held it to her lips. She drank it obediently, evidently conscious now that she was being cared for. But she was still restless, and presently she sat up in a listening attitude, one hand uplifted.

"Listen!" she said in a low, awed tone—"Thunder! Do you hear it? God speaks!"

She lay down again passively and was silent for a long time. The hours passed and the day grew into late afternoon, and Morgana, patiently watchful, thought she slept. All suddenly she sprang up, wide-eyed and alert.

"What was that?" she cried—"I heard him call!"

Morgana, startled by her swift movement, stood transfixed—listening. The deep tones of a man's voice rang out loudly and defiantly—

"There shall be no more wars! There can be none! I say so! I am Master of the World!"

XXV

A brilliant morning broke over the flower-filled gardens of the Palazzo d'Oro, and the sea, stretched out in a wide radiance of purest blue shimmered with millions of tiny silver ripples brushed on its surface by a light wind as delicate as a bird's wing. Morgana stood in her rose-marble loggia, looking with a pathetic wistfulness at the beauty of the scene, and beside her stood Marco Ardini, scientist, surgeon and physician, looking also, but scarcely seeing, his whole thought being concentrated on the "case" with which he had been dealing.

"It is exactly as I at first told you,"—he said—"The man is strong in muscle and sinew,—but his brain is ruined. It can no longer control or command the body's mechanism,—therefore the body is practically useless. Power of volition is gone,—the poor fellow will never be able to walk again or to lift a hand. A certain faculty of speech is left,—but even this is limited to a few words which are evidently the result of the last prevailing thoughts impressed on the brain-cells. It is possible he will repeat those words thousands of times!—the oftener he repeats them the more he will like to say them."

"What are they?" Morgana asked in a tone of sorrow and compassion.

"Strange enough for a man in his condition"—replied Ardini—"And always the same. 'THERE SHALL BE NO MORE WARS! THERE CAN BE NONE! I SAY IT!—*I* ONLY! IT IS MY GREAT SECRET! *I* AM MASTER OF THE WORLD!' Poor devil! What a 'master of the world' is there!"

Morgana shuddered as with cold, shading her eyes from the radiant sunshine.

"Does he say nothing else?" she murmured—"Is there no name—no place—that he seems to remember?"

"He remembers nothing—he knows nothing"—answered Ardini—"He does not even realize me as a man—I might be a fish or a serpent for all his comprehension. One glance at his moveless eyes is enough to prove that. They are like pebbles in his head—without cognisance or expression. He mutters the words 'Great Secret' over and over again, and tacks it on to the other phrase of 'No more wars' in a semi-conscious sort of gabble,—this is, of course, the disordered action of the brain working to catch up and join together hopelessly severed fragments."

Morgana lifted her sea-blue eyes and looked with grave appeal into the severely intellectual, half-frowning face of the great Professor.

"Is there no hope of an ultimate recovery?" she asked—"With time and rest and the best of unceasing care, might not this poor brain right itself?"

"Medically and scientifically speaking, there is no hope,—none whatever"—he replied—"Though of course we all know that Nature's remedial methods are inexhaustible, and often, to the wisest of us, seem miraculous, because as yet we do not understand one tithe of her processes. But—in this case,—this strange and terrible case"—and he uttered the words with marked gravity,—"It is Nature's own force that has wrought the damage,—some powerful influence which the man has been testing has proved too much for him—and it has taken its own vengeance."

Morgana heard this with strained interest and attention.

"Tell me just what you mean,"—she said—"There is something you do not quite express—or else I am too slow to understand—"

Ardini took a few paces up and down the loggia and then halted, facing her in the attitude of a teacher preparing to instruct a pupil.

"Signora,"—he said—"When you began to correspond with me some years ago from America, I realised that I was in touch with a highly intelligent and cultivated mind. I took you to be many years older than you are, with a ripe scientific experience. I find you young, beautiful, and pathetic in the pure womanliness of your nature, which must be perpetually contending with an indomitable power of intellectuality and of spirituality,—spirituality is the strongest force of your being. You are not made like other women. This being so I can say to you what other women would not understand. Science is my life-subject, as it is yours,—it is a window set open in the universe admitting great light. But many of us foolishly imagine that this light emanates from ourselves as a result of our own cleverness, whereas it comes from that Divine Source of all things, which we call God. We refuse to believe this,—it wounds our pride. And we use the discoveries of science recklessly and selfishly—without gratitude, humbleness or reverence. So it happens that the first tendency of godless men is to destroy. The love of destruction and torture shows itself in the boy who tears off the wing of an insect, or kills a bird for the pleasure of killing. The boy is father of the man. And we come, after much ignorant denial and obstinacy, back to the inexorable truth that 'they who take the sword shall perish with the sword.' If we consider the 'sword' as a metaphor for every instrument of destruction, we shall see the force of its application—the submarine, for example, built for the most treacherous kind of sea-warfare—how often they that undertake its work are slain themselves! And so it is through the whole gamut of scientific discovery when it is used for inhuman and unlawful purposes. But when this same 'sword' is lifted to put an end to torture, disease, and the manifold miseries of life, then the Power that has entrusted it to mankind endows it with blessing and there are no evil results. I say this to you by way of explaining the view I am forced to take of this man whose strange case you ask me to deal with,—my opinion is that through chance or intention he has been playing recklessly with a great natural force, which he has not entirely understood, for some destructive purpose, and that it has recoiled on himself."

Morgana looked him steadily in the eyes.

"You may be right,"—she said—"He is—or was—one of the most brilliant of our younger scientists. You know his name—I have sent you from New York some accounts of his work—He is Roger Seaton, whose experiments in the condensation of radioactivity startled America some four or five years ago—"

"Roger Seaton!" he exclaimed—"What! The man who professed to have found a new power which would change the face of the world? . . . He,—this wreck?—this blind, deaf lump of breathing clay? Surely he has not fallen on so horrible a destiny!"

Tears rushed to Morgana's eyes,—she could not answer. She could only bend her head in assent.

Profoundly moved, Ardini took her hand, and kissed it with sympathetic reverence.

"Signora," he said—"This is indeed a tragedy! You have saved this life at I know not what risk to yourself—and as I am aware what a life of great attainment it promised to be, you may be sure I will spare no pains to bring it back to normal conditions. But frankly I do not think it will be possible. There is the woman who loves him—her influence may do something—"

"If he ever loved her—yes"—and Morgana smiled rather sadly— "But if he did not—if the love is all on her side—"

Ardini shrugged his shoulders.

"A great love is always on the woman's side,"—he said—"Men are too selfish to love perfectly. In this case, of course, there is no emotion, no sentiment of any sort left in the mere hulk of man. But still I will continue my work and do my best."

He left her then,—and she stood for a while alone, gazing far out to the blue sea and sunlight, scarcely seeing them for the half-unconscious tears that blinded her eyes. Suddenly a Ray, not of the sun, shot athwart the loggia and touched her with a deep gold radiance. She saw it and looked up, listening.

"Morgana!"

The Voice quivered along the Ray like the touched string of an aeolian harp. She answered it in almost a whisper—

"I hear!"

"You grieve for sorrows not your own," said the Voice—"And we love you for it. But you must not waste your tears on the errors of others. Each individual Spirit makes its own destiny, and no other but Itself can help Itself. You are one of the Chosen and Beloved!—You must fulfil the happiness you have created for your own soul! Come to us soon!" A thrill of exquisite joy ran through her.

"I will!" she said—"When my duties here are done."

The golden Ray decreased in length and brilliancy, and finally died away in a fine haze mingling with the air. She watched it till it vanished,—then with a sense of relief from her former sadness, she went into the house to see Manella. The girl had risen from her bed, and with the assistance of Lady Kingswood, who tended her with motherly care, had been arrayed in a loose white woollen gown, which, carelessly gathered round her, intensified by contrast the striking beauty of her dark eyes and hair, and ivory pale skin. As Morgana entered the room she smiled, her small even teeth gleaming like tiny pearls in the faint rose of her pretty mouth, and stretched out her hand.

"What has he said to you?" she asked—"Tell me! Is he not glad to see you?—to know he is with you?—safe with you in your home?"

Morgana sat down beside her.

"Dear Manella"—she answered, gently and with tenderest pity—"He does not know me. He knows nothing! He speaks a few words,—but he has no consciousness of what he is saying."

Manella looked at her wonderingly—

"Ah, that is because he is not himself yet"—she said—"The crash of the rocks—the pouring of the flood—this was enough to kill him—but he will recover in a little while and he will know you!—yes, he will know you, and he will thank God for life to see you!"

Her unselfish joy in the idea that the man she loved would soon recognise the woman he preferred to herself, was profoundly touching, and Morgana kissed the hand she held.

"Dear, I am afraid he will never know anything more in this world"—she said, sorrowfully—"Neither man nor woman! Nor can he thank God for a life which will be long, living death! Unless You can help him!"

"I?" and Manella's eyes dilated with brilliant eagerness; "I will give my life for his! What can I do?"

And then, with patient slowness and gentleness, little by little, Morgana told her all. Lady Kingswood, sitting in an arm-chair near the window, worked at her embroidery, furtive tears dropping now and again on the delicate pattern, as she heard the details of the tragic verdict given by one of Europe's greatest medical scientists on the hopelessness of ever repairing the damage wrought by the shock which had shaken a powerful brain into ruins. But it was wonderful to watch Manella's face as she listened. Sorrow, pity, tenderness, love, all in turn flashed their heavenly radiance in her eyes and intensified her beauty, and when she had heard all, she smiled as some lovely angel might smile on a repentant soul. Her whole frame seemed to vibrate with a passion of unselfish emotion.

"He will be my care!" she said—"The good God has heard my prayers and given him to me to be all mine!" She clasped her hands in a kind of ecstasy, "My life is for him and him alone! He will be my little child!—this big, strong, poor broken man!—and I will nurse him back to himself,—I will watch for every little sign of hope!—he shall learn to see through my eyes—to hear through my ears—to remember all that he has forgotten! . . ." Her voice broke in a half sob. Morgana put an arm about her.

"Manella, Manella!" she said—"You do not know what you say—you cannot understand the responsibility—it would make you a prisoner for life—"

"Oh, I understand!" and Manella shook back her dark hair with the little proud, decisive gesture characteristic of her temperament—"Yes!—and I wish to be so imprisoned! If we had not been rescued by you, we should have died together!—now you will help us to live together! Will you not? You are a little white angel—a fairy!—yes!—to me you are!—your heart is full of unspent love! You will let me stay with him always—always?—As his nurse?—his servant?—his slave?"

Morgana looked at her tenderly, touched to the quick by her eagerness and her beauty, now intensified by the glow of excitement which gave a roseate warmth to her cheeks and deeper darkness to her eyes. All ignorant and unsuspecting as she was of the world's malignity and cruel misjudgments, how could it be explained to her that a woman of such youth and loveliness, electing to dwell alone with a man, even if the man were a hopeless paralytic, would make herself the subject of malicious comment and pitiless scandal! Some reflection of this feeling showed itself in the expression of Morgana's face while she hesitated to answer, holding the girl's hand in her own and stroking it affectionately the while. Manella, gazing at her as a worshipper might gaze at a sacred picture, instinctively divined her thought.

"Ah? I know what you would say!" she exclaimed, "That I might bring shame to him by my companionship—always—yes!—that is possible!—wicked people would talk of him and judge him wrongly—"

"Oh, Manella, dear!" murmured Morgana—"Not him—not him—but You!"

"Me?" She tossed back her wealth of hair, and smiled—"What am I? Just a bit of dust in his path! I am nothing at all! I do not care what anybody says or thinks of Me!—what should it matter! But see!—to save Him—let me be his wife!"

"His wife!" Morgana repeated the words in amazement, and Lady Kingswood, laying down her work, gazed at the two beautiful women, the one so spiritlike and fair, the other so human and queenly, in a kind of stupefaction, wondering if she had heard aright.

"His wife! Yes!" . . . Manella spoke with a thrill of exultation in her voice,—and she caught Morgana's hand and kissed it fondly—"His wife! It is the only way I can be his slave-woman! Let me marry him while he knows nothing, so that I may have the right to wait upon him and care for him! He shall never know! For—if he comes to himself again—please God he will!—as soon as that happens I will go away at once. He will never know!—he shall never learn who it is that has cared for him! You see? I shall never be really his wife—nor he my husband—only in name. And then—when he comes out of the darkness—when he is strong and well once more, he will go to You!—you whom he loves—"

Morgana silenced her by a gesture which was at once commanding and sweetly austere.

"Dear girl, he never loved me!" she said, gently—"He has always loved himself. Yes!—you know that as well as I do! Once—I fancied I loved Him—but now I know my way of love is not his. Let us say no more of it! You wish to be his wife? Do you think what that means? He will never know he is your husband—never recognise you,—your life will be sacrificed to a helpless creature whose brain is gone—who will be unconscious of your care and utterly irresponsive. Oh, sweet, Too loving Manella!—you must not pledge the best years of your youth and beauty to such a destiny!"

Manella's dark eyes flashed with passionate ardour and enthusiasm.

"I must—I must!" she said—"It is the work God gives me to do! Do you not see how it is with me? It is my one love—the best of my heart!—the pulse of my life! Youth and beauty!—what are they without him? Ill or well, he is all I care for, and if I may not care for him I will die! It is quite easy to die—to make an end!—but if there is any youth or beauty to spend, it will be better to spend it on love than in death! My white angel, listen and be patient with me! You ARE patient but still be more so!—you know there will be none in the world to care for him!—ah!—when he was well and strong he said that love would weary him—he did not think he would ever be helpless and ill!—ah, no!—but a broken brain is put away—out of sight—to be forgotten like a broken toy! He was at work on some wonderful invention—some great secret!—it will never be known now—not a soul will ever ask what has become of it or of him! The world does not care what becomes of anyone—it has no sympathy. Only those who love greatly have any pity!"

She clasped her hands and lifted them in an attitude of prayer, laying them against Morgana's breast.

"You will let me have my way—surely you will?" she pleaded—"You are a little angel of mercy, unlike any other woman I ever saw—so white and pure and sweet!—you understand it all! In his dreadful weakness and loneliness, God gives him to ME!—happy me, who am young and strong enough to care for him and attend upon him. I have no money,—perhaps he has none either, but I will work to keep him,—I am clever at my needle—I can embroider quite well—and I will manage to earn enough for us both." Her voice broke in a sob, and Morgana, the tears falling from her own eyes, drew her into a close embrace.

And she murmured plaintively again—

"His wife!—I must be his wife,—his serving-woman—then no one can forbid me to be with him! You will find some good priest to say the marriage service for us and give us God's benediction—it will mean nothing to him, because he cannot know or understand,—but to me it will be a holy sacrament!"

Then she broke down and wept softly till the pent-up passion of her heart was relieved, and Morgana, mastering her own emotion, had soothed her into quietude. Leaning back from her arm-chair where she had rested since rising from her bed, she looked up with an anxious appeal in her lovely eyes.

"Let me tell you something before I forget it again"—she said—"It is something terrible—the earthquake."

"Yes, yes, do not think of it now"—said Morgana, hastily, afraid that her mind would wander into painful mazes of recollection—"That is all over."

"Ah, yes! But you should know the truth! It was NOT an earthquake!" she persisted—"It was not God's doing! It was HIS work!"

And she indicated by a gesture the next room where Roger Seaton lay.

A cold horror ran through Morgana's blood. HIS work!—the widespread ruin of villages and townships,—the devastation of a vast tract of country—the deaths of hundreds of men, women and little children—HIS work? Could it be possible? She stood transfixed,—while Manella went on—

"I know it was his work!" she said—"I was warned by a friend of his who came to 'la Plaza' that he was working at something which might lose him his life. And so I watched. I told you how I followed him that morning—how I saw him looking at a box full of shining things that glittered like the points of swords,—how he put this box in a case and then in a basket, and slung the basket over his shoulder, and went down into the canon, and then to the cave where I found him. I called him—he heard, and held up a miner's lamp and saw me!—then—then, oh, dear God!—then he cursed me for following him,—he raised his arm to strike me, and in his furious haste to reach me he slipped on the wet, mossy stones. Something fell from his hand with a great crash like thunder—and there was a sudden glare of fire!—oh, the awfulness of that sound and that flame!—and the rocks rose up and split asunder—the ground shook and broke under me—and I remember no more—no more till I found myself here!—here with you!"

Morgana roused herself from the stupefaction of horror with which she had listened to this narration.

"Do not think of it any more!" she said in a low sad voice—"Try to forget it all. Yes, dear!—try to forget all the mad selfishness and cruelty of the man you love! Poor, besotted soul!—he has a bitter punishment!"

She could say no more then,—stooping, she kissed the girl on the white forehead between the rippling waves of dark hair, and strove to meet the searching eyes with a smile.

"Dear, beautiful angel, you will help me?" Manella pleaded—"You will help me to be his wife?"

And Morgana answered with pitiful tenderness.

"I will!"

And with a sign to Lady Kingswood to come nearer and sit by the girl as she lay among her pillows more or less exhausted, she herself left the room. As she opened the door on her way out, the strong voice of Roger Seaton rang out with singularly horrible harshness—

"There shall be no more wars! There can be none! I say it! My great secret! I am master of the world!"

Shuddering as she heard, she pressed her hands over her ears and hurried along the corridor. Her thoughts paraphrased the saying of Madame Roland on Liberty—"Oh, Science! what crimes are committed in thy name!" She was anxious to see and speak with Professor Ardini, but came upon the Marchese Rivardi instead, who met her at the door of the library and caught her by both hands.

"What is all this?" he demanded, insistently—"I MUST speak to you! You have been weeping! What is troubling you?"

She drew her hands gently away from his.

"Nothing, Giulio!" and she smiled kindly—"I grieve for the griefs of others—quite uselessly!—but I cannot help it!"

"There is no hope, then?" he said.

"None—not for the man"—she replied—"His body will live,—but his brain is dead."

Rivardi gave an expressive gesture.

"Horrible! Better he should die!"

"Yes, far better! But the girl loves him. She is an ardent Spanish creature—warm-hearted and simple as a child,—she believes"—and Morgana's eyes had a pathetic wistfulness—"she believes,—as all women believe when they love for the first time,—that love has a divine power next to that of God!—that it will work miracles of recovery when all seems lost. The disillusion comes, of course, sooner or later,—but it has to come of itself—not through any other influence. She—Manella Soriso—has resolved to be his wife."

MARIE CORELLI

"Gran' Dio!" Rivardi started back in utter amazement—"His wife?—That girl? Young, beautiful? She will chain herself to a madman? Surely you will not allow it!"

Morgana looked at him with a smile.

"Poor Giulio!" she said, softly—"You are a most unfortunate descendant of your Roman ancestors as far as we women are concerned! You fall in love with me—and you find I am not for you!—then you see a perfectly lovely woman whom you cannot choose but admire—and a little stray thought comes flying into your head—yes!—quite involuntarily!—that perhaps—only perhaps—her love might come your way! Do not be angry, my friend!—it was only a thought that moved you when you saw her the other day—when I called you to look at her as she recovered consciousness and lay on her bed like a sleeping figure of the loveliest of pagan goddesses! What man could have seen her thus without a thrill of tenderness!—and now you have to hear that all that beauty and warmth of youthful life is to be sacrificed to a stone idol!—(for the man she worships is little more!) ah, yes!—I am sorry for you, Giulio!—but can do nothing to prevent the sacrifice,—indeed, I have promised to assist it!"

Rivardi had alternately flushed and paled while she spoke,—her keen, incisive probing of his most secret fancies puzzled and vexed him,—but with a well-assumed indifference he waved aside her delicately pointed suggestions as though he had scarcely heard them, and said—

"You have promised to assist? Can you reconcile it to your conscience to let this girl make herself a prisoner for life?"

"I can!" she answered quietly—"For if she is opposed in her desire for such imprisonment she will kill herself. So it is wisest to let her have her way. The man she loves so desperately may die at any moment, and then she will be free. But meanwhile she will have the consolation of doing all she can for him, and the hope of helping him to recover; vain hope as it may be, there is a divine unselfishness in it. For she says that if he is restored to health she will go away at once and never let him know she is his wife."

Rivardi's handsome face expressed utter incredulity.

"Will she keep her word I wonder?"

"She will!"

"Marvellous woman!" and there was bitterness in his tone—"But women are all amazing when you come to know them! In love? in hate, in good, in evil, in cleverness and in utter stupidity, they are wonderful creatures! And you, amica bella, are perhaps the most wonderful of them all! So kind and yet so cruel!"

"Cruel?" she echoed.

"Yes! To me!"

She looked at him and smiled. That smile gave such a dreamy, spiritlike sweetness to her whole personality that for the moment she seemed to float before him like an aerial vision rather than a woman of flesh and blood, and the bold desire which possessed him to seize and clasp her in his arms was checked by a sense of something like fear. Her eyes rested on his with a full clear frankness.

"If I am cruel to you, my friend"—she said, gently, "it is only to be more kind!"

She left him then and went out. He saw her small, elfin figure pass among the chains of roses which at this season seemed to tie up the garden in brilliant knots of colour, and then go down the terraces, one by one, towards the monastic retreat half buried among pine and olive, where Don Aloysius governed his little group of religious brethren.

He guessed her intent.

"She will tell him all"—he thought—"And with his strange semi-religious, semi-scientific notions, it will be easy for her to persuade him to marry the girl to this demented creature who fills the house with his shouting 'There shall be no more wars!' I should never have thought her capable of tolerating such a crime!"

He turned to leave the loggia,—but paused as he perceived Professor Ardini advancing from the interior of the house, his hands clasped behind his back and his furrowed brows bent in gloomy meditation.

"You have a difficult case?" he queried.

"More than difficult!" replied Ardini—"Beyond human skill! Perhaps not beyond the mysterious power we call God."

Rivardi shrugged his shoulders. He was a sceptic of sceptics and his modern-world experiences had convinced him that what man could not do was not to be done at all.

"The latest remedy proposed by the Signora is—love!" he said, carelessly—"The girl who is here,—Manella Soriso—has made up her mind to be the wife of this unfortunate—"

Ardini gave an expressive gesture.

"Altro! If she has made up her mind, heaven itself will not move her! It will be a sublime sacrifice of one life for another,—what would you?

MARIE CORELLI

Such sacrifices are common, though the world does not hear of them. In this instance there is no one to prevent it."

"You approve—you tolerate it?" exclaimed Rivardi angrily.

"I have no power to approve or to tolerate"—replied the scientist, coldly—"The matter is not one in which I have any right to interfere. Nor,—I think,—have You!—I have stated such facts as exist—that the man's brain is practically destroyed—but that owing to the strength of the life-centres he will probably exist in his present condition for a full term of years. To keep him so alive will entail considerable care and expense. He will need a male nurse—probably two—food of the best and absolutely tranquil surroundings. If the Signora, who is rich and generous, guarantees these necessities, and the girl who loves him desires to be his wife under such terrible conditions, I do not see how anyone can object to the marriage."

"Then he poor devil of a man will be married without his knowledge, and probably (if he had his senses) against his will!" said Rivardi.

Ardini bent his brows yet more frowningly.

"Just so!" he answered—"But he has neither knowledge nor will— nor is he likely ever to have them again. These great attributes of the god in man have been taken from him. Power and Will!—Will and Power!—the two wings of the Soul!—they are gone, probably for ever. Science can do nothing to bring them back, but I will not deny the possibility of other forces which might work a remedy on this ruin of a 'master of the world' as he calls himself! Therefore I say let the love-woman try her best!"

XXVI

D on Aloysius sat in his private library,—a room little larger than a monastic cell, and at his feet knelt Morgana like a child at prayer. The rose and purple glow of the sunset fell aslant through a high oriel window of painted glass, shedding an aureole round her golden head, and intensified the fine, dark intellectual outline of the priest's features as he listened with fixed attention to the soft pure voice, vibrating with tenderness and pity as she told him of the love that sought to sacrifice itself for love's sake only.

"In your Creed and in mine,"—she said—"there is no union which is real or binding save the Spiritual,—and this may be consummated in some way beyond our knowledge when once the sacred rite is said. You need no explanation from me,—you who are a member and future denizen of the Golden City,—you, who are set apart to live long after these poor human creatures have passed away with the unthinking millions of the time—and you can have no hesitation to unite them as far as they CAN be united, so that they may at least be saved from the malicious tongues of an always evil-speaking world. You once asked me to tell you of the few moments of real happiness I have known,—this will be one of the keenest joys to me if I can satisfy this loving-hearted girl and aid her to carry out her self-chosen martyrdom. And you must help me!"

Gently Aloysius laid his hand on her bent head.

"It will be indeed a martyrdom!" he said, slowly, "Long and torturing! Think well of it!—a woman, youthful and beautiful, chained to a mere breathing image of man,—a creature who cannot recognise either persons or objects, who is helpless to move, and who will remain in that pitiable state all his life, if he lives!—dear child, are you convinced there is no other way?"

"Not for her!" Morgana replied—"She has set her soul to try if God will help her to restore him,—she will surround him with the constant influence of a perfectly devoted love. Dare we say there shall be no healing power in such an influence?—we who know so much of which the world is ignorant!"

He stroked her shining hair with a careful tenderness as one might stroke the soft plumage of a bird.

"And you?" he said, in a low tone—"What of you?"

She raised her eyes to his. A light of heaven's own radiance shone in those blue orbs—an angelic peace beyond all expression.

"What should there be of me except the dream come true?" she responded, smiling—"You know my plans,—you also know my destiny, for I have told you everything! You will be the controller of all my wealth, entrusted to carry out all my wishes, till it is time either for you to come where I am, or for me to return hither. We never know how or when that may be. But it has all seemed plain sailing for me since I saw the city called 'Brazen' but which WE know is Golden!—and when I found that you belonged to it, and were only stationed here for a short time, I knew I could give you my entire confidence. It is not as if we were of the passing world or its ways—we are of the New Race, and time does not count with us."

"Quite true," he said—"But for these persons in whom you are interested, time is still considered—and for the girl it will be long!"

"Not with such love as hers!" replied Morgana. "Each moment, each hour will be filled with hope and prayer and constant vigilance. Love makes all things easy! It is useless to contend with a fate which both the man and woman have made for themselves. He is—I should say he was a scientist, who discovered the means of annihilating any section of humanity at his own wish and will—he played with the fires of God and brought annihilation on himself. MY discovery—the force that moves my air-ship—the force that is the vital element of all who live in the Golden City—is the same as his!—but *I* use it for health and movement, progress and power—not for the destruction of any living soul! By one single false step he has caused the death and misery of hundreds of helpless human creatures—and this terror has recoiled on his own head. The girl Manella has no evil thought in her—she simply loves!—her love is ill placed, but she also has brought her own destiny on herself. You have worked—and so have I—WITH the universal force, not as the world does, AGAINST it,—and we have made OURSELVES what we are and what we SHALL BE. There is no other way either forward or backward,—you know there is not!" Here she rose from her knees and confronted him, a light aerial creature of glowing radiance and elfin loveliness—"And you must fulfil her wish—and mine!"

He rose also and stood erect, a noble figure of a man with a dignified beauty of mien and feature that seemed to belong to the classic age rather than ours.

"So be it!" he said—"I will carry out all your commands to the letter! May I just say that your generosity to Giulio Rivardi seems almost unnecessary? To endow him with a fortune for life is surely too indulgent! Does he merit such bounty at your hands?"

She smiled.

"Dear Father Aloysius, Giulio has lost his heart to me!" she said—"Or what he calls his heart! He should have some recompense for the loss! He wants to restore his old Roman villa—and when I am gone he will have nothing to distract him from this artistic work,—I leave him the means to do it! I hope he will marry—it is the best thing for him!"

She turned to go.

"And your own Palazzo d'Oro?—"

"Will become the abode of self-sacrificing love," she replied—"It could not be put to better use! It was a fancy of mine;—I love it and its gardens—and I should have tried to live there had I not found out the secret of a large and longer life!" She paused—then added—"Tomorrow morning you will come?"

He bent his head.

"Tomorrow!"

With a salute of mingled reverence and affection she left him. He watched her go,—and hearing the bell begin to chime in the chapel for vespers, he lifted his eyes for a moment in silent prayer. A light flashed downward, playing on his hands like a golden ripple,—and he stood quietly expectant and listening. A Voice floated along the Ray—"You are doing well and rightly!" it said—"You will release her now from the strain of seeming to be what she is not. She is of the New Race, and her spirit is advanced too far to endure the grossness and materialism of the Old generation. She deserves all she has studied and worked for,—lasting life, lasting beauty, lasting love! Nothing must hinder her now!"

"Nothing shall!" he answered.

The Ray lessened in brilliancy and gradually diminished till it entirely vanished,—and Don Aloysius, with the rapt expression of a saint and visionary, entered the chapel where his brethren were already assembled, and chanted with them—

"Magna opera Domini; exquisita in omnes voluntates ejus!"

The next morning, all radiant with sunshine, saw the strangest of nuptial ceremonies,—one that surely had seldom, if ever, been witnessed before in all the strange happenings of human chance. Manella Soriso, pale as a white arum lily, her rich dark hair adorned with a single spray of orange-blossom gathered from the garden, stood trembling beside the bed where lay stretched out the immobile form of the once active, world-defiant Roger Seaton. His eyes, wide open and staring into vacancy, were, like dull pebbles, fixed in his head,—his face was set and rigid as a mask of clay—only his regular breathing gave evidence of life. Manella's pitiful gazing on this ruin of the man to whom she had devoted her heart and soul, her tender sorrow, her yearning beauty, might have almost moved a stone image to a thrill of response,—but not a flicker of expression appeared on the frozen features of that terrible fallen pillar of human self-sufficiency. Standing beside the bed with Manella was Marco Ardini, intensely watchful and eager to note even a quiver of the flesh or the tremor of a muscle,—and near him was Lady Kingswood, terrified yet enthralled by the scene, and anxious on behalf of Morgana, who looked statuesque and pensive like a small attendant angel close to Don Aloysius. He, in his priestly robes, read the marriage service with soft and impressive intonation, himself speaking the responses for the bride-groom,—and taking Manella's hand he placed it on Seaton's, clasping the two together, the one so yielding and warm, the other stiff as marble, and setting the golden marriage ring which Morgana had given, on the bride's finger. As he made the sign of the cross and uttered the final blessing, Manella sank on her knees and covered her face. There followed a tense silence—Aloysius laid his hand on her bent head—

"God help and bless you!" he said, solemnly—"Only the Divine Power can give you strength to bear the burden you have taken on yourself!"

But at his words she sprang up, her eyes glowing with a great joy.

"It is no burden!" she said—"I have prayed to be his slave—and now I am his wife! That is more than I ever dared to dream of!—for now I have the right to care for him, to work for him, and no one can separate me from him! What happiness for me! But I will not take a mean advantage of this—ah, no!—no good, Father! Listen!—I swear before you and the holy Cross you wear, that if he recovers he shall never know!—I will leave him at once without a word—he shall think I am a servant in his employ—or rather he shall not think at all about me for I will go where he can never find me, and he will be as free as ever he was! Yes, truly!—by the blessed Madonna I swear it! I will kill myself rather than let him know!"

She looked regally beautiful, her face flushed with the pride and love of her soul,—and in her newly gained privilege as a wife she bent down and kissed the pallid face that lay like the face of a corpse on the pillow before her.

"He is a poor wounded child just now!" she murmured, tenderly—"But I will care for him in his weakness and sorrow! The doctor will tell me what to do—and it shall all be done! I will neglect nothing—as for money, I have none—but I will work—"

Morgana put an arm about her.

"Dear, do not think of that!" she said—"For the present you will stay here—I am going on a journey very soon, and you and Lady Kingswood will take care of my house till I return. Be quite satisfied!—You will have all you want for him and for yourself. Professor Ardini will talk to you now and tell you everything—come away—"

But Manella was gazing intently at the figure on the bed—she saw its grey lips move. With startling suddenness a harsh voice smote the air—

"There shall be no more wars! There can be none! My Great Secret! I am Master of the World!"

She shrank and shivered, and a faint sobbing cry escaped her.

"Come!" said Morgana again,—and gently led her away. The spray of orange-blossom fell from her hair as she moved, and Don Aloyslus, stooping, picked it up. Marco Ardini saw his action.

"You will keep that as a souvenir of this strange marriage?" he said.

"No,—" and Don Aloysius touched the white fragrant flower with his crucifix—"I will lay it as a votive offering on the altar of the Eternal Virgin!"

About a fortnight later life at the Palazzo d'Oro had settled into organised lines of method and routine. Professor Ardini had selected two competent men attendants, skilled in surgery and medicine to watch Seaton's case with all the care trained nursing could give, and himself had undertaken to visit the patient regularly and report his condition. Seaton's marriage to Manella Soriso had been briefly announced in the European papers and cabled to the American Press, Senator Gwent being one of the first who saw it thus chronicled, much to his amazement.

"He has actually become sane at last!" he soliloquised, "And beauty has conquered science! I gave the girl good advice—I told her to marry him if she could,—and she's done it! I wonder how they escaped that earthquake? Perhaps that brought him to his senses! Well, well! I daresay I shall be seeing them soon over here—I suppose they are spending their honeymoon with Morgana. Curious affair! I'd like to know the ins and outs of it!"

"Have you seen that Roger Seaton is married?" was the question asked of him by every one he knew, especially by the flashing society butterfly once Lydia Herbert, who in these early days of her marriage was getting everything she could out of her millionaire—"And NOT to Morgana! Just think! What a disappointment for her!—I'm sure she was in love with him!"

"I thought so"—Gwent answered, cautiously—"And he with her! But—one never knows—"

"No, one never does!" laughed the fair Lydia—"Poor Morgana! Left on the stalk! But she's so rich it won't matter. She can marry anybody she likes."

"Marriage isn't everything," said Gwent—"To some it may be heaven,—but to others—"

"The worser place!"—agreed Lydia—"And Morgana is not like ordinary women. I wonder what she's doing, and when we shall see her again?"

"Yes—I wonder!" Gwent responded vaguely,—and the subject dropped.

They might have had more than ordinary cause to "wonder" had they been able to form even a guess as to the manner and intentions of life held by the strange half spiritual creature whom they imagined to be but an ordinary mortal moved by the same ephemeral aims and desires as the rest of the grosser world. Who,—even among scientists, accustomed as they are to study the evolution of grubs into lovely rainbow-winged shapes, and the transformation of ordinary weeds into exquisite flowers of perfect form and glorious colour, goes far enough or deep enough to realise similar capability of transformation in a human organism self-trained to so evolve and develop itself? Who, at this time of day,—even with the hourly vivid flashes kindled by the research lamps of science, reverts to former theories of men like De Gabalis, who held that beings in process of finer evolution and formation, and known as "elementals," nourishing their own growth into exquisite existence, through the radio-force of air and fire, may be among us, all unrecognised, yet working their way out of lowness to highness, indifferent to worldly loves, pleasures and opinions, and only bent on the attainment of immortal life? Such beliefs serve only as material for the scoffer and iconoclast,—nevertheless they may be true for all that, and may in the end confound the mockery of materialism which in itself is nothing but the deep shadow cast by a great light.

The strangest and most dramatic happenings have the knack of settling down into the commonplace,—and so in due course the days at the Palazzo d'Oro went on tranquilly,—Manella being established there and known as "la bella Signora Seaton" by the natives of the little surrounding villages, who were gradually brought to understand the helpless condition of her husband and pitied her accordingly. Lady Kingswood had agreed to stay as friend and protectress to the girl as long as Morgana desired it,—indeed she had no wish to leave the beautiful Sicilian home she had so fortunately found, and where she was treated with so much kindness and consideration.

There was no lack or stint of wealth to carry out every arranged plan, and Manella was too simple and primitive in her nature to question anything that her "little white angel" as she called her, suggested or commanded. Intensely grateful for the affectionate care bestowed upon her, she acquiesced in what she understood to be the methods of possible cure for the ruined man to whom she had bound her life.

"If he gets well—quite, quite well"—she said, lifting her splendid dark eyes to Morgana's blue as "love-in-a-mist" "I will go away and give him to you!"

And she meant it, having no predominant idea in her mind save that of making her elect beloved happy.

Meanwhile Morgana announced her intention of taking another aerial voyage in the "White Eagle"—much to the joy of Giulio Rivardi. Receiving his orders to prepare the wonderful air-ship for a long flight, he and Gaspard worked energetically to perfect every detail. Where he had previously felt a certain sense of fear as to the capabilities of the great vessel, controlled by a force of which Morgana alone had the secret, he was now full of certainty and confidence, and told her so.

"I am glad"—he said—"that you are leaving this place where you have installed people who to me seem quite out of keeping with it. That terrible man who shouts 'I am master of the world'!—ah, cara Madonna!—I did not work at your fairy Palazzo d'Oro for such an occupant!"

"I know you did not;" she answered, gently—"Nor did I intend it to be so occupied. I dreamed of it as a home of pleasure where I should dwell—alone! And you said it would be lonely!—you remember?"

"I said it was a place for love!" he replied.

"You were right! And love inhabits it—love of the purest, most unselfish nature—"

"Love that is a cruel martyrdom!" he interposed.

"True!" and her eyes shone with a strange brilliancy—"But love—as the world knows it—is never anything else! There, do not frown, my friend! You will never wear its crown of thorns! And you are glad I am going away?"

"Yes!—glad that you will have a change"—he said—"Your constant care and anxiety for these people whom we rescued from death must have tired you out unconsciously. You will enjoy a free flight through space,—and the ship is in perfect condition; she will carry you like an angel in the air!"

She smiled and gave him her hand.

"Good Giulio!—you are quite a romancist!—you talk of angels without believing in them!"

"I believe in them when I look at You!" he said, with all an Italian's impulsive gallantry.

"Very pretty of you!" and she withdrew her hand from his too fervent clasp,—"I feel sorry for myself that I cannot rightly appreciate so charming a compliment!"

"It is not a compliment"—he declared, vehemently; "It is a truth!"

Her eyes dwelt on him with a wistful kindness.

"You are what some people call 'a good fellow,' Giulio!" she said— "And you deserve to be very happy. I hope you will be so! I want you to prosper so that you may restore your grand old villa to its former beauty,—I also want you to marry—and bring up a big family"—here she laughed a little—"A family of sons and daughters who will be grateful to you, and not waste every penny you give them—though that is the modern way of sons and daughters."

She paused, smiling at his moody expression. "And you say everything is ready?—the 'White Eagle' is prepared for flight?"

"She will leave the shed at a moment's touch"—he answered—"when You supply the motive power!"

She nodded comprehensively, and thought a moment. "Come to me the day after tomorrow"—she said—"You will then have your orders."

"Is it to be a long flight this time?" he asked.

"Not so long as to California!" she answered—"But long enough!"

With that she left him. And he betook himself to the air-shed where the superb "White Eagle" rested all a-quiver for departure, palpitating, or so it seemed to him, with a strange eagerness for movement which struck him as unusual and "uncanny" in a mere piece of mechanism.

The next day moved on tranquilly. Morgana wrote many letters—and varied this occupation by occasionally sitting in the loggia to talk with Manella and Lady Kingswood, both of whom now seemed the natural inhabitants of the Palazzo d'Oro. She spoke easily of her intended air-trip,—so that they accepted her intention as a matter of course, Manella only entreating—"Do not be long away!" her lovely, eloquent eyes emphasising her appeal. Now and again the terrible cries of "There shall be no more wars! There can be none! My Great Secret! I am Master of the World!" rang through the house despite the closed doors,—cries which they feigned not to hear, though Manella winced with pain, as at a dagger thrust, each time the sounds echoed on the air.

And the night came,—mildly glorious, with a full moon shining in an almost clear sky—clear save for little delicate wings of snowy cloud drifting in the east like wandering shapes of birds that haunted the domain of sunrise. Giulio Rivardi, leaning out of one of the richly sculptured window arches of his half-ruined villa, looked at the sky with pleasurable anticipation of the morrow's intended voyage in the "White Eagle."

"The weather will be perfect!" he thought—"She will be pleased. And when she is pleased no woman can be more charming! She is not beautiful, like Manella—but she is something more than beautiful—she is bewitching! I wonder where she means to go!"

Suddenly a thought struck him,—a vivid impression coming from he knew not whence—an idea that he had forgotten a small item of detail in the air-ship which its owner might or might not notice, but which would certainly imply some slight forgetfulness on his part. He glanced at his watch,—it was close on midnight. Acting on a momentary impulse he decided not to wait till morning, but to go at once down to the shed and see that everything in and about the vessel was absolutely and finally in order. As he walked among the perfumed tangles of shrub and flower in his garden, and out towards the sea-shore he was impressed by the great silence everywhere around him. Everything looked like a moveless picture—a study in still life. Passing through a little olive wood which lay between his own grounds and the sea, he paused as he came out of the shadow of the trees and looked towards the height crowned by the Palazzo d'Oro, where from the upper windows twinkled a few lights showing the position of the room where the "master of the world" lay stretched in brainless immobility, waited upon by medical nurses ever on the watch, and a wife of whom he knew nothing, guarding him with the fixed devotion of a faithful dog rather than of a human being. Going onwards in a kind of abstract reverie, he came to a halt again on reaching the shore, enchanted by the dreamy loveliness of the scene. In an open stretch of dazzling brilliancy the sea presented itself to his eyes like a delicate network of jewels finely strung on swaying threads of silver, and he gazed upon it as one might gaze on the "fairy lands forlorn" of Keats in his enchanting poesy. Never surely, he thought, had he seen a night so beautiful,—so perfect in its expression of peace. He walked leisurely,—the long shed which sheltered the air-ship was just before him, its black outline silhouetted against the sky—but as he approached it more nearly, something caused him to stop abruptly and stare fixedly as though stricken by some sudden terror—then he dashed off at a violent run, till he came to a breathless halt, crying out—"Gran' Dio! It has gone!"

Gone! The shed was empty! No air-ship was there, poised trembling on its own balance all prepared for flight,—the wonderful "White Eagle" had unfurled its wings and fled! Whither? Like a madman he rushed up and down, shouting and calling in vain—it was after midnight and there was no one about to hear him. He started to run to the Palazzo d'Oro to give the alarm—but was held back—held by an indescribable force which he was powerless to resist. He struggled with all his might,—uselessly.

"Morganna!" he cried in a desperate voice—"Morganna!"

Running down to the edge of the sea he gazed across it and up to the wonderful sky through which the moon rolled lazily like a silver ball. Was there nothing to be seen there save that moon and the moon-dimmed stars? With eager straining eyes he searched every quarter of the visible space—stay! Was that a white dove soaring eastwards?—or a cloud sinking to its rest?

"Morgana!" he cried again, stretching out his arms in despair—"She has gone! And alone!"

Even as he spoke the dove-like shape was lost to sight beyond the shining of the evening star.

L'Envoi

S everal months ago the ruin of a great air-ship was found on the outskirts of the Great Desert so battered and broken as to make its mechanism unrecognisable. No one could trace its origin,—no one could discover the method of its design. There was no remnant of any engine, and its wings were cut to ribbons. The travellers who came upon its fragments half buried in the sand left it where they found it, deciding that a terrible catastrophe had overtaken the unfortunate aviators who had piloted it thus far. They spoke of it when they returned to Europe, but came upon no one who could offer a clue to its possible origin. These same travellers were those who a short time since filled a certain section of the sensational press with tales of a "Brazen City" seen from the desert in the distance, with towers and cupolas that shone like brass or like "the city of pure gold," revealed to St. John the Divine, where "in the midst of the street of it" is the Tree of Life. Such tales were and are received with scorn by the world's majority, for whom food and money constitute the chief interest of existence,—nevertheless tradition sometimes proves to be true, and dreams become realities. However this may be, Morgana lives,—and can make her voice heard when she will along the "Sound Ray"—that wonderful "wireless" which is soon to be declared to the world. For there is no distance that is not bridged by light,—and no separation of sounds that cannot be again brought into unison and harmony. "There are more things in heaven and earth than are dreamed of in our philosophy,"—and the "Golden City" is one of those things! "Masters of the world" are poor creatures at best,—but the secret Makers of the New Race are the gods of the Future!

The End

9 781513 280110